RECKLESS DREAMER

Dion Alden

BANTAM BOOKS

TORONTO • NEW YORK • LONDON • SYDNEY • AUCKLAND

RECKLESS DREAMER
A Bantam Book / August 1985

ISBN 0-553-25264-X

Published simultaneously in the United States and Canada

Bantam Books are published by Bantam Books, Inc. Its trademark,
consisting of the words ''Bantam Books'' and the portrayal of a
rooster, is Registered in U.S. Patent and Trademark Office and in
other countries. Marca Registrada. Bantam Books, Inc., 666 Fifth
Avenue, New York, New York 10103.

PRINTED IN THE UNITED STATES OF AMERICA

0 9 8 7 6 5 4 3 2 1

She'd surrendered her romantic dreams for the promise of success, until the one man who loved her walked back into her life . . .

"Do you want a drink?" Alison asked.

"The usual."

"Oh," she said, and for the life of her could not remember what he drank. She reached for the bourbon bottle.

"You did remember . . ." He smiled.

She brought him the drink and when he took it from her, their hands touched. His hands, she thought, had never lost their authority, not once. She had to stop thinking about his hands.

"What are you thinking about?" he asked.

"Nothing." Did he know she was thinking about his hands? She had trouble looking at him. His direct gaze always aroused her and she did not want to be aroused. She was working, and had difficult choices to make.

"Now that we are through with the small talk," he said, "I only have one thing to ask you. Where are we, the two of us? Are you in love with me? 'Cause I sure as hell do love you."

Her "Yes" came out so small that he could hardly hear her. He kissed her. It was the one thing she had hoped he would not do, and when he did, she lost all qualms. Sam was the only man who could excite her and protect her at the same time. He was kissing her and his breath was sweet and, oh, God, she was anticipating making love with him again.

RECKLESS DREAMER

"An amazing achievement. Dion Alden has captured that edgy, glamorous jetset—rock star—Broadway—Hollywood scene and put it into her incredibly hip pocket. Enormous fun."

—Rex Reed

"Powerful and gutsy. This walk on the steamy side of show business throbs with erotic reality. It's harsh and tender and true and I loved it."

—Jimmy Coco

RECKLESS
DREAMER

Chapter One

Click! Click!

Alison Carmichael kept snapping the shutter of the Leica.

One more shot! And then another! And another! Hold it! Yes! This may be the perfect photo.

It was spring. It was Paris. The chestnut trees were in blossom just as the song said. And Alison Carmichael was very young and very beautiful, and totally unaware of the devastating effect she was having on Parisians. Right now she couldn't take enough photographs. Around every street corner there was something new and dazzling. Circus posters exploding against the medieval gray walls of the Latin Quarter. Bunches of flowers sunning themselves on windowsills. She only had eyes for these images, and the passersby only had eyes for her.

Alison had the long leggy look of a thoroughbred and could have been mistaken for a fashion model. Whatever she wore acquired an incredible chic, mainly because she wore it. Maybe it was due to the high cheekbones and the clear blue eyes, gifts from her father. Or the delicacy of her other features—her mother's gifts. Quite possibly it was her hair, which was the color of honey. It had been streaked by the sun on Vermont ski slopes in winter and salted by the spray on the centerboard sloops that left the Marblehead Yacht Club every careless summer Sunday afternoon. Jonathan Carmichael's estate was at Pride's Crossing, Massachusetts, ten miles from the yacht club.

1

Alison's look was all of these things, and one thing more. She wore clothes with the carelessness of people born to money.

At nineteen she was totally unaware of anything that she did not find by looking into the camera. Actually she had always been that way, from the time her father gave her her first camera on her seventh birthday. She had peered through the viewfinder and loved the world she saw there. It was a clear, focused world with well-defined boundaries.

She had taken her camera with her everywhere. She had gone to the correct New England preparatory school, the correct New England college, attended the correct coming-out parties, and survived the weekends at Yale. She had applied for admission to the Sorbonne for her third year of college. One day in the spring of 1967 there was a letter of acceptance in her mailbox. She would attend the School of Photography and Fine Arts in Paris.

She had dutifully kissed her mother—who had mainly spent her life telling Alison to wear white gloves—and then embraced her daddy—whom she adored.

"Take care of yourself, baby," he murmured. He was the only one who called her that.

"Oh, Daddy!" She grinned. "Haven't you prepared me for everything?"

And with a wave and the cruel self-absorption that goes with being nineteen, she left home, and parents, and childhood.

Chapter Two

Nothing had prepared Alison for the explosion of the senses that was Paris.

She arrived late in the summer to find a city deserted by the French, but filled with Americans. Her first night she met a boy from Yale who took her to the New Jimmy's, a wild discothèque hidden away in the dark of the city. From there they raced around the deserted streets in his rented Peugeot 404 to discover other night spots, which were filled with Germans, Scandinavians, rather kinky British, and Americans—Americans everywhere. Midwesterners still with their crew cuts. Easterners with the hippie look, now fashionable enough because it was outrageous. They all danced together, and apart, and in threes, while the music throbbed through the night. When the dawn was coming up over the still-hot city, Alison let the boy from Yale kiss her in his Peugeot. And then she left him, to search for an apartment.

It took two days, but the apartment she found was a dream. Of course, one had to walk up five flights of stairs, but after all, that was why one was in the Latin Quarter, on the Left Bank, in Paris. Parisians all lived in walk-ups, didn't they? And this one was special. Although it faced a narrow little street that was straight out of the eighteenth century, from the living-room window Alison could catch a glimpse of the Seine and the towers of Notre-Dame. There was a small bedroom with delicately patterned red rose wallpaper. There was a kitchen. There was the atelier, the living room that had doubled as an artist's studio. And, miracle of miracles, there was a private bathroom with a tub and a shower—unheard of in the student section of Paris.

Alison took the place on the spot and ran out and bought two framed posters. One was in lively red and yellow, announcing a Picasso exhibition, and the other was a tear sheet for a Fellini film. Like the thousands of posters that were slapped up on the gray stone walls where the words DÉFENSE D'AFFICHER were written, this particular sheet had fascinated Alison. There were flowers and balloons floating in midair. It was just the way she felt. She was floating in the wonderful French aura of late summer.

And then they returned, the French. *La rentrée*. From all over Europe they returned from vacation, hurtling down on the city with their children packed inside the cars and their beach chairs and luggage strapped on top. For two days the people of Paris were screaming and honking horns and threatening one another with either death or lawsuits. And then everyone settled down to the business at hand—which was making a living in the City of Light.

For Alison it meant registering at the Sorbonne. She stood in line, surprised that the French looked just like the Americans. Long hair and blue jeans. Lots of cigarettes. The girls were not as pretty as she had been led to believe, Alison found to her satisfaction. And the boys were cuter. They were fun. They talked more of revolution than the boys back home; they smoked more cigarettes. They seemed to be in training for nothing. No one was going out for the track team. They were all quite intense. They rode little motor scooters and whizzed around the narrow Left Bank streets at alarming speeds. And talked so fast. Everyone talked fast. But in a short time Alison found her Rosemary Hall and Smith French adequate for most social situations, and she began to pick up the slang.

However, as the fall progressed she discovered that the Sorbonne was not like Harvard, nor the Seine like the Charles. She grew a little homesick for those football weekends with Harvard boyfriends and the impromptu picnics along the banks of the Charles with the city of Boston rising across the river.

The classrooms were incredibly crowded. She had to arrive fifteen minutes before class to find a seat. There were only one hundred places, and often three hundred students were jammed into a room.

At first she thought the lectures were boring only to her—and that because of the foreign language. But then she found that most of the students were grumbling about the rigidity, the lack of imagination in the curriculum. The students were all ready for a dare. Ready for adventure. The authorities were ready only for fulfillments. Students were always filling out forms and then filling out papers, and filling out the lines for the different themes and assignments. One area alone was exciting to Alison: the darkroom. She learned in a very short while more than she had ever dreamed of—how to develop the negative, to crop the photo, to heighten the mood by exposure.

She became so engrossed with her work that the rest of the world disappeared. She hardly noticed that the afternoons were growing shorter, that the gold had disappeared from autumn and the leaves had disappeared from the plane trees. One day she went out, a beautiful, warm end-of-fall Saturday. She took her camera and became fascinated with the look and the light of the area. The posters, so gay against the somber buildings; the graffiti that seemed to appear from nowhere, stark red or shocking white against, again, the gray walls. She snapped these shots, then began to look around her: at the lovers, the grocer, the fishmonger, the concierge, and the *clochards*, the bums who fished in the Seine all year long. Because she was young and eager, they were willing to pose for her.

She was so engrossed in her work, she had no idea she was causing a sensation. She was dressed for the weather—in Massachusetts. She was wearing a heather-colored turtleneck sweater, gray slacks, and a heavy tweed hacking jacket, perfectly appropriate for a late-fall weekend in Boston. But in Paris she was so upbeat, so *américaine*, that had she been wearing a Balenciaga ball gown, she would have looked more ordinary. In her New

England country attire she was a showstopper. Of course, her honey-colored hair crowned everything. One couldn't buy that look. One was born into it. Or one was not.

It was early afternoon as Alison raced through the streets, eager to get to the darkroom, which was in the basement of a building close to the Sorbonne. A man named Noircet had permitted her to share it with him. Once there she took off her jacket and set to work developing the film, then printing a contact sheet. She could feel herself bursting with a great excitement. Part of it was being young and alive and in Paris. But there was also the premonition of— No, she wouldn't bring herself to think about it.

When the contact sheets came out of the fixative, she couldn't wait for them to dry. She glanced at them briefly, and her heart stopped for a moment. Some of the pictures were so good, they took her breath away. She could not bear to dwell upon them in the cold darkroom.

Again she hurried through the streets. The sun was setting. She stopped and bought herself a brilliant bouquet of autumn asters, fresh from the *marchand de quatre saisons*—the flower seller who kept his panorama of flowers fresh daily in the little cart he hauled around the streets.

Then she bought herself a bottle of wine. If the pictures weren't as good as she thought, at least she would have flowers and wine for consolation.

She ran up the five flights of stairs, and once in the little apartment, she stopped. In the room there was that faint glow of Paris at dusk. She quickly lit a fire, meticulously took out a vase—not an expensive one, but a nice one that set the asters off beautifully—poured herself a glass of wine, and placed the contact sheets facedown on the table. She turned on a light and searched for a magnifying glass.

Oh, God, she thought, *let it be true, that what I thought I saw, I did see. . . .*

She sat down at the table, picked up the first contact sheet, and scrutinized it under the magnifying glass.

What first caught her eye was a shot of an old bum who had been fishing along the Seine. He was facing the camera, dressed in rags, his face grizzled, a butt hanging from his lip. But there was also a grin on his face and a tough-city twinkle in his eye as he showed her the poor excuse for a fish he had just hauled out of the river. Behind him was Notre-Dame.

What had she done? she wondered. Why was the photo so arresting? It was. There was no doubt. It had to do, Alison decided, with the look in the old man's eye, a look of pride combined with self-mockery. The misbegotten little fish and the gesture as he displayed it. The indomitable sense of survival of an old man in rags. And behind him one of the most incredible glories of the Western World.

Was it a fluke, this one shot? She poured over the pictures. No. No, it was not a fluke. Out of perhaps one hundred frames, she had at least twenty powerful photographs.

She gulped the wine and kept examining the contact sheets through the magnifying glass as if to confirm that the sheets were not lying.

It came to her, then, the realization, as clear as any one of the prints. This was her life. This was what she would follow, would work at, would devote her passion to. She was a photographer. And suddenly she had no doubts. She was going to be wonderful. Brilliant.

She had the Eye. She could distinguish the daring and courageous from the merely gaudy and cheap. She could separate the tragic from the sentimental.

And so she passed the winter, camera always at hand. She shot for the Decisive Moment. She either got it or she got nothing. But like gunmen in the Old West, she learned to shoot fast.

She photographed Versailles, the Hall of Mirrors and the glorious paintings. Under the guise of mythology, of Hercules and Apollo, the plushest of kings and rosiest of females cavorted, while beneath them the real Louis XIV and his court gambled and gamboled, chattered and connived, until two Louis later it was all swept away in the Revolution of 1789. All those pretty birds of paradise with their heads chopped off by the guillotine, stripped of their ribbons and silks and lace and plumage and thrown into wagons and dumped into ditches. Still left were the gardens, the buildings, the grandeur of Fontainebleau and the palace of Versailles.

But another revolution was brewing.

It started in the hallways, in the classrooms, in the Latin Quarter itself. *Les événements de mai,* it came to be called. This revolution started out so innocuously. As at the University in Nanterre, the Sorbonne Library contained only four thousand seats for forty thousand students. More than inadequate facilities, though, it was true—in the eyes of the students of the sixties—that the curriculum was outmoded.

On a Friday afternoon, as cold and mean as May can be in Paris, the head of the Sorbonne was forced to call in the Paris police to clear the university courtyard of a small and disputatious student meeting. Violating the sanctuary of the courtyard, of the university—something which had been maintained for centuries—brought about a protest. Violence exploded when students and some of the professors saw other students being hauled off to a police station. By Saturday night there was marching in the streets. By Sunday morning ten students were dead, fifteen hundred wounded. Several students had been sentenced to two years in prison. The news whizzed through the university like the bullets of snipers. Within hours the entire student body along with some members of the Sorbonne had risen in a fury.

Overnight the City of Light became the City of Outrage. The workers, eight million of them, almost half the labor force, joined the students. Paris was all but immobilized by strikes. Suddenly there was no more mail delivery. No newspapers. The telephone service was sporadic. Workers took over their factories. There were demonstrations every day and every night. Conflicts erupted between groups. Cars were overturned and set on fire. The Latin Quarter blossomed with slogans. SOYONS CRUELS— "Let us be cruel"—was painted on the walls of the Sorbonne. Young students, armed with garbage-pail covers and wearing white masks splashed with red paint to protest the bloodied faces of their comrades, confronted the elite and despised Compagnies Républicaines de

Sécurité, who wore futuristic anti–tear gas goggles and were armed with truncheons and tear gas.

The students built huge barricades from cobblestones. The C.R.S. tossed in the tear gas. The students fled, running up the staircases of the houses. They began fighting from the roofs, tipping parapet stones onto the enemy below. Some members of the C.R.S. indiscriminately pursued, arrested, beat anyone in the streets. Students, workers, bystanders. Men, women, children.

And through it all, somewhat as though she were on a summer-camp tour and therefore not susceptible to injury or violence, Alison floated, snapping pictures, catching in her camera the faces of the impassioned students; the horror of the onlookers; the bewilderment of the bourgeoisie, whose tranquil world had just exploded; the anger of the police; the viciousness of class hatred; the glowering hostility of the workers. It was all there. Exultation, passion, sorrow, death, resolution.

For two weeks the revolution continued to rip the country apart, to threaten the government of Charles de Gaulle. There was very little sleeping at night, and during the day one roamed the streets, never sure what was around the next corner. A demonstration? A roundup?

Therefore it was not surprising when, late one evening, Alison heard the racing of feet up and down the hallway outside her apartment. There were cries and muffled curses, commands and commotion, and then a pounding on her door.

It frightened her. The pounding was so insistent, so desperate. At first she kept quiet. Perhaps they would go away. But they did not. The pounding continued.

"Who is it? What do you want?" she called out. Her voice sounded tiny.

"Ouvre la porte!" came the cry from outside. It was a man. It sounded like a young man, a frightened man.

She overcame her own fear and undid the latch. A boy of eighteen pushed his way in, proceeded to the kitchen sink, and began washing his hands. There was tar from the paving blocks on his dirty fingers. His dirty fingers would convict him.

"*T'es pas française. . . .*" he whispered at her, lacking breath. Alison shook her head no.

"*Anglaise? Américaine?*"

"*Américaine,*" she said.

He had time for one more word. "Help!" he said, wiping the dirty black ringlets from his forehead and lighting a cigarette.

There came a second knock on the door.

"*Police!*" Another angry rap. Again Alison opened the door. Immediately there was a babble of French that she only half comprehended. She pretended she understood nothing at all.

"What is it? Why are you here?" she asked.

"*Américaine?*" the policeman questioned her.

Alison reached for her bag. Miraculously she found her passport. She held it up in front of her as one held a cross before a vampire. It would, she felt, protect her from all evil.

The agent examined the passport, returned it, and nodded in the direction of the young man.

"*Et lui?*" he asked.

A phrase came to her, though she wasn't sure why.

"Make love, not war," she said, and smiled. The agent looked at her curiously and then at the boy.

"*Faire l'amour, pas la guerre,*" the boy translated, then added, "*C'est du Viêt-nam.*"

The officer looked at their hands. Clean hands. Unpolitical hands. He left. She closed the door and bolted it, then turned around.

"*Merci,*" the boy said, and Alison merely nodded. She felt she had run ten miles. She was gasping for breath and her hands were shaking.

"*Calme-toi,*" the boy reassured her, and smiled. Then, in English, he said, "It's okay." The word sounded ridiculous but charming. There was something in his tone and manner that made Alison feel everything *would* be okay.

"Whatever is going to happen?" she asked tentatively. "Can we continue this in English? At least till I get my bearings."

"Okay," the boy repeated, and grinned. "This was

something, *hein*? You never experience this . . . thrill . . . of danger before?"

"No. I guess I always kept my distance."

"Kept your distance?" The words confused him.

"Kept away. To myself." She was floundering. He lit another cigarette.

"That is too bad. 'To keep to oneself,' " he said mockingly. "It is better to be involved." There was a gentle insinuation in his voice that made her look at him.

Under the dirt and exhaustion that came from two weeks of street fighting, he was handsome, Alison noticed— and perhaps more a man than a boy. He was dark, with dark brown eyes, his hair snarled now but naturally curly. He had not shaved in two or three days, and his face was pale. She looked at his hands. They were strong; the veins stood out. She gathered that he was powerful, although slight.

"Shall I go?" he asked. His eyes were amused. He seemed to be reading her mind.

"No, not just yet," she said, flustered.

"You are alone here?" he asked.

"Yes. I live alone."

"You keep to yourself."

"Yes. So far." He blinked. He was on the verge of collapse.

"Stay the night. It will be all right," Alison said impulsively.

His smile was self-mocking. "Ah, yes, you will be safe tonight," he said, and looked for a place to lie down. What he saw was not encouraging. Three chairs and a table in the living room, and in the bedroom only the bed and the dresser.

He started to lie down on the floor.

"Take the bed," she said. "I'm not sleepy. I can sleep in the chair if I feel like it."

He was too tired to protest. He nodded his thanks and headed for the bedroom. He lay down on the bed and was asleep immediately.

Alison watched him for a moment. She could not believe what she had done. Who was this young man she had let in? Who was *she*? She was suddenly someone she could not recognize. What kind of behavior was this?

Outside the crashing of glass and the sound of sirens continued. Shouts and cries carried through the darkened streets. Periodically she could hear the sound of running feet. Another chase.

The boy slept on.

Suddenly the electricity went off, but she was used to this. All the services in the city were on a makeshift basis. She sat in the living room staring out at the night, aware of the sounds below but not caring. She grew cold. The weather was particularly bitter for May. She longed for bed, to sleep under the warm coverlet. Still she hesitated. The cold won out.

She slipped into the bedroom quietly, took off her shoes, and approached the bed. She was surprised to find that in his sleep the young man had somehow found his way under the coverlet. She listened to his soft, easy breathing for a minute, then timidly, got into bed. She slipped under the covers and lay motionless, afraid to move, but he did not stir. She relaxed. The warmth crept back into her body and she dozed. Before she fell asleep she thought, how strange to be sleeping in a bed with a man and not to know his name.

She woke first. It was morning, though the sun was not shining. For days, for as long as the revolution had lasted, it had been sullen and gray. Today was no exception.

Alison got out of bed, careful not to wake the man. She went into the kitchen and prepared some coffee. The aroma must have awakened him because suddenly there he was, standing in the kitchen doorway.

"You want coffee?" she asked him.

"God, yes," he said, then added politely, "if you have enough."

"Of course, there's enough. I stored up on coffee beans. I have enough to get me through this whole mess."

She poured him a cup. It was strong and black, and he grabbed the mug and drank two or three sips before putting it down.

"This mess, as you call it—do you know what we are doing?"

"I only know what I see," she said stiffly. "I am a photographer. The reason I'm in Paris is to study."

"Then you are a student too?"

"Yes. At the Sorbonne."

"You don't know my name!" he cried, then he laughed. "All this time we have been talking and you don't know my name. I am Alain."

"And I am Alison."

They shook hands.

"But this is crazy," he protested.

"But I like it," she said simply.

"So do I." He smiled, finished his coffee, and rose. "I must go."

"I could make you some breakfast."

"I have no time. I shall be late. There is a meeting." He glanced at his watch.

Alison was feeling very bold. "Do you have a place to sleep tonight?" she asked.

"Not really. I live with my parents, but that is in Neuilly, and since there is no transportation, I sleep wherever I can. Besides, if I went home, my parents would never let me out. They would lock me up and say, 'Be a good boy until this affair is ended.' "

"You could stay here," she offered.

He looked at her. She blushed at the directness of his stare.

"That is very kind of you."

"I'm a kind kind of person," she said, but the play on words was lost on him.

"But it is not necessary."

"No. Not necessary. But it is an offer."

He made a quick decision. "All right. I will come back. And tonight I will bring you a bottle of wine. We will have dinner."

She giggled. "If the gas is on."

"*On se débrouille*," Alain said. Alison had heard that phrase everywhere in Paris. We'll make do, we'll struggle through. It evoked a way of life that was as characteristically French as the shrug.

"*Salut*," he said suddenly, kissed her on the cheek, and was gone.

It was as though he had never been there—except for the feel of his lips on her cheek. She put her hand there. He had given her such a casual kiss, the most casual kind of kiss, and for some reason she just stood in the middle of the room, stunned and breathless.

She felt dizzy. Was she in love? she wondered. In love with a boy whose first name was Alain, and whose last name she did not know? He lived somewhere outside of Paris. He was involved in *les événements*. They had spoken only maybe twenty sentences to each other.

First dizzy and then exhilarated, she tried to eat a croissant but wasn't hungry. She could not forget the look in his eyes.

These were crazy times, she said to herself. She tried to blame her feelings on the excitement, the enormous turmoil that existed around her. But all that really existed was the touch of his lips against her cheek and the look of him asleep in the bed, relaxed and no longer the street-fighting revolutionary.

She shook herself free of her daydreams. This was the morning she was going to develop the photos she had taken the previous three days. Noircet, the man with whom she shared the basement darkroom, would have nothing to do with the rebellion. He stayed clear of it all, somewhere safe in the suburbs. But Alison had her own key, and now the luxury of all that space to herself.

Cold. Everything was cold. Only in bed had she felt warm at all. Here in the darkroom the cold seeped in through the door and down the basement steps. The air was stale and dank.

She mixed the chemicals and proceeded to develop the negatives. Then, once she had completed that, she moved to the enlarger to make prints. She dipped the white paper in the solution and stirred gently. Patterns began to emerge, black-and-white shadows forming figures, and then backgrounds and expressions and drama. The Moment. She had captured the Moment.

The results were beyond her dreams. It was all there. The anger, the antiquity of Paris, the passion of the students, the callousness of the police, the hauteur of the leaders, the puzzlement of the shopkeepers. Barricades of burning autos, a young girl—as fierce and triumphant as a statue—holding up the black flag of revolution. The photos spoke of grayness and despair and flashes of triumphant resolution; of the exhaustion and the defiance of the times. Alison could not believe what she had done.

She hurried home through the mangled streets, dodging craters and police barriers. Under her arm were the prints. In her pocket were the negatives.

It had started to rain, and it was almost impossible in the gloom to tell what time of day it was. She glanced at a clock as she passed a store. It was past five o'clock. She had spent the entire day in the darkroom.

Her mind returned to Alain. Curious. She had forgotten about him as she worked. But now the thought of seeing him again made her walk faster along the glistening sidewalks. She found, miraculously, a *boulangerie* that was open and bought bread. The baker told her of a *charcuterie* that still had some meat left. She ran there and bought some stew beef. At home, she calculated, she had some spring onions, some spices. She would make a *bœuf bourguignon*. That should take away the chill, Alison thought.

At her building she sprang up the stairs, unlocked the apartment door, and ran in. She threw the photos on the bed and headed for the kitchen. Everything was there. Flour. Garlic. She peeled the potatoes, cut up the onions and sautéed them in butter, sliced and floured the meat, and then browned it. She added some red wine and set the mixture to simmer.

There was no electricity, but fortunately the gas was still on. She went to the telephone. The line was dead. Still on strike. It was growing dark. She found candles, lit them. She placed two of them on the table in the living room, one in the kitchen, and carried one into the bedroom. As she did this she found herself blushing. Her imagination had carried her far beyond dinner. She pictured herself in bed with Alain. He would be kissing and loving her. And there her mind had stopped.

She knew about sex, had heard the girls in the dorms talk about it. But Alison was still a virgin. "When the time comes . . ." her mother had once said vaguely, then stopped. It seemed as though the time was at hand, Alison thought, and *she* was totally unprepared.

Alain caught her in the bedroom. He burst through the door, waving the bottle of wine.

"*Voilà,*" he said triumphantly. "Nothing is impossible." He glanced at her in the bedroom. "Ah," he said, grinning. "You have preceded me."

"There's no electricity. I was putting candles . . ." she said lamely.

"So I see." He sniffed the air. "But there is gas, and there is something marvelous cooking on the stove, and I am so hungry, I could eat—" He stopped. "I could eat *you!*" He lunged for her neck. The roughness of his beard scratched her skin, but she didn't mind. He was catching her off-guard though.

"You seem so happy," she said, and then, making a joke, asked, "Did things go well at the office?"

He looked puzzled.

"Isn't that what wives always say to their husbands?" she asked.

"Oh, yes," Alain replied, and he joined the joke. He assumed the role of the tired businessman. "Well, it was— you know—meetings and conferences." Just as quickly he stopped playacting and grabbed her arm.

"I think we are winning since the leaders of the unions have joined us. The strike by all these workers must force de Gaulle to come to terms. Ah, I can't believe it. Us—we are such little kids—and the workers—they all look so old. Even our accents are different. Everything— totally different. And yet the anger is the same. And the determination. You should see it."

"I'd love to," she said. Then, quite shyly, added, "I have something to show you. Can you see in this light?"

"Barely," he admitted.

She showed him her pictures. He looked at them slowly and in silence. Then he looked at them again, examined them more closely.

"But these are good!" he said in amazement. "They are better than that!"

"Are they? Are they?" Her voice changed, and she said in wonder, "They *are*. Yes, they are good."

"They are the truth. They show exactly what is happening."

She took the photos and put them on the dresser, then turned to him. He was staring at her.

"What are you looking at?"

"You amaze me," he whispered. "And you are beautiful."

She waited, then, for him to come to her, to put his arms around her, but he did not. He grinned.

"You think a bottle of wine was all I brought with me? No. Look." Out of his pocket he brought a razor. "I am so filthy. Can you let me have a shave?"

"I have a surprise, Alain," she said. She opened a door off the bedroom. Under the eaves was the small bathroom.

"Soap!" He touched it, held it up as though it were silver. "Towels!" he exclaimed as though he had never seen any. "Water!" he said as he turned the faucet, then shrugged. "Not hot, but water still the same. I will—may take a shower?"

"Certainly," she said, and shut the door on him. She put the kettle on and when the water had boiled, carried it into the bathroom. He was still in the shower.

"Leave it there," he shouted over the water, and she did. She gathered up some napkins, set the table, and waited.

Fifteen minutes later he emerged from the bathroom. He had wrapped a towel around his waist and slung another over his shoulders. He carried the empty tea kettle in one hand and his clothes, which he had washed, in the other.

"Can you turn on the oven?" he asked. "Perhaps they will dry. I had to wash these clothes. They were sticking to my skin. Eh, how do I look?"

He was totally unselfconscious. He looked . . . *shining* was the word that came to Alison's mind. His black curly hair had been slicked down. His skin had been scrubbed. He glowed with good health and youth. But it was his eyes she was drawn to. They were shining with happiness.

She took his clothes, stretched them over a chair in the tiny kitchen, lit the oven, and opened the oven door.

"This will make us warmer too," she said, and served the dinner. He took his plate, but instead of sitting down at the table, he removed the candles and the two glasses and placed them on the rug. Then he sat down.

"It is easier on the floor. At table, it is too formal. I did not dress for dinner, as you can see. Have you a . . ." He was at a loss for the word. *"Tire-bouchon,"* he said.

"Corkscrew," she translated. "Yes, of course." She brought it to him. He uncorked the wine and poured it. It was delicious and made Alison dizzy. She had not eaten anything all day. They both attacked the *bœuf bourguignon* greedily.

Outside the serenade of sirens and nightsticks and whistles and cries continued. But here, by the candlelight, they dined cozily.

Whether he was dressed for it or not, that was what they were doing—dining. Alison felt elegant. Her blond hair was spun gold in the candlelight, and to him she shone like a goddess in the night. They each put fork to mouth, raised a napkin. He watched the delicate movement of her arms. She noticed the hair on his chest. She drained her glass of wine. He poured another, and their hands touched. She sighed softly. Her eyes closed, and then his lips were on hers. She could taste the wine. She had been dying to feel his lips, and now she let her own lips explore his face. His hands were roaming her body. They kissed. She had been kissed before, but allowed it only through some kind of duty—college-etiquette, end-of-the-date kissing. Here she was kissing back. She was as greedy as he was. Before she knew it, she had stripped off her two sweaters and he was holding her breasts in his hands and kissing them. Putting his tongue to them.

Dizzy from wine and passion and exhaustion, she responded totally. They were naked and did not bother to move from the floor. He cradled her in his arms. It seemed to her their two bodies were glued together. And more than that she could feel his maleness, the hardness of him between her thighs. She thought she did not know what to do with her hands, but she was wrong. She stroked him, nuzzled him, felt the strength of his muscles, the smoothness of his back, and then her legs opened to receive him. There was a moment of pain, but it was a kind of glorious pain, and he was inside her, thrusting inside her, making love to her. She did not think of anything else from that moment. He made love to her, made her burn and pant and cover his face with kisses. Her body obeyed every movement of his, and then, as though a great barrier had been overcome, she cried out to him. Their cries mingled, their bodies mingled. This was ecstasy, Alison told herself. This was completion. This was the reason she had been born. To receive a man and give to him, to take him inside her and to gather his love.

And they were spent then, on the rug, both of them breathless from the passion that had engulfed them.

There was blood. He saw it.

"You— This was your first. I am so sorry. . . ."

"No! No!" She covered his mouth with kisses. "Never be sorry. Never be anything but what you are. You are my lover. My lover."

He carried her into the bedroom and they lay in the darkness. He cradled her and stroked her skin and whispered in her ear, and she found she was crying, and he was crying too.

"I love you," he said, surprised. "I honestly love you."

"Is this what it is? Is this what it always is?"

"No, my angel. It is almost never like this. This is something so special, so rare. You will never forget it, nor shall I. So long as we live."

He made love to her again, this time with more delicacy. He waited for her response, brought her to a tingling peak. She thought she would faint, and then they froze, their bodies motionless, until he started again. Time after time he brought her to a point and paused—then finally he swept her over the edge and she beat on his shoulders with her fists and writhed under his demanding body.

They slept after that, for a few hours. He woke her in the middle of the night with a curious question.

"Those photos, what are you going to do with them?"

"I don't know," she said sleepily.

"You should sell them. They would bring you money. You are a photographer, no?"

"That's what I want to be."

"No, no," he corrected her. "That's what you already are. You may want to be more than that. That is up to you. You may go as far as you like. That is what all this fighting is about. No one should tell us our limits. What we can and can't be. We have no limitations—but ourselves. That is how it should be." He turned in the bed and stroked her hair. "Sell your photographs. Go to a news agency tomorrow. You may be surprised."

Chapter Three

Alain turned out to be right. Alison was not only surprised. She was dumbfounded.

The man at Magnum—which was only the largest news-photo service in the world—took one look at her pictures and whistled.

"Where did you get these?" He was not trusting.

"Get them? I shot them," Alison answered.

"You're kidding. Nobody else has come up with stuff like this. You're sure these are yours?"

"Of course, I'm sure." Suddenly she was Boston-angry. With clipped tones she began gathering up the materials. "If you don't want them—"

"I didn't say that. I just didn't believe a woman could—"

"Oh?" She looked at him. "What are you saying? A woman can't snap a shutter?"

"You were in some pretty dangerous territory."

"Well, I came out unscathed. Perhaps it is better to be a woman. Now, do you want these?"

"Yes," the man from Magnum said. "And anything else you have."

Fifteen minutes later they had a deal. Alison had never been offered so much money in her life. She was surprised how easily it had come to her. But from somewhere back in her Yankee forebears also came the trader's instinct.

"That amount of money will do for this first batch,"

she said. "But I want double for what I bring you from now on."

"So long as we have the exclusive."

"You have my word on that."

"I want more than your word. I want your signature."

An advance was paid, money was put in a bank, and Alison walked home with a profession. She was now a photographer. She had no inkling that even as she was walking, the photos were being sent out over the services to *Life* magazine. In two weeks she would not be just a photographer. She would be a recognizable name. But she had no way of knowing that as she made her way through the chaos back to her apartment.

Two weeks.

For two weeks she became accustomed to the sound of running feet on the stairs; shouts; smashing glass; sandwiches and scraps of food; and love on the run with a man whose last name she wasn't sure how to spell.

The nineteenth of May was Alison's twentieth birthday, and when she mentioned it to Alain, he told her he would spend the day with her. They walked, for hours, holding hands and talking. They visited Notre-Dame, and although Alison had been there before, she was overwhelmed, awed. She held onto Alain tightly, and felt closer to him than ever before.

They ended up in a cafe near Notre-Dame, where they often went for coffee. This time, though, Alain ordered Benedictine and Brandy and they toasted her birthday.

A week later they were lying in bed one night when she suddenly asked him, "What are you? What are your parents like?"

"Why do you ask?"

"Because I know nothing about you."

"I have parents. A mother and father. They are, unsurprisingly, a woman and a man."

"Do you see them much?"

"I live with them. But I do not see them much."

"What does your father do?"

"He is a *fonctionnaire*. He works in an office."

"Then you're not rich."

"No. Not rich."

"I think my parents are rich. Do you work in the summer?" All the boys she knew had summer jobs. It was supposed to strengthen their character. They were mostly lifeguards or worked at the Marblehead Yacht Club. Sometimes they were counselors at summer camps in Maine. They were not like Alain.

"Work? No. In August we go on holiday."

"Then you must be *some* rich."

"But no. Everybody goes on holiday. My parents have a place in Normandy."

"Is it an estate?"

"It is a cottage."

"Do you have pictures?"

"Of course." He got out of bed and brought her his wallet. She looked at the photos.

"This is your mother?"

"No, that is Aunt Thérèse. *This* is my mother. Behind her, of course, that is Papa. And that is my brother, Joseph."

She handled his wallet. It was the most intimate thing she had ever done. More intimate than lovemaking, Alison thought. More private. Inside were his possessions. Scraps of paper he had collected before he met her, the pictures, the smell of the leather. It was an old wallet, worn from use, but the leather was expensive. It smelled of Alain, or was it the other way around? She returned the wallet to him. It was like giving a life back. He tossed it on the chair by his clothes, which he had also tossed off.

He smiled. "Satisfied?"

"No." She shook her head. "It makes me more curious. I feel I don't know you."

He put his arms around her. "But you do know me. You know me better than anyone. You know me the way I know you. How we feel together. The odor of our bodies. I know when you are angry. It shows right here, on your cheek."

She was silent and he caressed her cheek. Outside, far away, the chant was heard. "C.R.S.—S.S.!" It was a rhythm used everywhere in Paris, sounding to Alison like shave-and-a-haircut-two-bits.

"Do you swim much at your summer place?" she continued.

"I don't swim."

Alison knew no one who didn't swim.

"What do you do then? You don't go to the beach?"

"We are not by a beach. There is a river nearby, but it is very dirty. What do I do? I sleep in the sun. There is a field, and there are strawberries."

"Do you dance?"

"Of course, I dance."

"We've never danced together."

He laughed. "Do you want to dance now?"

"No. I want to stay here in bed with you. Do you like the Beatles?"

"Yes. And Vivaldi. String music. I like chamber music. Quartets."

"Do you have a record player?"

"Yes. I should bring it here. You do not have one. Perhaps someday there will be electricity again."

They didn't mind. They were lovers, and lovers love candlelight.

She was very shy when he began to make love to her that night. Now that she knew more about him, he was a stranger. And perhaps the nicest thing about Alain—as opposed to the most complex thing—was that he understood her shyness. He took the time to woo her, something she was grateful for. He feminized her, feminized the valley where her waist joined the round curve of her hips. He was a young man who adored making love to women, and in the process he made them even more beautiful.

She was amazed by his strength and his size. He did not look strong, but how safe she felt within his arms, how warm she felt when he was inside her! She knew so little about sex, yet her body seemed to know so much. Perhaps because she wanted to continue feeling him, she would move counter to him, they would meet in counterrhythm. She could adapt to his rhythm. He was a steady lover, a wonderful teacher. She clasped him to her after their orgasms, her legs around his body to try to keep him there longer. Forever. But her lover was always on the go, having to leave for some meeting, some demonstration.

The next morning, the twenty-fourth of May, which was a morning like all others, he put on his clothes, slipped his wallet in his pocket, and kissed her.

"Nothing was ever this good," he said. She thought he meant the lovemaking, but she questioned the nostalgia in his voice.

"You will be back tonight?"

"Tonight and every night. Watch yourself on the street today. There may be trouble."

He was gone. Since there was still no transportation, Alison was always on the street when she was not in the apartment. Disregarding the danger of being caught up in the *manifestations*, she photographed the guerrilla theater that was taking place. The week before she had brought a second series of photos to Magnum. Magnum had grabbed them.

But on this day, the twenty-fourth, de Gaulle spoke to the nation. On this day the workers split apart from the students. After all, the workers did not want to destroy society, only to have their proper place within it. On this day Alison walked through the troubled streets with a troubled heart, and by nine o'clock, when Alain had not returned, she knew something was wrong.

Next morning, she was told—by an acquaintance—that Alain had been killed. Shot in the head. She could not hear any more of it. She ran, ran from the sound of the voice. Ran through the twisted, narrow little streets of the Quarter. She wanted to run from the eyes that haunted her. She ran to her apartment, but he was there. And not there. The smell of him, the remembrance of him was there, everything except the living breathing person. And that person was living and breathing no more. He was gone, wiped out of her life forever.

"Nothing was ever this good," he had murmured to her the morning before. The phrase tormented her. Through the night, as the sirens whined and the glass shattered she sat in the darkness, too sad for tears. For the next two days, almost like the city itself, she was stopped, stalled. Nothing functioned. She lay in bed and kept seeing Alain bursting with life, coming through the door, full of stories about the events of May, the events of the day. *Nothing was ever this good.* But the door remained closed. Then she would shut her eyes and hope for the sleep that never came.

At the end of the week the divided nation collected itself. Order was restored. Alison pulled herself together and booked passage home on the *QE2*.

Chapter Four

Alain! Alain!

She could see him in the river—he was swimming—but why had he gone in the water? He knew he could not swim. Where were his mother and father? Why could no one help him? He was suddenly small, a child. A child and her own Alain, and she watched his arm stretch toward her. She glimpsed his face, the terror in his eyes. She was running to him. She could save him, *she* could swim. And then he disappeared beneath the surface. She was frantic, running along the riverbank. Where had he gone to? Where was he? The eyes had been looking to her for help. The eyes she had loved, the hands that had so moved her.

Alain! Alain!

She woke up crying out his name. Slowly she realized where she was. The stateroom was spacious. The soft pink coverlet and the luxurious sheets spoke of first class. But first-class staterooms did not erase the pain. And sleep did not erase the pain. She slept most of the time since she had boarded the ship, waking to order meals that invariably arrived accompanied by a single cheerful red rose in a slender silver vase. But neither rose nor food was consolation. She would ring for the steward, who took the tray away, shaking his head in disapproval.

He was distressed. On the third morning he spoke up.

"Beautiful morning, mum."

"Is it? I hadn't noticed."

"Why don't you take a walk around the deck? Perhaps the sea air might do you some good. You're looking a bit pale, if you don't mind my saying so."

Alison sighed. "I don't feel like walking."

A change of tactics. "I notice you have some quite nice camera equipment 'ere. Would you be takin' some pictures maybe?"

"I hadn't thought about it."

"You could always come back to bed now, couldn't you?" he `said reasonably.

He bowed out, and Alison rose from her bed to take a scalding shower. To try to wash away the past. To try to begin again.

After her shower she selected a red turtleneck, a blue blazer, and white flannel pants. Totally nautical, especially the long skinny red-, white-, and blue-checked scarf that she tied and threw over her shoulder casually. She automatically slung her camera over her other shoulder, looked at herself, and smiled wanly. *Très sportive*. But yes, the steward was right. It was better to get up, dress, and go out and see what the world on board ship had to offer.

It was chilly on deck, but the sunlight was brilliant and the sea air brought the color back to her face. Her hair whirled in the breeze, and she roamed the ship, oblivious to the stares of the passengers. The *QE2* was like a small town, a very exclusive one. By the third day everyone knew everyone else, at least by sight. The group had little to do but examine one another and gossip.

There was a schedule. Activities for all, at all possible hours. After breakfast there were card games, followed by a midmorning café of croissants and many kinds of jams and jellies, fresh peaches and grapes, mounds of cheeses. *Pâtisserie*. Followed by lunch. Followed by afternoon tea. And then the cocktail hour in the bar. Then change for dinner. After dinner—second sitting naturally—dancing. And drinks. And laughter. Then a nightcap and a final stroll around the deck. Then to bed. A simple life. Wonderfully simple and terribly expensive. But money was no object to these people. On land they might have fought tooth and nail to amass their wealth, but here on board they lived in a play world of fun and games—lolling on deck chairs while attentive stewards brought bouillion or Bloody Marys, and dozing under a warm June sun as the sleek ship sped across the bright blue Atlantic.

Alison strolled twice around the deck and for a moment was indecisive. Perhaps she should return to her cabin. Close the door and retreat under the covers again.

Then something caught her eye. A pattern. An angle of shadows and sunlight, vertical strips of wood.

She took out her camera. Interesting. An abstract. After weeks of seeing nothing but the faces of the *enragés* and the demonstrations that had all but overthrown the French government, it was a welcome change to photograph patterns. No people. No faces. No passions. Just patterns. She raised the camera to her eye and in a matter of minutes had become absorbed in her work.

"My heavens!" a voice suddenly rasped from behind her back. "What do you think you're doing?" The voice was deep, challenging, dry, amused. Alison turned to see who had spoken.

The woman she faced was incredibly ugly and incredibly chic, Alison thought, perhaps fifty years of age, but ageless. Wise slits of eyes, a lined face, a jutting jaw. Obviously disdainful of plastic surgery, this woman had let her face fall where it may. And yet there was no denying her allure. Was it the Dior scarf tied peasant-fashion, pulling her hair straight back and accentuating the face? Was it the cloth jacket with the collar up to keep out the cold? Or the trim figure? Or the jangle of gold bracelets that hung carelessly from the wrist, while the hand, holding a Gauloise, waved in the air?

The question had been direct. The woman had been direct. Immediately Alison responded to her.

"I'm photographing angles," she answered simply, brushing her gold locks away from her face.

"Of course, you are, my dear," the woman said ironically, then muttered to herself, "I think I have discovered a genuine looney. . . ."

She puffed on her cigarette and exhaled. "What do you find fascinating in angles?"

Alison explained what had caught her eye. At the end she asked, "Do you see?"

The older woman was sizing her up.

"I think I do. I think I understand very well. Tell me, do you take these photographs for fun? Or do you make a living at it?"

Alison faced her squarely. "More than a living. I intend to make a life out of it."

"Oh, my dear, how dangerous that is. To put such a burden on any one aspect of life. Still, I suppose I did the same thing. I'm Myra Van Steen."

The name was supposed to evoke some response, but there was no recognition from Alison.

"Of *Charm*," Myra Van Steen continued.

"Oh, do you work for *Charm*?" Alison asked.

"I *am Charm*," Myra Van Steen said flatly. "Why is it I haven't seen you before now?"

"I've been hiding."

"Oh? That sounds intriguing."

"It isn't. Only self-pitying."

"You're an interesting girl. Would I have seen any of your pictures?"

"I can't believe so. I've been studying in Paris for a year," Alison said, then added, "But I did sell some pictures to Magnum. Photos of the riots in Paris."

"There were some fabulous photos in *Life* of the riots. I don't suppose those were yours."

Alison shrugged. "I wouldn't expect so."

"Come, come with me. I still have a copy. It was last week's. We flew over to Milan for the showings. . . . I remember buying a copy of *Life*. Let's see if they are like your photos."

All the while they were wending their way through corridors, finally arriving at Myra Van Steen's stateroom. She unlocked the door and breezed in.

"Forgive the mess." There were newspapers scattered on the floors, papers in French, English, and Italian. Magazines. Swatches of material. The suite itself was sumptuous. Two huge beds, a cream-colored sofa, two overstuffed chairs, a glass coffee table. Seated in one of the chairs was a very slim dark woman, leafing through a magazine. She was petite, no more than five feet tall, with eyes the shape of almonds and a vaguely Oriental cast to her.

"This is Trevina," Myra said, waving airily. "We have decided to endure the torture of this ocean crossing together."

The small woman nodded. There was no need to explain her name to Alison. Trevina was the latest rage in fashion; a designer who designed for women, not against them, who allowed her fashions, her gowns, to flow with the body. She used exquisite materials, some of them rather exotic, reminding one of *The Arabian Nights*. Exotic fabrics but simple designs. She was the new answer to the excesses of the miniskirts and the Pop rebellion.

"My name is Alison Carmichael." Alison extended her hand and Trevina shook it with a good grasp. Meanwhile Myra was making more of a mess of the room.

"I am looking for that copy of *Life*. Did you see it? It must be here somewhere. I remember buying it at the airport on the way to Milan. Don't you remember? I said I refused to be bored with one more jet trip and all that ghastly food and—ah, here it is."

There was a picture of John Lindsay on the cover.

"Now, isn't that a handsome man? *Divine*." Myra held the magazine out for inspection. "I don't know what kind of mayor he is, but Lord knows he could raise my taxes any day of the week. Merely joking," she rattled on as she thumbed through the magazine.

"Yes," she said, stopping and holding the magazine out to Alison. "See these?"

Alison could not believe her eyes. There they were: ghostly white and smeared in the bleeding fury of blood-red paint. Two masked policemen striking university students. And the detested *gardes mobiles* swinging their truncheons, the students choking on tear gas, the streets strewn with rubble and burning automobiles. Her photographs! It suddenly struck her that never in all this had she taken one photo, one remembrance of Alain. He was gone, and there was no trace of him, only the battles in which he'd fought.

"These are mine," she said quietly.

"But you are famous!" Trevina cried.

"I am?"

"Of course. These photographs have been printed everywhere now. This issue of *Life* is a collector's item. How is it that you do not know?"

"Because so much has happened—so fast. I had no idea." Alison had to sit down, and she did, amid the litter of the room.

"You see," Trevina continued, showing her the Italian magazine she had been holding, "they have also been printed here."

"Guess what I found her doing," Myra said to Trevina, lighting another cigarette with the gold Dunhill lighter. "Photographing *angles*. I thought she was some kind of lunatic."

"You are very talented," Trevina said softly. "These photographs are extremely moving. You have a good eye—"

"That's what I was saying," Myra interrupted. She did not take kindly to being upstaged in any way, Alison noticed. "I was remarking what a discerning eye you had for structure and design. Have you ever shot fashion?"

"No." Alison laughed. "Forgive me, but the models always seemed so silly, frozen in those outlandish poses. So heartless. I guess I had no interest."

"Hmm." Myra Van Steen peered at Alison through the curtain of cigarette smoke. "Heartless, eh?" That kind of mannequin pose had been her trademark, her inspiration. "Well, how would *you* shoot them?"

"Give the models more freedom, I suppose. Women should not be such dolls. This is the sixties. Lord knows, there has been more than one revolution. Liberate the models. Get them out on the town and into rock concerts— and on ocean liners and striding down Fifth Avenue."

"I suppose you would put them on motorcycles?" Myra snapped testily.

"Of course. It would show off the clothes well. Motorcycles are very sexy."

"Mmm." Myra appraised Alison, then turned on Trevina. "What do you think?"

"She has a fresh eye."

"I don't know if what I want is a fresh eye," Myra muttered. "My own eye has been sufficiently au courant—"

"Yes, for a long time," Trevina said mischievously.

"That will do!"

"Oh, Myra." Trevina gave a little tinkle of a laugh. "You are nothing but *Charm*."

"As many a gossip columnist has reminded me." She turned to Alison. "Will we be seeing you for dinner?"

"I don't know," Alison said, startled by the abrupt switch.

"Do come," Trevina coaxed. "It must be no fun at all, alone on a crossing."

"No, not unless you're alone with a man," Myra said.

"There are fascinating men on this ship," Trevina said.

"I assume you refer to that lawyer," Myra said sharply.

"Ben? Is that whom you meant?"

"It's come to that already, has it? Ben and Trevina."

"Not at all. He has no interest in me. You can see he is involved with Diane."

"The glorious Diane Landers," Myra murmured sardonically. "Well, trash is trash, darling, although she has covered it up very well. Only once in a while does something slip—nothing so embarrassing as a shoulder strap, just the mere trace of an accent. Some locution that is not quite of the *haut monde*. Her *a*'s are a bit too flat. I suspect a touch of the Bronx there."

"Snob!" Trevina said.

"Incurably!" Myra admitted. "Particularly with cruel kinds of climbers. Which is what Diane Landers is." Turning to Alison, she said, "See what fun you're missing. Plus the fact that—if you're alone—you have no one to gossip with. Or about."

"Well, I'm sure I will see you again, whether or not it's tonight," Alison said with a smile, her hand on the doorknob. "I do thank you for showing me the magazine. I wonder whether I can get a copy somewhere."

Myra's laugh was raucous. "You poor lamb. You do need someone to take care of you. The answer is yes, I think when we land in New York, *Life* might spare you a copy. Now, so long. I need my nap or I shall look a wreck tonight."

Alison left the stateroom. Not all the naps in the

world, she thought, but then stopped. The lady was kind
and forthright. And successful. And somehow generous.
Alison could not explain why she thought so.

Her instinct proved correct.

When she returned to the stateroom, she found the
steward had taken the liberty of reserving a table for the
second sitting, leaving her a note to that effect. She read
the note and put it down.

Suddenly the depression flooded over her, pressed
her down. She closed her eyes. *I can't go on with this*, she
thought. *It's too painful. It's all too painful. I can't make
conversation. I don't want food. I don't want to keep up
the pretense.*

But she imagined Alain saying, *Nonsense, you must
continue to live. You must learn to live without me. You
will never forget me, but you will learn to live without me.
Live, Alison, live. That is what we are put on this earth to
do.*

She picked up the note again and smiled. It would
not do to disappoint the steward. She took great care in
choosing something suitable to dine in fashionably. Her
inventory was not encouraging. During her year in Paris
she had been too busy to buy—but not too busy to
observe—the latest in fashion. The cheeky invasion of the
miniskirt had been complete. There was the same kind of
saucy insouciance about fashion that had characterized the
twenties.

She cast her eyes on the collection of sensible tweeds
and cocktail dresses she had brought from Boston and
rejected them. There was only one possibility. She had
bought it in Paris, a dress of white silk. It flowed to the
waist, then hugged in, then draped with a hem cut on the
diagonal. It was quite short.

She tried it on and admired the effect in the mirror.
Quite right for coming out of mourning. She applied a
little light lipstick, took another look in the mirror, ran her
fingers through her hair, freeing it, and left for the Queen's
Grill—the first-class dining room.

The Queen's Grill stretched the width of the ship
with two gigantic picture windows at either end, lined
with banquette tables for two. Below in the center, rather

like an enormous sunken living room and circled by a railing, were larger tables that seated up to eight people. The entrance to the Queen's Grill made everyone highly visible. That had been deliberate. Everyone, indeed, could make an entrance. But not quite like Alison's.

She entered a bit hesitantly, looking absolutely smashing in her white dress.

"Miss! Miss!" An exceedingly officious maître d' was bearing down on her, the panic in his voice reducing the Grill to silence. "No miniskirts! No miniskirts!"

Alison turned in confusion. "What?"

"I regret"—the maître d's voice rang out through the room—"I regret that miniskirts are not permitted in the first-class dining saloon."

For a moment Alison was stunned, then realized that the entire assemblage was staring at her. She looked down instinctively to check the length of her hem. It was short, but surely not outrageous.

"This isn't a miniskirt," she began, but stopped. Incredibly the maître d' was on his knees with a yardstick, about to measure the length. Alison flushed.

"What are you doing?" she asked him.

"Regulations, miss. As to length. I am following instructions."

Suddenly she heard Alain's voice again. Laughing. *Get the bastard,* he was saying. *Don't let him get away with it.* And before her appeared a blur of *manifs*— demonstrations—street parades, students and gendarmes, police with helmets, students with mocking masks. Whenever they had protested, Alain in the forefront, they had carried it off with style.

Alison faced the maître d' and spoke very clearly.

"Let me give you a lesson in fashion. This is not a miniskirt." She pointed to what she was wearing, then raised her skirt to midthigh and stood there in front of this man on his knees. "*This* is a miniskirt."

There was a moment's stunned silence. Even the maître d' was taken aback. Then a laugh a familiar voice cried, "Bravo!" and Myra Van Steen was up from her table and approaching Alison.

"I believe that little lecture-demonstration was necessary," Myra said. "It seems as though this bloody ship is not aware of its own country's fashions. However"—she looked icily at the maître d'—"since one must follow rules, darling, take this coat, since I have nothing to show. Therefore nothing to hide." She tossed Alison her incredibly sumptuous sable coat. "That is to dispel whatever chill might remain in the air," she added loudly.

Alison gratefully wrapped the coat around her and whispered, "Don't you think you might be thrown off the ship?"

"Boat, darling. Call it a boat. They hate that. Yes, I suppose there's always the danger that I might be lowered away like Captain Bligh, but I don't intend to worry about it. Come along with me. Now is not the time for you to be alone at a table."

She threaded her way through the tables, apparently oblivious to the stares—some of consternation, some of amusement—of the other diners. Alison followed, not realizing how beautiful she looked. The embarrassment and her subsequent anger had given her face high color. Her hair glinted gold in the elegant lighting of the Queen's Grill. And a sable coat never hurt.

At the table for six Alison recognized Trevina. Her photographer's eye quickly took in the other couple.

First the woman. Jet-black hair, oval face. Tan. Beautiful. Calculated to look like a passionate gypsy. Lip gloss accented the cruel curve of the mouth. Eyeliner added mystery to eyes that were more covetous than mysterious. Dangerous lady, Alison thought.

And then the man. His grin was boyish and open. He belonged on ski slopes, she thought, with his wild blond hair and that happy-go-lucky glint in his eye. Was he an actor, a movie star? Or a ski bum? He could be any of the three. Prep school, Ivy League college, she guessed. But not uptight about it, therefore not from the East. The West? California maybe?

Myra introduced them.

Diane Landers—the gypsy—gave a cool nod. Ben Sawyer—her ski bum—rose and pulled out a chair for Alison to sit.

"Great legs!" he said enthusiastically by way of introduction.

"Yes, that was quite a performance," Diane Landers said, not nearly so enthusiastically.

Alison laughed. "Not quite what I had intended for a debut."

"Well," Myra said, "you have brightened the entire crossing. Your little contretemps is worth perhaps two days of gossip over bridge and drinks."

"I hadn't found the trip so dull," Diane said sweetly.

"Perhaps you have more inner resources than the rest of us." Myra lit a cigarette.

"Perhaps my interests are more varied," Diane retorted, flashing a smile at Ben Sawyer, who remained noncommittal, seemingly unaware of the war of words flashing past him. Actually his attention was on Alison. He was taking her measure. She felt his gaze but refused to respond to it.

Trevina spoke up. "Ben, Alison took the photos you admired so much in *Life*."

Suddenly there was new respect from Diane. It was obvious she could not decide whether to continue a course of bitchiness or pursue a potential client. So she tried both at once. "I hope those terrific shots weren't just beginner's luck," she cooed.

Alison ignored the dig. "You liked them? I'm so glad. Those are kind words from so severe a critic."

Ben was much more direct. "You surprise me, because quite honestly I can't imagine a girl your age running through the streets of Paris in the midst of all that violence. Weren't you scared?"

"No, I was too inexperienced. I suppose I have always felt that nothing would ever happen to me. As Miss Landers says, I'm just a beginner."

"Call me Diane." Diane was being quite tolerant.

"Alison," Alison countered. If they were to be rivals, they were well matched.

Myra Van Steen was thrilled. There was nothing more fun to watch than a genteel catfight . . . unless it was a vicious one.

"Ah, here come the *hors d'oeuvres*," she said, "just in time. I'm famished!"

The dinner that followed was so dazzling that Alison forgot any unpleasantness. First there were the hors d'oeuvres: a *pâté en croute*, then an incredibly delicate *mousse de truite*, made by pressing the flesh of the trout through a fine sieve. Each one was served separately, followed by the ritual of changing plates and silverware and cleansing the palate after each new dish with a *sorbet*. Then the fish course, a *turbot au champagne*, and for the climax an *entrecôte* with a mustard sauce, the beef tender and just the right pink-red on the inside. Then there was a cornucopia of cheeses, *glaces* and more *sorbets, marjolaines*, pastries, tarts. Finally a choice of fruits with the coffee.

To celebrate the occasion Ben ordered a '61 Montrachet to accompany the *hors d'oeuvres*, Dom Perignon '59 for the turbot and to be reprised for the desserts, and the famous bordeaux, Château Lynch-Bages '62, to complement the entrecôte.

The food and the wine dulled the combativeness and sharpened the wit of all. However, Alison noticed that Diane decidedly monopolized Ben's attention. The two of them had just returned from Europe—Munich and Rome to be exact—where she as agent and he as lawyer had assembled a motion-picture venture that seemed to involve the total resources of at least three countries and twenty banks. Chase Manhattan was to supply the financing up to the first four million. More money had been raised by deals with foreign distributors—hence the stop in Munich. Although Ben answered her questions, Alison noticed he divulged little information that was not asked for directly. Oddly enough, rather than being bored by these business details, she was fascinated. She had never considered movies as a business venture, and she was intrigued with all the intricacies—the imagination, the power deals, the checks and balances that went into financing a product that she might rather carelessly plunk down two fifty to see. Or might not. "Flicks" had been part of the college scene, and there were those who went only to art movies in little theaters that served Colombian coffee but no popcorn. And no Nestlé bars.

How films were made, produced, and financed had never crossed her mind. Now, what she was hearing excited her.

The director of this movie was obviously new. *"Nouvelle Vague,"* Diane kept insisting—the director was her client—"but *commercial.*"

"A little grandiose," Ben said.

"Why not? He's a genius. He thinks big."

"He *lives* big," Ben continued.

"Why not? Why not? He has a right to. Paul Masland is Hollywood's future!"

"He, and maybe ten others," Ben reminded her.

"There's no one who can touch his talent!" Diane said hotly.

"Hey, what are we fighting about? I put the package together. Your guy is going to make his film."

"But don't you understand, Ben?" Diane purred. "I *like* fighting with you."

Ben blushed slightly under his tan.

"I'm through," Myra interrupted. "What's next on this marathon?"

"Drinks! Dancing! Follow the regime!" Trevina answered.

Alison demurred. Although she had been intrigued by the conversation, her interest was waning. She felt the need to be alone again, not to put any more effort into being sociable.

Do it, Alain's voice urged. *Go on. I insist.*

Obediently she followed the others from the table as they made their way to the lounge, where a small trio was playing. In the dim light one could see stars outside in the dark night. Ben asked her to dance. Diane's eyes cast gypsy curses. Alison, in defiance, accepted Ben's invitation.

He took her in his arms and they danced. She had never danced with Alain, she remembered. There had never been enough time.

Ben was apologizing. "Diane's all business, I'm afraid."

"That's one thing I like about her. She loves her business."

"Yes," he admitted. "She's a good agent."

"And you, what about you?"

"I'm also pretty good in my way."

"Law?"

"Yeah, that too."

"That's what I meant."

"Oh, sorry."

"Why sorry?"

"Sorry that that's what you meant." He held her a bit more closely. His skin smelled of the outdoors. She tried to remember the odor of Alain's skin. She couldn't. It was fading. She could not quite grasp, sense him.

"Do you ever go to court?" she asked.

"And say 'ladies and gentlemen of the jury'? No. No trial work. I tried it once and was terrified. Tongue-tied. I leave that to others. The only time I can wax eloquent is on politics. Where are you from?"

"Massachusetts," she said, a little startled at the sudden switch.

"I thought I heard New England in that voice."

"You seem kind of New England to me too—but not quite."

"Well, I went to school there. Andover. Then Dartmouth."

"Ski team?"

"How did you know?"

"My first impression. Ski bum."

"It was a choice. Law or the slopes. Law won. For the time being."

"You're originally from California."

"Correct. Pasadena. A native."

"Then you've been around these movie people all your life."

"Never!" He feigned shock. "We were never allowed to play with 'them.' When I joined this firm that dealt mostly with the entertainment industry, my family practically disowned me."

"But you love it?"

"Love it all. Love my life, love my work, love this trip, and I think I love you." He said it lightly and grinned good-naturedly. He wasn't prepared for the tears that suddenly filled her eyes.

"Hey, what did I say?"

"No, it's nothing like that. It's just—I've just been through a bad experience."

"Do you want to stop dancing?"

"No, please, please, let's keep dancing. I'm sorry. I didn't mean to cry. I don't know why I am. . . ."

He held her closer to comfort her, and they danced in silence for a few minutes.

"Any better?" he asked quietly.

"Thank you."

"I'm not used to playing good friend."

"Sorry. I'm not up to anything more than that."

"Don't be sorry. It's good discipline for me. Like cold showers at school."

She laughed. "Or porridge at breakfast. 'It's good for you. Sticks to your ribs.'"

"I think we went to the same school."

"Hardly. We saw boys only on Glee Club weekends."

"Don't forget the Fall Dance. Or the Winter Dance. Or the *Spring* Dance."

"This may sound silly, but do you remember the code? If you were really serious about someone and didn't want anyone cutting in, you danced—"

"Like this." He swung her right arm down and bent it behind her back. "I used the same grip in wrestling."

"Oh?" she said. "Well, I never got pinned." She extricated herself.

"You think we should join the others?" he asked finally.

"You join them. I'm really tired. I think I'll go to bed."

His eyes reflected his desire to join her there, but he kept silent and nodded.

They returned to the table, where Alison bade the group good night and went directly to her stateroom. Once inside she leaned against the door and closed her eyes.

I did it, she whispered to Alain. *I did what you wanted.*

And it wasn't so difficult?

It was horrendous.

The next time will be easier, he promised. *And the*

time after that. His voice was gentle and soft. She wept
for him that night, but her tears were those of release. It
was the first night that she did not dream about him.

The next two days were interesting because Alison
was welcomed into "the group." There were several cliques
on board.

"But we're the money table," Myra said positively.
"We're where the action is."

And indeed, it was fun. They played shuffleboard and
a crazy kind of *Alice in Wonderland* croquet, making side
bets on shots with one another. Trevina was definitely the
croquet champion in a game that had its own risks, with
the pitch of the ship making every shot chancy. The five of
them walked the deck together, much to the annoyance of
Diane, who really wanted to keep Ben to herself. But Ben
was not the kind of man to be kept. In any way.

And as Alain had promised, the next day was easier
for Alison than the first, and so it went. She still felt his
presence, but not such grief.

They played water polo in the ship's pool. All except
Myra, who refused to be seen in a bathing suit and therefore refereed, making outrageous calls and never taking
the cigarette from her mouth. "I call them as I see them,
darlings, and I am terribly astigmatic."

The time passed until the day arrived for the Captain's Dinner. The four women were in the steam room,
discussing what they would wear, when Diane suddenly
turned to Alison. "It's formal," she said. "You don't have a
formal gown, do you?"

Alison, remembering the imbroglio with the maître
d', simply shrugged. "I can always buy a gown. They do
have shops on board, you know. Or maybe I won't go. You
can tell me all about it in the morning—and I'm sure you
will."

Myra suddenly remembered an appointment and
quickly left the steam room. Trevina followed soon
after. Diane and Alison were left, in steam and in silence.
But not for long.

"You find him attractive?" Diane asked. She didn't
have to mention who.

"Of course," Alison said. "When I first met him, I thought he was either a movie star or a ski bum."

"Yes, you're quite right. He could have been either."

"Is he good at what he does?"

"Yes, in that crazy world of film financing and mergers and conglomerates, Ben is the best. We use only the best."

"We?"

"The people I work with." Diane kept it deliberately vague, and Alison did not pursue it.

"When we reach the States, where are you going?" Diane asked.

"Nowhere. Just home, I guess. Back to school."

"Surely you're not going to just stay there. Not with the break you just had." This was the professional agent speaking.

"I don't know. I'll have to think about it."

"Don't think about it too long. When you get a break, make the most of it. Who's your rep?"

"I don't have one."

"I'll give you my card," Diane said, adding, "*And* my private number." Alison did not realize at the time the compliment she was receiving. No one whose name was not instantly recognizable to the entire world possessed Diane Lander's private, unlisted, hush-hush number. And those who did were sworn on pain of death not to reveal it.

Once outside the steam room Diane wrote down the number and handed it to Alison. Alison found Diane's attitude amusing in its ambivalence. She put the card in her wallet and promptly forgot all about it.

Back in the stateroom her phone was ringing. When she lifted the receiver, she heard Myra Van Steen's voice commanding her.

"Alison, where have you been? Come to our stateroom at once! We don't have much time!"

"For what?"

"No questions. Come immediately." That was an order and Alison followed it. She found the two women in a mess of creativity. Trevina had a mouthful of pins and yards of various materials were strewn like banners over both beds.

"You are going to the Captain's Dinner tonight!" Myra said the moment Alison entered the room. "And what's more, you'll wear a Trevina original. Right?" Trevina nodded confirmation.

"Now, take off those clothes." Alison again followed the order. Myra and Trevina set to work. They held up various materials against Alison's body, discarding them one after another, until Trevina suddenly had an inspiration.

"The peacock!" she shouted. "You told me I was mad to buy it. But you shall see."

The material she was referring to was diaphanous, a myriad of greens and blues and golds, a jungle of shimmering hues.

"Perfect!" Myra pronounced. "Now, create!"

With great economy of movement Trevina draped the material around Alison's body, then stood back a minute, casting her eye over the contours, making a mental note of the flow of the material. Then she took the pins and began to model a gown, folding material in toward the waist, gathering it, bunching it, letting it drape so that, while it was a full-length evening gown, it was also slit above the knee to allow full movement. She carefully accentuated the curve of Alison's buttocks, emphasized the delicious rise of her bosom by creating a daring and yet modest cleavage, and finally the masterstroke: She gathered the material around the arms.

"Raise your arms," she commanded, and as Alison did, the diaphanous material cascaded into breathtaking wings.

"A butterfly," Trevina said. She was finished. That was it. The confection.

"*The* Butterfly. . . ." Myra immediately sensed the commercial possibilities. "A new look. Sensational." Then, teasingly to Trevina, she said, "You see what a good deed can do for you. It can make you a million dollars."

And that was what Alison looked like that evening when she appeared at the Captain's Dinner. They had all been invited to sit at the captain's table. Alison had been about to make her entrance when Myra grabbed her.

"Too early!" she whispered harshly. "Go back and wait half an hour. *Then* you make an entrance. And, darling . . . make an *entrance!*"

Alison did.

With her hair swept up to the top of her head, she resembled a goddess. Her long neck was adorned with a simple ruby-and-diamond necklace Myra had lent her. It was hard to believe that this was merely a twenty-year-old girl.

The dress itself caused a sensation. Its simplicity and subtlety made the European designer gowns look a bit old hat, a bit stodgy. Every other woman in the room suddenly felt like Queen Elizabeth wearing one of her horrible hats. The ladies' looks were of envy and admiration. For Alison it was just fun. It was playacting. It was getting dressed up for a party, the kind of thing kids did on rainy days. She had not the slightest idea that she was starting a New Trend.

The gentlemen all rose and the ladies all nodded to her at the captain's table. Even Diane, although her nod was almost imperceptible. Alison sat down and was up a moment later, invited to dance.

She had hardly time to taste the champagne—which was a Veuve Cliquot and a good vintage naturally—and she hardly had time to sample the cuisine—which was magnificent—between dances. She danced with the captain, who found this the least onerous of his chores.

"At last a lady who can follow," he said appreciatively.

Alison looked at him with sympathy. "These evenings must be difficult for you."

"There are delights." He smiled and Alison inclined her head at the compliment. She happened to glance to one side, and what she saw warmed her heart. Diane was watching, the expression on her face not what one would call cheery. Opposite her Myra was beaming, enjoying the scene so much. And Trevina was thronged by women.

It was Carnival, Cinderella's Ball, New Year's Eve, and Homecoming Weekend. It was every good party combined. At the end of it Ben managed to slip away with Alison for a quiet drink. He ordered another bottle of champagne and toasted her.

"To us," he said. "I don't intend to let you out of my life so quickly."

She smiled. "How do you propose to keep us together? Are you going to practice law in Boston? Teach at Harvard?"

"I wasn't thinking of coming east. I was wondering why you weren't coming *west*."

"There's nothing to take me there. No reason to go."

"No," he said quietly. "Not yet." They drank their champagne in silence, then he began to speak, no longer in his usual bantering tone.

"Alison, you don't realize that you are on the verge of being *somebody*. You've just had your work printed in a national magazine, where it received tremendous exposure. Now is the time to capitalize on that—if you want a career. You had a lucky break. You were good, very good. But people forget so quickly. Everything is disposable. We live in a disposable society. Last week's news is out the door and into the trash heap, since everything happens so fast in today's world. Yo ought to be where the action is."

She laughed. "I don't know. The action seems to find me."

Ben didn't smile. "I wouldn't count on that. You need connections. I have connections. For instance, you ought to come to California and cover the primaries."

"What primaries?"

Then Ben did laugh. "Whew, you have been out of touch. The Democratic primaries. Haven't you heard? This is 1968. We have an election every four years to see who will be President. Remember? I've been working on Robert Kennedy's campaign. I think he's going to win. I *know* he's going to win the California primary. You're from Massachusetts. Do you know the Kennedys?"

It was another one of his abrupt switches.

"I never met them," she confessed. "My family didn't approve of the Kennedys."

"Good Lord, you ought to meet Bobby, then. He's fantastic! And so far as I can see, he's our only hope. What with Vietnam and the civil rights movement and the student riots, Bobby's the only one who can bring us all together. He's *doing* it, in fact. That's why I've been working so hard to get him elected."

Alison sighed. "I don't know."

"I'm not asking for your vote, for God's sake. I'm not even putting the touch on you for a donation. I'm just saying you ought to meet him, photograph him. Get involved. Look, there's a dinner at the Biltmore in L.A. on June fifth. Come with me. Bring your camera. Come on, kiddo, it's time to get you launched."

"We haven't even docked yet, and you want to get me launched!" She laughed evasively, shaking her head. "You and Diane. You're both so full of drive! I thought Californians were supposed to be laid-back."

"I have other reasons," Ben said. "I don't want this to be just a shipboard romance."

"It wasn't," she reminded him gently.

"Friendship, then."

"Our friendship won't end," she promised.

"Then, tell me, what are you going to do when we land?"

"I frankly don't know."

"You have no plans?"

"No."

"Then come to California. You don't have to stay if you don't want to. But on the other hand you might like it. What the hell? It could be an adventure."

That was the word that appealed to her. *Adventure.* It was true. She had nothing in mind, nothing in view. She was beginning to be released from the pain of Alain's death. She had never seen California, and there was the possibility that it might be a career move for her. Who could tell?

"You're on!" she told Ben impulsively.

"Let's drink to that!" he shouted.

"No wonder you're so successful. You're very persuasive."

"Only with the mergers I'm truly interested in. Like this one." He grinned and poured the rest of the champagne.

The two of them sat in the bar until dawn, watching the sky lighten outside the huge picture window, watching

the sea emerge from the shadows, the night fade and the
stars disappear. And they talked about the future. Ben
made it sound so rosy and wonderful. A new beginning. A
new country. A new day.

And so it seemed after they had docked. There was a
flurry of good-byes. Kisses on the cheeks for Myra and
Trevina. Promises of correspondence. Hugs. Farewells.
And then the three of them, Alison, Ben, and a glowering
Diane, sorted luggage, tipped porters, supervised the loading of limousines, drove madly to the airport, boarded a
flight, and found another limousine waiting when they
landed. The East Coast limo had a television. The West
Coast one also had a fully stocked bar. So much for the
differences between the coasts, Alison mused.

In California Alison hardly had time to orient herself
in terms of what day it was, let alone what time of day,
before it was the fifth of June, the night of the Kennedy
dinner, and she found herself on the arm of Ben Sawyer,
who looked, she thought, extraordinarily handsome in formal wear. Outside the Biltmore they braved the spotlights
and flashbulbs of photographers. Inside the crush of people was fantastic—and everyone seemed to know Ben. He
introduced her to all of them. There were famous names she
knew, faces she recognized from the screen. There were
other names she had heard of, and some who preferred
privacy. But this was her introduction to the world of the
affluent, the handsome, the wealthy, the powerful people
of the West Coast. Alison found herself exhilarated by the
company, as well as the promise of the evening. After the
dinner they were going to a party hosted by Peter Lawford,
which the Kennedys were also attending.

Ben had seen to it that they were seated at a table
fairly close to the dais where Robert Kennedy would speak.
It was also close to the kitchen. Alison realized Ben had
placed them there for a reason—so that she could snap
away without disturbing anyone.

Ben surveyed the glittering assemblage, then winked
at her. "A night to remember?" he said.

"I love it!" she whispered. "I love the excitement of
all this."

The room darkened and the introductions began, the

speeches. Alison lifted her camera and began to take pictures. She focused on Bobby Kennedy, in profile. He was waiting to speak. In repose his face showed the fatigue of campaigning. His eyes were pensive. He reminded Alison of the football players at Harvard, third quarter, time out. The big push coming. The concentration was on winning. That was it. Kennedy's eyes had the same look, the winner's look. She had seen it at the Marblehead regattas and on the football field. At track meets. At debates. She had seen it when she looked in the mirror. It suddenly struck her that she had never seen that expression in her father's eyes. Was it because he had nothing more to win? She had no time to dwell on that. She unobtrusively kept her camera trained on Kennedy's face.

The atmosphere was all dark and dazzling light. The senator rose to an ovation, and his famous grin transformed his face. Indeed, Alison noted, it transformed the room into a victory celebration. Television cameras were grinding away, flashbulbs were popping, people were shouting. Then the crowd hushed to hear Kennedy's words. They were brief, but bold and jubilant. Everyone roared his approval and encouragement.

Smiling with characteristic boyish charm, alternately waving and gesturing triumphantly, Kennedy plunged into the crowd, his aides furrowing a narrow path for him. Alison and Ben moved in tandem with the Kennedy party. Keeping first Ethel then Bobby in her viewfinder, Alison snapped away, jostled by the throng, guided and protected by Ben.

There was a crack, no more than a small explosion, then another, and suddenly Kennedy was no longer moving. He had crumpled. Fainted? Tripped? Injured? There was a violent scuffling around his body. It took Alison only a second to realize what had occurred: The candidate was wounded, shot, his blood staining the white tiles of the kitchen corridor's floor. She never ceased photographing.

Around her was pandemonium. From the banquet room she could hear the screams, the howling voices at the microphones attempting to restore some order. She was aware of a tussle. Someone cried that the assassin had been captured. She concentrated on Kennedy. The look in the eye had changed.

It was the hunting season, Alison thought. The dying stag. The wounded, wondering, glazed look in the eye. She continued to snap the shutter. Then she raised the camera and caught the madness and the horror that had been unleashed.

Kennedy was taken away and in the early hours of the morning, as Ben was driving his black Mercedes SL 150 up the canyons above Sunset Drive to his house, they heard on the radio that Kennedy had died. Ben drove on in silence. Only when they had reached the drive and he had parked the wonderfully sleek little car did he give way to his emotions and begin to sob.

Alison reached over and cradled his head in her arms, trying to soothe him.

"Yes, cry," she said. "It's all right, Ben. Let it out. It's all right. It will be all right."

Of course, it wouldn't be all right, and Ben was crying for a whole age, for a whole movement that had been systematically gunned down. All the men had been young, powerful, and wise. Not cynical, but street-smart and idealistic at the same time. They had known how to wield influence. Black and white, they had used their power in search of the same goals. They had attracted large masses of the population. There had been the same zest to the way they lived. And for every one of them, the same ending. The same shattering, smashing of life.

Ben was weeping for this, and Alison was weeping for Ben. She understood only too well the pain of loss, the bullet in the head that exterminated all dreams. So they sat there in the car, in the saucy sports car with the red leather and the fancy gearshift, and cried.

Suddenly Ben raised his head and looked at her. "You've got to get that film developed."

She shook her head.

"Of course, you're going to develop that film." His voice was savage. "And sell it. And let the whole world look at what just happened! What else is a photographer for? To grab the great moments in time. This was a great moment. This was the end. The end of a great fucking era!"

He slammed out of the car and into the incredible house that sprawled over half a canyon. By the time Alison had followed him through the heavy mahogany doors, he was on the phone, snapping out curt, peremptory orders while the lights of Los Angeles blazed below him.

Now the drive was fury, as it had once been elation, and in less than half an hour Alison was in the darkroom of a publisher, Ben pacing behind her, his face hard and impassive in the light of the one red lightbulb. He was waiting for the results of her work. He was not waiting patiently. She wouldn't like to be his adversary.

The prints began to appear out of the solution and together she and Ben watched, as if in slow motion, a repeat of the horror. First the exhilarated, yet exhausted, face of the vibrant politician. Next the blaze of light, the exultation of victory. Then the fallen hero, the kitchen and the blood, and the last look in the dying man's eyes.

"You got it. You managed to get the whole thing." Ben's voice was soft and deadly, his rage tangible. She could feel his body throbbing beside her. "Now, let's get it out to the world."

Ben handled the deal. Suddenly as cold-blooded as the assassin had been, he called the various wire services, set the bidding in motion, and got the highest price possible. And credit whenever printed. There was no bargaining. The highest price won. Alison watched, passive, disturbed by what she was seeing.

This was not a world she wanted to be part of. She wanted to flee this pain and this anger. Flee this horror. She wanted to run away from business deals. From Los Angeles. From Ben.

The deal completed, he slammed down the phone.

"A certified check will be deposited in your account in the First National Bank of Boston. They'll pick up the prints in fifteen minutes."

They were now seated in his modern, slick, cold office that rose high above the Sunset Strip. His face was harsh in the early morning light. Neither of them had slept.

Alison rose. "I'm leaving, Ben," she said. "I'm going back home."

"What's the matter? No guts?" His voice was like a whiplash.

"No, not enough for this," she murmured, trying to hold herself together.

"I'm sorry, Alison," he said. "I didn't mean that."

"I know you didn't, Ben. I'm going home to straighten things out. And you—you don't need a further complication in your life." He did not refute this.

"Good-bye Ben," she said. And then he did a very L.A. thing. He took a card from his wallet and handed it to her.

"You don't have my number. It's not listed."

They stood there in the dawn. She took the card and put it beside Diane's.

"Of course, you can always reach me through the firm," he said sadly, "if you ever need me."

She left. There was nothing more she could do to help him. Or herself. She had to go back home for a while and put her life into perspective—without the aid of a viewfinder.

Chapter Five

Alison sought shelter in the wonderful old mansion—all granite and slate and inviting windows—that had been her childhood refuge. She roamed the estate with its twenty-six acres and its own pond and pine grove, and she wandered from the gatehouse and the stables up the driveway of crushed blue rock to the main house, looking for herself.

She remembered that a little over a year ago—could it have been so recently?—she had strolled these grounds with her father, and the trees had been a light-green cobweb against a cloudless blue sky. The lilacs, lining the path to the formal gardens, had been a frothy purple. She could remember the head gardener busily clipping the hedge while his helper pruned the forsythia. She could remember how, arm in arm, father and daughter had climbed the hill where the land fell away to the blue strip that marked the Atlantic Ocean and Marblehead. The two of them had paused to inhale the delicious mixture of salt and first flowers that made the spring day so memorable. She could remember saying (that innocent Alison), "I want life always to be like this. To be just like this day. Oh, how wonderful life is!"

"Baby," her father had cautioned her, "never take anything for granted. Not this day, nor the way we live, nor our love for each other. Happiness is not just given. It is earned."

And she, so young only a year ago, had joked with him.

53

"Are you worried about me, Daddy? Well, don't be. You have prepared me for life! What else was Rosemary Hall for? And Smith? And summer camp? Why, you can drop me in the middle of the Rocky Mountains and I'll find my way out. You sent me to Survival School. I even learned to skin a rabbit."

That had made Jonathan Carmichael laugh. Together they had returned to the gray slate house, where dinner waited for them in the dining room with its dark paneled walls, a fire warding off the evening chill, the Baccarat crystal shining in the firelight, and the chandeliers gleaming on the long mahogany table.

Now they were together once more, Alison and her parents. But, having loved, Alison was much more conscious of the relationship between Jonathan and Phyllis Carmichael. She looked at the two of them. He was the handsomest man she had ever known—silver hair, crinkly eyes, slight mustache, and the tanned face of the outdoorsman combined with the casual elegance of Old Money. Her mother was the perfect picture of the Former Deb. Chin and neck still graceful in a world where grace did not readily accompany pedigree. Skin that was as young as a schoolgirl's. Even her gray hair was still worn in the pageboy style that went out with the Big Band era.

The Perfect Couple.

Why, then, were dinnertimes so strained, her father so preoccupied, and the occasional attempts at joviality so miserable? Why did she notice her mother chattering to the woodwork, making conversation? Alison could see that both her parents were attempting to talk with her, but were avoiding talking to each other. There was a sadness about them. How strange that she had never noticed it before. But then, how young she had been, how innocent. So much had happened in a year's time that she found herself no longer able to communicate with her father. She realized that she and her mother had never communicated. Phyllis Carmichael had merely supervised her daughter's life. Packing for camp and arranging the debutante parties, sewing on name tags and making checklists for college. She had run the house and garden. But about her mother's feelings Alison knew next to nothing. Nobody did.

She had once found the sound of their voices comforting, as she had found the pines and the wild flowers, the trails she had sauntered down most of her sheltered life. But now she felt oddly out of place, no longer a child. What *was* she? she asked herself. That was what she was trying to discover.

At the yacht club the old crowd welcomed her back—a bit uneasily, she felt. She had become an odd sort of celebrity. She passed most of the month of June at the prow of a racing sailer, feeling the spray wet her face. She welcomed its sharp sting as she welcomed the blazing sun and the spanking breeze.

It was on a Sunday that Dick Bailey, who had once squired her to a weekend dance at Yale, asked her to go along with him as crew, and she agreed. She observed him at the tiller. He looked Just Right. He had light brown hair cut in a conservative fashion, and why not? He was being groomed to take over his father's brokerage house. He had faithfully put in his time learning the business as he had dutifully put in his time at Andover and then at Yale. In a year or so, of course, he would zoom to the top; his place was waiting for him. Next would come a suitable marriage and a comfortable life with winter vacations skiing in Switzerland, or sunning in the Caribbean, and then after that vacations "with the kids"—in the same spots probably. And finally, as he got older, more subdued holidays in Bermuda. His life was already charted out.

"You can tie the jib line if you want to," Dick said to her. They were two or three miles out from land, and there was nothing but glorious blue sky, the gently swelling ocean, and the sun of a Sunday noon.

"You were looking at me funny," he added.

"Was I?" she said. It was true; she had been adding up his assets. Smooth dancer, solidly good-looking without being too handsome. A good game of tennis. Excellent boatsman. He had been a considerate escort. He had always kissed her good night without pushing it. The kiss had been sufficient. A good kisser, she remembered. She

wondered what he was like now. Then he had been a boy.
Now he wasn't. He had caught her in midthought.

"What are you thinking about?"

She avoided the question neatly. "About the time
that's passed since I last saw you."

"New Haven—two years ago," he reminded her,
grinning.

"Oh, I'd forgotten New Haven. I was remembering
those Glee Club Weekend dances at Andover."

"Lord, we were kids then!"

"Yes, that was what I was thinking. And wondering,
you know, what are we now?"

"Well," he said, slightly mockingly, "I am the man-of-
the-world at the helm. Could I pose for you?"

"You were always so neat," she murmured to herself,
but he caught it.

"Hey, I spent my time bumming around. Fort Lauderdale spring vacation. That was a blast. Although it's
gotten pretty grimy now, and Bermuda's not much better.
And I hitchhiked through Europe last year. With Perry
Knowlton. Remember him?"

Of course, she did. He had been the boy who had
escorted her to New Jimmy's that first late summer night
in Paris.

"We were in Paris at the same time," she said.

"How about that!" he said. "I remember now, Perry
told me he'd met this swell ginch."

"Was that what he called me?"

"Yeah. Hey, we could have had fun."

"I did."

"Actually I wasn't all that crazy about Paris. Were
you?"

"Yes," she answered in a faraway voice. "Yes, I was
all that crazy about Paris."

"Coming about," he said, and she ducked her head.
The boom swung around. They began a leeward tack.
"You want to go to the dance at the club with me next
Saturday?"

She had to laugh. He was still using that prep-school
terminology. He mistook her laugh.

"It's not all that hilarious, is it? Asking a girl to a dance?"

"No," she said. "Oh, no, Dick. It's just I've been away from this world so long."

"Well, I guess you are a celebrity. I don't know how to deal with that," he said rather stiffly.

"I'm not. And you don't. It's just that we've had such different experiences this last year. I feel like a stranger."

"That's crazy. You know everybody there. It's the old crowd. Mimi Cabot has been asking about you, by the way."

"I haven't seen Mimi in ages." Alison felt the pattern of country-club patter coming back to her, but at the same time she was laughing at herself inside.

"Well, you'll see her Saturday night. I'll pick you up at seven. It's a dinner-dance. Formal, of course."

"Of course."

"You can loose the jib. I'll head downwind."

Of course, she would go on Saturday. She remembered Mimi. Everyone called her a "darling girl," which meant she wasn't really beautiful, but cute and no bother to anyone. Just the way Dick was considered a "good catch."

Saturday night she was surrounded by darling girls and good catches. Nothing had changed. The music was still tinged with the Society Beat; even the Beatles tunes became a kind of dignified fox-trot. And the darling girls all wore their hair the way they had in prep school. They talked the same way, although there was, Alison noticed, more purpose in the flirtations. More careful aiming at that good catch. Everyone had a few drinks before dinner. Dinner consisted of roast chicken and canned peas. They couldn't get fresh peas in the summer? she thought. Strawberry shortcake for dessert. The strawberries were just out, and the shortcake was real and New England and Alison was the only girl who touched dessert.

She sat to Dick's right. Mimi sat on his left. They talked across him. Mimi was full of questions.

"Wasn't it awful being there when he was shot?" And, "My goodness, how did you have the presence of mind to

keep photographing like that?" And, "What kind of life
was that in Paris? It sounds super, living on the Left Bank.
I always wanted to go to Paris, but my grades weren't good
enough."

Alison looked at her blankly. Was she kidding? No.

Dick asked her to dance. Alison noticed a slightly
chilled expression on Mimi's face. Oh, well, she thought.
It was every girl for herself in this life.

She had remembered correctly. Dick was a smooth
dancer, as good as he had been at Andover. She suddenly
asked him if he remembered a Ben Sawyer.

"Lord, yes," Dick said. (He was fond of saying "Lord."
In the locker room among the boys he would allow himself
a "God" and a "Christ" occasionally. On the whole he was
careful not to offend. Who knew what might offend a good
prospect?) "Ben was a couple of years ahead of me. Skied
a lot, as I remember. California man? Never quite fit in.
He was always attracted to townies, if you know what I
mean. Well, we all had our fling, but Lord, Ben Sawyer
really went after the town ginch."

"Oh," Alison said, and the band swung deftly into
"Night and Day." "Night and Day." How many times
throughout her childhood had she watched her parents
dance to this sentimental yet sophisticated Cole Porter
song? Her grandparents undoubtedly had danced often to
it too. Alison sighed, wistful for the simplicity of life of
previous generations. Oh, her parents and grandparents
had known the turmoil of World Wars, the Great Depression, but those events had merely disrupted the timetables—
not the basic patterns—of their lives. They "knew" the
fundamental order of things. Why couldn't she believe?
Why couldn't she settle for what they had just as Dick and
Mimi and all the rest of the Just Right set? Life seemed
hopelessly complicated to her.

She wondered vaguely whether Dick would kiss her,
and how he would kiss her when he took her home. They
left the party early, and Alison felt that Mimi's good-night
was a shade too cheery. *She has her eye on Dick*, Alison
thought, *and believes I'm taking him away from her*. Her
own problem, she realized, was that she could take none

of this seriously. Was it because she had known another kind of life?

Rather cold-bloodedly she decided to play the game. It was almost an experiment. It involved none of her feelings, because she had none. She was an actress playing the part in the Saturday Night Follies.

Dick drove her home. Past the beach, where he did not stop the car to take a look at the ocean or suggest a walk. He took her straight home. She was disappointed. He came around to open the door for her. She got out. The evening smelled of all the night flowers in the garden. When he took her arm, she was curious. What would happen if she took the initiative? How would he feel? Threatened, she decided. Let him make all the moves in this game. How detached she was.

He did exactly what was expected. Told her how much he had enjoyed the evening and kissed her. It was the good-night kiss, perfectly proper for two people who had known each other a long time. Perfectly proper, and yet she was intrigued to find that his kiss was not a proper one. Oh, it started out in the correct fashion, but then got away from him and he let himself go and devoured her lips, kissed her, caressed her, let his hands roam over her body just as though he had *not* gone to the right schools. She felt nothing. But she was fascinated that she could rouse this feeling in him. Thank God he didn't apologize when he came up for air. Instead, he said, "Hey, I liked that. Could we do that some more?"

She smiled. "Yes, but not tonight."

"Well, next Saturday, then? And if the weather's good, we could go sailing next Sunday. I'm busy this Sunday," he added by way of apology.

"Fine," she said, "if you're sure Mimi wouldn't mind."

He looked confused. "What does Mimi have to do with this?"

"I've been out of touch. I thought maybe you two—"

"Are just good friends," he hastened to assure her.

And so the summer passed. Most of the time she didn't have to talk, only tie lines and handle the jib sheet. Return the serve. People remarked that she had changed.

Amid so much laughter and gaiety her silences were seen
as merely mysterious. They made her more beautiful. She
had grown so detached that she was like some goddess.
After three weeks—golden-tanned, hair almost white-blond
from the sun and spray—she was a Dietrich, a Garbo. She
smiled but did not laugh. She answered but did not really
respond. And Dick Bailey continued his pursuit of her.
He was wild about her that summer. And wilder because
her lack of response made him desperate. She allowed his
kisses, enjoyed them even. She had been right. He was a
good kisser. But it was meaningless to her. And yet she
allowed it, not even considering that she might be hurting
him. He was so totally serious about his intentions, why
did he so frequently inspire in her an insane desire to
laugh? Either she had to straighten up or stop. This was
like living a double life—her real self watching this pretend self playing.

At first there were some calls. From New York. From
Paris. From Los Angeles. Again her pictures of the Kennedy assassination had created a sensation. The agencies
were after her. Would she cover the political conventions?
Go to Chicago? No, she would not. In August Myra called
to ask if she was all right. To ask after Ben. And most
importantly, to ask whether Alison would take some fashion shots. These had to be rush-rush. The shots she had
ordered were disastrous, Myra confided to Alison. And
she intimated the entire magazine might fold if Alison did
not come to her aid.

"Whatever you wish to shoot. Wherever. What I
need is clean, fresh lines. These fashions are a bit—*un peu
de nostalgie*, shall we say. They recall old times and sim-
pler ways. They're resort clothes for this winter. Is it
possible to help me out?"

Alison told her she'd call back. That afternoon Dick
Bailey called to tell her he had to travel to California for
an extended time. The possibility of setting up a branch
office in Los Angeles. The possibility of his heading the
office. She wanted to share his excitement, but merely
wished him the best of luck. The moment she hung up he
was out of her thoughts.

Alison mulled over Myra's words. *Old times and sim-*

pler ways. She remembered thinking, as she had danced to "Night and Day," of the generations of club members who had circled the floor to that tune. She had an idea and called Myra back.

"Come up to Massachusetts," she said, "and I will get you results."

Myra Van Steen's arrival at Pride's Crossing caused as much comment as Alison's entrance to the Queen's Grill on the *QE2.* Fashion wasn't considered quite the thing. And female fashion editors—indeed, any woman who did more than charity work—were not really suitable. But Myra was keen and very shrewd.

For instance, it took only five minutes to win over Jonathan Carmichael. She merely had to admire the quality of his hunting dogs and the pedigree of his horses. Mrs. Carmichael was a slightly tougher case, but Myra was an authority on roses. She admired exactly the right hybrids, the pink and yellow fragrances, even the more common primroses that Mrs. Carmichael had so carefully nurtured. After that the deep voice, the constant cigarette in the mouth was accepted. Even promoted. Myra Van Steen could do no wrong. She was a fine honest woman and, more than that, protective and terribly concerned about Alison. With Myra's arrival Alison seemed to brighten.

The shooting itself took only two days. The first day, the models arrived in Boston and were driven out to the estate. Myra and Alison had already agreed on the location. The country club. Alison's idea was to mix the models with the female members of the club. At first the female members had been hesitant. Again Myra won them over. They grew to like the idea of appearing in *Charm*—as long as there would be no pay. After all, they were not models. The models understood that and were amused. The "civilians," as they called the club members, were titillated and thrilled.

The Victorian furbelows of the country club made a perfect background for these summer fashions. Polka dots and puffed sleeves. Organdy. Light white cottons. The sea breeze seemed to liberate the models. They became like children at play. Their hair streamed out behind them. They grasped their floppy picture hats. They were charm-

ing and delicious, and after fifteen minutes totally unselfconscious. The civilians—and Alison had chosen them
wisely—were the perfect counterpart. Mimi, for instance,
had a piquancy about her face that no professional model
could hope to duplicate. Some of the mothers had an
aristocratic bearing that no modeling school could teach.
The older women, some in their golf togs, and Mimi and
some of the younger girls in their tennis outfits, assumed
poses they thought were "professional." Alison took this
disaster and put it to good use. She made them all play
living statues. The models knew what she was up to. The
results, of course, showed hoydens frolicking among the
prototypes of the Social Set. Alison took advantage of
everything and shot away.

Looking through the lens, she saw another world.
This was the world of illusion. Yes, the sky was truly blue,
the grounds clean and windswept, the models beautiful,
and the dresses delightful. But she was creating a world
where the sun would never go behind a cloud, or the
dresses be mussed up, or the time pass on. Young women,
older women. All were enjoying a perennial summer.

She used that phrase on Myra, who immediately wrote
it down in her little notebook. When the pictures appeared in the following issue, that was the title.

On the second day of the shooting, while the models
were taking a break, Mimi approached Alison.

"I have something to say to you," she said seriously.
Alison was truly puzzled. "It's by way of an apology, I
guess. When you first came back to Pride's Crossing, I
thought you were putting on airs. I thought you were
some kind of celebrity and that you were trying to take
Dick away from me. What I'm trying to say is, I thought
you were laughing at all of us."

Alison kept very still, because everything Mimi was
saying was true. Mimi continued. "Alison, I do understand it now. You really are different from the rest of us.
The moment you get behind that camera, something happens to you. Well, for instance, I know in a tiny way what
you're doing. I can arrange flowers. I can't do much else,
but I can do that. I can make patterns with flowers, and
they look better than anyone else's. So I do understand

about you, that's all." And then she left, embarrassed. Alison sat alone for a minute, and then Myra appeared.

"You seem different, Alison," she said. "Sad. What is it?"

"It's nothing, Myra. Maybe that's it. I feel nothing."

"I don't believe that for a moment. But whatever it is, we'll talk about it later. In the meantime continue shooting this extraordinary group. I mean, I do love those sharp-nosed Puritans in their golf clothes. Formidable!"

Later that night, when the shooting was finished and Myra and Alison were sipping coffee on the front porch of the Carmichael house, Alison confessed. They were sitting in shadows in wonderful New England rockers. The evening was balmy and the little peepers were singing in the pond beyond the thicket.

"I think I feel guilty," Alison began.

"About what, for heaven's sake?" asked Myra, who had never felt guilty about anything in her life.

"It has to do with Robert Kennedy's assassination. No, more with Ben. You see, when it all happened, I kept clicking away. I didn't stop. I didn't concern myself with a dying man. I was *photographing* him. I didn't realize it at the time, but my instinct was to keep getting frame after frame."

"Because that is what you are, my dear. Your life, all the life around you, is attached to the camera."

"But somehow—and it wasn't until later, in Ben's office—he said nothing, but I felt he was disapproving. I felt he considered me unfeeling. Self-serving. It was almost as though he were saying, 'Well you got what you came for.'"

"That's nonsense, my dear," Myra said gently, "but I do understand. We women are a strange lot. If we don't go after what we want, we feel angry. And if we do go after what we want, we feel guilty. Be careful though. That feeling of guilt can lead to dangerous positions. I've seen it before. Great artists throw themselves away on the wrong man. Actresses run away from the theater. Writers turn themselves into baby machines. Why? To compensate. To expiate the sin of talent. Of ability. Don't let that happen to you, Alison. You're too fine and too special to waste. And now, my dear, I must go to bed. The sea air is better than Demerol."

It was a brief conversation, but it stayed in Alison's mind. It did not change her mood however. She could not shake the lethargy that possessed her. The summer came and went. She refused to cover the Chicago convention, and when—again—she saw the pictures of the bloodied young heads and the old men pontificating, the nightsticks and mounted police, the riots and the anger, she sat alone by the sea until the images ceased burning her mind.

The fall passed. She didn't return to Smith, although she still joined in the Harvard football weekends, the impromptu picnics in station wagons, the Bloody Marys and bullshots, the postgame celebrations. The fall was one long golden season, but to Alison it was a season she could not recapture.

She had grown older than they—the Class of '69—older and different, and after the Thanksgiving Day game, with Dick Bailey still away, she stopped going out. She refused dates. She holed up in the Carmichael estate, and while the snow whirled around the windowpanes, she read. She read the classics, Jane Austen, Willa Cather, Emily Brontë. She read Emily Dickinson. She even tried her hand at poetry. The images that flowed from her pen were interesting, but not the same as those that came through her lens. Still, she did not touch the camera.

Christmas came and went. And New Year's. Finally Jonathan Carmichael roused himself from his own apathy and decided it was time for action.

"You're coming with me," he said to Alison. "I want you to look at some investments."

"Where?" she asked.

"Never mind," he said swiftly, "but dress warmly. And bring your camera. I may need some pictures."

They drove to the White Mountains in New Hampshire, to a section of undeveloped land outside North Conway, which was the principal ski resort for the Boston area. Jonathan stopped the car, they got out, and he asked her to take several shots of the landscape.

"Well, what do you think?" he finally asked her.

"The scenery is beautiful. What do you want me to think?"

"Essex Valley. Condominiums. An entire mountain, sixteen trails. Tennis courts year round, under a bubble. And the condominiums can be built at a premium. There will be nothing like this east of Aspen."

"Is it a gamble for you?"

"A challenge, darling. At last a challenge. You're young. You have a feel for all this. In ten years—well, who can tell me what will happen in ten years?"

"Do you know the other investors?" she asked. She was concerned. This seemed so unlike her father, the conservative, practical man. Of course, ski areas were booming. The spread of condominiums was nationwide, particularly in resort areas. North Conway had at least three seasons when the area was booming with tourists. Skiers, summer vacationers, and visitors to the fall foliage.

"What can I say?" She laughed. "It feels good to me. And if it feels good to you, then *do* it."

"I think I will. There's a meeting at three o'clock this afternoon, and I promised I'd be there. Do you think you can find enough amusement here until the meeting is finished?"

"Don't worry about me, Daddy," she said. "Are you sure you have enough pictures of the terrain?"

"Thank you, yes, Alison. Now, drive me over to that horrendous-looking edifice at the edge of the road. And then the car is yours. Pick me up at—oh, say, four o'clock."

It was now two. Alison sighed. She had time on her hands and nothing to do. She returned to the slopes. Perhaps she could find something of interest to while away the hours.

There was a slalom race taking place, between the instructors and the townies. The ski instructors were dressed like *skiers*. They had the helmets, the goggles, the right kind of down vests, Roffe pants, Hansen boots, Rossignol skis with Salomon 727 bindings. In other words, the works. The townies, on the other hand, wore tight-fitting jeans, plaid wool jackets. Hand-me-down skis from the end-of-the-season trade-ins that take place annually at the high school. Unfair. Some advantaged, some not.

But it made no difference when it came to racing. The townies had been on the slopes since they could walk. They had schussed the mountain at age five, sometimes crying because the surface wasn't icy enough. They were fearless. They were used to spills and hard knocks, and most of them worked after high school in the shoe factories or garages, or did odd jobs. They became handymen or house painters. Or moved away. And, after the brief wonderful springtime of their lives, they settled into bitterness and alcoholism and Saturday-night brawls. And had kids they couldn't quite support. These townies grew up early, and burned out early. The rest of life was a long middle-age. Their wives grew fat and sullen. Their houses fell into disrepair. Their automobiles rusted from the salt on the roads in winter, the mud in springtime, the dirt in summer. But, for a time, a little time, they lived—for the ski season and the hunting season. They lived with nature. Nature was the only beautiful thing in their lives. Nature was the reason they remained in this poor section of the country.

Alison watched the skiers weave in and out between the flags. All the young men possessed amazing grace and agility, but one stood out. He cut corners the most sharply, hurtled down the mountain at breakneck speed. It appeared that he was trying to kill himself.

"There goes Crazy Kenny," somebody in the crowd said, and to Alison it seemed that he had to be crazy to take such chances. She unconsciously picked up her camera and adjusted the range finder. How odd, she thought. What was she doing?

The difference between the ill-equipped and the well-equipped skiers fascinated her. Their faces, also, which glowed with their exertion when they reached the bottom of the hill and whipped off their protective goggles. The townies, she noticed, wore no gloves. This was evidently a macho image. The competition, she further noticed, was not deadly. It was a camaraderie of the mountain. Each side admired the other's skill.

There was to be one last run down the mountain. The last of three heats, which would decide the winner. Alison watched the men clamber onto the chairlift and disappear.

Fifteen minutes later they started their descent, one by one, zigzagging down the icy mountain, the evening shadows already making the trail treacherous. This slowed up the more cautious. The times were slower than the previous heat's. Not by much, usually fractions of seconds, but as in any race, those fractions were what changed winners into losers.

There were good times, slow times, and two spectacular times. One belonged to Hannes Bruns, the head of the ski school. The other was the last contestant, who came flying down the mountain, sometimes lost in the sharp shadows, disappearing into ravines, emerging again, weaving, the hips swaying slightly, never too little, never too much. Alison had never seen such grace and such control. He skimmed down the mountain, and the crowd started to cheer. As he came closer she recognized the young man someone had called Crazy Kenny. She stepped closer to the finish line. She wanted a shot of his face.

He twisted and turned between the last poles, then it was straight downhill at the end. He shot for the finish line. Alison was so intent with her camera, she didn't realize how far she had moved. Kenny saw her just in time and managed to swerve, having crossed the finish line, missing her by a hairbreadth. He sprayed her with snow, then fell to avoid crashing into the group gathered at the bottom of the mountain. For a moment there was a tumble of skis, poles, goggles flying off, particles of snow. And then the body was still.

Alison was horrified. She had killed him. It was her fault. She rushed over to the prone figure.

"Oh, I'm sorry, I'm sorry. Are you all right? Please forgive me!" she babbled. She bent over the figure to see if he was breathing.

Suddenly he wrapped his arms around her, drew her down, and kissed her. Not just a brush on the cheek, either. He parted her lips with his tongue and gave her a real *kiss*. Alison was nonplussed. She found herself thrilling to the touch of this man, furious that he had upset her, relieved that she hadn't killed him. So she stayed there and let herself be kissed. And when he was through kissing her, Kenny released her.

"It was worth it," he said. She couldn't see his eyes through the snow. Then he shook his head and she was able to glimpse his face.

An Indian. That was her first impression. Like the carved figures. His face was so strong and, with the winter tan, the color of mahogany. The nose was straight and strong, the cheekbones almost Oriental. And the hair, long and pulled back in a ponytail, was blacker than any white man's hair. An Indian savage. That was her reaction, her impression. She was not far wrong.

Kenny Buck was half-Indian. The Abnaki tribe. His mother had been French-Canadian. A beauty once, with a photograph from Thetford Mines, Province of Quebec, to prove it. She had come down to Maine looking for work in the mills and had met Kenny's father. The two had found each other and had become each other's total destruction. He introduced the French beauty to hopelessness and she introduced him to liquor. They had sat across kitchen tables, drinking up the Saturday nights, spewing abuse on each other. So they passed the years, pulling themselves together for temporary jobs. Sometimes she clerked at the five-and-dime and sometimes he worked for the town in the woods or, during the summer, on the roads. Then their anger would flare up at each other. She would bring other men into the house to taunt him. Twice he went to the men's reformatory for the winter, emerging in spring with a new pair of shoes, courtesy of the State of Maine. When Kenny was twelve, his father left and never returned. The men around his mother increased. The sounds in the night—the laughter, groans, cursing and weeping—all became more frequent. Kenny would recognize the men during the day, sitting on the curb during the summer, hanging around the post office during the winter. He became known as the son of a whore, and a half-breed to boot. Looking at those men, he was looking at his future—if he was lucky.

He needed an escape. And he found one when he almost collided with Alison Carmichael.

Everything might have been left just where it was—a near accident, nothing exceptional—except for one thing. Alison laughed.

She hadn't meant to. She had been extremely concerned, even frightened. But she laughed at the outrageousness of Crazy Kenny.

And when she laughed, he was intrigued.

"Who are you?" he asked her, still lying in the snow. "And are you rich enough so I can sue you for a lot of money?"

"Is that what you want?" she asked, and found he was looking hard at her.

"No," he said finally, after he had taken in the beauty of her face, the soft blondness of her hair, the lovely fragile quality of her skin. He had never been close to a woman like that. He had been close to many women, the town girls—sometimes their mothers too—but they had already been roughened by life. Now he was looking at another kind of female altogether.

"Help me up." It was an order. She obeyed.

"Can you walk?"

"Some," Kenny Buck said. "But not twenty miles."

"Twenty miles?"

"That's where home is."

"How did you get here?"

"Thumbed. Everybody knows me."

"Then thumb home," she said with spirit.

"I may be crippled," he said, looking down at her.

"I doubt that."

"Take me home," he said softly.

Home was a teepee. Crazy Kenny had built his own teepee out in the woods, but close enough to the road so that he could hook into the Central Maine Power Line. He had a lightbulb. He had his guitar and an amplifier. He could cook his meals. And he had no one to bother him.

"Why did you come out here?" Alison asked. Her fingers were itching to take some photographs, but she wasn't quite sure. Not yet.

"It's cheap. I don't pay no tax. I don't pay no electricity, so long as they don't know about it. And I'm free here. I do whatever I want. What about you? What are you doing here?"

"You asked me to bring you home."

"Yeah. But you didn't have to," he said with an easy smile. He knew women, and he had learned of his power over them. This one was no different, he thought. He was wrong.

"I felt obligated."

"Big word."

"Don't play dumb with me."

"Okay. No games. Either one of us. What do you want to do with that camera?"

"Take your picture."

"Is there any money in it?"

"Ten dollars."

"That's better than a kick in the head. You want me to pose?"

"No. I don't know what I want. What would you do if I weren't here?"

"I'd be playing my guitar. Shit!" he interrupted himself. "I forgot my trophy. I won that freakin' slalom. See what you made me do! You made me forget all about winning."

Alison snapped the shutter. The defiance, the sudden anger. His blazing eyes were full on her.

He turned away slightly, his face glowering. Snap! There seemed to be no way for him to escape. Like a caged animal he looked back at her, then ripped the bandanna from his hair. It swung free. He was the savage, his hair around his face. He spoke no more, but proceeded to take off his workshirt. Underneath that was thermal underwear, soaked with sweat. He took that off, too, and rubbed his body with it. His muscles were hard, his body lean. There was no room for fat. There was too much energy stored up inside that body. An animal, Alison kept repeating to herself as she took shot after shot. He was more animal than human.

As though he were reading her mind, he suddenly spoke. "What do you see when you look at me?"

"A wild Indian!" She laughed, continuing to snap the shutter.

Kenny did not laugh. A shadow came over his face. "Yeah, that's what I am," he muttered bitterly.

"But that's wonderful!" she said. "Are you really an Indian?"

"Abnaki. My father was a full-blooded Abnaki."

Alison suddenly felt uncomfortable. They were reenacting some historic moment, the Puritan and the Primitive. She was exploiting him, giving him words that were like little worthless glass beads, and he was giving her, showing her without knowing it, his life.

"My mother was—*is*," he corrected himself—"a full-blooded whore. Have you got what you want?"

"Yes, yes. I guess so." Alison was flustered. There was something so disturbing, so contradictory about this man. Never had she met someone so blatantly male. So reckless. So threatening. And inside a voice was saying, *So attractive*. For the first time in months she was aware of her own sexuality. She found her breath coming in little short gasps.

"You better go now," he said.

He was dismissing her. She allowed it.

"Here's your ten dollars," she said with some asperity, sure that he would refuse it, but wanting to humiliate him.

"Thanks," he said, taking it and stuffing it inside the front of his jeans. He was still bare-chested. The gesture brought his nakedness back to her. In contrast to the straight black hair surrounding his head, he had no hair at all on his body. His skin was smooth. Polished mahogany. . . .

He was smiling at her, so aware. She hated that smile, the knowingness of it.

She turned and left, gunned the station wagon, and headed back to Daddy. And safety.

Jonathan Carmichael was more worried than angry.

"Where have you been?"

"Oh, I got caught up in some local color," she muttered. "I'm sorry. Have I kept you waiting long?"

"Not as long as I am going to have to keep you waiting. We didn't finish all the business. We have another meeting at nine tomorrow morning. At the bank. But I promise you that will be the end of it. Meanwhile I made a reservation for us for dinner. Are you hungry?"

"Starved."

"Then, let's go eat."

They went to the Bell Buoy North and were escorted to the cellar, which had been converted to an attractive dining room, a cross between a wine cellar and a rathskeller. There were candles on the table, efficient waiters.

The dinner was healthful and robust, a combination of New England and French. Clam chowder, steaming hot. Popovers with butter that melted gloriously into the crevices. Steak and matchstick French fries. A fresh salad and a sturdy red wine. And for dessert home-baked maple-sugar pie. The chef came from Montreal. They offered their compliments. Jonathan paid the check and left a large tip. He was feeling expansive. The meeting had gone well. The future looked good. The mountain air and the vibrancy of the little resort town stimulated him. He felt young again. And for the first time in months his daughter had that glow. There was an aura about her that radiated health and good spirits, and it had been sadly lacking of late.

That was why he suggested they look in on the bar upstairs. There was live music. He could hear the whine of a guitar and the throb of drums. It was the only alternative to an evening of television, probably with poor reception. Alison agreed. They were ushered into a crowded, dimly lit dancehall and shown to a table fairly close to the stage.

It was hot and smoky, and the noise was deafening. Ordinarily Jonathan would have fled, but tonight he felt like observing this new world he might soon be entering. He noticed, to his amazement, that Alison was not at all discomfited by the music. Rather than being put off by it, she seemed drawn to it. He followed her gaze. She was staring at the lead musician, a guitarist with wild black hair. A musician? Jonathan felt that did not describe the sounds the man was making. Caterwauling. Howling. And the movements of his body as he steadily stroked the guitar were . . . suggestive. This was not singing. This was some kind of exhibition.

Jonathan looked around him. No one else seemed to be taking offense. The floor was crowded with dancers, whose movements matched the singer's, except they lacked the same grace. The other "musicians" in the band appeared to be farmboys—local yokels dressed up like scouts in the West. Mustaches and long hair. Wild Bill Hickok on the drums and General Custer on the long guitar that resembled a bass.

Meanwhile Alison had taken out her camera. This was a most amazing coincidence, she thought. Her crazy Indian was a rock singer. Only it wasn't rock, she decided, as she started taking pictures, but something beyond. Along with the rock bite, it had a country-and-western punch to it. It was honky-tonk. There was little of the Beatles influence here, or even the blues that had influenced the Beatles. It was mocking, this music, savage and intense. Primitive.

God, he was sexy, Alison thought. She couldn't keep her lens away from him. His movements, the way he attacked the guitar, lunged toward the mike, then suddenly caressed it. Once in a while he would croon. The words weren't always distinguishable, but the meaning was. There was a cruelty that never quite left his face.

The group finished the set and left the stage, drenched in sweat. Kenny Buck came right over to their table.

"Who said you could take pictures?" he demanded.

"No one," Alison retorted.

"Now, just a minute, young man," Jonathan Carmichael began.

Kenny Buck ignored him.

"You didn't pay the ten dollars." A slight smile curved his lips. Alison opened her mouth to say something, but her father suddenly spoke up.

"What do you mean? Do you know who my daughter is? She's Alison Carmichael, the photographer. Did you see those pictures in *Life* of the riots in Paris? Did you see the pictures of the Kennedy assassination? Why, my daughter could make you *famous* if she put her mind to it!"

Alison was both amused and awed. She had never heard her father speak so passionately before. Certainly not about her career. It delighted her. Her father was proud of her, defended her. He thought she was good! What a marvelous feeling. She turned to him.

"Never mind, Daddy. We know each other. This afternoon I almost killed him. And he practically saved my life. The ten dollars is just a joke between us."

"No joke." Her noble savage was reverting to his sketch.

"Oh, well, do you want another ten dollars?" She reached for her wallet.

"Can you make me famous?" he asked suddenly. His ambition was naked on that strong face.

"What do you want to be famous *as*?"

"As *me*."

"Well . . . as what though? Actor? Singer? Male model?"

He looked doubtful at that. "You can help. You know people. The right people." He was testing her.

"Some," she said.

"What's your name again?"

She told him, and he wrote it down on a matchbook cover.

"When I'm ready to be famous, I'll come to you," he said, not joking. "In the meantime keep the pictures."

Then he was gone. Jonathan Carmichael was nonplussed. He looked at his daughter. "Am I out of touch? Does everybody behave like that? Is this whole world suddenly crazy?"

"No," Alison said. "I think you were looking at a genuine original. There aren't many in the world like him."

The following morning Jonathan Carmiahael concluded his business. Essex Valley was a reality. An investment in a condominium ski community. Risky perhaps, but what was life if not one adventure after another? For Jonathan it had been too long between adventures.

That afternoon he and Alison drove home to Pride's Crossing, neither aware of the effect the previous twenty-four hours would have on their lives.

Chapter Six

As though Kenny Buck and his fierce energy had released her, Alison began taking an interest in life—and her camera—again. She did another fashion spread for *Charm*, and in March *Rolling Stone* contacted her. A reclusive celebrity was fascinated with her work and had agreed to do a sitting for *Rolling Stone*—if Alison agreed to be the photographer. She did.

The portraits were praised for their sensitivity, insightfulness, and honesty. *Rolling Stone* was thrilled, and in the middle of August Alison found herself trapped in the Holiday Inn in Liberty, New York, where a Sleepy Hollow valley had suddenly become the center of the music universe. Woodstock. *Rolling Stone* had hired her to photograph the scene. Not merely the performers, but everything.

And she had. The lines of the young and vibrant waiting on the blocked roads. A girl with a rabbit on her knee. The indoctrination course in adoption. The nude swimming at Filippini Pond where a waterfall was the only shower within fifty miles. The young who banded together to set up a first-aid stand on Route 17B, cooking potatoes over a fire to give to the hungry.

Everyone was there. Drugstore waitresses, fraternity brothers, leather dudes. Philosophical state troopers. Farmers. Farmboys. The Midwest and Alabama, and everyone going through changes. Thousands of changes during a weekend. There was love and there were good vibrations—

not yet so commercialized—and there was hope. And most importantly there was a resurgence of that wonderful energy Ben Sawyer had felt.

Alison had a wonderful time photographing the outrageous and the simple. The brilliant performance of Jimi Hendrix, the innocence of lovers sleeping in each other's arms.

She spent the weekend and then was rescued from the Holiday Inn by helicopter. She developed the pictures and sent them to California, while she returned to Massachusetts. *Rolling Stone* gave her a by-line and devoted four pages to her work, and she promptly forgot all about it. Diane and Ben had been right. Everything was disposable. Everything happened so fast, it was all forgotten before the week was out.

The experience did finally give her the impetus to move out of the Carmichael mansion and into an apartment in Cambridge. She furnished the three rooms with very little. The house itself was one of the old dark buildings along Brattle Street, with high ceilings and endless rooms with a great deal of space. Most of the walls were paneled.

She bought an antique brass bed for fifteen dollars at a country auction, then spent a fortune on pink and white Porthault sheets. The most delicate of flowers, the subtlest of shades. A bed was important to Alison. She did her best creating there, snuggled under the covers with a fire in the grate. She loved the gloomy weather that periodically blanketed Cambridge with a Londonlike fog.

It was on such a night in late November that her doorbell rang, surprising her. She looked at the clock. Nearly midnight. Late for her, although most of her new acquaintances were just rising. They were night people who frequented the strange after-hours dives that were springing up all over town. There were so many scenes in Boston. The folk scene. The rock scene. The drug scene. Alison observed all of them, and was part of none of them. Her apartment, however, was a hang-out. She was in that strange netherworld of the almost famous. Everyone in Boston knew her. She had a nationwide reputation. Her name was used by others to impress. And yet she was not

Milton Greene, Scavullo, Richard Avedon, Marie Cosindas. She was just on the brink.

She opened her door to find the Indian. Kenny Buck was standing before her, his rain-wet hair plastered to his head. He wore no coat and his shirt was clinging to his body. His face was glistening.

"Well, I'm ready," he said, as though almost a year had not passed. Alison couldn't help laughing.

"Come in," she said, "or you won't last the night. You'll be dead of pneumonia before anyone has ever heard of you."

He was making puddles on the newly waxed floors. What would she do about the puddles? she thought. The puddles, hell. What would she do about the maniac in her house who was standing dripping before her?

"I'm used to the wet," he said nonchalantly. "And the cold. I sleep out a lot." Alison made no comment.

"How did you find me?" she asked finally.

"I went to Pride's Crossing. They told me. Everyone knows you. Your family's rich." There was a touch of awe in his voice.

"Well, fairly well off. I wouldn't say rich."

"I would. And everyone else does. Rich, that's what they say."

Another awkward silence.

"I wish you'd take off your things . . ." she began.

"I will," he offered.

"But I don't have anything for you to wear."

"I don't mind if you don't."

"I do."

"Maybe you got a towel?"

"I do. Yes, I have a towel."

"Or a sheet?"

"I have both. Which would you prefer? A sheet or a towel?"

"It don't matter to me. You're the one who's bothered." He grinned.

"A towel," she decided. Then, "*Two* towels. That ought to cover it." She could have bitten her tongue off. She had never felt so awkward. It was *her* house. She brought him the towels and busied herself while he stripped and wrapped one towel around his hips and draped the other one over his lean shoulders.

"What are you doing here?" she asked uneasily when she could turn around.

"You're going to make me famous," Kenny Buck said confidently.

"Oh, that was a joke. That was fun."

"No," he said flatly. "You can do it. I saw your stuff in *Rolling Stone*. You're good." He stared at her, and she noticed that his long hair was soaking the green towel.

"And I'm good," he said simply. "I know it. I know I got whatever it is. What I need from you—" He paused. It was difficult for him to put it into words.

"I've seen what every successful performer has. I mean, besides what makes you get up and do it in the first place. There's a picture about them . . ."

"An image," Alison prompted.

"Yuh. Image. That's a good word. You mention the name, you get an image. I don't think that just happens. I read. I study. I know it doesn't just happen. It's people like you—"

"I just take pictures."

"What about my pictures?"

"I never looked at them," she answered untruthfully.

"You're lying," he said. He was used to women not telling him the whole truth.

"I don't remember them."

"You are lying," he repeated.

"Well, I'm not sure where I put them."

"I don't believe you."

"All right, I'll find them," she said in exasperation. It wasn't difficult. She had filed them. She knew right where they were. The filing cabinet was in the bedroom.

She spread the pictures on the bed, and Kenny examined them. There was no vanity involved. He was looking at the "product," himself.

"Is there a story there?" he asked her.

She looked at the photos: the skier, the man in his teepee, the performer. If he were a star, if he had a record, *Rolling Stone* would be interested, Alison thought.

But there were so many singers and so many stories to be told. What would make Kenny Buck's different?

She turned to him. He was sitting on his haunches. The pose triggered something in her mind.

The Indian.

Was that the image? She looked again at the pictures, then at the subject. She never questioned why she was doing this. It was—what?—another adventure.

"How did you get here?" she asked.

"Motorcycle."

"Where are you going to sleep?"

"I got a sleeping bag."

"But it's raining."

"I don't have to sleep outside," he said craftily. "There's room in here."

"I don't have a couch. I just moved in. I haven't gotten around—"

"I can sleep on the floor."

"Yes, I suppose you can." She knew she was weakening. What was happening to her? she wondered.

In two minutes he had moved in. Bedroll, some changes of clothes, guitar. The sleeping bag was laid out in front of the living room fireplace.

"You certainly make yourself at *home*," she said.

"I got no time to waste."

"Whatever it is you want—" she began.

"Success," he said succinctly.

"—it won't happen overnight. It doesn't happen that way."

"We'll make it happen." He grinned at her. His smile was dazzling. He smiled so seldom. She shrugged helplessly. He was relentless.

"I made a demo record. Do you have a stereo?"

"I have a record player."

"Listen."

He put the record on. She tried to take into account that it was a little record made in a little studio in some little town, where no one had much experience. But the magic just wasn't there. Whatever Kenny Buck had in person didn't show up on the record. She had a hunch it would never come across on a record. Yes, the voice was still husky and sexy. But Kenny could not be categorized, and in the record world there were categories. Records were put into bins. R & B, country-and-western, folk. He wasn't rock, or country, or pop.

The record ended. Kenny looked at her face. "You have lousy equipment," he said.

"It's a lousy record," she answered. He didn't take offense. He agreed with her.

"Then what am I?"

"I don't know yet."

"Make me an image." He was giving orders again. "How you see me."

"What do you want me to be? Your manager? You want photos and phone calls and images and all the rest. What do I get out of it?" She was teasing. He wasn't.

"What do you want?" His voice was very low and very direct.

"A piece of you." She had heard Diane use that phrase, and it sounded right. Everybody has a piece of somebody. She had heard it, and it was obvious from his smile that somewhere in his life, he had heard it too.

"You can have whatever piece of me you want."

She blushed. "It's late. Let's talk it over in the morning."

"No!" He jumped up. "I don't want to wait until morning. I want to start now. Where's your camera? Shoot me! Tomorrow—"

"What about tomorrow?"

"Tomorrow I'll go to the theaters. You got theaters in Boston? I'll get a job."

"The theaters bring in everyone from New York. They're either opening shows or trying them out here, or they're playing road companies."

"Nothing else?"

"The Brattle. The Charles. I don't know. Maybe they could use someone."

"You know the people there. You'll come with me. You'll introduce me."

"Kenny—"

"Sure, you will, and if there aren't any jobs here, and if they don't want me, to hell with them. Then we'll go to

New York, where the companies start from, and I'll go around there and get a job. And if I can't get a job there, we'll go to Hollywood."

"You're moving too fast for me. . . ."

"It's all possible. I know, even now, in the back of your mind, there's an idea. I can see it."

It was as if he himself were making the idea grow. He scared her with his intensity. She had nothing. She knew of nothing. She just stared at him.

And just as suddenly it came to her. Myra had written her a letter two, three weeks ago, asking for a series on American Primitives. The New Sophistication. *Primal* was the operative word. Myra was always a little vague about particulars, but at the same time, always sure of the trend.

Alison pictured Kenny Buck in *Charm*, amid all the fashions and poses of female couture and talk of skin lotions and exclusive tours of the wine country.

She moved the two chairs in the room toward the fireplace. They were early American, real period pieces. One was a rocking chair. Next a delicate little table with a candle. The wall was white plaster.

She set up her camera and told Kenny to sit in the chair. The effect was more than she had hoped for. He was still damp from the rain. His torso glistened. His blue jeans clung to his thighs. And he possessed the chair he sprawled in. The Savage invading the Puritan household. She began to shoot very quickly as he looked around the room, taking in the richness of the moldings, the wood paneling in the dining room beyond. His glance was greedy. To a boy from a milltown in Maine the room represented wealth and power, and he was determined to get both.

When he looked back at the camera, there was defiance and challenge in his face. Alison kept snapping away. She would stop for a minute, remove a roll of film, and insert another, but they did not speak to each other. From time to time she moved the candle or turned his head a certain way. He allowed this.

By four in the morning she was exhausted.

"I can't see anymore," she said. She unstrapped the camera and set it on the bare floor. "I'm tired, exhausted.

I've got to go to bed" She felt totally drained. Without realizing it, this man was demanding everything from her.

He came over to her and kissed her. No, it couldn't be called that. He took possession of her mouth. His body was hard against hers. All of him was animal hard. She could feel the muscles of his chest as he strained to her.

There was no resisting him. Before she knew it, she was down on the hardwood floor and he had stripped off their clothes and he was dominating her body. She felt herself aflame. No man had ever simply taken her. He entered her, filled her with such heat as she had never known. He was moving—this man, this animal—moving over her and through her and into her, and she found herself caught up in it. She was no longer the Puritan from Pride's Crossing. She was his squaw. She was locked into his fantasy. He was totally male and she succumbed totally. They reached a climax together and she cried out and scratched at the powerful shoulders, then lay there panting.

"Wild," she said sleepily.

"What?" His voice was thick.

"The Wild Indian," she murmured. "My Wild Indian. That's what you are." She spent the rest of the night in his sleeping bag on the floor instead of in her nice warm pink-flowered bed.

Chapter Seven

Success was not supposed to happen overnight. Everyone knew that. But Kenny's started almost immediately.

Alison called Myra, and after Alison had explained her idea of using Kenny, Myra guaranteed magazine coverage. Then, on a sudden inspiration, Alison took Kenny to Brooks Brothers.

The conservatism of the white Oxford-cloth button-down shirt, the four-in-hand russet tie, the suit, only accentuated Kenny's primitivism. Never had a man done more for a suit. Men's fashion could once again do royal battle with beads and blue jeans. One shot was of Kenny standing by the fireplace, mockery and sensuality playing across his face. It was an expression that endlessly intrigued Alison.

Another shot came about quite by accident. It was a nude photo of Kenny standing in semidarkness just behind her bed. White starched ruffles on the canopy and the dark muscular shadow of a naked man. Light and dark. Feminine and masculine. There was something shocking about the photo, but not because of the nudity. In truth most of Kenny's body was in the shadows. Only the contours of his flanks, one arm, his chest, and his cheekbones were touched by light. But it was what the photograph evoked, the subconscious desire that was illuminated. Alison studied the print for an hour, then shrugged and included it with the others for Myra.

A chance meeting occurred two nights later. Alison

had received an invitation to a private, pre-opening party at Roscoe's, a new discothèque—one of the first in Boston—scheduled to open in February.

"Come on," she said to Kenny. "This is where you get introduced to Boston society."

He had no money, so she bought him a second suit. Something in her rebelled at the thought of buying a man clothes, but she dismissed it.

The discothèque was filled with flashing lights and pounding music, all new to New England ears and eyes. Half of Boston stood to one side, goggle-eyed. The other half plunged in. Wild and willing bodies gyrated on the floor. The laughter and the free-wheeling motions of the couples and singles was seductive. Alison and Kenny joined this second group, and the night passed in a blaze of red and yellow and purple lights and throbbing bass.

On the way out a voice called Alison. It was Michael Butler, the producer of *Hair*.

"What brings you to Boston?" she asked as she kissed him on the cheek. "Surely not another disco bash."

"No," Butler said. "We're casting a company of *Hair*. I'm only here for today and tomorrow. Gerald is doing most of the actual casting." He waved a vague hand in back of him. A bearded boy, maybe twenty, reveling in his new power, nodded, not deigning to speak. This didn't stop Kenny.

"You're holding auditions?" he asked. "You mean, you're looking for actors? What do you have to do?" Nothing shy about Kenny.

Butler smiled. "Come in with two rock songs, preferably something that could relate to *Hair*, and be prepared to read a scene."

"Where are you holding these auditions?"

"Tomorrow at ten at the Wilbur."

Gerald broke in, looking at Kenny in his suit. "I don't think you're the type."

"Why not?"

"Because I just don't."

"What makes you so sure?"

"It's my job to be sure." Alison was keeping out of

this. So, she noticed, was Michael. He stood to one side, smiling.

"The auditions start at ten?" Kenny asked.

"Yes, but don't bother." Gerald was holding his own. "I wouldn't hire you."

"Let's see about that." Kenny smiled. It was the smile of a savage. He took Alison's hand and they left.

It was only in the car on the way to Cambridge that he asked, "What is *Hair*?"

"You mean, you don't know?"

"No."

"Well, it's the hottest thing to come along since *My Fair Lady*, and it's called an American Tribal Rock Musical and there's hardly a person left in America who will admit to not having seen it."

"Tribal, huh? Tribal like in Indian?"

"Actually, yes."

She filled him in on the style of the musical, the kind of revolutionary spirit that had catapulted it to such success. Kenny kept nodding, taking it all in.

The alleyway to the Wilbur was filled with kids. Kids with guitars, kids with peace stickers, with feathers, with rawhide, with jeans. Middle-class kids who were trying to be hip, hip kids who were already high.

Kenny Buck stood in the alley and watched. It was easy to distinguish the fake from the real. The fake ones came out of the stage door, crestfallen, their faces mirroring middle-class disappointment. The real ones came out a little more stoned than when they went in.

Finally Kenny made up his mind. It was noon, and he was beginning to feel a heat, a kind of pressure. He clutched his guitar to him and shouldered his way through the crowd.

"Is your name on the roster?" a stage door attendant asked him.

"Yeah," Kenny said, and kept on walking.

"Well, you'll have to wait your turn in any case."

"Yeah," Kenny repeated, walking toward the music that was coming from the stage.

"You can't go in there," said another attendant.

"Yeah," Kenny drawled again, and kept right on going.

"Did you hear what I said?" The voice was outraged. A hand was on Kenny's shirt.

And then there was a brawl. Kenny didn't like to be touched. He liked to do the touching. He grabbed the hand that was restraining him and threw it off. Another restraint came from the right. The shirt started to rip. Kenny swung with his free hand, clutching the guitar with his left, and kept on walking. By the time he reached the stage, he was bare to the waist, the tatters of his shirt like battle scars around him. His hair was disheveled. He was the wild Indian, no doubt about it. Hanging on to him were the two attendants.

"What's going on here?" Kenny recognized Gerald's voice.

"I came to sing for you," he said.

"You can't do this."

"Well, I'm going to, so you might as well sit down and listen."

"I don't have to—" Gerald began, but another voice came out of the darkness. It was amused and authoritative.

"Gerald, sit down and listen." It was Michael Butler.

Kenny was alone on stage. He was where he belonged. He could feel it. He took the guitar out of the case and began to sing. He was making a kind of war chant, improvising as he went along, carried by the anger he felt inside him. He sang, and he chanted, and he moved. As primitive as stone and as primitive as his forefathers. Out of his mind, too, because he suddenly leaped off the stage, found Gerald, and clutched him by the throat with one muscular hand.

"Now tell me I'm not the type, you son of a bitch!"

Gerald could say nothing; he was in danger of being strangled. Kenny held him for a minute, then threw him back down in his seat. He leaped back on to the stage, packed his guitar, and started off.

In the silence Butler's voice said, "Read!" And Kenny knew at that moment he was in.

They made him read four scenes. The director worked with him for an hour. By six o'clock he had the job.

*   *   *

Michael Butler's press agent saw that it made all the papers. Not just the Boston papers, but the national press as well. Anything to do with *Hair* was news. The fact that a real Indian had come in and demanded a job, forced his way into the theater, made a good story.

Kenny worked like a demon. And like a demon, he also possessed Alison. Caught up in the work at the theater, he came home still high from the experience and made savage love to her. Often they had no dinner. He would open a bottle of wine and take her to bed, where he possessed her with his incredible energy. Alison found herself living in his shadow. And enjoying it.

One afternoon in February the phone rang. It was Dick Bailey, back from California.

"I heard you had moved to town," he said, "and I'd love to see you."

"Oh, I don't know . . ." she began.

"We had a good thing going . . ." he said. A little bit of California had rubbed off evidently. "I won't take no for an answer. How about Wednesday?"

She agreed. When he arrived to pick her up, she was waiting and didn't let him come in. What was she hiding? she wondered. She had made the bed, but the evidence of Kenny was everywhere. Even in his absence he permeated the room. She shut the door as if to shut him out.

"I'm starved," she said by way of apology. Dick accepted this and they went to a little Italian restaurant in Boston's North End. This was, Alison realized, Dick's idea of bohemian living. He ordered for them both, selected a sensibly priced wine. She looked at him. His hair was a bit longer. It was all right now, even fashionable, to have long hair, and Alison thought it was an amusing contrast to the three-piece Brooks Brothers suit and the blue button-down shirt. School tie. Really—the school tie. He looked a bit older, more interesting. He carried himself with more authority.

"I like California," he was saying, "I didn't realize how much until I came back home. Remember once you told me you felt like a stranger? Well, I feel the same way now. I got together with the old crowd at the club the other night and, Lord, we just didn't have that much in common."

The wine came and he sampled it, nodded his approval, and continued talking. As a matter of fact he never stopped talking. He was full of enthusiasms. His new life. Tennis. Sailing out to Catalina. The houses in Pasadena. San Francisco, where they really had fine food. You would have thought *he* had discovered the cable cars and Nob Hill and Marin County.

California took them through dinner. His prospects took them through the walk to the car. He was indeed going to head up the California office. His future was secure. All he needed now was someone to share it with.

"Where should we go?" he asked, once he was behind the wheel of the car.

"Home," she said. "I think I should be getting home."

"I thought maybe there was a nightspot you might like to visit," he said, a bit crestfallen.

Perhaps it was that word—*nightspot*—that did it for Alison. It symbolized how far apart their lives had become.

He stopped the car by her apartment, turned off the ignition, and kissed her. Yes, he was still a good kisser, Alison thought. Better now than before. California had helped him out there. There was nothing wrong with Dick Bailey. Any woman would be lucky to have him. He would be attentive. He could be aroused. He could be amusing. But he couldn't be Kenny.

And Kenny was in her blood. It was Kenny she was kissing, Kenny's body she felt. Kenny inhabited her mind and her soul. He was savage and selfish, and sometimes he wounded her. But he excited her, made her feel like no man ever had, because there was no man at all like Kenny Buck.

"I have to tell you something, Dick," she said, pushing him away gently. "I'm involved. I'm sorry, but I can't continue to see you."

"Do you mean, it's true what I've been hearing about you?"

"What?" she asked, piqued. She'd never realized how small a town Boston was.

"That you've taken up with some half-breed. My God, it sounds like *White Cargo* or something."

"I'm living with Kenny Buck. He's an actor and a singer, and yes, he's part Indian."

"Good Lord, Alison, I hope you know what you're doing." It was already evident in his voice that there would be no Pasadena, no flights to San Francisco for combined business-pleasure trips, no formal wedding at St. Anne's High Episcopal Church for *them*. He was already getting out to open the door for her. He did not kiss her good night. An awkward grasping of her hand sufficed. She was the most intriguing girl he had ever known, but still . . .

When she let herself in, Kenny was waiting for her. Half a bottle of wine was left. He was sitting cross-legged on the floor watching television, eating an Italian sandwich. The blue reflection from the screen was playing over his naked body.

"You want some?" he said, gesturing with the sandwich. She shook her head, then, impulsively, threw her coat down on the floor and rushed to him. She needed him, his kisses, his lovemaking. He continued to eat, drank the wine, watched television, and made love to her all at the same time, until finally the passion overcame everything else and he took her there on the floor. She was glad the taste of onions had completely erased any trace of Dick Bailey. It was true. There was no other man for her except Kenny Buck.

When *Hair* opened a month later, Kenny received rave reviews. The show, of course, was a smash, and Kenny a Boston celebrity. When the phone rang now it was for Kenny, not Alison. Invitations. Guest appearances. Radio interviews. Television. Groupies who somehow found the number and hung up when they heard Alison's voice. Who was Alison? She had become, she realized, Kenny Buck's Old Lady. She was somewhere in the background, her own career abandoned for the moment. She reveled in his success, attended most of his performances, saw for herself how the crowd reacted to his galvanic personality. Something wonderful had happened to Kenny. Now that he had stopped rejecting the Indian in him, it made for an incredibly imposing presence.

Dynamite was the word the New York group used after they had made the Eastern shuttle trip up for a matinee. The group was imposing. Sam Cohn from CMA, Biff Liff from William Morris, and two dark trim men who were never introduced but always referred to as "the guys from the Coast."

The following week a very small, mild-mannered looking man stood in the back of the theater. Alison watched him watching Kenny. After the performance he went backstage.

"You're good," he said to Kenny.

"I know."

"Can you do anything else?"

"Besides what?"

"Besides be a wild Indian."

"I can do what I put my mind to."

"Do you know who I am?"

"I know your name," Kenny said.

"I would like you to come down to New York and read for me," the man said nonchalantly.

"Why don't you sit down and I'll read for you here?"

"Because I want you to come down to New York and read for me. And I want you to read with somebody else I have in mind for the girl. So next Monday you can take the shuttle and be back in time for your show here. You'll come to the Brooks Atkinson Theatre."

"Where is it?" Kenny asked.

The man looked stunned. Didn't everybody know which street every theater was on? Evidently not.

"Forty-seventh Street," he said, then added, "west of Broadway." And then, having visions of the Wild Indian lost in the Minnesota Strip, he became more precise. "Between Broadway and Eighth Avenue. Don't cross Eighth Avenue!" It was a warning.

Kenny was amused. He told Alison.

"Are you going?" she asked.

"Why not? You go with me?"

"Why not?"

They were both awfully careless with their lives. Everything was so easy. Maybe they would go, maybe they wouldn't go. What did it matter? Life was too wonderful. If this didn't happen, something even better would.

As it turned out they did go to New York on Monday morning. Kenny had never seen the city and was determined not to be impressed by it. But he started laughing as soon as they got stuck in a traffic jam just across the 59th Street Bridge, and he continued laughing until they got to Broadway.

"I want to see Eighth Avenue," he told the driver.

"You don't want to see Eighth Avenue," the driver said balefully. "What's to see on Eighth Avenue? Only scumbags. That's all."

"What do you mean?" Kenny asked.

"I can't say in front of the lady, mister. But you don't want to see Eighth Avenue."

The first thing they did after leaving the cab was to head for Eighth Avenue. The hookers were out in their little shorts and their high boots, and they were bold and funny and suggested a threesome. Kenny invited three of them to join him and Alison for a drink at the Play Pen. After two drinks everybody wanted his picture taken, which was what Alison was waiting for. She snapped the bartender in the half-jaundiced light coming through the dusty pane, and the three hookers, all black, one with a yellow wig on, looking at life through already lost eyes. The music was playing and the girls smoked up a pack of Lucky Strikes, then Kenny suddenly lost interest and paid them each twenty dollars. The day turned sour for a moment.

Alison looked at him when they were out on the street.

"Where are we?" she asked him.

"On Eighth Avenue," he said, laughing.

"No, I mean, you and me," she said. Seriously.

"Don't ask me that now."

"I will ask you that now. We don't have any contract. Any kind of contract. About anything. About our business dealings. About our lives."

"So?"

"So you're going in to read for America's foremost playwright, and suppose he asks you to do the play and you do it, where am I?"

"You got my word, I told you that before. You got that piece of me. Red Man never lie." He was grinning again.

"I love you," she said, and it sounded strange and lonely in the middle of Eighth Avenue where the phrase must be worked a thousand times an hour.

"Come on." He took her around the waist. "Come with me to the Brooks Atkinson, wherever the hell it is."

They found it, and used the backstage entrance.

"Where will you be?" he asked her.

"I'll go out into the orchestra. I'll see you afterward."

"Okay. Don't get lost."

She did, however. She ended up in the basement of the Atkinson and had to climb the stairs again. By the time she parted the velvet curtains opening into the orchestra, Kenny was already reading opposite a girl with red bangs and a gamine face.

For a moment Alison thought she had wandered into the wrong theater. Here was some light and rather funny comedy, newlyweds having a spat in a walk-up apartment. The playwright, Alison guessed, was planning a revival of *Barefoot in the Park*. The scene ended with the newlyweds falling into each other's arms, loving with laughter.

Alison was impressed. Kenny was totally at ease. He was charming. He seemed to throw the lines away, which made them funnier than they were. Most of all, he was carrying on an affair with this girl right on the stage.

The mild-mannered man was alone in the theater, except for Alison. He was chuckling to himself. He was in Authors' Heaven. Two "dynamite"—to use the New York word—performers were saying his lines.

At the end he stood up.

"Terrific!" he said. "I loved it. I loved both of you."

The two on stage were still locked in each other's arms, laughing. Then Kenny threw the script up in the air.

"Oh, man," he said. "I can't do this. I'm sorry, but I can't do this kind of shit. I thank you and it was fun reading here, and it sure do beat freezing my ass off in Millinocket, Maine, but I'm not the right man for this."

"Now, hold it." The man was no longer mild-mannered. "I want you for this part. And I want her. I want both of you." He was used to getting what he wanted.

"Sorry," Kenny said, "but I don't want you. I'd like *her*," he added, nodding at the girl, "but I don't want you." He walked off the stage.

"Who is he?" the girl said rather breathlessly. "Listen, I would follow him to the ends of the earth. He's some terrific!"

The author turned to Alison. "You talk to him. You evidently have some relationship with him. I don't want to know about it. I know too much about everybody already. But I want him for that part."

"If he said no, then he won't say yes," Alison said.

"But nobody says no to me," the playwright protested.

"Kenny Buck did," she said, and left the theater.

She found him back at the Play Pen. He was playing a guitar. The bartender had turned off the jukebox. Two or three regulars and a couple of off-the-street trade were drinking and listening. Kenny was singing "Molly Malone," and an old Irish lady in the back was crying, the tears streaming down her face.

"Oh, Christ," Alison muttered, and extricated Kenny from the Play Pen, headed him toward the Boston shuttle, and got him to the theater in time for the performance.

That night, in bed, his body against hers, he murmured, "I like New York. I like all that. I betcha I like Hollywood better."

Alison laughed. "Are you going to Hollywood?"

"Won't be long now," he said, and settled down for some serious lovemaking. This was the other part of Kenny that she found difficult. He was insatiable. He was a wonderful lover because he loved women and loved making love, but he never stopped. Alison was curiously resentful. She couldn't call her body her own. It belonged to him.

And with the appearance of the April issue of *Charm*, Kenny's body belonged to the world. Myra had turned Alison's photo essay into as clever a piece of pornography as any high-fashion magazine could hope to disguise. Alison's intuition had been right. After pages of girls in various stages of undress, modeling gowns and furs and underwear, Kenny Buck's dark virility was indeed shocking. Myra had entitled the piece, "American Native," and the last photo was the one of Kenny, naked in the shadows, half hidden, half exposed by Alison's canopy bed. It was a full-page spread, and its immediate result was to bring another group of agents, managers, and producers up to Boston to take a look at *Hair*.

Kenny Buck was suddenly hot. Everybody wanted him. Women wanted his body. Producers wanted his person. Everyone was after a piece of him. Even Mimi Cabot.

She phoned the second week in April, ostensibly to ask Alison to be maid of honor at her wedding to Dick Bailey.

"Did you see the announcement in the *Herald*? Wasn't that a heaven picture? I know Dick is going to make an absolutely dreamy husband."

Alison thought of her dinner with Dick a month earlier. "I didn't know, Mimi. Congratulations. But I'm not sure . . ."

"Oh, Alison, you have *got* to be my maid of honor. I will not take no for an answer."

"Well, if it means that much to you . . ."

"To both of us. Dick too." Afterthought. "Oh, and *please* invite Kenny."

Alison got the picture. She and Kenny were Famous People in Boston. She could hear Mimi saying casually, "My best friend in the world is Alison Carmichael—you know, the photographer—and she and Kenny Buck are going to be at the wedding. They're living together. . . ." It was 1970 and maybe not quite the right thing to do in Boston. But it was titillating, and it somehow made the Cabot-Bailey nuptials seem more important, more glamorous. Daring even.

Alison accepted. Reluctantly.

There was to be a formal party the next week at the Somerset Club for both families and the wedding party.

"I do hope Kenny is coming," Mimi said to Alison, a little too anxiously, the day before the party. They were shopping for the bridesmaids' gowns.

"Mimi, I don't know," Alison said. "He has two shows tomorrow."

"Please, *please* persuade him. We would love to meet him. We'll even have a limousine pick him up at the theater."

Alison felt compelled to say "Oh, that wouldn't be necessary. Kenny has his own limo now."

"Oh. Well, tell him not to dress."

"Mimi," Alison said in exasperation, "I haven't even asked him yet."

"Well, ask him!" Mimi said. "Otherwise you're going to be the only single one at the party and that would just be too awkward."

As if that mattered, Alison thought. She asked Kenny anyway, even though she knew the answer.

"I don't think so, babe," he said. "I know those people."

"Mimi will be really disappointed."

"Oh, God, who cares? I know those people. She just wants to show me off." He reflected. "I waited on enough of them."

"You wouldn't be waiting on them now."

"That's right."

"Well," she said, hiding her disappointment. "I said I'd see this thing through and I will. I won't be home too late."

The four bridesmaids, the ushers, and John Collier, Dick Bailey's best man, were all being put up at the Ritz-Carlton—at the bride's parents' expense, of course. It was easier than chauffering the girls to and from Pride's Crossing, and it gave everyone a sense of having a postgraduate slumber party. Most of the men, stockbrokers now, had flown in from Chicago and New York, and they hadn't seen each other for more than a year, so there was a great deal to talk about. Comparisons of the Onwentsia Club, for instance, with the Myopia. The best restaurants in Chicago. Real estate prices in the suburbs.

Everyone got slightly sloshed—that is to say, not falling-down drunk, but just pleasantly numb. The older generation, Cabots and Baileys, watched with tolerant amusement the mild flirtations, the traditional silliness of the traditional prewedding dinner.

Alison was supremely bored. She had a headache. She wanted to leave. She wondered why she had ever accepted in the first place. She left in search of some aspirin. In her absence the conversation naturally focused on her. And Kenny.

"Jesus Kee-rist, what's he got?" John Collier asked.

Dick Bailey, more sloshed than the rest, said, "Heap big—"

Mimi cut him off. "Please! Dick!"

"Well, that's what you told me. You went to see him."

"I went to see him because he's in *Hair*," Mimi explained. "They have a nude scene."

"Kee-rist," Collier repeated.

"Heap big . . ." Bailey was measuring trout.

"The fact that he couldn't show up makes me slightly *porked*," Mimi said.

But Kenny did show up, just after midnight. He made an entrance, dressed, as they all were, in formal attire. Alison had to look twice to recognize him. His face was shining, and his hair was combed back and fastened in a ponytail. Alison made the introductions. Without meaning to, Kenny stared down every woman in the place and every woman blushed. He took the measure of every man and every man felt diminished.

Mimi's voice showed her disappointment. "Oh," she said upon meeting him, "I didn't think you'd dress for the occasion."

"What did you think I'd wear?" he asked her.

"Something outrageous. Or maybe nothing at all. I saw your show three times."

The interrogation began.

"My God, what does it feel like," John Collier asked, "coming out on a stage abso-lutely naked?"

"It feels like—nothing at all." Kenny laughed it off,

but Collier—being a bit more sloshed and Dick Bailey's best man—was out for more than that.

"I mean, doesn't it feel degrading? Out there in front of all those people—bare-ass *naked*?"

"What's he saying about naked?" Mrs. Cabot asked. She hadn't been to the theater in twenty-six years.

"That man appears on stage without any of his clothes on," her sister told her. "John is asking him about it."

"No clothes on? In Boston?" Mrs. Cabot was more disbelieving than shocked.

Kenny gave Alison a look. She motioned with her head. Did he want to leave? He signaled no.

"Are you really naked?" a bridesmaid inquired.

"He really is," Mimi replied with the authority of a three-time viewer.

"Good Lord, I'd never do that. Not for any amount of money." Collier snorted, dismissing the whole thing.

"Why? I'm not ashamed of my body," Kenny said, a bit more sharply than he had intended. In spite of himself these people were getting to him.

Collier laughed. "That's what Lili St. Cyr told me at the Old Howard."

"Who?" Mrs. Cabot asked someone.

"A stripper," somebody answered.

Mimi was getting flirtatious. She, too, was sloshed now.

"I thought you might come in buckskin," she said, trying to cuddle up to Kenny.

"Why would he come in buckskin?" Mrs. Cabot wanted to know.

"Because he's an Indian."

"Who invited him?" she asked promptly.

"He's my escort, Mrs. Cabot," Alison said crisply.

"Alison dear," Mrs. Cabot said, "is this a *prank*?" She knew these wedding parties sometimes went the limit, but this was going beyond.

"Oh, Mother, this is 1970!" Mimi said dizzily.

Mr. Cabot tried to save the day. "You've had quite a success, young man," he said to Kenny. "Are you enjoying it?"

"Yes," Kenny answered. "I like limousines. I like money."

Another gaffe. Nobody mentioned money in these circles.

"Are you from Boston?" Mrs. Bailey asked. "Did you perform in high school?" What she really wanted to know was what were his roots, his family, his *place*.

Kenny looked at her steadily. "No, ma'am. I never performed in high school. I didn't really go to high school much. I spent most of my time in the woods."

"In *Boston*?" Mrs. Cabot was now shocked.

"No, ma'am," Kenny repeated. "I didn't grow up in Boston. I grew up in a milltown in Maine." Here was a gauntlet, he realized.

"Well," Mrs. Cabot said, "what would your mother say about your running around naked on stage?"

He turned on her, on them all. "What would she say? My mother? The Canuck whore? Listen, people, she wouldn't say anything. My mother never had nothing to say to me, except 'Get out of the bed.' And that was when she was busy fucking millhands Saturday nights when they got their pay. When I was little, the millhands used to bounce me outta the bed and beat me up in the mornings. They beat up my mama, too, until I got big enough to beat them up. And then I was big enough to leave. So I left."

He looked at Alison. "Which is what I'm gonna do now. White woman follow brave?" She nodded without hesitation.

He had only two more words for the lot of them.

"Disgusting bastards," he said. Then walked out on an outraged Boston. They got what they wanted, Alison thought.

"I'm sorry," she said to Kenny as the limousine took them home.

"Don't be," he said.

"I am. I didn't realize."

"I know. Alison, you got your choice."

"What do you mean?"

"Them or me."

"Oh, you, Kenny. You!" she said with such passion

that he began to make love to her in the backseat of the limousine, then finished it in the riotous sensual carnival that was their bed.

But it was not as simple as that. After their lovemaking Kenny Buck, the possessor, began to cry. She had never seen that. He didn't want her to see him now. He turned his back to her, but the sobs racked his body. He got out of bed and left her. She followed him and put her arms around him. That broke him completely. He began to pour out to her everything he had kept inside so long— the image of his mother, of those nights and drunken arguments and strange men in the bed, the cries and threats. He had wanted to kill her. He had wanted to love her. And she had been too drunk to want either. She hadn't cared at all how he felt or what he saw. He saw men fornicating with his mother on sofas, in cars, late at night and early in the morning. He saw her beaten and cuffed by those men, and when he had come to her defense, those same men had beaten him too. And she had laughed. He had loved her and she'd never loved him. That's what it came down to. And somehow, some way, someday, someone would pay. Alison held him in her arms, cradled him, rocked him, calmed him finally.

The subject was never mentioned again.

Alison called to tender regrets. She would not be Mimi's maid of honor. Not after what had happened. Mimi's mother sounded relieved on the phone. The ceremony took place without Alison Carmichael.

One night, a week later, Ben Sawyer called. The sound of his voice shocked Alison. It was coming from another world and another life.

"Surprised?" he said.

"Rather. I guess we lost touch."

"I haven't lost touch with you. I've watched what's been happening. Now, I take it you're on to a hot property."

"Oh, Ben, don't make fun of me."

"I'm not making fun, Alison. I just find it a rather comical coincidence that David has asked me to find out whether your Wild Indian has a contract with a studio."

"He doesn't have anything. Except me," Alison said. "Who's David?"

"David Sampson. He *is* Vanguard Studios."

"Oh."

"This contract, is it on paper?" There was a serious note in Ben's voice.

"Of course not. We just agreed. We're—" She hesitated.

"Living together?" he suggested.

"Yes."

"A little free advice. Better get it on paper, kiddo," he said, then got back to the business of the call. "Tell your fella that David sent some scouts out, and they reported back—"

"Dynamite?" Alison said.

"You took the word right out of their mouths. So I'm calling to see if there's interest."

"Of course, there's interest. But in what? What do you want to do with him?"

"Make him a star."

"Well, that's what he wants," she said wryly. "What plans?"

Ben laid out the contract over the phone—the options, the provisions, the money, the selection of scripts. Alison was smart enough to say merely that it sounded intriguing and that she would get back to him. They were about ready to hang up when she suddenly asked, "What did you mean about getting it on paper? Are you talking marriage or business?"

"Either way I guess."

"But I trust Kenny."

Ben laughed and laughed. "Oh, Alison, do get it down on paper."

After hanging up she immediately telephoned Myra for advice, and as always, Myra was extremely precise.

"You know why they want him? They saw those pictures in *Charm*. You made him look both dangerous and fun. That seems to be the right combination for the seventies. God forbid anyone should be as lovable as Cary Grant. So what they see is a Wild Man for the kids, with a sense of humor for the grown-ups. Very valuable. The terms sound right. I don't say this about many people, but I would say it about Ben. You can trust him."

"When I mentioned trusting Kenny, Ben laughed," Alison said.

"He was being polite, darling. One can never trust Kenny. But that's his appeal. It is why, my dear, he will be in the movies and Ben never will. Take the deal."

"Myra, let me ask you something. Is Kenny real, or did I just make him up?"

There was a pause while Myra considered how to put it. "Alison, Kenny's qualities were always there. But you saw them, and you showed others how to look at him. You made him. *Esquire*, incidentally, is furious. They feel we're doing a send-up of their girlie poses. I couldn't be more delighted."

Alison was silent.

"For God's sake, Alison," Myra said, sounding a bit annoyed, "go and have a wonderful time with your Wild Indian. Go to Hollywood. Go Hollywood all the way with limousines and wild pool parties and everything else I read about that ghastly place. Go and enjoy it and see what happens. It's an adventure. Grab it. Now, I must get off the wire and fire someone. I love you, darling." She hung up.

An adventure. Life was one adventure after another, or it was nothing. Alison had to remind herself of that. She approached Kenny.

His reaction was "Great. When do we leave?"

"Wait a minute. You have a contract here with the theater. You can't just leave."

"Oh, what do I have to do?"

"You have to honor your contract."

"Oh," Kenny said, and smiled at her. He was smarter than that, and far less innocent than Alison.

On Tuesday he developed a cold. By Wednesday night he could hardly talk. Two numbers were cut. He missed the Saturday matinee and evening performance. He could hardly whisper.

A doctor was called in.

"Nodes on the vocal cords, plus the cold," the doctor

said. "He should rest the voice. Two to three months. Otherwise there might be permanent damage."

"Oh, no!" Kenny wheezed. Alison did not find him convincing. Whether Michael Butler was convinced or not Alison never found out, but he talked to her.

"Let him go. *Hair* doesn't depend on any one performer. *Hair* itself is the attraction. Let him go to Hollywood and maybe kill himself. But," he added, "don't expect me ever to hire him again. Tell Kenny that."

Alison sighed.

That evening she called back Ben Sawyer. "We're interested. When do we talk money?"

"When you get out here, we'll sort things out. David tells me he is very, very, very interested."

"That's three *very*'s. I counted," Alison said. "What does that mean?"

"It means six-figure interested. David doesn't get more interested than that."

"We'll come."

"Good. You know, kiddo, I can't believe your luck. How come you're *always* where the action is?"

Alison called her parents to tell them, but before she could say anything, her mother suggested—no, ordered—a luncheon engagement. At the Ritz-Carlton naturally.

One prelunch sherry and Phyllis Carmichael came straight to the point.

"Fortunately," she began, "your father does not open the pages of *Charm*, or read the gossip columns, or listen to women chatter in the beauty parlor. Otherwise I do believe there would be one less half-breed in this world. Now, Alison, for heaven's sake, what are you doing with your life?"

Alison began her Generation Gap speech, but her mother was having none of it.

"Oh, sleep with the man if you will. But you're risking more than reputation with this."

Alison smiled in spite of herself. Her mother's advice was so Victorian. Of course, in those days it had been said by father to son.

"What are you smiling at? The man could ruin your life."

Alison shrugged. "I love him."

Phyllis sipped her sherry. "Ah, yes. Love." She took a deep breath. "Alison, we have never been close, the two of us, never talked much, you and I. Perhaps now it's too late."

"It is, Mother," Alison said with the arrogance of youth. "Kenny and I are going to California." She might as well have said Sodom. Her mother's "Oh" was faint.

"Los Angeles," Alison added. Gomorrah.

"And what will you do there?"

"Oh, Kenny is going to be very successful."

Her mother's voice cut through like ice. "I said, what are *you* going to do there?"

"Live with him, love him, look out for him." Alison talked on and her mother said no more. It was like dealing with an addict, Phyllis Carmichael thought. There was nothing to say, no way she could express her fear for her daughter's future. Allison was so radiant, so vulnerable, and didn't know it. Schemes for the future stretched out across the table like the fabled mirages of the desert preceding L.A. Oh, there were ways of cutting off inheritances. That had worked in the days of the fortune seekers. But Kenny Buck was his own future. That wasn't what was worrying Phyllis Carmichael. She sensed a destructive, self-destructive, streak in her daughter that was coming to the surface. She couldn't help. She paid the check and mother and daughter left the Ritz, two out of a number of proper Bostonians who had just had lunch.

"You went to town." Jonathan's statement was more of a question.

Phyllis nodded. "I had lunch with Alison," she said lightly.

"And could not convince her," Jonathan concluded.

She looked at him sharply. "Then you know."

"Yes. I met the man in question." He shook his head and looked, really looked, at his wife for the first time in years. "Ah, Phyl," he sighed. "We do try. We hope things will turn out for the best, but there's no way to shield her from hurt or disappointment. Tragedy . . ." He took his wife's hand. "There's no way to protect anyone from anything."

And so they sat, comforting each other in the huge mansion in Pride's Crossing, closer than they had been for several years.

The next morning Alison and Kenny took the nine o'clock flight to the West Coast.

Chapter Eight

Los Angeles was Life Beyond Belief. So was the house Alison and Kenny had rented.

Consider the bedroom, for instance.

It jutted out from the Santa Monica Mountains, high above the gardens and pools of Bel-Air. The walls were mostly glass. It was like living on a springboard. The room was open to the world, but the world was kept at bay by two electronic systems that guarded the estate.

The glass wall on the right was a sliding door that led to a bathroom that had been fashioned from a boulder and was open to the sky and mountains. It had been designed to resemble a leafy jungle bower. The sunken tub was a rock pool. The shower that spurted from a ledge resembled a waterfall. Many tropical plants flourished there, and the shadows from their leaves formed pretty patterns on the smooth slate floor.

The glass wall to the left was another sliding door, and it opened onto a pool area that also hung over the mountain. The real wall of the bedroom was ribbed with long wooden shelves that housed books, tape decks, and telephonic systems connecting four continents. A console to the left of the huge ornate bed controlled everything. Push a button and the ceiling slid back to offer midnight stars. Push a button and heavy green velvet drapes glided across the glass walls to shut out light and sound. Push a button and a screen descended and a projector emerged.

Consider the bed.

The headboard was made of gold leaf. Little pieces of wood were supposed to resemble the antlers of stags. Perched on the gilded antlers were gilded angels and cherubs. They looked down beatifically on the bed, blessing its occupants. Above them a canopy, draped in pink satin and topped by a crown, protected the angels and cherubs. Porthault sheets bore a monogram in forest green to accompany the pink. The bed was the twenty-thousand dollar kind of joke that the New Hollywood loved to play on the world of Old Hollywood. Admiring and mocking the ancient opulence at the same time.

Naturally it appealed to Kenny Buck. He and Alison spent the first three days they were in Los Angeles in that bed. They watched films in that bed. They made love in that bed. There were servants who served them meals and who changed the sheets and who picked up the dirty clothes and wet towels. For three days Alison allowed herself to be just a female enjoying the maleness of the man she loved.

Everything excited Kenny. He could feel that the world was ready to open up for him, and it kept him in a constant state of stimulation. Alison satisfied him for three days and three nights. Mornings and afternoons.

On the fourth day he was restless. Where were the contracts? Where were the calls? No one had noticed him. He badgered Alison with questions. What were they waiting for? Who was David Sampson?

On the fifth day he rented a car and smashed it up in front of Ma Maison, severely damaging a Rolls-Royce that belonged to someone whose license plate spelled out HIYAWL. A cowboy star. Who cared?

While he was gone, Alison phoned Ben.

"What's happening?" she asked. "Or more to the point, why is nothing happening?"

"David has been in Europe. He just got back, and he asked me to extend an invitation. Come over Sunday afternoon. He wants to meet his new acquisition. And the food is fabulous. And . . . I'll get a chance to see you again."

"In order of importance."

"Starting with the last," Ben said smoothly. "Sunday. Shall I send a driver?"

Alison laughed. "Why not?"

"It never hurts to be seen emerging from the boss's limousine," he said.

"I'll remember that."

It was just another Sunday afternoon get together at David Sampson's. Three hundred people, all of them tanned, all of them slim, except for David Sampson himself, who was almost monstrously fat. His hair was quite long and bleached blond. He wore a caftan, granny glasses, and went barefoot. He was the power of the New Hollywood. His mansion was also in the hills and built on several levels. There was a main house, then a pool area as big as Encino, and below that a lanai where the sumptuous buffet was being served. David loved all these things. He loved Hollywood. He loved power. He loved food. He loved foreign cars, especially his new emerald-green Mercedes with the white leather seats.

Alison and Kenny's arrival was a letdown. No one noticed them. Just another limousine pulling up. Valet Parking. The boys were busy moving the unchauffeured cars from one side of the canyon road to the other. The chauffeurs took care of their own. The chaos was incredible. It was no wonder they got lost in the shuffle.

That was not to last for long. Leaving Alison behind, Kenny strode through the main house, down past the pool. Above the pool and shielding it from the road was latticework covered with bougainvillea, and the garage, with the prize Mercedes on display. Everyone was admiring the Mercedes. No one was noticing him.

"Who is David Sampson?" he asked a pretty blonde.

"What do you mean, who?" she asked incredulously.

"I mean, point him out to me."

"You must be new here. That's him." She pointed to the man in the caftan.

At that moment Alison arrived with Ben Sawyer by her side.

"You ran through this place like a brushfire," she said. "I want you to meet Ben."

"Hey," Kenny said.

"That's good enough." Ben grinned affably. Then, seeing the expression on Kenny's face, asked, "What are you sore about?"

"I been here five days now, no, six. I betcha he don't know who I am."

"Of course, he does."

"I'll betcha."

"God, he has taken to the L.A. way," Ben said to Alison. She was looking at Kenny.

"What's on your mind, Kenny?" she asked.

"He's gonna notice me," Kenny said. "You'll see." He suddenly leaped away from them and disappeared in the crowd.

"Are you a little scared of what might happen?" Ben asked Alison.

"No," she said. "I came out here for the adventure."

"You bring your cameras?"

"Of course. Why do you ask?"

"You seem submerged. Under a spell, maybe."

She didn't want to consider that. "I love him," was all she answered.

There was a commotion and they looked up. Kenny reappeared, dressed in a Valet Parking uniform, calling David Sampson.

"Hey, Mr. Sampson. Mr. Sampson."

Sampson turned around.

"Do you know who I am?" Kenny asked.

Sampson looked peeved. "Why should I? You're Valet Parking."

"Yeah, that's what I mean. I'm Valet Parking. There's this car which is kind of fucking—excuse me—everything up. And I need your permission to move it. Okay? Is it okay?"

What was his game? Alison wondered. He was really playing the ingenuous little kid.

"Do whatever you have to do," Sampson said, and turned away, dismissing him.

"Okay, those are your orders, Mr. Sampson."

The party continued to flow. Diane came over and kissed the air close to Alison's cheek. "Where is your boy we've heard so much about? I've looked forward to meeting him."

"I'm sure you'll be seeing him soon," Alison said.

Diane laughed. "Oh, is he going to make an entrance?" No sooner were the words out of her mouth than there was the sound of a powerful engine and of wood splintering.

And before everyone's eyes, the latticework gave way and David Sampson's beautiful new emerald-green Mercedes appeared with Kenny Buck at the wheel. He drove it through the wall, gunned the motor, and aimed it straight at the pool.

It sank. David Sampson screamed. There was then utter silence. Kenny Buck climbed out of the pool dripping wet and extended his hand to David Sampson.

"Hi, I'm Kenny Buck. Your other acquisition."

Maybe out of instinct Kenny had discovered the one way to gain favor with David Sampson. A meeting was arranged for the next morning.

Kenny Buck arrived. And Alison found that again she was known as his Old Lady.

She tried not to think of the consequences of that.

Chapter Nine

Kenny soared and Alison submerged, a victim of L.A. lassitude.

At first she strolled the Strip, camera in hand, snapping the action. The billboards; the music; the Sunkist kids who were high on everything America was high on that year, wandering the few blocks of legend, barefoot and dreaming, searching for the frontier beyond the New Frontier. But the scene depressed her; she remembered Paris. She recalled Alain and the passions of '68, and after three nights on the Strip she returned to the house in the hills and waited for Kenny to come home. Or if he was home, she waited for him to get off the phone. Or if he was asleep, she waited for him to wake up and make love to her. When he did, he seized her with a quick ferocity that sometimes excited her and as often left her unsatisfied. But he was already occupied elsewhere with a telephone call, a meeting. With David.

David Sampson was the key to this world. He and Diane were panning gold. There was pure gold streaming down the canyons of L.A. in the form of gold records, Golden Oldies, waste and luxury, fantasy gone public. All the images, the gods, were male and barely twenty, outlaw figures with long hair, bare chests, leather vests, tight jeans, hot tubs, hard beats, beads, chains, grass, dope, H, coke, highs, blows. They were stars, replacing Doris Day and Cary Grant in popularity. And they were recording names. These recording names had never before reached the moviegoing public.

That was what David wanted from Kenny; that was Diane's involvment. They were intent on owning a million——*multi*million——dollar commodity called Kenny Buck. Alison didn't realize that she was standing in their way. As the weeks went by she was content to drift. She slept a lot, dreamed a lot. Her excitement came from Kenny. It accompanied him home. He could excite her by looking at her, by grinning suddenly, by grabbing her, kissing her neck, stroking her buttocks. By a word. And by his body. In a land of great bodies and sexual energy Kenny was a standout, and Alison was a beachcomber on a desert island, nourished by nothing but her intoxication with his body.

Until an actor named Avery came along. She met him at one of David Sampson's parties. She recognized his face from a television series. He had been the second lead, the series was successful, and he was stuck in Los Angeles with his wife, making money and doing very little. Photography was his hobby. Alison's name impressed him, and he asked what she was doing while she was in Los Angeles. She fumbled for an answer. He recognized the symptoms.

"Don't do this to yourself," he said sharply, causing her to look at him closely.

"Do what?"

"Waste yourself. It's too easy here."

"Well, what do you do?"

"To keep from dying there's a bunch of us—mostly from the East—who've formed a workshop. Actors, writers. We take turns directing. . . ."

"Mmm," Alison said, looking around for an escape.

"It's like calisthenics. Keeps you in shape. Why don't you come?"

"Perhaps I will . . ." Her voice drifted off.

"Do you want the address? It's in the Valley." He was writing it down for her. When he finished, he looked up and said, "If you don't come, I won't be hurt. Or surprised."

But she did show up—just as a couple were preparing to do a scene from *The Rainmaker*. Alison was introduced to Lynn, the person in charge, a woman of forty with lively eyes, dark hair and bangs, and an easy smile.

"Do you know the play?" she asked Alison. "It's about a family in the midst of a drought. And Lizzie, the heroine, is in danger of becoming a spinster. Along comes Starbuck, who promises rain, and Lizzie falls in love with him. In this scene she's waiting for Starbuck to take her to a dance. Okay? Let's go."

The two actors walked on to the tiny stage and began. The girl playing Lizzie kept twirling a daisy throughout the scene and at the end finally stuck it in her hair with a flourish.

Lynn called for comments. Members of the group discussed moments of truth, as well as places where the scene lost impact or where the intention was diffuse. Lynn nodded and looked at Alison.

"Do you have anything to say?"

Alison frowned. "One thing bothered me. You said this was a drought?"

"Yes."

"Where did the daisy come from?"

Lynn burst out laughing, and the group applauded. The actress playing Lizzie flushed. Alison immediately began to apologize.

"I'm sorry. I didn't mean to make fun of you. I was just curious—"

Lynn shook her head. "No, you were correct. You saw what we all missed, and it was an essential element of the scene. The drought. Where did a wonderful fresh daisy come from in the middle of a drought? It's true. Sometimes we actors don't consider all the conditions of the play. We get the relationships and the action and then overlook something absolutely important. Thank you."

At the end of the session Lynn asked Alison if she'd like to direct a scene.

"I've never directed anything," Alison said.

"That's why this is a workshop. A place to try things out. Actors play parts they would never be cast in. Writers find out what it's like to act. Why shouldn't you direct? You're a photographer, aren't you?"

"Yes."

"Well, now make pictures on the stage. I've seen your work, and it's very powerful. Somehow you felt what your subjects were feeling or were able to capture it. Try this. If you fail"—she laughed—"you can count on our letting you know."

She picked *Our Town*, though she wasn't sure why. Was it the New Englander's homesickness, a longing for some scent of pine and lilac in the middle of diesel and mimosa? Or was it because she missed her father, thought about him a lot, and was losing touch with him?

Whatever the reason, she selected a scene from the last act in the cemetery, and chose her actors. Emily Webb, married to George Gibbs, has just died in childbirth and joins others in the graveyard. As the scene begins she implores the Stage Manager to allow her to replay one day in her life. She finds it too painful and welcomes the world of eternity as her husband comes to her grave to grieve. The Stage Manager then ends the play simply and movingly.

Something had always disturbed Alison about that scene. She was not at all sure that death stopped one from caring about the earth, the sound of rain, or the smell of flowers.

She went to work on the scene. It was simple to make pictures. She recollected daguerreotypes from the Victorian era, family portraits. Why should they not be grouped in death as they had been in life? The men a bit stiff and severe, the women patient and resigned, sometimes the slight strain of bitterness in the eyes. And the loners, a bit off from the others as they had been in life, chairs turned almost sideways. Sloping. The pictures were there.

The next two weeks absorbed her completely. She took to directing as she had to photography. But here she had Mr. Wilder's help. And the actors'. They became as stimulated as she was, offering suggestions, which she listened to carefully. Some she kept and some she tactfully discarded. At the end of two weeks the scene was ready, and she drove the old Oldsmobile she had bought in a used car lot over the mountains to Glendale and found herself, ludicrously, in a panic. What if it didn't work?

Three scenes were presented before hers, and to her

the discussions were interminable. "Let's get on with it," she kept whispering to herself. Finally the actors set the stage for *Our Town*. The lights went down, then came up, revealing the actors seated in the cemetery grouping on stage. The picture was striking—the clusters of families. The scene began. Emily relived painfully her twelfth birthday. George walked up the hill to the graveyard, carrying a cluster of fresh lilacs, prostrated himself by Emily's grave while the other dead watched with detachment, then left again. It was time for the Stage Manager to give his final speech.

He picked up one of the blossoms and, after describing the nightfall, the course of the planets, and the struggle of this one, paused for a second to inhale the aroma of the lilac sprig. The gesture was simple and devastating. It symbolized the ease with which we could accept the beauty of this world, the carelessness of our existence, despite its preciousness.

At the conclusion there was silence. A clearing of throats. Oh, Alison thought. Oh, terrible. Oh, disgrace.

Lynn spoke first. "The play never fails to move me," she began, then stopped. "But I don't want to be the one to talk." She looked at the group. "What are your reactions?"

Alison discovered something about actors. No matter the performance, they always apologize. This hadn't been fulfilled, that objective had not been reached, the next moment had been incomplete. Doubts and apologies. Alison grew impatient. Lynn noticed it. "How do you feel?" she asked Alison.

"Terrific!" Alison said. "I tried something, and I think I made it work, so I feel good."

"And well you should," Lynn agreed. "I'm not sure if Mr. Wilder would have approved of the lilac—as you know, there were no conventional sets, no props at all. But what does that matter here? I happen to think the lilac was a brilliant choice. Where are you from incidentally?"

"New England."

"It figures. Well, congratulations. I hope you'll work with us more."

Alison floated back over the mountain, up the winding canyon road, and into an argument. Diane and Kenny.

She was being persistent and hardly acknowledged Alison's entrance.

"But David wants this for you," she was saying. "I think you should do it."

"I don't like the role."

"Do this one, and then you'll be able to do the one you like." He was sitting cross-legged on the huge couch and Diane was hovering over him, pushing too hard. Alison eyed her Wild Indian. Somehow David and Diane had managed to tame him a bit.

"What do you think?" Kenny asked her.

"I think you could say hello," she said.

"About what David wants," he persisted.

She smiled. "I don't care what David—"

"Oh, she's of no use," Diane interrupted angrily.

"Yes, she is," Kenny said obstinately, then said to Alison, "read these scripts."

"Sure."

"But this isn't her business. She doesn't know about all this," Diane argued.

"I trust her," Kenny said simply.

"Is it possible for either of you to give me a name? My name is Alison."

Diane was up and ready to fling herself out the door. "Listen, I don't need this temperament. I get enough from stars. Kenny, let me know in the morning."

"When I'm ready," he said.

"David's waiting," she reminded him.

"Let him," Kenny said. Diane left.

Quite suddenly Alison was tired. This had been happening frequently lately—sudden bursts of energy, then exhaustion. Maybe she had been working on the scene from *Our Town* too intensely. But now she was thinking, this was Kenny's choice. Let *him* make it. Let *him* deal with David Sampson.

By coincidence Kenny said, "David says it's all right to buy this house."

"Why bring that up?"

He shrugged. "It's your money, after all."

Yes, of course. Over the weeks she had forgotten. She had staked Kenny, she was supposed to be his manager. She looked at him now and saw a stranger. She had never told him about her little project. On the other hand he had never asked her where she'd been. They met in bed. Or if he wanted something else from her, as he did now.

"When can you read the scripts?" he asked.

"Tonight. After I've called home."

"Are you hungry? How about I send out for Chinese?"

"Sure," she said, and went into the library, where there was a private line. She dialed home, anxious to hear her father's voice. She'd been uneasy for weeks and needed to talk with him. Phyllis answered the phone.

"Where's Daddy?" Alison asked.

"He's in New Hampshire again. . . ." Her mother sounded tired. "Another trip."

"Is everything all right?"

"Yes. Fine. And you?"

"Fine." Three thousand miles of phone wire, Alison thought, and all one could say was fine, fine. She hung up, having accomplished nothing. She still felt uneasy.

After dinner she read the scripts. The choice was obvious. One was a rehash of *Easy Rider* with a leftover sixties rebel. That was David Sampson's choice, and a bad one. The other role was not the lead. It was a·three-scene part of a film that had already began shooting—the actor they were looking for would have to be brought in at the end—but it was Kenny. The character, selfish and driven, would make a tremendous impact. This was the Savage. Amoral. The times of the Causes were over.

Diane was furious when they told her the next day.

"It's not a lead. It's three scenes. He's disgusting. The audience will have no sympathy."

"I liked the script," Alison said, smiling.

"But do you know who's directing the other film?"

"I don't care."

Diane turned to Kenny. "She doesn't care. It's your career and she doesn't care."

"I didn't say that, Diane. I said I don't care who's directing the film."

"Who do you think you are? His manager, for God's sake?"

"Yes," Alison said. That left Diane with her mouth open.

She turned to Kenny. "You'd be a fool to turn down a Paul Masland film. David says so. *I* say so. You can't be too careful in this town. Not with your first film," she cautioned him, and left.

As it happened, the choice was made for Kenny. Paul Masland didn't want him, and a young director with one film for the American Film Institute to his credit saw in Kenny what Alison saw. The problem was solved and Kenny began his first film role.

About a week later Alison went to the doctor, thinking she was anemic. He told her she was pregnant. She was going to have Kenny's baby. At first she was dumbfounded, then exhilarated. She began to laugh. It was wonderful. She couldn't wait to tell Kenny. Perhaps they would even get married. She could picture the ceremony now. Quite surrealistic. Very much in tune with the times. Her parents would come, but stand to one side, probably disapproving. There would be a whole section of disapprovers. She visualized them. Myra, haughty and disapproving; Diane, malevolent and likewise; David Sampson . . . the list was enormous. She drove home. The house was empty. Her house? Her money had paid for it. His house? The papers had been signed under a corporation David Sampson had set up. It was their house, their baby. She recalled Kenny's mentioning that there was a conference that day at David's—David loved to hold conferences on his estate—so she drove there, announced herself at the gate, was buzzed through, and parked in the drive.

The house was quiet. She entered the pool area. Nothing stirred. The water was an impossible blue. Not a stray leaf marred the surface. Blazing peonies guarded the borders that led to the garage. Of course, she would know if their cars were there. On the way she passed by the lanai that was used for changing clothes or for intimate parties. David Sampson had many fantasies, one of them being that he was a modern-day Marie Antoinette. As she approached she heard moans from the screened-in room. She opened the sliding door.

Later she wished that she had brought her camera. It might have saved her a great deal of grief.

Kenny, stripped naked, whip in hand, was beating David Sampson, who was down on his knees in his floral caftan, moaning with pain and delight. She caught Kenny's expression. He was a whore who enjoyed his trade, Alison noticed; he liked using the whip. A lot.

The two of them stopped, startled at the interruption.

"Oh," Alison said, turning to go. But David was far too clever for that.

"No need to go," he said. "You have, certainly, changed the mood, but I am nothing if not adaptable. Certainly in this kind of situation. You have caught us naughty boys"—he stopped to sniff some cocaine and passed a straw to Kenny— "although your boy is naughtier than most. He won't let me touch him. Admire him, yes. But touch him, never. That is exquisite pain." David kept talking while Kenny stared at Alison and she at him.

"Join us," David suggested. "Kenny will make love to you and I would certainly enjoy watching that. Is he wonderful? Thrilling? I can tell he must be thrilling."

She stood immobile.

"Well, go or stay," David said with annoyance, "but don't just stand there." He took another blow. "Look at him," he whinnied. "Look at Kenny Buck. He's going to be a big star, you know."

She found the energy to leave. Those were the parting words, probably everybody's parting words in that City of Great Promise, and they followed her through the winding roads, back to the house that was her house, their house, overlooking Bel-Air. She sat in the living room whose furniture was outsize, whose proportions were all too grand, and she did not move. Even when Kenny strode in, she didn't move. The room had darkened; he turned on a light. She could feel him looking at her. Then he moved in front and stared into her face. The skin was stretched taut over his cheekbones.

"I would do anything to get where I'm going," he said. "I wouldn't let anything get in my way. If I had to kill, I think I would do that. And if I had to get down on my knees and kiss ass all the way to Santa Monica, I would do that too. But all he wants to do is look at me, so I let him. That, and a little whipping."

"You liked it," Alison cut in. "I could see it in your eyes. You liked the whip, didn't you?"

He laughed. "Oh, yeah, I didn't mind that at all. You don't know how many people I want to cut with that whip. How good it feels to get back, even a little. . . ."

"You'll never get even."

"Probably not. And I do have to be careful when I see him down there on his knees, because I want to see blood."

"Does he want that too?"

"Probably. He wants more, he tells me he wants more, but the point is you never give everything, right? You never give at all."

This was a nightmare, Alison thought. She tried to end it by leaving. Kenny caught her by the wrist.

"You're not going anywhere," he said, "except where I want you to go. And don't judge me. And don't lie to yourself. Whatever it is about me that's *me* turns you on."

She knew she couldn't escape him; his grasp was too strong. Moreover, she didn't want to. He was right. She wanted the cruelty, his unpredictability, whatever it was that was raw, that was sexual, that was savage, that was Kenny Buck. She responded to him. In the living room with the preposterous furniture and grandiose fireplace, he kissed her on the mouth, and she wanted more. He teased her, played with her, threw her down on the couch, toyed with her, excited her, made love to her, and it was more than ever, better than ever, and she wondered why she didn't hate him for it, or hate herself. Then she gave up wondering altogether and just gave in, for it was so easy to give in. Only for a moment did she think about how far they had come. How different they had become.

Two days later, when Kenny was out, the phone rang. The Massachusetts State Police were calling to tell Alison her father was dead. He had taken the car and driven off to the woods where he loved to hike during the fall, looking for deer, and in the spring, looking for flowers. He had parked the car, walked into the woods, not far, and shot himself in the head.

She left Kenny a note, packed a few things, and booked the next plane to Boston. Somewhere over Kansas it occurred to her that she had forgotten to tell Kenny she was carrying his baby. Had that been an accident?

Chapter Ten

Fury saw her through the funeral. She selected the coffin, arranged for the flowers for the service, picked out the gravestone. She shepherded her mother through the ceremony at the small church and then accompanied her on the bumpy journey to the grave site.

But as soon as the last words were said over the casket suspended above the empty grave, she left her father and took her mother back to the Carmichael estate, then sped off in the convertible to the nearest beach. It was very hot—early heat for June, but it was spring and it was New England. Her mind returned to the last act of *Our Town* and the smell of the lilacs. Had that been a premonition?

She tried to picture her father on that last day. What had made him abandon her? What had made him give up hope? Was there no more fun to be had from this world, no one he really wanted to share the day with, neither mother nor daughter? Was it all, day after day, one relentless night after another, nothing but muted pain that had finally become intolerable? Were there no consoling words? Even at the last moment had he not had some urge to return to his home? To dinner? To a martini? To make a telephone call? Nothing? Had he thought about her mother? Had he, in those last moments, thought about her?

She faced the ocean and waited for tears to come, but they did not. Merely curses.

She soon discovered that Jonathan Carmichael had

failed. He had no money, no future. His speculation in the New Hampshire resort condominium venture had wiped him out, and the pressure of loss had driven him to his death. He had lost everything, and even the insurance was not enough to see his wife through comfortably. Everything was used up to pay off his debts. He had made his escape.

Alison saw that the furniture was sold at auction. Fat strangers hauled away the green leather armchair that had been his favorite. An oil of a nineteenth-century sailing vessel fetched a thousand dollars and started its voyage to New York. The Ivers & Pond piano (*Randall Thompson Easy Books*, "Kitten on the Keys," hours of drudgery hunched over the keyboard) went for five hundred. Alison was surprised she was sorry to see it go, the onetime scourge of her existence. Then a parade of chairs, dishpans, china, bedsteads, chiffoniers, that were carted off in a flood of bidding, the prices rising on a river of fives and fifties. Alison watched the bits and pieces of her childhood disappear into station wagons and vans with New York and Connecticut license plates. When the auction was over and the house stripped of its belongings, when it was growing dark, she sat on the floor because there was no chair to sit on, sat in the dark because there was no light to turn on, and finally the tears came. Great heaving sobs, and the thought of life without her father, the anguish and pain of having people die and having to go on living. The picture of Alain—just another body, anonymous in a Paris morgue—came to her suddenly. It was more than she could bear. Her weeping echoed through the empty house. Finally, long after it was dark, she stopped. Exhausted from crying, and from living, and from coping, she found herself panting for breath.

She rose to her feet, shut the door on the house she had grown up in, and left. Another part of her life was over, forever.

Amazing, how tangled, how involved, the wreckage of her father's business affairs had become. There were lawyers—always lawyers—and with lawyers came their bills. There was the business of finding an apartment for her mother, one she could afford. Luckily Alison discovered a floor-through on Commonwealth Avenue with high ceilings and a big bay window that/ would accommodate the draperies from Pride's Crossing and a few other ornaments of the past. There was the china and silver, and the sideboard to keep them in. There was the crystal. There was a chandelier her mother had refused to part with.

In the first week of August Alison joined her mother for a last dinner together. She was returning to California the next day.

There had been a few phone calls between Kenny and her. He had described the progress of the film, the first rough-cut preview in Denver, the enthusiastic reaction; executives who had never known of his existence had shaken his hand and smiled the smile of money. She noticed he never mentioned Diane. She noticed she never mentioned the baby. It never seemed to be the right time.

The two women were silent. Spoon clicked against soup plate. Her mother had taken to playing the radio, syrupy music, the kind one hears in beauty salons.

"Have you told him?" Phyllis asked out of the blue.

"Told him what?"

"That you're pregnant. It is his baby, isn't it?"

"Of course." Alison was shocked at her mother's image of her.

"And you're going to have the baby?"

"Certainly," Alison declared.

Her mother was more matter-of-fact than she. "Well, it's very difficult to understand people's behavior nowadays. Relationships. Marriages. So many brilliant people around who seem insistent on throwing their lives away. I hope you're not one of them."

She rose to clear the dishes. It struck Alison she had never seen her mother lift a plate. There had always been servants.

"Oh, yes," Phyllis said, noticing Alison's expression and laughing. "I can do for myself. I always managed." She took the dishes into the kitchen, still talking.

"I managed to get by. When your father had other women. He did, you know. One of them was my best

friend. That's the classic story, isn't it? And when the affair
was over, *she* took to drink. I never did. *She* became an
alcoholic. Died of cirrhosis of the liver." Her mother's
voice was triumphant. "And here I am, still managing. I
never let things get to me. Not even your father's death.
And I did love your father. But there was a weakness in
him. It's not easy, understanding men. They can be de-
ceiving. And I do wonder about your young man." She
was returning with a strawberry mousse. Alison had not
known her mother was capable of boiling an egg. Or of
being so direct.

"Your father hated him. For taking you away, of
course. But also he considered him to be dangerous."
Phyllis put down her spoon and considered this. "Perhaps
he feared Kenny's strength."

"Kenny is a fighter," Alison said.

Her mother continued her own train of thought. "Or
perhaps he felt you had inherited his weakness."

Her mother rose to clear the dessert dishes. Dinner
was over. So was the conversation.

"I don't think I did," Alison said evenly.

"No, I don't think you did. But I don't want to see
you waste your life, Alison. You're in danger of doing
that."

Alison returned to Los Angeles the next day.

Chapter Eleven

Kenny sent his chauffeur, Giorgio, to meet her at the airport. Giorgio doubled as bodyguard to ward off an occasional persistent fan. Soon Kenny would need Giorgio to keep the groupies away.

All because of three scenes. Alison had been right. Kenny's impact on the screen was enormous and immediate. And the timing had been just right. The movie was a smash hit and Kenny its sensation. He was famous. And his life had changed totally in the time she was away.

First of all, the chauffeur-bodyguard informed her, dinner that evening was to be at Edward's Steak House, the new restaurant on Little Santa Monica. Be ready at 7:15, he said. Miss Landers and Mr. Sampson had flown in a European director for Mr. Buck's approval. Dress, casual.

An electronic gate had been installed at the entrance to their house. Giorgio manipulated a gadget and the gate swung open. Inside the house she found stacks of unopened mail, some of it for her. One letter was from Dick and Mimi Bailey. It was a condolence letter that also managed to insinuate that they would love to see both Kenny and Alison. Their address and phone number in Pasadena were included. Alison stuffed the letter in her purse. It would have to be answered. She doubted that Kenny would suffer another evening with the newlyweds, but she was curious about them. They had arrived in California soon after she had, yet they had never been in contact until Kenny's film had come out. She looked again at the familiar Choate Rosemary Hall penmanship and realized she had missed Mimi. And missed, the way many misplaced Bostonians do, the sound of a New England accent. She would definitely call them. In the meantime she hurried to get ready for Kenny.

When he arrived, it was in a whirlwind of energy. He was tearing off his clothes and taking a shower and greeting her all at the same time. He was late. She was ready. He had been delayed. He loved her. How was the trip?

"Kenny," she blurted out, "I'm pregnant. I'm having your baby."

There was a beat missed. He looked at her. "No shit! My baby? Fucking unbelievable!"

Was he smiling? She thought so. Was he pleased? She couldn't tell. He didn't have time to react. It was just another piece of information and he had to get dressed. His outfit was white buckskin, making his dark skin darker, and he added a tight red bandanna around the jet-black hair. Very conscious of his image. The Primitive Male.

He took her hand. "Come on, we'll talk about all this later," he promised. He led her to his new sports car and soon they were on that roller coaster, winding down canyon roads, smelling mimosa, sweet evening smells. Sunset on Sunset Boulevard, the world bathed in golden light. They arrived at Edward's. They made five at a table for four. Diana had not expected Alison; she barely masked her annoyance.

"You're late," was her greeting.

Kenny shrugged. "I was signing the papers."

"Congratulations." David lifted his glass to Diane. She smiled like a gypsy and nodded. A chair was brought up. Alison and Kenny sat down, and Diane introduced them to Nagy, the European director.

Alison knew his name. He had made films in London. He was a Hungarian who had lived under the Nazis, and following the war had moved to Paris. He had just made one enormously successful American film that everyone swore would be nominated for an Academy Award. He was wearing a casual workshirt and pants, his face was grizzled, his eyes squinting from the smoke of the cigarette dangling in his mouth. Short, wiry, he was always grinning, she found. But the eyes were very sharp. He saw everything.

"Your agent thought it important that we meet," Nagy said to Kenny, indicating Diane. Alison kept her cool. Since when had Diane become Kenny's agent? Since that afternoon, she figured. That was the signing of the papers, the congratulations from David.

"Okay. We met. When do we make the movie?" Kenny said. He was sprawling in his chair, his legs too long for the delicate seat.

Nagy raised his eyebrows. "You approve? So quick?"

"Sure. Tear up your round-trip ticket."

"Ah, that I never do." Nagy laughed. "Whatever country I am in, I always keep passage out."

"Then it's a deal?" Diane said quickly.

"Deal," Kenny said. Nagy nodded. Diane raised her glass.

"Let's drink to that." They did. Half the room turned to watch.

The other half was on the prowl and smiling. Strolling from table to table, touching cheeks, slapping backs, hoping to make connections. The smiles flashed on and off like neon. Beautiful busboys smiled, anticipating TV series; maître d's anticipated tips; women anticipated presents of preferred stock. There were other more interesting smiles. The smiles of those who promised luncheons their secretaries would later cancel; the smiles of those who were refusing offers. Who said no to agents, smiling; who sent back food, smiling; declined co-production deals, canceled careers, decided fates, always smiling.

Lookin' good was the phrase. Prospects, pictures, the economy, real estate, one another—all were lookin' good. They, the easily powerful and calculatedly casual, kept at it in health clubs and on tennis courts, in plastic surgeons' parlors and beauty salons. Everyone in the room had the comfort of knowing that, should he die from food poisoning that night, he would be lookin' good in his casket the next day.

"Tout le pays-ci," Nagy murmured, and Alison laughed.

"What did he say?" Diane asked quickly. "Why did you laugh?"

"It's a French phrase," Alison explained. "Louis the Fourteenth built Versailles to keep the nobility as close to him as possible. *Tout le pays-ci* meant Versailles, the center of the world. *Tout le pays-là* meant anywhere else in the world. In other words nowhere."

"I was just comparing this to Versailles," Nagy said with a shrug.

"It must be all the mirrors," Diane decided.

"No," Nagy said. "All the smiles."

Diane was smiling.

"To cover the intrigue," he added. Diane was stuck with her smile. She lit a cigarette, talked to David, talked to Kenny. Alison closed her eyes.

Perhaps it was jet lag, she thought as they ordered. She could not keep up with the voices and the gossip and laughter. Finally it was over and, relieved, Alison was standing by Kenny's side as Valet Parking delivered their various automobiles. Kenny's Porsche 935, white. David's Mercedes SL 150, flaming red. Diane's MGB, black, naturally. Nagy's rented American compact. They bid one another good night and departed, deals accomplished, and she and Kenny wound their way up the hillside through the lush and fragrant California night.

It was cooler up in the mountains. The pool was still lit. Kenny walked out to it, stripping off his clothes as he went and turning on the stereo. The music blasted over the mountains. Naked, he leaped on the parapet that kept the pool from sliding down the mountain.

"What are you doing?" Alison asked nervously.

"I'm gonna piss all over L.A., babe," he said, and proceeded to do so. The night air and the wine had aroused him.

"Diane wants to ball me," he said, facing out into the night. "Everyone wants to ball me. Everyone in the whole fuckin' world."

"Is she your agent now?" Alison asked.

"Yeah."

"And what am I?"

"What you've always been." He grinned and swayed

on the parapet. "Don't be scared. Indians never fall. There's a lot of us Indians on construction jobs. We never fall." He suddenly swung around, gave a war whoop, and plunged into the pool. He came up laughing at her.

"Come in," he invited.

"It's late, Kenny."

"I want you to," he ordered, and when she turned away, he was out of the pool in a second, holding her in his wet arms, undressing her before she could protest. But she didn't want to protest, for as he was stripping her he was making love to her.

"I want to talk," she protested. "We have to talk."

"Tomorrow," he mumbled, his mouth against the sweet skin of her neck.

"No. What about the baby? What about Diane?"

"Tomorrow," he repeated. "Everything solved tomorrow." He was picking her up in his arms.

"What am I to you?" she asked.

"I'll show you," he answered, and then they were together in the pool. The water was much warmer than the night air, and she clung to his body. His tongue was inside her mouth, sucking on her. She could feel the hardness of his body brushing against her in the water. Suddenly he dived beneath the surface and began to nibble at her underwater. She felt herself floating, totally protected and relaxed as he stroked her legs. She rolled over, and they kissed again, the warm water cushioning them. Excitement flowed from him to her and back again. She needed to envelop him. She tried to touch him. He laughed and swam out of reach, then lunged back, touched her, lifted her. She was out of the water, and the night air and his caresses made her body tingle. He grabbed the towel and began to rub her. She moaned at this opulent world where the pool was shining turquoise and stars were glowing in the California sky, and Kenny was rubbing her arms and shoulders and breasts, breathing against her neck, kissing her shoulder, enfolding her first in the towel and then in his body.

She wanted him. He knew it. He laughed again and disappeared into the bedroom while she lay looking at the night, too far gone in her desire to move. In a minute he appeared again, dancing naked in front of her. On his head was one of her straw beach hats, with an absurd pink plume stuck in it. He was the savage playing the plumed cavalier, Louis XIV. *"Tout le pays-citte!"* he mocked in French-Canadian dialect, and impulsively hurled the hat off the parapet into the night. It sailed out of sight, the plume waving at the stars. It would land in some patio below, just another unsolved nocturnal Bel-Air mystery.

Alison's pleasure was in gazing at Kenny. He was her drug as cocaine was becoming his. She could tell from the glitter in his eye that he had just taken some and wondered if he had been free-basing. He was now wild beyond wildness. Alison watched the muscles in his thighs, the grace of his body. This man was meant to be naked, she thought. He was more beautiful naked, and she waited for him to come to her now. He took his time. He stalked her, advancing slowly, standing over her. She reached one arm up his leg to stroke his thigh, then pulled herself up and kissed it. She could inhale everything; him, the night smell of flowers that bloomed mysteriously in secret canyons.

Kneeling, he offered his chest to her, his nipple. "Kiss it," he ordered. She obeyed. "Kiss it, kiss it," he continued, offering various parts of his body to her until suddenly he could take no more. He thrust her back on the towel, spread her legs, and entered her with such a savage lunge that she cried out more in pain than in ecstasy, though her pain was part of the ecstasy. She welcomed him, feeling him fill her, feeling the throb of his desire. The greatest kind of lovemaking is selfish, Alison reasoned; he no longer cared what she wanted, if he ever had. He was satisfying himself with her breast, her lips, her arms. Whatever he touched turned electric, and the greedier he became, the more it excited her, and still he moved in rhythm, insatiable.

All of him was hard and pulsing against her, and when it burst, it glowed from him in words from his tongue and lips, from all of him into all of her and she grasped it all, received it all gladly. They lay together in the night, feeling the touch of body to body. The slightest movement excited them both again. He remained hard inside her and traced with his fingers maps of worlds yet to conquer on her shoulders, traveling the mountains of her breasts, while her hands ran up and down his broad, satiny body, the firm buttocks, hoping to hold the memory. But that was impossible, she realized. Her hands forgot as soon as the stroke was finished and had to begin again.

Later she was aware of his laying her on the bed, aware of the smoothness of sheets, the smoothness of his skin. Her body strove to remember him as he made love to her—the way his hands caressed her thighs, the feel of his belly against hers, the way his mouth surrounded her breasts and his teeth nibbled her nipples. Small bites, like eating juicy raspberries. But the memories blurred, and after a time she was aware only of one continuous orgasm that did not stop because he did not stop, because he kept on loving her until she fell asleep under his weight, feeling him still inside her, moving, exciting her, drugging her.

When had he left? When had he gone away from her? She had no memory of that. She remembered only his lovemaking and then the sound at the door that was more a peremptory order than a knock. Still half asleep, waiting for Kenny to yell "Go away. Leave us alone," she reached out. There was no body beside her. Where had he gone? Where was he?

She had no time to search for an answer before the bedroom door opened and she was invaded. An avalanche of uniforms, sunglasses, boots, weapons. Men waving papers before her. Documents. Madness. A nightmare. Papers, boots, weapons, pistols, documents, Nazis, war movies. And in the midst of it all, smiling only slightly, dark and triumphant, Diane. She had brought along Charlie, who worked for her, who did her dirty work. Charlie, whose skin refused to tan, whose thinning hair and fattening middle made him ridiculous in leisure suits and gold chains and blow-dried hair. Laughable. She was laughing at him now, shaking with hysteria and laughing at the same time. Out of control. Beneath the laughter she was remembering glances, conspiracies between David Samp-

son and Diane. Ah, the smiles. *Tout le pays-ci*. And
Kenny's promise. *Everything solved tomorrow*.

"What is this, Diane?" she yelled from the bed. "What
are these people doing breaking into my room?"

"This is *Kenny Buck*'s room!" Charlie shouted on cue
and louder than necessary. He was saying this for other
ears. He flashed papers before Alison's eyes.

"These are *Kenny Buck*'s orders. You are to leave the
premises within a half hour or the sheriff will arrest you
for trespassing."

Alison laughed again, in disbelief, but found she was
laughing alone. None of the uniforms were doing any
laughing. Their sunglasses shone serious. Only Diane smiled
and held her silence.

"This is the sheriff," Charlie said, "and *this* is the city
marshall. And *these* are the deputies." Alison looked from
one pair of sunglasses to the next. The sunglasses kept
silent. Charlie did not.

"You are not to take any property—neither the vehicles in the garage, nor the bankbooks, nor any of the
belongings in this house!" he shouted in officialese.

Alison finally found her fury.

"This is my house!" she screamed. "Paid for by me,
you ignorant little creep!"

In contrast Diane's voice came though softly and perfectly controlled. "The papers are in Kenny Buck's name.
Kenny Buck is the owner of this house and its belongings."

She looked to the sheriff, who nodded.

"She's quite right, miss." His voice was surprisingly
young and high. "It's all official, if you want to look at the
documents."

Alison shook her head in anger. "Get out and let me
get dressed," she said.

They waited outside the door while she pulled herself
together. The first thing she did, as she had done every
day of her life—whether she was being thrown out of her
own house or not—was brush her teeth and comb her
hair. Then she pulled on a pair of jeans and a shirt, then a
linen jacket she had tossed over the back of a chair. She
gathered up her traveler's checks and put them in her
purse. Packed her suitcase. That was easy. Actually she

had not *un*packed it. All the while her mind refused to function. This was like nothing she had ever experienced. Never had she been humiliated before. Her hands were shaking with rage. She tried to control them. Another knock on the door gave her a start.

"I'm coming," she said, and actually hurried, gathering up whatever cash was lying around—it wasn't much—and ran to open the door. One of the deputies took her bag. They all followed her to the front door. Sheriff, deputies, sunglasses, Charlie and his gold chains. And Diane. All making sure she left the premises.

Outside the door the burst of sunlight and then the flashbulbs. She hadn't expected that. The drive was filled with photographers snapping at her like ferocious dogs. She put her hands up to her face, momentarily blinded, and stumbled, falling against the jagged brick that formed the border for the pachysandra. More flashes. She could envision the headlines. LIVE-IN LOVER TUMBLES. UNSTEADY STEADY. A sharp pain tore at the insides of her body. A torn ligament, she thought. Goddamn it, she had torn a ligament in the midst of this. Hands offered help; she refused. She picked herself up. The taxi was waiting. The cab driver opened the door and she got in. Somebody dumped her bags in beside her. The photographers were surrounding the cab and the reporters were jabbing her with questions. And out of all of it the only distinct impression she got was of Diane, supreme and smiling, the winner.

The cab driver asked her where she wanted to go.

"Just drive!" she yelled at him. "Just get me out of here!" He stepped on the gas and they were gone, curving down the narrow road. Halfway down she put her hands up to her face to shield her eyes. The sun was violent. She was crying. Quite possibly Alison Carmichael was the only person in all Los Angeles who did not possess a pair of sunglasses.

At the bottom of the hill the driver stopped. She had to make a decision. She could think of only one address.

"Take me to the Sunset Marquis," she said.

That was a mistake.

Chapter Twelve

The Sunset Marquis was not a bad hotel. It was merely the center of the Hollywood rock scene. From her useless little balcony Alison could look down at the pool area where young and not so young girls lolled in their lounge chairs, reading *Record World* and *The Hollywood Reporter*, moving only to answer the phone or go to the machine for another soda. These girls she knew too well. They were waiting in the unblinking California sun for their men to finish a gig. They lived in not-quite-comfortable suites where the bar doubled as a dining table and the ice machines were always down the hall.

They formed a lazy, catlike group. They were stoned a lot; they went to bed at dawn and ate breakfasts of Chinese food at three in the afternoon. Sometimes they attended all-night recording sessions. To Alison they all looked alike. Muffled and secret-eyed. And they were, every one of them, somebody's Old Lady. As she had been Kenny's.

Buying the afternoon paper was a mistake, too, because there it was. Diane had seen to it. Alison's picture was on the front page. Stumbling, hair mussed, disheveled in jeans and jacket with a hand up to her face as if warding off a blow. She looked underneath. AP. That meant it had gone out over the wire services. Kenny was big enough that this picture could make the front page of the Chicago papers, and the *New York Post* and the *Daily News*. And obviously Boston. And what would the caption be there? she wondered. FORMER DEB SLIPS? What would she be called? One time photographer? Socially prominent? Live-in lover?

She bought all the papers and crossed the pool area, passing all those sun-tanned limbs, oiled and waiting, like parts to machines. She walked under the blazing sun and climbed the concrete stairs that led to her room, entered it, and locked the door. She pulled the drapes shut and stared at the photos. She didn't move, didn't comprehend.

She was like a child asking, *Why?* Why had Kenny done this? Why had Diane engineered this to hurt her? The answer to that was obvious. Diane was out to destroy her because she was standing in the way. And Diane had found a weapon, one better than a gun or knife, to eliminate her. But why had Kenny allowed this to happen? There she drew a blank. Maybe the answer was in another photo she found in the next morning's paper—a photo of Kenny and Nagy getting off a plane in Seattle. In the background was a young blond groupie, described as a traveling companion.

Or was it because she was having his baby? She remained in her room in the Sunset Marquis, turning the pages of the newspaper over and over as if she could find the answer to her questions. But there was no answer to be found. She pictured the other women of the Sunset Marquis, and their suntanned bodies and bored faces mocked her. They were a reflection of her.

Was this what she had become? she wondered. Once she had been Alison Carmichael, the prominent photographer, the well-brought up debutante. Once she had been Jonathan's daughter, but he was lying in the earth and had abandoned her. As Kenny Buck had abandoned her. *Abandoned her! They had abandoned her!*

She felt rage well up inside her, like a scream that was pushing against her, trying to release itself. The rage became a pain, as sharp as a knife. The knife was inside her and turning slowly. When she stumbled, she thought, had she seriously injured herself? The pain continued to build, and she doubled over, clutching her abdomen. She closed her eyes and could see the man over her, turning the knife slowly with sadistic pleasure. How much pain was it possible to inflict on any one person?

She opened the door and left, instinctively seeking help. The pain . . . She stumbled against the wall of the corridor and followed it to the iron bannister that led to the ground floor. That was as far as she got.

They found her at the top of the staircase. Luckily she had not fallen down the concrete steps.

She lost the baby. And lost a part of herself too. The doctor took the time to explain to her she had suffered an ectopic pregnancy, that she had almost died. They had been forced to remove the Fallopian tube and the adjoining ovary. That did not mean she could not have another child, the doctor assured her, as sunny as a songbird. She was young, she was healthy, and accidents do happen, he said. Too bad. And, having done his duty, he left her in the hospital ward.

She wanted to die but hadn't even the strength to accomplish that, so she lay in the hospital bed and waited. She watched the sunlight travel across the room, morning sunlight a bright color, afternoon sun harsher and whiter, evening sun edged with shadows until the shadows took over and then were erased by neon light which had no color and no substance. Finally night would arrive and she could be alone. She didn't need to close her eyes anymore to pretend she was sleeping. She could stare at nothingness while time passed.

The doctors grew edgy. They needed the bed.

She couldn't pay the bill though. The surgeon's bill, the hospital bill. The management of the Sunset Marquis brought her things. She looked at the traveler's checks. Not enough. Well, someone would have to go without. They could draw lots.

The next morning the nurse came in and told her she was leaving that day. She wondered what had happened.

Ben Sawyer had happened.

He came into the ward on a wave of sighing, adoring nurses, but wasn't the Ben she remembered. He wasn't smiling. Handsome, yes, but angry now. Angry with her, she thought.

"Come on," he said roughly. "I'm getting you out of here." She was dressed and rolled in a wheelchair to where his car was waiting. They drove along the winding strip of Sunset Boulevard.

"Why didn't you call me?" he shouted at her. "Why didn't you let me know where you were?"

"I thought you were part of it!" she yelled back. "You work for *them*."

"Who's them?"

"David Sampson. And Diane. And—" She couldn't say his name. Suddenly all the emotions she had been holding back burst forth. She began sobbing there in his convertible in the middle of Sunset Boulevard.

"Oh, Ben, he left me. He left me. He didn't even do it himself. He had them do it. He left me, and I loved him, and Ben, oh, Ben, you don't know how much that hurts. It hurts so much. What am I going to do? I can't keep crying for the rest of my life."

"Alison, I happen to love you. I can't bear to see you hurt. I wouldn't have let anything happen to you!"

"Don't say that. Don't say you love me." The sound of her own voice chilled her. "I never want to hear that again in my life."

"Alison—"

"Ben, don't. Don't ask for feelings. I don't have any more. I just want to be left alone." She had stopped crying. It was true. She felt nothing.

"What are you going to do?" he asked.

"I don't know. I need my things. My car. My cameras. That's all I have. You're a lawyer. Their lawyer—"

"You still think I had something to do with this?"

"How could you not? There were legal documents. Sheriffs. City marshals. You must have known."

"I swear. Nothing."

"Well," she continued tonelessly, "Kenny Buck now possesses everything I have. I want what is mine. Nothing more."

"It has to go through a court order," he said.

"Yes. Of course. Don't explain the procedures to me, Ben. Just get me what's mine."

"You know, you do have a case . . ." he started to say.

"Against Kenny? No thank you. I don't want legal fees, publicity, humiliation. I've had enough of that."

"You'll need a certificate of ownership for the car. For the cameras. . . ."

"Ben. Get me what's mine," she said. They continued in silence to his place.

Alison watched him dial a number. He gave no name to the person who answered.

"Alison Carmichael is here," he said. "There were some things left behind."

He was silent a moment, listening, his face betraying no emotion. Then he continued.

"If you want trouble, she is perfectly capable of making it. She's left her automobile—a 1960 Oldsmobile—and her photographic equipment, which is her means of livelihood."

There was some comment from the other end of the phone.

"Look," he said, irritation showing in his voice, "it's possible to get a court order. She has proof of ownership. I suggest enough is enough. All this can be cleared up in fifteen minutes."

Pause.

"Yes, I will accompany her. In twenty minutes. All right, half an hour." He hung up the phone.

"Thank you," Alison said, but her tone was that of a woman thanking a salesman who had finally located an order that had been mislaid.

Diane was at the door. She waved and called "Hi," as though they had come to play doubles. "I hope this won't take too long. Do you know where everything is?"

"I think so," Alison said over her shoulder as she brushed past Diane.

"Good," Diane said.

"This is mine, this Leica," Alison said.

"One Leica." Diane continued the charade, writing everything down. Alison controlled her emotion.

"And this Fujica. This Rollei. A light meter. These three cases. This film." She looked around her.

"I think that's it," she said, facing Ben and Diane. "Except for the car."

"The car?" Diane asked. "What car is that?"

"The Oldsmobile."

Diane giggled. "That? You came to collect *that*? I thought it belonged to the gardener."

"Diane . . ." Ben's voice had warning in it.

"Of course. Do you have the keys?" Diane asked.

"No," Alison said. "The keys were . . ." Her memory deserted her for a moment. She looked around the house, this whole part of her life, this palace of madness. Redwood. Stonewall. Shiny surfaces. Chrome. All of it hardedged. The house was deserted. No trace of Kenny Buck. No sign he had ever lived there. Everything had been erased. She wanted to get out as fast as possible.

"The keys," she repeated. "On a hook in the kitchen."

The cars shone in the driveway. Above them the dusty red-clay canyon, hung together with arroyo and sagebrush, looked as though it might collapse, tumble down and crush them all at any moment. Diane's sports coupé, black and compact. Ben's car, more curves to it. Behind the gate her car, in need of a paint job, in need of polish. Bought for a lark, a kind of protest against all the foreign two-seater prestige bullshit that had surrounded her, the Olds was now her only means of escape.

She opened the door and got in behind the wheel. Like most old cars, it smelled of beat-up upholstery and other owners. She turned the key in the ignition. The motor kicked over and died. She pumped the gas pedal.

Diane was watching her, the cool smile below the sunglasses. Alison prayed the Olds would start. She tried it three more times. Ben came forward to assist, but just at that moment, the engine caught. She gunned the motor and turned to back the car out of the garage.

"Just a moment," Diane said as they approached the gate. "I'm afraid you'll have to sign these."

"What are they?" Alison asked.

"A statement saying these are your possessions."

Alison signed.

"And this."

"What is this?"

"Swearing that this is your automobile."

Alison signed.

"And this."

Ben was looking at Diane curiously.

"What is this?" Alison asked. The heat in the car was overpowering.

"A document stating that you will no longer harass Kenny Buck at any time," Diane answered smoothly.

"No longer?" Alison shouted.

"If you want your possessions, you will sign this," Diane said. Alison proceeded to. "After all," Diane continued, "I must protect my client."

"Is that all?" Alison said, her voice trembling. She grasped the steering wheel.

"I think that takes care of everything." Diane smiled.

"Then let me out," Alison shouted. The gates had been locked again against intruders. A button had to be pushed. Some electronic device.

"Let me out! Let me out of here!" She hit the horn. It wailed.

From an invisible power the gates swung open.

"Alison," Ben began.

"Don't talk to me. Don't say a word. Not a word."

"Bye!" Diane cooed. Alison could not lose that word, it echoed in her ears. She steered down the winding road.

"Let me out!" she continued to shout to herself, as though she were still locked inside some madhouse from which there was no escape.

But she had been freed. Like many former inmates, though, she realized with panic as she reached the bottom of the hill where Sunset turns west toward the Pacific or east, she had nowhere to go.

There are worse places in which to be lost and penniless than Los Angeles.

Siberia might be one of them.

*   *   *

Ben Sawyer returned to his office. On a hunch he contacted the Sheriff's Office of Los Angeles County to check on an eviction proceeding at 814 N. Faring Way. It took the clerk two minutes to return to the phone and declare that no such procedure had ever taken place.

Diane had used Central Casting. A setup. And she had gotten Alison's signature.

Swell town, swell people, Ben thought as he looked out over Los Angeles baking in the heat of August.

Chapter Thirteen

Alison called her mother to reassure her.

"But are you all right? I saw the pictures in the paper—"

"I stumbled, that's all. No, I'm really okay. There's no need to worry."

"Then why don't you come home?"

Alison had no answer for that. She only knew she couldn't. She couldn't always be on guard and keep her emotions in check. Here, at least, she could sit in the car and when one of the rages came upon her, she could weep and no one would pay any attention. This town was full of weeping women.

"I'll call you or write you when I get settled. But don't worry. I'm all right," Alison said again, and hung up the phone.

She made other calls.

It was amazing how well Diane had succeeded in spreading the word. Alison Carmichael was some demented groupie who had literally been kicked out of a film star's mansion. She was a drunk. She was a junkie. She had flipped. She had suffered a breakdown. She was not to be trusted. What did it matter? No one would return her calls. In L.A. as in no other city in the world, you're either on top or you're nothing. At the moment Alison was nothing.

It was when she called Mimi and Dick Bailey that she realized nothing could hurt her anymore.

"I wanted to thank you for your note," she said to Mimi.

"Oh, think nothing of it," Mimi said hurriedly.

"I thought maybe we might get together. Lunch or something like that."

"Oh . . ." There was silence at the other end of the line.

"Hello, Mimi? Are you there?"

"Of course, I'm here. I don't know about lunch."

"Well, it doesn't have to be today. It could be anytime."

"I just don't know about lunch."

Alison began to get angry. "What do you mean, you don't know about lunch? You mean, you're booked solid for a year? Two years?"

Mimi retreated. "I think you better talk to Dick."

Dick got on the phone. He was no longer the Andover-Yale sweet-talker. Now he was the executive.

"Alison," he said, "Mimi doesn't want to hurt you, but I might as well tell you. We can't afford to be seen with you. I am sorry you took the route you took, and I'm sorry it ended the way it ended. But I have a position to look out for and I can't be mixed up with drugs and sex and alcohol and the police and all the rest of it."

"All the rest of what?" Alison shouted.

"Don't yell at me," Dick said. "I've got a future, and I won't jeopardize it in any way. Don't call us again, Alison."

She hung up first. She was sure she was the one to hang up first. She hung up and then clung to the phone. She was in a phonebooth by a parking lot, and the cars shining in the sunlight dazzled her eyes. She began to panic.

It was all very clear to her. She had no money. She had no prospects for a job. She thought, quite clearly in fact, that maybe she was going crazy. No, maybe she was crazy.

No, I'm all right, she said to herself. *I'm really all right. I will be all right in a minute or two.*

The rage hit her again. She wanted to kill. She looked out of the phonebooth. There was a salesman on a used-car lot. She wanted to kill him. How confident he looked.

He was a liar and a cheat in a lying and cheating business. He was a man and a liar and a cheat.

"I will be all right," she said to the phone. "Please God, I will be all right."

And then it was a matter of getting to the car. It took all her effort to open the door and sit inside. She closed the door and locked it and sat there. The words came back to her. Drugs. Drunk. Breakdown.

Alison did have a breakdown, without recognizing it. The streets became longer and flatter, distances insuperable. For two days she slept in the car, huddled in the back seat. She was awakened the second night by a tap on the window. A face was peering in at her. She screamed. The doors were locked. Two men were trying to open the doors. The face continued to stare at her. They made gestures. The heat in the car was suffocating. She came back to reality.

It was the L.A. police.

She had to explain why she was sleeping in the car. Produce the registration. Proof of ownership. She was constantly having to prove her existence, it seemed. The police lectured her on the dangers of sleeping in an automobile and suggested she locate the Office of Human Resources.

"Wait a minute," she said. "You are talking to a person here who is not indigent, who is not in need of welfare, who is perfectly capable, a woman from Massachusetts who has a career, who has been to Europe, who has connections, friends, influence. . . ." She realized she was sounding like a looney.

"Call them," the cop suggested, his eyes challenging her.

She pretended to make the call, with his eyes still observing her, and said to an imaginary person, "Oh, they're away in Paris? I'll call later."

The police let her go. They had no grounds for holding her. What was her crime, after all?

What was her crime, she thought. What was she punishing herself for? For falling in love, for being tricked, for being taken?

For being innocent, she decided.

No one should be so innocent, so trusting. That was her crime. And she had now sentenced herself to prison.

Prison consisted of sleeping in the car and using the public toilets at Rancho Park. Prison consisted of shoplifting. She stole a can opener and ate canned tuna for a week.

She had also sentenced herself to solitary confinement, but discovered she wasn't alone. There were many people who lived on the beaches in Venice, slept in the park or under the pier, shit in Texaco toilets, panhandled on Sunset and Santa Monica.

Oh, it could have been worse, much worse, she thought. She could have sentenced herself to the heavy security pens of Chicago or New York or St. Louis in the heat of the summer.

No, L.A. was the paradise of penitents. And Venice the inner sanctum. There she found she could sleep undisturbed. Daylight woke her. She washed herself in the ocean. There was a shower by the curb. She stood under it and let the free water clean her. The sun dried her for nothing. She could do with a cup of coffee for most of the day. She ate fruit. It was cheap and plentiful, peaches in particular. She would spend the day on the beach. Men passed by and had greetings, smiles, suggestions, propositions, but she never acknowledged them, not their hellos, their good-byes, nor their curses when she ignored them.

Silence was her other punishment. She talked to no one. Never said thank you, never asked directions, never said a word. She stared at the blue Pacific, which for days wasn't blue at all but the color of light soot, of fog, a washed-out gray. And when the heat of the day finally wore off, three or four hours after darkness, she returned to her car, which was like an oven and crept in. She felt herself, night after night, slipping away, as though with the tide. She was drifting out to sea, a little more each day. It was painless, this drifting. It involved no feeling at all. One disappeared bit by bit.

There comes the time when one gives up, goes under, capitulates, dies. Or one takes hold, looks up, fights back, and lives.

For Alison it came out of curiosity. She noticed the

rather casual drug dealing that was going on. Light drugs or heavy drugs, she wasn't sure what anyone was puffing or sniffing. But the entire ceremony of the transaction intrigued her.

The dealers were mostly men. Young, very young. Sometimes eighteen. Usually handsome and sun-kissed. She would have used them to model beachwear. They lived well, but in the same manner she did. They lived from car to car, swam in the same ocean and washed off the salt with the same shower, but they made money for their dreams. They were hard businessmen. They had their clients and their products locked away in little secret dream compartments with keys that they hid in their bikinis. The casualness of their faces caught her eye.

One day it occurred to her to take out a camera.

The object was unfamiliar. Her hands fumbled with the case. It was heavier than she remembered. She looked at it as though it belonged to another life. There were dials with numbers on them. The machine moved backward and forward with a touch. With a click a moment was recorded on film. The process could be repeated thirty-six times. Thirty-six exposures. She took off the lens cover and examined the lens. It was clean. Its eye stared back at her. She could see a distortion of her reflection. Her hair was tangled and hung down her neck. Her nose was peeling.

She put the camera up to her eye. What did she see? Crumbling buildings. An antique waterway. A fantasy fallen on hard times. Here everything disintegrated, decayed before its time. She turned with the camera to her eye and focused on a face—two faces. Intent on dealing. Instinct took over. She snapped the shutter.

They looked up and in two seconds were on her. They knocked her to the ground, causing her elbow to bleed. The larger one, beefy, with blond curly hair, grabbed her camera.

"Give me that," she growled.

"Who are you? Shooting this fuckin' film!" The skinnier, darker one was angry.

"Take the film. Gimme the camera," she said.

"Why?" They started to question her. What was it

worth? Was it to be held for ransom? What? What was it worth?

"Let me open it for you," Alison said. "I'll give you the film."

They tantalized her by handing the camera to her, then withdrawing it. Suddenly her rage against Kenny, Diane, Ben, the L.A. Police Department, the world, erupted from her. She brought her knee in to a groin; she scratched, bit, punched. They fell as she had fallen. Beefy One looked at her in amazement. Lean One recovered first and started to his knees, but she kicked him in the face. Kicked him! She had never kicked anyone in her life before. He went down on the black pavement, and by then, the yelling had brought the cops. They asked her if she had been attacked.

"Yes," she said.

"These were the perpetrators?"

"Yes."

"You want to press charges?"

She looked at the two of them, then at herself. Three of a kind. Bums and drifters. "No," she said.

The cops turned belligerent. "Don't get yourself in this situation, girlie. Someday you won't be so lucky."

"No, I don't think I'll be in this position again," she said. And from that moment on she began to feel better.

It was not easy finding work. *Look* had gone. *Life* was going under. Everyone remembered her work, but she was now known only as Kenny Buck's Old Lady, down and out and in trouble, and not worth the risk.

She joined the unemployment line. When asked about her last job and her occupation, and she said photographer, the lady questioning her looked at her in disbelief. They hear all kinds of stories in the unemployment line, Alison thought.

"Can you type?"

"No. I'm a photographer."

"How about bookkeeping?"

"I can try. I don't know."

"What kind of work are you looking for?"

"I applied to *Life*."

"I see. Perhaps you should lower your sights a bit. Who was your last employer?"

"Nobody employed me. I was free-lance."

"Oh, well, you can't expect unemployment compensation. You have been self-employed. Your best bet is welfare. There's nothing we can do."

"I don't have any money."

The woman just shrugged.

Alison turned to the newspapers. She read the employment listings. The Sorbonne had not prepared her for this. She couldn't type or take shorthand. She could take pictures. And it seemed nobody needed that.

She learned her way around town. She discovered how to present herself and how to get past the first secretary or the first employment officer. She did get to see vice-presidents and department heads, but she couldn't hide her lack of experience.

Early one Monday morning a word in the classifieds caught her eyes. *Bilingual*. She read the ad.

BILINGUAL

GIRL FRIDAY needed by up-coming ad agency, commercial house. Call and send resume to X-Clu Melrose Avenue

She waited until ten o'clock and presented herself at the address.

The office was not exactly an office. There were file cabinets, but they were scattered around the room. There were two desks, each facing a wall, each littered with papers. A telephone was ringing. Alison looked around. She could see no telephone, nor anyone to answer it. A door burst open and a slim blond man brushed some papers aside, found the phone, and in slightly accented English answered it. In a moment he switched to French. Obviously he was talking to an applicant. The man began to use some technical French terms, then shrugged and hung up the receiver. The applicant had failed. He swore.

"No need for that," Alison said, and the man took

notice of her. They regarded one another. He had nice eyes and a rather silly mustache. He was wearing a faded chambray shirt to go with his eyes. He was obviously meticulous about his wardrobe. California casual with the French touch, Alison thought.

At the same time he was thinking, nice eyes, good face. Was it possible she had a sense of humor? The clothes were not right. There were too many creases and wrinkles.

Also the skin was burned. The nose was peeling.

"Are applying for the position?" he asked her flatly.

"Yes, I read the ad."

"It said to telephone."

"I thought I'd see what kind of place it was. After all, you did give an address."

He switched to French. "Some dump, eh?" he said.

"Everything's a little scattered. What it needs is a little organization," she answered, looking around the wreckage. She realized the desks had no chairs. There was no place to sit down.

"What is this establishment?" she asked.

"Good question. We are a production house."

She looked at him blankly. He had switched back to English. He switched to French again.

"I don't understand you," she confessed.

"Commercials. We make TV spots."

"Oh." Alison found her interest reviving. "You mean you actually—"

The man nodded. "Yes, get the actors, find the locations, shoot the commercial, edit it, and collect the money. No, we get the money first."

"What would I do?"

"Clean this place up—type, answer the phone." Her face was not too happy. "Learn the business . . ." She looked doubtful.

"What's the pay?"

"Seventy-five a week."

"Oh, no," she said. "You need someone very badly. You pay me two hundred."

"Impossible!" The phone rang. Alison answered it. Another applicant. She did precisely what the man had done. She asked questions, first in English, then in French. She began to talk about lenses and photographic equipment. The girl on the other end of the line sank into silence. Alison said crisply, "Sorry. I'm afraid you are not what we require," and hung up the phone.

"A hundred," the man countered.

"A hundred fifty," Alison bargained. They switched to French, both of them enjoying the transaction. The phone rang again. Alison picked up the receiver. "No, I am sorry. The position has been filled."

They shook hands on it and the man introduced himself as Raymond.

"I want you to meet my partner," he said.

"What do you do? What does he do?"

"He is the business end."

"You can hire me just like that?"

"Well, he must approve. But I'm sure he will."

"I can't type."

"Don't say that!" Raymond said in horror. "You mean you can't type at all?"

"Well, I can use the two-finger system. But I can't type."

"You can type. You tell him you can type. Shorthand?"

"Of course not."

"Fake it."

"How do I fake it?"

"You want the job?"

"I want the money."

"Then fake it."

Alison decided he was right. They looked at each other, and she drew herself up and became Miss Efficiency.

"By the way" she asked, "is your partner French?"

"Doesn't speak a word."

"Then how did you two get together?"

"Because we're crazy. We got one account. I was in Creative and he was in Personnel, and we came up with a couple of good ideas. Cheaper than the rest. He knew how to deal with unions. Cut corners, all that. Go to music houses for the music. Get things on spec. Buy-outs."

Alison was listening to a new language and learning fast. She would have to know all about this. She had already made the decision she was not just going to answer the phone and take dictation. First of all, she figured Raymond's partner was no dummy. Sooner or later, he would find out she wasn't your run-of-the-mill girl Friday.

"One more question," she said.

"What? What?" Raymond was growing impatient.

"Why French? What do you do that's French?"

"*Publicité.*" He shrugged. In every French cinema there are filmed advertisements before the feature. "It costs less here. And now, you know, everything *there* is American. Jukebox. Cowboy. Fast food. Drugstore. We shoot the locations here and then dub them if we have to. Now, come meet Bert."

Bert was short and squat and harried. He did not look as though he were in advertising or commercials. He walked toward her like an accountant with flat feet, duck waddling.

"This is Schecter," Raymond said. "Schecter, this is Alison, our new sec—girl Friday."

Alison looked from one to the other. "Is that what you want me to call you?" she asked Schecter.

"What else should you call me? That's my name. Schecter."

"No, I mean—*Mr*. Schecter?"

"Oh, okay, if you want. . . ." Schecter had never considered it.

"And I am Miss Carmichael."

"Okay, Alison," Schecter said agreeably, wondering why they were wasting time.

"Okay," Alison said. "What do I do?"

Schecter looked a little apologetic. "Could you make an office out there? Like other people's offices?"

"You mean with chairs and magazines?"

"Yeah." Schecter was delighted. "Gimme the homey touch."

"Let me have some money."

Schecter looked at Raymond. "We got any money?"

"Wait a minute," Alison interrupted. "I thought you were the business person."

"He is," Raymond said. "He's terrific when it comes to making deals."

"I just never bother with the banking," Schecter said, then added, "that will be your job. And you can also sort things, you know, like what's paid and what's owed."

Alison was doubtful. "I don't know if this is going to work out."

"Oh, come on," Raymond said, almost pleading. "Give us a try."

Everything was upside down, Alison thought. She should have asked for more money. As it was, she said, "I'll give it a week."

It shouldn't have worked out, but it did. Schecter lacked organization, but he was tenacious. In his bargaining. In his soliciting of accounts. But he needed someone around at all times to take notes, to remind him of his next appointment, who the client was. Once he had struck a bargain, he lost interest. Then it was up to Raymond, and Raymond had style, flair, and a good deal of luck.

Alison spent her first afternoon ordering and organizing. She made a plan for an office. She commandeered Raymond to move the file cabinets. The wonderful thing about Los Angeles was instant delivery. She ordered four chairs and they were in place by three in the afternoon. She distributed some fashion magazines, sighed as she looked at a back issue of *Charm*, placed it beside *Paris-Match*.

She got rid of the can of cocoa that was filed under *C*. She proceeded to go through the accounts. Actually X-Clu wasn't doing too badly.

At the end of the week, when she got her pay check, she decided she would stay another week. By the end of three weeks, she decided she was indispensable.

This was the other side of Los Angeles, a not unpleasant existence, if one kept one's sense of humor. She rented a furnished apartment and moved in. As a woman alone, working at a job, she discovered a routine. The supermarkets were like automated palaces, and were open twenty-four hours a day. The clerks always looked fresh. As did the produce. It wasn't like Paris. In some ways it was better. Where could you find an avocado in Paris? Never had she seen such a multitude of pineapples, huge peaches,

mangoes, oranges, sweet tangelos, all mellowing under
the neon tubing that was on at all times.

She also discovered the superdrugstore—also open all
night—and the Laundromat. And how to make deals.

It wasn't that Schecter taught her. She just listened
and remembered. She heard him deal with the unions,
handle the contracts, make up the budgets. Fortunately
for her there were very few letters to write and the
contracts were mostly printed up. What letters there were
appalled her.

"Take a letter," Schecter said one morning. It was the
moment Alison had been dreading. She found a pad and
pencil and sat tensely. Schecter gazed into space.

"To Jim Braddock, BB D and O. Check the address
in the directory. Dear Jim—" He stopped. Alison waited.

"Dear Jim," he repeated. "A deal is a deal and you
are an asshole. Don't try to change terms on me. Sincerely
yours and all that crap."

Alison looked up. "This is a business letter?"

Schecter stared at her. "Of course it's a business
letter."

She sat down in front of the typewriter. Instinct told
her to make a carbon copy. She put the carbon in wrong
and the letter came out backward. She redid it. After four
attempts she had a passable letter. Before mailing it, she
conferred with Raymond.

"Should I send this?" she asked him.

"Oh, sure," Raymond said. "Schecter's right. Jim is
an asshole. Oh, get me a cowboy who can ride for
Thursday."

She looked at him blankly. "How do I do that?"

"Call up SAG and say you want cowboys who can
ride. Age twenty to twenty-five. It's a drugstore commercial. We shoot on Friday."

She called the Screen Actors Guild. She expected
they'd consider her request odd. They didn't.

"Do they have to provide their own horse?" the
woman on the other end asked matter-of-factly. "That's
extra."

"No," Alison said, though she didn't know. "We'll
provide the horse."

When she talked to Raymond about that later, he said, "Thank God you said that. Can you imagine all the horseshit there would be in the parking lot?"

Thursday they auditioned cowboys who could ride.

"Now, what I want you to do," Raymond said, directing them, "is ride down the aisle, have the horse rear at the end, then jump over the counter. You got that?"

Thirty-five men were standing there; blond, dark, short, tall, all in chaps and hats, full cowboy gear. All thirty-five nodded.

"And"—Raymond distributed the scripts—"here's the copy." All but five bit the dust when it came to copy. Finally one was chosen.

"Shouldn't you have a standby?" Alison suggested.

"A standby!" Schecter shouted. "For a stuntman?"

"Well, suppose something happens? I mean, you have a horse riding through a drugstore. . . ."

"Nothing will happen." Schecter dismissed the thought. Alison was not so positive. She looked down the list of prospects. Tim Ramsey had been second choice. She remembered him. He was tall, blond, and really from Texas. He had the accent. He was the prototype of the all-American cowboy.

She sidled over to him. "What are you doing tomorrow morning?"

"As of now, nothing," Ramsey said, shrugging. "I sure figured I had this one."

"Well, if you're not doing anything," Alison said, "maybe we could have a cup of coffee. You could kind of hang around. We could talk." She wrote down the location on a piece of paper.

Ramsey looked at her with his piercing Lone Star eyes.

"I surely would appreciate that, ma'am."

She smiled. He smiled.

"Wear your boots," she advised him. "They're so great-looking."

"You know I will."

The next morning Alison drove to the location. The drugstore, rented for the day, was on Paramount Avenue in Downey. Even though it was seven o'clock in the morning, the store was far from empty. The group of extras was already in makeup and prepared for rehearsal. The crew was standing by. There was a long table with a huge coffee urn and a mountain of crullers. Who were all these people? What were their jobs? she wondered. She looked around more carefully. It was very early in the morning; perhaps she was dreaming.

She was back in Paris. There was the *marchand de quatre saisons* in his smock. An artist. A baker. A concierge. A washerwoman. Two French children dressed for school. A young French housewife and a business type. She had seen his kind tooling around l'Étoile on a motor scooter, trying to be American. Raymond stood beside the cameraman, chatting, smiling. He was focusing on the cowboy who was eating a cruller. The horse was there, and the horse's trainer.

The entire effect was bizarre. The crew had set up for the shoot. An American drugstore, a cowboy on horseback, and a group of your average French customers.

"What is this all for?" she asked Raymond.

"I thought you knew. It's a new product to relieve hemorrhoids."

She laughed at the joke. He was putting her on.

"It's called Ledoux," he added. She was not so sure.

Then Raymond called rehearsal and she watched the extras assume their roles. French shoppers in a drugstore. Business type and housewife with two children suddenly became a family. The concierge belonged to the baker. They all assumed attitudes of distress, searching through the aisles of the drugstore for relief.

Suddenly, down the center aisle galloping on horseback and holding up a package, came the cowboy. On cue the horse reared up, the cowboy moved his lips, and Raymond cried out in French, *"Même nous, les cowboys, sont des souffrants! Voici Ledoux pour le soulagement!"* The cowboy whooped *"Yahoo! Ledoux!"* and all the extras cried in unison, *"Ledoux! Ledoux!"*

Alison decided that Raymond was indeed not joking and was probably some kind of genius.

"Not bad!" Raymond said to the cowboy. "But raise

the box up higher. Even in closeup, I can't see the name. I got to see the name. They're paying for the name."

The cowboy asked what he was supposed to be saying in French.

Raymond translated for him. "Even cowboys have hemorrhoids. Get Ledoux for relief!"

"Oh. I wanted to know what my motivation was," the cowboy said.

"You are like the Lone Ranger. You come to the rescue of all these people. You bring them Ledoux. It is more valuable than gold."

"Then I should be happy . . ." the cowboy persisted.

"You should be triumphant. You have saved the village from the Indians. You understand?"

"I get it." The cowboy nodded. Raymond then circulated among the extras, switching back and forth from French to English. More vigor was needed from the boulanger. The children *un peu plus sportifs*. Their mother appeared from another aisle.

"Eh, what did I tell you?" she shouted at them. "*Vifs! Vifs!*" Raymond signaled Alison. She got the message and approached the mother.

"Madame, I have some papers here for you to sign. Would you like a cup of coffee?" The woman was all graciousness.

"*Mais certainement!*" she cried, and Alison took her to one side where she could sign the release.

"You don't know how difficult it is," the mother confided. "They miss school. Sometimes they do two commercials a week, and then for months, nothing. It is no life."

"Cream? Sugar?"

"*Un peu de crème. Pas de sucre, merci.*" Sighing, she continued her complaints. Alison gave her the release to sign.

"Hi. Here ah am," a voice said behind her. It was Tim Ramsey. The French widow sighed again, this time with envy. Tim only had eyes for Alison. His eyes were twinkling and it was only eight-thirty in the morning. He looked rarin' to go. Alison gave him a cup of coffee and he sat down beside her. The French widow reluctantly returned to her children and the shoot continued.

"I see you wore your boots," Alison said.

"Wouldn't be caught without 'em," Tim said, smiling and stretching his long legs. "Except on certain occasions." And then his attention was taken up with the rehearsal. He cast a critical eye on the cowboy who once more rode down the aisle lined with cosmetics and lotions. Tim watched as the horse reared and the actor held up the package of Ledoux.

"*Même nous, les cowboys, sont des souffrants. Voici Ledoux pour le soulagement!*" Raymond yelled. The cowboy grinned triumphantly and fell off his horse. There was a scream from the French widow and pandemonium in the lotion department.

"Oh, fuck!" cried Raymond.

"The horse! How is the horse?" cried the trainer. "That horse is very valuable."

There was general shouting. Alison noticed Tim Ramsey's face was expressionless. He stood up to get a better view of the situation.

The cowboy emerged from out of the melee. He was cradling his Ledoux arm. "The arm's broke," he said. "Goddamn horse . . ."

"That horse is worth ten of you, so don't try to sue!" the trainer warned him.

"I hope that fuckin' horse breaks his fuckin' neck!" the cowboy shouted.

"You heard him. There are witnesses. If anything happens to that animal, you are responsible!"

Raymond walked over to Schecter. Alison joined them, Tim Ramsey right behind her.

"It's true," Raymond said. "The idiot fell off the horse and broke his arm."

"How about he holds it in the other hand?" Schecter said. "No one will care."

Raymond turned to the stunt man. "Can you hold it in your other hand?"

"How'm I gonna hold the reins?" the man asked.

"I don't know," Raymond said. "Do you have to hold the reins? Can't you steer the horse with your knees?"

The stuntman looked at Raymond. "No," he said flatly. "I can't."

"Are we covered by insurance?" Raymond asked Schecter.

"We're covered for the injury, but not for the shoot. We still have to pay all these extras. And get the drugstore some other time. And that's not cheap."

"Not necessarily," Alison said. "Remember Tim Ramsey?"

"No," Raymond said irritably. "Who's Tim Ramsey?"

"This is Tim Ramsey," Alison said, pushing Tim forward. "He was number two."

Raymond pounced. "Oh, that Tim Ramsey. Of course. Hey, how are ya?"

"*Ah'm* fine," Tim Ramsey said, smiling. "You're the one in trouble."

"Tim just happened to be here. I asked him to drop by," Alison added. "How's that for luck?"

Schecter cut through. "You think you could do this?"

"Ah know ah could do it. Ah want twice the money."

Schecter protested. Alison interposed. Raymond countered. Ramsey rejected. Alison suggested a compromise. In fifteen minutes it was done.

"Who's the agent on this deal?" Schecter asked.

There was a moment's hesitation. Ramsey looked confused. Alison thought of all the coupons she had cut out of the paper, all the bargains she had shopped for, all the movies she had gone without . . . and the meals.

"I am," she said.

"You?" Schecter said.

"Aren't I?" She turned to Tim.

"That's right." Tim nodded. "She's it. She managed the whole thing." Raymond gave her a secret nod of approval, and they all began to work again.

The shoot lasted all day. Alison was fascinated by the attention to detail, the extraordinary number of takes that were required. Raymond, who seemed to be so casual, was a perfectionist. He knew exactly what he wanted. He had a series of camera shots on the faces of the extras; he shot from under the horse, from around the horse.

"Okay for sound."

"Okay for picture."

Airplanes overhead would ruin perfect sound takes. Falling tubes of hair lotion would ruin perfect picture takes. The process was infinitely tiring.

At five o'clock the children had to be dismissed. There were union rules covering them all, even the horse. But by then Raymond was satisfied. He nodded to Schecter, thanked the cast and crew, and dismissed everybody.

"Can ah buy you dinner?" Tim Ramsey offered Alison.

"Yes, you may," she said.

"Someplace we can relax."

"Wherever you say."

Wherever you say turned out to be a rather dark, small, intimate bistro on Santa Monica Boulevard where the martinis were fifty cents until nine o'clock.

"Just what ah needed," Tim said when the first two drinks arrived. They toasted each other. Those Lone Star eyes looked into hers.

"Thank you, ma'am," he said.

Alison smiled. She had the feeling that later he would be difficult. Horny cow puncher arrives in Hollywood. He probably thought—and with good reason—she had asked him to come to the location just to see him again. He downed his drink as though it were a shot of Scotch and immediately ordered another round.

"Just what ah needed," he repeated. He had relaxed. The long legs in the skin tight jeans were stretched out, revealing the prodigious boots.

"Hand-tooled?" Alison asked.

Tim regarded them. "You bet your ass," he said. "Three hundred bucks."

"For a pair of boots?"

"Keeping up the image." The second round of martinis arrived. He took the glass, looked at it, examining its frostiness and the glint of the liquid.

"Ah love martinis," he said, and then without a pause asked, "how was ah?"

"Terrific."

"Was ah really? Was ah really terrific?"

"I thought you were really terrific."

"Ah thought ah was really terrific too. But sometimes ah need another eye. Sometimes ah'm not terrific when ah think ah am." He was sipping steadily now. "Ah *loved* working today, being up there on that mount. Ah loved bein' in power like that. Ah *love* your dress."

The third round of drinks came and went very quickly. Alison was still on her first. Tim, she noticed, was loosening up fast.

"Ah love the cut of that dress," he was telling her. "The women out here are tacky, tacky, tacky. No sense of style. Ah *love* a person with a sense of style." He needed no one to help him with the conversation. He was doing all right on his own, so Alison said nothing.

"Hi, Tim," another cowboy said. The bar was crowding up now, Alison noted, mostly men in Stetsons, plaid shirts, tight jeans, and boots. Sleeves had been rolled up and biceps were showing. Shirts unbuttoned to display proud pectorals.

"Shall we eat?" Alison suggested. She felt uncomfortable. Tim, on the other hand, was feeling nothing at all.

"Whatever you want. Order anything you want. Mah treat."

There wasn't much on the menu. Tacos and enchiladas. She ordered tacos. He ordered another drink. When they were done, he offered to take her home and she told him she had her car.

"Can ah see you again?" he asked. She immediately felt that familiar flush of rage. What did he want from her? Want out of her? He noticed it.

"Hey," he said softly, "ah just want to see you. Nothin' complicated about that."

"I guess not," she said, and they made a date for the following week. She went out to her car and he turned back to the bar full of boys who were flexing their muscles.

The next two months of her life she found convenient. She learned a great deal about editing film from Raymond. She learned about wheeling and dealing from Schecter. And Tim Ramsey was the perfect squire. He never came on too strong, despite his appearance. He showed her a side of Los Angeles she had not been aware of. Restaurants that were cheap enough, where the extras and featured players hung out. Unpretentious places in out-of-the-way neighborhoods. On their third date—and it was hardly that, more just getting together to eat and talk, and for Tim to drink—he put an arm around her. She flinched and he removed it.

"Sorry," he said.

"No, *I* am," she said. "Gun-shy, I guess."

"Well, don't you worry about it."

Gradually she grew stronger. The time came when she realized that she had little more to learn from Raymond and Schecter, that she should find her own way in the business.

It was nearly Christmas, a depressing holiday in Los Angeles. Tim took her to the bar they had gone to on their first date. Alison made sure that they split the check. She knew Tim didn't have that much money. Jobs were scarce and stuntmen plentiful. The usual martinis appeared. Alison looked around. Tinselly Santas and little blinking Christmas lights made the bar look lonelier than ever. Groups of men with the same strange cowboy look, red bandannas, biceps and pectorals, macho mustaches and tight pants, passed by. Ricky passed by. Nicky passed by. Teddy passed by. They all flashed Tim a greeting. He always flashed one back.

"I think I may go back to New York," Alison said, and was surprised when he took offense.

"What about me?" he asked.

"What about you?"

"What are you doing about me?" She thought he must be drunk already, but he didn't seem to be.

"I don't know what you're talking about."

"Look at me!" he said. She did. "Ah should be a star! Can you tell me why ah shouldn't be a star? A superstar? Can you give me one good reason?"

"I can't give you any reasons at all."

"Ah thought you were goin' to help me. Ah need someone like you. You got me that job. Do you know how long it's been between jobs?"

"I can't help you. I can hardly help myself," she said apologetically.

He wasn't even listening. "Ah should be in the Hall of Fame. Have you ever heard me sing?"

She shook her head.

"Well, then, you just listen!" He yelled to the bartender to shut off the jukebox.

"Oh, mercy, Mary!" one of the other men said. "Timmy's off and at it again."

Tim ignored them and sang. She didn't recognize the song, only that it was a country tune. It struck her that he was doing a good imitation of some country female vocalist. And then she realized her cowboy was gay. This was a gay bar. She was the only woman in the place. What had he wanted? A woman, yes. A mother, maybe. A strong lady to make him a star. She had fit the bill, and had not known it.

He was still singing. She got up to go.

"Don't go!" he pleaded. "Listen to this. Here's a Christmas song."

She was passing Ricky and Nicky and Rod.

"Alison, what am ah goin' to do with mah life?" Tim was calling to her as she left.

At a taco stand somewhere near Santa Monica and Fairfax, Alison stopped for a chiliburger. *What am I doing with my life?* she asked Pete's taco sign. The Jiffy Car-Wash. The Amigo Motel. They didn't give her a clue.

The next morning, she gave Raymond and Schecter notice. They offered her their blessing.

By four o'clock she was on her way to New York. She looked down from her seat in the tourist section. So long, L.A.

Alison had had it.

Chapter Fourteen

What a shock to find it was almost the real Christmas. Alison had forgotten about winter and cold weather.

New York reminded her none too gently. The wind swept down through Central Park and along Fifth Avenue. Crowds of shoppers hurried along 57th Street. Alison wanted to hug every single one of them. Why should she feel so elated? she wondered. She had practically no money, no job, no place to live, not even a real winter coat. She was standing on the corner of 57th Street and Fifth, shivering in the cold, and joyous.

That was what New York could do for you, Alison told herself.

She had an appointment with Myra Van Steen that afternoon. The voice on the phone had been cool.

"My, I thought we had lost you out there."

"I'm very bad about writing."

"Or phoning."

"I'm sorry."

"Yes." Myra had paused, then said, "What can I do for you now?"

"You can stop trying to make me feel guilty."

Myra had laughed. "You come and see me, Alison. This afternoon. Three o'clock."

It was now one. Alison looked at her reflection in the Bergdorf window. She saw a tangle-haired ragamuffin who had been out in the sun too long. She compared herself to the rest of the passersby. All success stories. Every woman sleek and sabled, foxed, or Burberryed. Every man's business suit, topcoat, briefcase, spoke of winning cases, top-echelon positions, executive accounts.

Alison examined the people a bit more carefully. It was hard to tell secretary from society matron. They both dressed in style. She was well aware that some women were wearing originals and others were wearing copies, but everyone exuded the same confidence. She turned back to her reflection for corroboration. Yes, she had better do something about herself. This was an important appointment with Myra Van Steen. The voice had been amused, but not cordial over the phone. Alison decided she had to risk all. She crossed the street and entered the Hermès shop at Bonwit's. One thing she had learned in Paris was never cheat on your accessories. The suit may be old, the skirt a bit worn, but the shoes and the pocketbook must be first class. And there was nothing more chic than Hermès. Not everyone recognized Hermès. Only the best, like Myra Van Steen, would appreciate it.

As she entered the shop she noticed several disapproving stares from the clerks. No one more snobbish than sales personnel. What was *she* doing at Hermès? Looking for the ladies' room?

As a matter of fact, she was. Once there she appraised herself in the mirror. A sharecropper who had just wandered into town after the fruit-picking season. The nose had stopped peeling, but it was still sunburnt. The hair was clean but tangled. The fingernails? She had work to be done and very little money to spend. How would she start?

First by combing her hair. Thank God for her hair. After all those months in the sun it had turned that wonderful honey shade that was the exclusive property of debutantes. No frosting or streaking of the ends could achieve the same results. Sun-bleached was sun-bleached. Alison was a thoroughbred and it showed. Now she just had to help it along.

In three minutes she was presentable. She returned to face the sales personnel in the Hermès boutique. Everyone seemed busy writing up sales slips or checking merchandise. She was ignored. She gave them exactly a minute and a half, then said rather loudly, "Is there any-one here who will wait on me?"

The well-groomed, well-tailored man who came out from behind the counter was not happy about it.

"Yes?" he said.

"A pair of shoes."

"Perhaps you would be happier in Miss Bonwit's."

"Why?"

"That's where the lower-priced shoes are located. This is Hermès."

"I know what this is and I know what I want."

The man seemed a bit defensive. "I just think our selection would be too expensive for you."

Alison decided this was it. She was definitely in New York. "Are you happy with your job?" she asked. "Are you happy working here?"

He looked shocked. She continued. "Because if you aren't, I can have someone else wait on me, someone who is happy and who would like to be of service. I can also inform the people who run this place that you are not happy waiting on people, and you also are not making me happy. Now, do you want to help me or not?"

The man figured he had misjudged. Here was possibly one of the rich eccentrics. Maybe she had been out in the sun in the Bahamas too long. Perhaps her yacht had been marooned. Who was he to question?

"What is it you wish? Alligator?"

Alison figured quickly. Alligator shoes would run any-where from four to eight hundred.

"No," she said. "Not this year. I want a calfskin shoe."

"Town and country?" he suggested.

"Town. Even more than that, city. For walking. Cordovan."

"Of course." He brought out several styles, then knelt and took off her shoes. In doing so, he looked at her feet. They were callused. He pretended not to notice. She wasn't going to let him get away with that.

"Beachbombing," she said. "It was fun."

"Oh," he said. "Where were you?"

"Africa."

The clerk decided she was French.

She tried on all the shoes and asked the price of everything, then selected a pair with a medium heel. She noted with approval that her legs had never looked better. It was all that walking on the beach and climbing up Hollywood hills.

"Fine. I'll take these."

"One pair?" the clerk asked.

"For the present. And a bag. I want a matching bag. What do you have?"

He displayed them all. She selected the cheapest. Fortunately it also looked the best.

"Will there be anything else?"

"No," she said carelessly, and then saw one of the really lovely Hermès scarves. She tried it on, tied it like a bandanna. Fortunately these were the casual years. Everything went with everything. She looked sensational.

"I'll take this."

"Cash or charge?"

"Cash." The clerk's brows raised. No one paid cash anymore. She *must* be eccentric. Perhaps an heiress.

"It's not safe to walk around New York with too much money," he warned her.

"Don't worry," she said with a smile. "I won't."

She paid for the shoes, the bag, and the scarf. And then noticed the little Hermès agenda, its pages tipped with gold, and the silver pen.

"Include that," she told the clerk, pointing. As she walked out the door she thought, what if Myra wanted only to chat, or worse, suppose she was holding a grudge? Well, it was too late to worry about that. The clerk had noticed her hands. Hands were a dead giveaway. She needed gloves.

She bought some at Berdorfs for twenty-five dollars. She couldn't sit with gloves on all afternoon though. She would have to have a manicure. She counted her money. She had exactly twenty-five dollars left. A manicure would cost eight. What would she do about her face?

The idea came to her at the manicurist's.

"They're having such wonderful sales at Bloomingdale's," the girl said. "My girlfriend and I went in to buy a compact, you know, and they were trying to give us everything. A massage, a facial—for free. It was crazy. I bought a lipstick." The girl looked up. "Gee, you sure could take advantage of that."

"What?" Alison hadn't been listening.

"Those free offers. The facial, for instance."

"I've been in the sun," Alison said.

"Yeah, it sure looks it. The sun is murder on your skin. Where you been? Florida?"

"Rio."

"No kidding. Gee, what's it like? I always wanted to go there."

Alison wondered what Rio was like. And Africa. And the Caribbean. How many girls ever got to go to Rio, or Africa?

"There. Finished. You look like a new woman," the manicurist said, admiring her work. Alison agreed. She looked at her reflection and then at her watch. She had one hour left before meeting Myra.

She gave the girl a good tip. As she was leaving she asked casually, "Where did you say cosmetics was?"

"What?"

"In Bloomingdale's. Where is cosmetics?"

"Where it's always been. First floor. A little to the left."

Bloomingdale's was an Arab bazaar. Eager hands were holding out samples. Alison had been right about the accessories. The sales personnel took one look at the purse and shoes and went for the kill.

"Try this new moisturizer. For oily skin, and this for dry skin. Yours, of course, has been overexposed. Skiing?"

"Surfing."

"What fun! Would you like to see how it works?"

The demonstrator applied the moisturizer, and then a liquid base. Alison looked in the mirror. She was coming along.

"Doesn't that make a difference?" the woman said. By now there were several people watching the process. To hell with it, the demonstrator thought. Even if she didn't sell anything, this was a wonderful case of before and after.

"How about a little cheek rouge? Light for the top of the bone"—she was already applying it—"and darker underneath. You see how it brings out the facial structure." Alison was thrilled. What luck! She was in good hands. More women were stopping to watch the process. The demonstrator gave it her all.

"Now a little eye liner—to accentuate those wonderful blue eyes."

Oohs and aahs from the women. Alison was enjoying herself. "Should I use eye shadow?" she asked.

"I recommend two shades. A gray, and then a blue above. What do you think?"

"I trust you completely."

The woman was flattered. She applied the shadow with the concentration of a brain surgeon, then stood back to examine the effect.

"Now," she said dramatically. "For the lips."

Two minutes later the woman was finished. Alison turned around. The crowd applauded.

Laughing with delight, Alison addressed the group. "This woman is fabulous," she said. "A half hour ago I arrived looking like the wrath of God." She took the woman by the hand. "I want to thank you."

"Thank *you*," the woman said effusively. Out of the corner of her eye she could see ladies lining up, examining the products, waiting for another demonstration. She wasn't sure quite what had happened, but she was not about to question it. One thing for certain, her day was made.

Heads turned as Alison walked down Third Avenue. Good. So far, the gamble had paid off. Now it was just a question of Myra. And that was a big question, she thought as she entered the building where *Charm* was located.

Myra did not get up from her desk. She was smoking a cigarette in a long ivory holder. She eyed Alison up and down for what seemed like an eternity.

"I must say heartbreak does agree with you," she said finally.

The remark caught Alison off-guard. "What do you know about it?"

"I have had many messages from Ben Sawyer. He seems to have mislaid you, if that is a possible word, in the urban sprawl of Los Angeles. From what he said, I expected one of the hundred neediest cases to come crawling up to my door."

Alison struggled to regain her composure. "I didn't think Ben was that interested."

"Interested? That was a frantic man calling from California."

"Well, he had cause to be."

"You'll tell me everything over dinner."

"Dinner?"

"Of course, you little idiot." Myra rose from her desk and embraced Alison. "It's so good to have you back. God, we did miss you."

Suddenly tears started to fill Alison's eyes. Oh, no, she thought. She couldn't ruin the makeup. She didn't have the money to get herself repaired. Stop crying, she told herself. It felt so good to have a friend, but she had to stop crying.

"I want to go back to work," she said after a moment, blinking back the tears. "And I was at my happiest here."

"Why not? *Charm* is the best place in the world to work. And I am the best person in the world to work for. But you could have come back when all that mess was happening out there."

"No." Alison shook her head. "I couldn't have." Myra was wise enough not to pursue it.

"We will meet for dinner at La Goulue, the three of us. I phoned Trevina. She would love to join us."

Alison took out her agenda from her cordovan bag to write down the address.

"Ben told me your father had died," Myra added. "I am sorry. He also told me you were broke."

"Obviously he was misinformed," Alison said icily.

"Obviously," Myra agreed. "The price tag is hanging from the agenda," she said casually. "Maybe you'd like to take it off."

Alison bit her lip.

"One thing about Ben," Myra continued. "He is never misinformed. Now, we'll make plans over dinner. In the meantime could you use a slight advance?"

Chapter Fifteen

The restaurant was cozy. Certainly Belle Époque, with its mahogany-wood paneling and its frosted glass, the slight separations between booths, the proximity to the street where there would be a sidewalk café in the summer. It had been transformed from part of a hotel to this in a matter of three months at enormous cost. It was this month's new place, where all the Beautiful People congregated. In Paris the diners would have been more serious about the cuisine. Here when the plates arrived, they glanced at the food and nodded, ate without caring, perhaps without tasting. Which was a pity, because the chef, Alison felt, was extraordinarily talented.

The carrots, for instance, had been freshly steamed, not overcooked, not underseasoned. Vegetables were always the test. In most kitchens they were left in the warming oven and they arrived either soggy or falling apart.

Alison was keenly aware of the restaurant's luxury: the richness of the linen napery, the clarity of the wine, the dexterity of the service. The cutlery shone. The lighting cleverly softened the faces of the women. Right now the restaurant was perfect, Alison thought. Fresh, unspoiled. How long would it last? How long before the management cut down on the staff, the profits outgrew the quality, and the restaurant was another famous name with an overrated reputation? She speared another carrot.

"What are you thinking?" Myra asked her.

"I was thinking how wonderful this restaurant is," she said.

"Yes, it is good, isn't it?" Myra said. "Everyone comes here."

"That's the trouble."

"You've changed, Alison," Trevina said. She was smiling, not disapproving.

"I guess I never knew what it was like not to be rich. I mean I never was rich-rich," She added hastily. "But I must say, I took a lot for granted. The rich take everything for granted. They never notice—" She stopped.

"What?" asked Myra. She lit another cigarette.

"Their carrots." Alison looked at the two other women. They burst out laughing.

"My God, the Boston puritan," Trevina exclaimed.

"Yes, I guess I am. You know what I think it is? I think there are spoilers."

"Spoilers?" Myra said, leaning forward. Alison was on to something interesting.

"Yes, just as there are Doers and Fixers, there are Spoilers. Everything they touch turns rotten. Everywhere they go."

"Who are these people?"

Alison laughed. "You want to get me in trouble?"

"Oh, definitely," Myra said. "*Charm* would love to get you in troble. Name me a few f rinstances."

Alison did. The effete little writer in Provincetown who had established a gay colony on the dunes. A rock group who had turned one of the Caribbean islands into its own drug haven. The bikers at Walden Pond. A restaurant in the village close to a famous off-Broadway theater. A hotel in Los Angeles.

Trevina had her own suggestions. "Who's got a pencil?" Myra said.

Alison produced her new Hermès agenda. "How about a new silver pen?" she asked.

Myra took it. "We'll call this piece 'The Spoilers,' " she said, writing on the tablecloth. Trevina and Alison looked at each other and said nothing. When dinner was finished, Myra grandly took the tablecloth with her. She wasn't a legend for nothing.

* * *

"The Spoilers" caused a sensation many months later when it appeared. Several people threatened lawsuits, a great deal of publicity appeared thanks to the gossip columns, and that issue of *Charm* sold out in its first week on the newsstands. The article was the talk of beauty salons—one of which was threatening suit—and restaurants—three of which were trying to suppress the issue. The French Government complained of the treatment of Cannes. Brazil talked of an embargo on Coca-Cola. Corsica and Sardinia both hinted at Mafia reprisals. None of that occurred, of course, because the piece only made each place mentioned more sought after. Was it really true what they said? Was there a chance that by going there one could see the notorious Spoilers?

Alison hadn't started out to do a hatchet job. But when she walked in to the Plaza and saw what they were doing to the Edwardian Room, the last of the grand hotel dining rooms, she was horrified. The exquisite carvings, the heavy sumptuousness of the rooms with their great expanse of windows overlooking Central Park on one side and the Grand Army Plaza were all being changed, covered up, turned into garden-party pretty. Out came the camera. Alison was back in action. The management was enthusiastic, encouraged her to record the transformation. "Trendy and fun" was their description. The Plaza had taken itself too seriously for too many years.

She photographed before and after the opening, the clientele, whose regalia was as bizarre as the room. So much for the Plaza.

In Jamaica the rock group couldn't give a shit. That was their quote. Alison could shoot what she liked. The island was a paradise. The beach with the bleached white sand and the incredible ocean—streaks of sapphire, then, closer to the beach, emerald. The sky cloudless. The moon at night a haunting oval. Stars burned in the skies while other stars burned out on the land. Stars and groupies and roadies and druggies. Strung-out drummers, British blond accents, cockney twangs, designer tops, and cut-offs. The rock stars hopped on arriving yachts and cruised the azure waters, their eyes glazed over, their

lives a strange tangle of sexes and bed partners. In the soft
dawn, bodies lay strewn about like driftwood. Emergency
helicopters disturbed the serenity by taking away two
bodies, one overdosed, the other murdered. No one knew
why; no one cared.

The sun and moon continued to shine; the flowers burst
into blossom; the incredible high would go on forever.
Only Alison seemed to notice the litter, the garbage, and
recorded the decay around her.

Gazing on Walden Pond was like looking through a
discarded beer bottle. Thoreau's tranquillity had been vio-
lated by cigarette butts and transistor radios. Unshaven
bikers astride their Harleys stared Alison down. Their
women, wearing snug clingy T-shirts, grinned, showing
bad teeth and nasty faces.

Provincetown was another story. Willowy male nudes
posed against the grandeur of the dunes. The older men
sat in beach chairs, floppy hats keeping the sun off, and
watched their young lovers cavort. Behind the beach gray
New England disapproved.

"Well there goes one third of our readership," Myra
said with a sigh when she saw these pictures.

In New York Mayor Linday had opened Central Park
to the people, and on Sundays it became a carnival. Bikers, joggers, string quartets, blue-grass music, lovers, black,
white, Oriental, East Side, Haitian, all mingled. At night
there were concerts in the Band Shell and theater in the
Delacorte, with the shadow of Belvedere Castle blessing
Joseph Papp and his players.

The air smelled of meat being grilled and smoke that
was rising from hibachis. Groups of people set up bars
under the trees and nodded out on rum and tequila and
Budweiser and chicken. Sunday evenings, they packed up
and left their litter behind.

One of the most devastating shots of the entire series
was a panoramic view of Sheep Meadow taken the morning after a rock concert. Overnight the field had blossomed
with crumpled cups, soft-drink cans, bottles, napkins, plastic containers. A lone figure from the Parks Department
was raking up the debris like some peasant harvesting his
crops. But this debris stretched all the way to the towers

of Central Park West. Alison's photograph made a statement: this debris was the aftermath of the sixties, when everyone cared. Now life was as hedonistic as the twenties without the twenties' sense of style. And the magazine that was the epitome of style made this glaringly evident. There was no Style anymore. Only Fads, Trends, and Cults that led nowhere.

Alison's work was as angry and passionate as its subjects were sterile. She worked with a concentration and ferocity of purpose that made her cohorts apprehensive. She was so single-minded. She absorbed everything and recorded it, selecting what she wanted. But she let no one near her.

One night, after the series was finished, when Myra was supervising the layout and Alison had gone home, Trevina dropped in to view the results. She examined each photo closely and at the end sighed rather wistfully.

"I wish Alison were in love," she said.

"What a frivolous remark!" Myra exclaimed. "This work is brilliant!"

Trevina nodded. It was true. The work was brilliant, but it was angry and it was cold.

Chapter Sixteen

In 1972 everyone seemed to be living the High Life—except the troops in Vietnam.

There were parties in Beverly Hills and soirees in Antibes. Yacht adventures in the South Pacific. All potentates somehow mixed and matched. For every Greek industrialist there was a rock star. For every oil tycoon an international film beauty of either sex.

All the exploits were chronicled. The paparazzi were an invaluable part of the scene, photographing with telescopic lenses the famous—walking down steps, bathing, dancing, smoking cigarettes. Every so often there would be a shot of a handsome film star decking one of the photographers. Suits and countersuits were threatened and, of course, dropped. It was all part of the High Life.

In 1972 everyone seemed to be successful—except George McGovern.

Diane Landers was the best-known agent in the business. And the most powerful. She had bought out the second largest agency for talent in Los Angeles, and it was rumored she might join the corporate force of a film company. The stories about her rise to power were legend. Upon acquiring the talent agency, she had immediately dropped five famous film stars of the thirties, who now existed on cameo appearances in films and rare spot episodes on television. "Spring housecleaning" was what Diane termed it. "Getting rid of the old bags in the attic." Again there were threats of lawsuits, but nobody was seriously going to sue Diane. On the other hand no one ever had a good word to say for her, except that she was the Best Lady Agent in the Business. She was a Phenomenon.

As was Kenny Buck, who had come along at the right time to soothe the national social conscience. The Plight of the Red Man in the White Man's world had taken over the civil rights scene. He became its symbol. Beauty and masculinity were an effective combination, and helped make him the number-one box office attraction in the country. He recorded an album that hit the charts and stayed there for sixteen weeks. He was a Phenomenon.

David Sampson produced the first truly successful movie musical since *The Sound of Music*. It was a celebration of life. It was a Phenomenon. Sampson was a Phenomenon. Kenny. Diane.

And Alison Carmichael. Her position was unique. She was the Daumier, the Hogarth of the twentieth century. Her photographs were both searing portraits and social documents. Her secrets were as unfathomable as those of Marie Cosindas, who used a box camera and then Polaroid to shoot her extraordinary color photographs. Alison's were now all black and white. There was no one who would not sit for her. It was proof of status. She, too, was a Phenomenon.

After the success of "The Spoilers," Myra suggested Alison do one called "Phenomena." It was like classifying butterflies. Alison went to the South of France to photograph the Rolling Stones and Elton John, who was recording in a château near Paris. Callas. Nureyev. Elizabeth Taylor—with and without Burton. George Cukor. Jean Paul Getty, gnarled and wizened against his extraordinary castle in England. A last portrait of Lyndon Baines Johnson with most of Texas as a background, most of the Texas he owned; the sexual glint in the eye, the rapacity, the humanity, the combination of toughness and honor that had so confused his country.

By the fall of 1972 Alison was almost as well-known as her subjects. She had climbed back; she was more successful than ever. Her private life remained a mystery though. She bought and renovated a loft in SoHo, which was a combination studio and apartment. It was full of light, and every time she approached the windows, she expected to see the rooftops of Paris. Paris still haunted her, and she tried to keep the haunts at bay by feeling nothing. She became an expert at that while managing to seize other people at their vulnerable moments. They opened up to her, but she kept to herself. She never laughed and rarely smiled. The secret self was contained.

Myra Van Steen set up an appointment early in October.

"You know there are several subjects you have been avoiding," she started off briskly. "Is that intentional?"

"I don't know what you mean," Alison countered.

"Several Phenomena you have neglected. Is it because you know them too well?"

Alison was silent.

"Or do you fear a confrontation?"

"Are you talking about Kenny? I've already shot Kenny."

"Perhaps not as literally as you might have wished," Myra said dryly. "What about David Sampson? Surely he is a phenomenon of the film industry. And outrageous enough to be interesting. And Diane?"

Alison faced Myra. "All right. You set up the appointments. Where is Sampson?"

Myra picked up the phone. "I'll have my staff find out. And Diane?"

"If I can photograph them together, Diane and Kenny," Alison said calmly.

Myra's eyebrows shot up. "Really? Are you sure about that?"

"Yes. Together or not at all."

David Sampson was expansive. He wore an orange and blue caftan and looked like an enormous butterfly. The playroom of his Goldwater Canyon mansion resembled a tropical bar from a Bogart-Greenstreet movie. Enormous rattan chairs, lazy flowing fans, a white player piano. Portraits of old stars hung on the walls, Maurice Seymour photographs with key lighting and soulful poses. Alison knew immediately how she wanted to pose David.

"Where do you want me?" he asked. "In my Sydney Greenstreet chair?" He picked up a fan. "How about the Shanghai Gesture?" He was ill at ease and was being arch. Alison's control unsettled him.

"Don't worry, David. We'll know when we have it."

"Would you like a drink?"

"Sure," she said. "Whatever you're having."

"Piña coladas. Jeb!" he called. A sweet-looking boy of eighteen with melancholy eyes appeared. "Would you make us two giant piña coladas, and don't go easy on the rum." The boy nodded and went to the bar. David adjusted his caftan.

"Thirty more pounds and it's off to the Costa del Sol. Have you ever been there? It's fabulous. You get nothing but a rose for breakfast. And then they pound at you and make you dance for exercise and walk three miles a day."

"Dance?" Alison asked. "How do you mean dance?"

"My darling, like Isadora Duncan. Expressive dancing. It's supposed to be aerobic with a lot of lunges, I guess."

"I can't imagine what it's like."

Jeb served them the drinks.

"It's like this," David cried, and began to move around his stage set. His caftan flowed and so did he. Alison began shooting. David giggled. "Oh, God, Alison, don't shoot that. It's so silly!" He took a large gulp of his drink.

"Well, if you're going to photograph me that way, I need music. Jeb! Put on the music!" Jeb flew to the stereo, and soon David was bobbing to the throb of the L.A. beat. "I have . . . always . . . loved music . . ." he puffed as he moved. "Ever since I was . . . a child . . . I wanted to be in the movies . . . Norma Shearer . . . *Idiot's Delight* . . . and those musicals. That's why . . . I am so successful. I want . . . to bring back . . . that glamour. I am bringing it back."

Sweat was pouring down his forehead. His caftan was wet with it. The phone rang.

"I'm not here!" he shouted to Jeb, but Jeb returned in a minute with a white phone and whispered in David's ear.

"Oh, shit!" David said. "Excuse me, Alison. It won't take a moment."

He squatted in the rattan chair, knees apart, the caftan grotesque, his face dripping. He was screaming into the phone, his face contorted with fury. Behind him, like the tiniest of pretty birds, hovered the androgynous Jeb. And behind Jeb was a glamorous shot of Fred and Ginger dancing their way through the thirties. *Click!* Alison had captured David Sampson.

After he got off the phone, for the sake of appearances, she shot another roll of film, allowing him to change caftans and pose by the Olympic-size pool with the bathhouse that had once been part of the set for *The Teahouse of the August Moon*. She dutifully recorded all his Hollywood memorabilia. At last she began to pack up her gear.

"All finished?" David sounded disappointed. He could have posed like this for hours. The business appointments could wait. Jeb made another piña colada.

"Forgive and forget?" David asked Alison.

"Oh, David, you don't know me very well," she said. "I never forget anything. And neither do you."

"No, I don't." He gulped his drink. "I admire you, Alison. You made it back."

"Surprised?" she asked him coolly.

"Yes, I misjudged you. And God knows, I never thought you would come here. Now I understand you're going to photograph Kenny and Diane."

"Yes. Well, they are Phenomena, are they not?" She continued to pack her equipment.

"It was a matter of money, you know," he said by way of apology.

"Money?" She looked at him. "I don't think so, David. It was power. You showed me that."

"Forgive and forget?" he asked again.

She just laughed at him. "You do ask a lot, don't you?"

"I'm having a party—" he began, but she interrupted him.

"Sorry," she said, still smiling. "I'll be back in New York."

She kept that smile on her face until she was well out of his fabulous mansion.

Diane and Kenny.

They looked like gypsies in the midst of the Victorian clutter of their brownstone sublet. Alison's first instinct would have been to hide the silver. They inspected her warily, anticipating—what? Bitchiness? Frostiness? A scene? Anything but the pure concentration Alision brought to her craft.

Odd, she thought, that she felt so calm, so in control. Maybe because the camera was between them. She looked at the two of them framed by the lens. Both dark and handsome. Lean. Something wolflike in the eyes.

"You look uncomfortable in the chair," she said to Kenny. "Find someplace comfortable," she added, knowing no place was comfortable for either of them. She wanted them ill at ease, on their guard.

"There's always the bedroom," Diane purred.

"I've already done that," Alison said flatly. "Diane, how about the wingback chair by the window? Why don't you sit there?"

Diane settled herself in the chair. The sunlight that was streaming through the window accentuated her heavy makeup. She did resemble a storefront fortune teller, Alison thought as she looked through the camera and snapped the picture.

"You know, Kenny's going to do a play," Diane said, "On Broadway."

"Oh. What?" Alison asked.

"Richard the Third."

Kenny, so far, had said very little. Did he find the situation amusing? Then Alison remembered. She remembered him with whip in hand. Richard III, she mused. Appropriate.

"Do you have a copy of the script?" she asked.

Diane looked around the room. "Well, there must be one somewhere. Everybody has a copy of Shakespeare."

"It doesn't matter. Any book will do," Alison said. "Would you feel uncomfortable with a book in your hand?" she asked Kenny innocently.

"No," he said.

"Good." As he posed by the window she was aware that he was looking at her body. He knew her body better than anyone in the world. At one time she had been willing to die for him. He had stroked her hair, put it in his mouth. . . .

"I think it's extraordinary that you wanted to picture us together," Diane said.

"Oh? But you made him what he is today," Alison said. "Kenny, sit down by the side of the chair."

He obeyed her. He naturally took the cross-legged Indian position.

"Don't look at the camera," she instructed them. "Look to the right." She focused on them. Silence filled the room.

"Are you happy?" she asked suddenly, and they both turned their heads abruptly as she snapped the shutter. She knew she had gotten what she wanted.

"Thank you," she said.

"That's it?" Diane asked incredulously. "I thought this would take a long time."

"Some do. Some don't. But, after all, I know you two pretty well."

Diane became all business. "When will this appear? Will it coincide with Kenny's appearance on Broadway?"

"Consult Myra." Alison smiled. "I have no control over those matters. Kenny, it was nice seeing you again. Diane . . ." She found herself at a loss for words. "Enjoy New York."

"I will. I love New York. I intend to make this my base of operations. So much more happens here. Which reminds me." She buzzed the intercom and asked her secretary for the messages that had come in. Alison and Kenny had a moment alone.

"Everyone has a secretary," she said. "You too?"

"No."

"Oh, I forgot. You have Giorgio."

"Not any longer. You should come see my place." She knew that smile.

"Why?" she asked.

"Because I'd like you to."

"Why?" she repeated.

"Because I still want you," he said simply.

She looked over at Diane, snapping out orders. "I can understand that."

"Oh, there's never been anything between Diane and me," he said.

"You do have the instinct for preservation."

He laughed. "So do you. They never thought you would survive."

"They? What about you?"

"I knew you would. How about dinner?"

Her smile was radiant. "Love to. A little restaurant called Trattoria da Alfredo. It's on Bank Street in the Village. Seven o'clock."

That night she stayed home.

The phone rang at seven fifteen and she listened to it ring.

The phone rang at seven twenty-five.

At seven-forty.

At eight o'clock.

She sat there in the gloom and listened to it ring. And only when it had stopped, when there was silence in her dark apartment, did she let the tears go, let out the pain that she had been holding inside her for more than two years, let it flow from her in gulps and cries. Her body rocked back and forth. And suddenly it stopped, the spasms, the emotion. She went to develop the film.

Chapter Seventeen

It wasn't nice what Alison had done. She realized this as she watched the photographs appear in the solution.

David Sampson, in his tropical fish tank, looked like a bloated guppy. A specimen at a country fair. A freak. Behind him was the portrait of Astaire and Rogers, cool and classic. Style and beauty. No comment needed.

As for Diane and Kenny, Myra Van Steen was particularly pleased with the results.

"Good," she said. "You show her with her claws into him. Oh, and look at her face. Guilty as sin. Caught poaching, a thief in the night. Oooh, and here, the Reader."

She was looking at Kenny perusing a leatherbound book with the light pouring in through the window. The book was lying uncomfortably in his hand and his look was self-conscious.

Myra kept riffling through the shots. "Ah." She pulled one out. "This is it. This is the essence. Wicked, wicked girl."

Diane and Kenny were both looking into the camera. Startled wolves. No smiles. No seductiveness. They were predators caught in the act. The greatness of the photograph was that they were both still beautiful. But the savagery showed. Both bodies were taut, ready to spring. And behind them lay civilization—bibelots, paperweights, charming gewgaws, collector's items, expensive curtains.

"We'll print this as the first. What a rogue's gallery.

How well you do delineate these rather gruesome times."
Myra was laughing and noticed that Alison was not.

She cocked an eyebrow. "Satisfied?"

"Almost," Alison said. "Not quite."

"This exposure?" Myra was astonished.

"This exposure will do them nothing but good." She
was right.

David Sampson was annoyed for maybe thirteen minutes when he saw the issue of *Charm*, but then the phone
calls came in from *really* famous people—from Washington circles, Wall Street, and Bond Street. International.
He was a new Diaghilev, a *monstre sacré*. He threw an
Exposure Bash on the spot. *Sunset* magazine called it the
best party of the year. Fourteen people were arrested for
indecent exposure, and there were two auto accidents,
one of them serious enough to ruin a career.

The photograph of Diane and Kenny became a classic. Cupidity. Greed. Avarice. It was a new generation,
and this picture, more than any nude centerfold, glamor-
ized the industry. Diane was now expected to ask for
rougher terms, harder deals. Opponents were disappointed
if they couldn't say, "Whew, Diane's incredible. She
stripped me. I was lucky I got out with my credit cards."

As for Kenny, he discovered how masochistic one
sector of society had become. Perfumed letters, elabo-
rately arranged meetings. Half of whatever was left of
European royalty, male and female, wanted a little pain
inflicted. They lusted to tangle with the Savage Beast.
Which made him, in the well-worn phrase of his well-
worn publicity agent, "hot as a pistol."

And it helped with reviews of *Richard III*. "Vulpine,"
"animal cunning," "stealthy," "capturing the savage essence of a monster" were some of the phrases critics
used to describe a performance that was often inau-
dible, many times amateurish, and never moving. Yet
there was something innately correct about casting Kenny
as Richard. He knew how to listen, and he could make his
inner thoughts easily apparent to the public. His plotting
to kill the two little princes was chilling. His portrayal of
Richard's manipulation of power, his greediness and cunning, was probably how Shakespeare had envisioned it,

Alison thought as she watched the performance. But there was no glorying in the beauty of the English language here. There was no majesty.

The joke around theater circles was that Kenny Buck's Richard III had gotten away with murder.

The week after the photographs of Diane, Kenny, and David had been published, Trevina met Alison for lunch at the Museum of Modern Art. She finally spoke her mind.

"When are you going to take charge of your life?" she asked.

"Oh—est," Alison scoffed. "Is that what you're into?"

"Don't be snide and silly with me, Alison. First of all, you seem to be on the outside—always."

"Isn't that the photographer's role?"

"You know better than that. I'm talking about a life role. But I'm also talking about something else. Everything in your career comes to you by chance. By whim. You need a press agent. A showing. You need to be a name. What am I?"

"A dress designer."

"Wrong. I *was* a dress designer. Now, I am a commodity. I will soon have a line of perfumes, scarves, the lot. I will design everything. What are you?"

"A photographer."

"But you are so much more. You know, they call you the Hogarth of the Camera."

Alison laughed.

"Don't laugh. It is valuable, to be known. Seize the moment, I am telling you. You do not have too many chances. Kenny knew that."

Alison's face clouded. Trevina noticed and persisted.

"Well, I *will* talk about him. Myra was very clever forcing you to face him. And indeed she got what she wanted. But you . . . you are very passive, Alison. You cannot handle your life like that. Kenny—and I do not defend him—seized what he wanted. I have done that. We all do, we who are successful. *You* have been lucky—"

"Lucky." Alison echoed the word, remembering the lost and lonely motel rooms, the squalid sunsets.

"Yes, and luck must play a part. But there is more. You must guide what you are doing. Otherwise you are a fool. Anyone can have you. Right now, everyone talks of you. No, I correct myself. They talk of your work, of the series in *Charm* about the Phenomena. They know you to be clever. But you are not—and this is what counts—you are not a name."

Trevina looked around the museum café.

"You should have a showing. Of your work. Are you really such a silly goose? You have a collection now. Let us put it together and see what this young girl with the flair for Cartier-Bresson's 'decisive moment' has done with her camera."

And that was how, a few months later, the exhibit at the Marlborough Gallery came about. From her photographs of the Paris uprisings to those in the early seventies, Alison's work had maintained its special quality. It had power and beauty. Most of all, it had an innate drama.

Because of Trevina the exhibit proved inordinately successful. She persuaded her press agent to promote Alison, and Alison found herself "in" with the Beautiful People.

She also happened at the right moment. Everyone began to want this "Hogarth of the Camera." Magazines, naturally, but it was also the era when novelists were making home movies and movie directors were planning Broadway musicals and rock singers were essaying classical dramatic roles. Anything was possible. Even for a photographer to direct a play.

Nagy, whom Alison had met only that one time in Los Angeles, came to the exhibit opening with a very tall, young, balding, hawk-nosed man. Nagy was enthusiastic. He hugged Alison. "You never told me you were an artist!" he exclaimed.

"We didn't have too much time to talk among the barracudas," Alison said.

"Oh, that was a meal to remember." Nagy laughed. "Six thousand miles to smell each other out. Like dogs. You should have seen me," he said to his companion. "It was my second American film, I believe, and I needed approval from this—savage. But I must say I enjoyed working with him enormously."

He turned back to Alison. "But you—you talked about *Louis Quatorze!*" He hugged her again. "You are so talented. I am pleased."

Alison looked at the other man, who had remained silent. "Do you say hello?" she asked him.

"Yes. Hello."

"I gather you'd rather not be here," she said.

"This is Jonas Brackman," Nagy interposed. "He has problems. He runs this theater, it is very big in New York. No money, of course, but very prestigious. And he has lost a director."

"Fired," Brackman corrected him.

"So he is upset," Nagy finished.

"Comatose," Alison said. Nagy smiled, but then he always did. Brackman remained like an abandoned heron. Alison decided to put an end to this.

"Enjoy the exhibit," she said to Nagy, and ignored Brackman.

"Wait," Nagy said. "I've been following your work. I brought Brackman here for a purpose."

"What purpose?"

"I think you should direct. I think he should have you do his *Threepenny Opera.*"

Alison felt a thrill of excitement. She'd always loved the play. "Whose *Threepenny Opera*?" she asked.

"Brecht's," the monosyllabic Brackman said.

"Oh," said Alison, staring at him. "I thought perhaps you meant Kurt Weill and Brecht's."

"Weill did the music," Brackman said offhandedly.

"And anyone could have accomplished that?" Alison asked mockingly.

"Brecht was the *force*," Brackman said.

"Bullshit!" Alison said sweetly.

"I knew the two of you were right for each other," Nagy said, smiling.

"I do not like women directors," Brackman said.

"I am not a director," Alison said.

"I would not consider you."

"I couldn't work with you. I don't like you."

"Made in heaven," Nagy crowed. "It is obvious. Look at her pictures. Look at the power she has. It is a new eye."

"I don't trust women," Brackman said flatly.

"And I bet they don't trust you." Alison smiled and turned to leave.

"Women don't make good directors," Brackman said to her back. "They are not strong enough."

That turned her around. "Wrong again," she said. "Women can be strong. Give them the opportunity."

"Then you'll do it," Nagy cried.

"Do what?"

"*The Threepenny Opera*."

"Why do that?" Alison asked.

"Because it's already been booked into the theater."

"Do you have a cast? Do you have a set? How far along is the production?"

"We have everything," Brackman said with satisfaction, "except a director."

"Then I'm not interested."

"Not interested?" How can you not be not interested?" Brackman exploded, mixing up his syntax.

"Because, if I did it, I would want to do *my Threepenny Opera*." Ideas were already beginning to form in Alison's mind.

"Have you ever directed?" he asked. It was his first sign of interest.

"I directed one scene for a group in Los Angeles. I have never directed a musical piece. I have never directed a full production. But I presume you have a competent staff."

"I have the best."

"Do you want me to meet them?"

"What could it hurt?" Brackman said hopelessly.

"You see how he masks his enthusiasm," Nagy said, nudging her. "You will love each other. You will work well together."

"By the way, how do you function in this theater?" she asked Brackman.

"I come in from time to time to see that everything is the way I want it," he said.

"Not when I'm directing, you don't. I'll tell you when you can come in."

"You don't have the job yet."

"I didn't say I wanted the job yet. First you'll have to show me what you have done. And then you'll have to listen to my ideas. And then you must make up your mind. And if you make up your mind, then you must stay away until I tell you you can come in and watch." Nagy was quite taken aback by Alison's directness. So, in fact, was Alison.

"Shall we have a drink," Nagy asked convivially, "and talk?"

"You're asking me to gamble on a woman who has done nothing!" Brackman said.

"It's impossible to have a drink now. I must meet some people," Alison said.

"We will go to Lady Astor's," Nagy insisted. It was a bar downtown with great pillars of marble. Windows that Henry James would have admired, and just the right mixture of funk and Victorian grandeur.

The three of them sat at the little table looking out on Lafayette Street and argued.

"I don't know any women in the theater," said Brackman, "except stars. And they're impossible."

"How about Tharon Musser?"

"And lighting designers," he added grudgingly.

"And Theoni Aldredge?"

"She's costumes."

"And Cheryl Crawford."

"And producers."

"And Agnes De Mille."

"She's a choreographer."

"What you're telling me is that no one is a director."

"Directress?" Nagy was trying out terms on a third martini. "Like mistress."

"Shut up, Nagy!" Brackman said.

"Isn't it time there were a few directors then?" Alison said.

"Well, there have been a few, but they have all been downtown and off-Broadway and not really important."

"Aren't you downtown?"

"Well, yes, the theater is located downtown. But it is important."

"I see. Well, can we go see your important theater?"

They walked the few blocks past Fifth Avenue and into Washington Square Park.

As they crossed the park Nagy ogled the pretty long-haired girls in blue jeans and Brackman walked with his head down, lost in his own problems of production. Only Alison took in the scene. There was a great amount of dealing taking place out in the open. Money changed hands and dope changed hands. It was dusk, and the hookers were coming out. And the boys on the Meat Rack. Most of the hookers were black, wearing white boots and hot pants, and often sported extraordinary blond or orange wigs. As Alison looked closer she realized that some of them might be transvestites. The idea amused her. It obviously amused the hookers themselves. They offered their wares with a great sense of mockery. They were outlandish, outrageous, Alison thought.

At the far end of the park, toward Sixth Avenue, a fight suddenly erupted. The effect was startling, and Alison's mind flashed back to Paris. Nagy grabbed her arm and put himself between her and the combatants. And then it wasn't just two, it wasn't just a junkie fight. The police had arrived, and there were the makings of a full-fledged street battle. The whole mood of the park had changed. Knives and broken bottles were flashing. Weapons appeared—from where? Most of the young men wore vests and no shirts. Did they carry their weapons in their boots? Alison wondered. Slipped into their jeans?

It was over as quickly as it had started—an argument over five dollars. Calm settled over the park again and the dealing and hawking and selling went on as before. Old men returned to their chess games in the fading light.

On the fringes of the park the panhandlers were asking for money. They were young. And hip.

"Hey, man, spare a quarter? I gotta get to Jersey. . . ."

"Say, friend, how's about letting me have . . ."

"Mister, you got the time?"

The theater was on Seventh Avenue just off Sheridan Square. It had once been a garage, then a bar, then a nightclub, then a coffee house. In 1970 it had been taken over by a repertory company that, with two Ionesco revivals and one new Sam Shepard play, had established itself as a theatrical force. First-string critics reviewed the openings. Broadway actors and young movie stars agreed to perform for a hundred twenty-five dollars a week just to be seen on its stage.

The Board of Directors included both Joseph Papp and Betty Ford. The only thing lacking at the moment was the new production.

Brackman rather apathetically showed Alison more than she wanted to see. The lighting board, which was operated electronically; the lighting instruments. He showed her the sketches for the costumes, and of course, they were bawdyhouse Victorian, true to the nineteenth-century London setting of the play. He showed her the set pieces for the brothel and the jail, which were very well drawn, Alison thought, but had nothing to do with present conditions.

Why would people want to see *The Threepenny Opera*? Alison asked herself. When it first appeared in Berlin in 1928, it was a sensation because it *was* revolutionary, the text and the music—tangoes, marches, and two-steps— perfectly mirroring pre-Hitler Germany. And later, in its 1954 New York revival, it had been a revelation to audiences who had grown up on Gershwin, Berlin, Porter, and Youmans.

But now? Despite the riots of the sixties, the racial confrontations, the emerging scandals in government, society's confusion and instability, Brackman was content to present a safe, traditional production. He was looking at the costume sketches of nineteenth-century London with solemn satisfaction.

"They won't do," Alison said to him sharply. She enjoyed watching him flinch.

"Won't do? They are authentic. Nobody does Victorian beggars better than Gina."

"Would you put this production out in the street?"

"Why would I want to do that?"

"We were almost involved in a riot when we crossed

the park. There were panhandlers, hookers, pimps—the same characters that are in the play. Didn't you see them?"

"See them!" Brackman shouted. "I pay people to keep them off the streets!"

Alison laughed. "Brackman," she said, "you are the perfect person to present *The Threepenny*. Do you want to hear my ideas?"

Brackman was intrigued in spite of himself. They sat until two in the morning and she told him of her concept. She wanted to set it in New York, not London. She wanted the set to be a reviewing stand for a Fifth Avenue parade. She wanted to use projections. She wanted a cast that was primarily black or Hispanic. She felt instinctively their bitter laughter would best express Brecht's mockery.

Weakly Brackman agreed. He was trapped. What else could he do? The timing could not have been worse. Any production should open mid-May in order to survive the summer. Here was one that would be casting over the Fourth of July weekend and not open until August. But he needed the show.

Alison had a lot of homework to do. She borrowed a script from Brackman and bought a recording of the play. She studied the script, listened to the songs, until she felt she could do the entire play herself. Then she talked to Nagy, to a few other directors he introduced her to. She bought the definitive books on stage directing by the definitive stage directors and read them long into the night. There was great power in *The Threepenny Opera*, with its cast of beggars, thieves, deceivers, and hookers—and Macheath, of course, at the center, the biggest thief and deceiver of them all—and she began to see how she would focus, exploit that power. She had to create pictures on stage, pictures that moved but that would still capture the Moment.

She prowled around the "Minnesota territory" of Eighth Avenue and the Forties, where the young girls, the runaways, the tough pimps, the johns, the farmboys fresh from the bus station, the old men cruising the alleys, the black hustlers and pimpmobiles and the bright-as-a-funeral-parlor white neon sweatbox hotel lobbies where they con-

gregated. Always in her mind she was translating this turf
into the Brechtian world of the twenties. The similarities
were both apparent and evidently undiscovered.

This Manhattan netherworld fascinated Alison. The
most brilliant lights in the world sparkled on those few
streets between Eighth and Broadway. Times Square was
a giant pinball machine. Eighth Avenue itself was down
and dirty. Limousines parked in front of the theaters to
collect their passengers while the hookers on Ninth Avenue worked the cars that were headed for the Lincoln
Tunnel and New Jersey.

For two weeks she walked the blazing nighttime alleys, snapping the limos, the hookers, the pimps, the
johns, the politicians, the celebrities. She caught the lights
and shadows, mounted policemen and the second-story
hotels that were Manhattan's answer to the brothels of
Wapping.

When she was finished, she showed the results to
Nagy. At first he was hesitant. But not negative. He
peered at the images. The eyes—giant close-ups—were of
all descriptions. Greedy, dope-glazed, excited, laughing,
heavily made up, brooding. And the lights were headlights and ambulance lights, glittering lights of the theater
marquees and naked lightbulbs in fleabag hotels.

Nagy was silent while Alison watched him. When he
finished, he thought for a moment, then came to a
conclusion.

"Cut the number of slides in half. You are using too
many. You overpower the music, and I never thought that
possible. Set the slides to the music. The music is jagged,
yes. Acrid almost. Now, what happens if that eye—yes,
that one—stares at you. Let it come in focus. Who is that,
by the way?"

"A girl who was singing in the streets. She couldn't
have been more than twelve."

"My, such knowledge is contained there," Nagy marveled. "So, well, gradually, let her eye get in focus, and
then rest there. At the end of the number, bring in those
bright lights, see, fast, yes, in tempo with the music."

"I know what you want." Alison jumped up in her

enthusiasm. She superimposed the bright dazzling lights over the one haunting eye.

"That is it! That is splendid, Alison. Now, be judicious with the use of these visuals. Your photographs are very strong. No," he corrected himself. "I am mistaken. Your job is to bring the performance up to the strength of the slides. I am sure you will do it."

The rehearsal period was very stormy. The set designer, Steven Lang, was fresh out of Yale Drama School and was also going to do the lights. He was fascinated with Alison's concept and knew he was either going to make a fool of himself, or make history. The costume designer left in the second week because nothing "coordinated." The mostly black and partly Hispanic cast often resented Alison because she was white and a woman and a director. She seemed unable to communicate to them what she wanted. They were also disconcerted by Weill's discordant jazzy twenties music.

"What kind of note is *that*?" they would question. "It say, 'blues-tempo.' That ain't the *blues*. That ain't nothin'. That be *shit*! Man, what you playin' under me? I can't get no note from that!"

For a while Alison thought she would fail. Then one day it worked. The cast had never sung all together before, and they were to rehearse the second act finale. The finale was a furious cry of the poor. It warned the rest of the world to feed the face first, and then talk about right and wrong. The pianist, Maurice, started off with the opening chords, which were as ponderous as the tolling of Judgment Day. Irresistibly, as a group, the cast was caught in the force of the music. They began to understand Alison's ideas. They sang as one, and when the music ended, they stood motionless on the stage, shaken by the power, their own power, the power of the music, the power of the piece. Alison decided everything would turn out all right.

The next day, though, the actor who was playing the Street Singer quit. Alison spent hours auditioning other actors. The part was important. Besides singing the famous "Ballad of Mack the Knife," which opened the show and set its tone, the character represented the Street. None of the actors she auditioned had that special impact.

At the end of the day, dissatisfied and unhappy, she took a long walk to release her frustrations. She found herself walking toward the theater district. Midsummer heat had overpowered the city. Even the pimps were like worn-out cats, only their eyes alert. West of the Hudson, the setting sun was an angry orange ball, and after it had disappeared, the heat still stuck to every lamppost and ginmill. Traffic was blocked. It was time for the evening's theater performances. Outside the Helen Hayes a street violinist was performing. He played well, both his instrument and his audience. They were amused by his audacity and impressed by his talent. Alison guessed he made a very good living.

Further on, she noticed two black boys playing on makeshift drums and a young girl singing. The girl looked familiar to Alison. She had the kind of voice that cut through traffic, taxi horns, and pedestrian chatter. The energy was amazing—amazing because it was under control. Alison had the feeling the girl could—and probably did—sing all night, outside the theaters and the bars.

And then Alison realized why the girl was familiar. She was the one she had photographed—the girl with the big eyes.

As she watched, the craziest idea formed in her mind. She examined the performer. Already, the underarms were dark with sweat. Her hair was pulled back. So severe, this girl—still, a little girl. She had no breasts, no sexuality. Only that energy. She sang with detachment, watching her effect on the audience, playing to the crowd and yet never pandering to it. She ended her song and one of the boys lifted the hat. Broadway was not paying well enough that night, not for *this* performer. She snatched the hat from the boy.

"Cheap muthahs!" she yelled at the crowd, and then to the boys said, "Let's move to Eighth. They be good for more'n half a buck."

"Wait a minute," Alison said. The girl turned, her eyes lighting up at the prospect of more money.

"You know 'Mack the Knife?' "

"Everybody *know* it," the girl said, implying no one was going to sing it for free.

Alison took out a five-dollar bill. "I want to hear it."

The girl examined the bill; she didn't want to be conned. A five was too much for just a song. There must be another reason. However, she would sing and then she would see.

"What about us?" one of the boys asked.

"Lay out for now," the girl commanded, and began to sing.

Eight bars were enough. In most auditions you can tell after eight bars if it's right or not.

"Okay," Alison said. "Come with me."

"No way." The girl stood defiantly. The two boys gathered closer.

"I want someone to hear you sing."

"We be around. Let 'em come here," the girl said.

"I don't have time for that. Do you have a mother? Call her and let her come with you."

"I got a mother. She ain't gonna mess around with that. What do you think I'm on the street for?"

"Well, if you're on it for the money—and why else would you be on it?—you and the boys come to this theater. How much do you make an evening?"

"Twenty dollars." The girl lied fast as that.

"That's what I'll pay you."

"How long this take? And where we go?"

"To the Village."

The girl looked doubtful. The Village didn't offer the protection of Broadway and Eighth Avenue.

"Lemme see your money," she said sullenly.

Alison showed her a twenty. The girl reached for it, but Alison shook her head. "I've been on the streets too," she said. "You come with me, you sing the song, then you get paid. All three of you, come on."

The atmosphere in the cab was tense. The driver was black and protective of the kids.

"Where you say you going?"

"Seventh Avenue and Sheridan Square."

"I need a definite destination," he insisted.

"It's a theater."

"Which theater is it?" He had the flag on the meter still up.

"The Manhattan Repertory Company. Do you know where it is?"

"Ah know where it *is*," he said, and decided he could take them there. But he looked into his rearview mirror with suspicion. What did this white woman want with these three black children?

Fortunately the theater was still open. They were loading in the skeletal set.

"Is Maurice here?" Alison shouted. The stagehands ignored her.

"Where's Brackman?"

"In the bar next door," someone said.

Maurice was in the bar too. Brackman was pumping him, Alison was sure. Brackman looked too guilty and Maurice too relieved when they saw her.

"Come, both of you," she said. "Yes, you, too, Brackman. I want your opinion on something."

"You want my opinion?" Brackman asked caustically.

"Yes." Alison grinned.

In leaving the bar, Brackman almost swept over the three black children. "Get out of the way," he said irritably.

Alison put her hand on his shoulder. "This is what I want your opinion on," she said.

"On what? On children? I don't know anything about children. I loathe children."

"Good. Then I know I'm on the right track."

They entered the theater again. Alison shouted for silence. There were protests.

"This is the load-in," Brackman said. "These men will be working overtime. I can't afford—"

Alison cut him off with a wave of her hands. "Sit," she said. "Listen." She talked to Maurice at the piano, then approached the girl.

"What's your name?"

The girl was cautious about even that. "You can call me Lillie Mae," she said. Alison had no idea whether that was her real name or not.

Well, Lillie Mae, I want you to sing that song. I want

you to stand right here. This man is going to play the piano—"

"I don't need no piano," Lillie Mae said proudly.

"No, but we do. I need to hear you with a piano. By the way, do you know all the words?"

"To what?"

"To 'Mack the Knife.' "

"I know what was on the record. You got more?"

"Don't worry about it."

"What about them?" Lillie Mae pointed to the boys.

"They'll sit down here with me."

"I don't like that. They's always with me." Lillie Mae was already showing some temperament. The theater was stifling. Alison could hear grumbling from the stagehands.

"Okay, kids. You sit down there beside her. No, Lillie Mae, I want you to stand. And I want you to sing. Now go ahead."

Evidently Lillie Mae decided it was better to sing than not to. There was, after all, maybe that twenty dollars at the end of it, and a sound in the woman's voice reminded her of her mother when she got mad. She started to sing.

Maurice was caught unprepared, but being the musician he was, he found the key in no time and started to accompany the girl.

Lillie Mae looked even smaller on the stage. It wasn't a bad idea having the boys there with her. Lillie Mae was all business. She was singing as though she were in the middle of Times Square. After one verse Maurice flicked a glance of approval at Alison. Brackman sat unmoving, astonished. Maurice began to add the complicated Weill accompaniment.

Lillie Mae obviously thought he was trying to trip her up. She gave him a glare that could kill, but never stopped singing.

It was the real thing. A street singer, and a shocker. Alison knew it at once. So did Maurice. Lillie Mae reached the end of the song. There was a moment of silence.

"Do I get my twenty now?" she asked.

"Right now," Alison said, pulling out the money. "But I also want you and the boys to wait. Then I'll take you back uptown."

"Well?" she asked Maurice.

"I say yes," Maurice answered. "She's got the voice. I can get the style. That won't be hard."

"Are you all crazy?" Brackman hissed. "You think I don't have enough headaches with the production. We open with a child who isn't even an Equity member, who knows what problems I'll have."

"Did you like her?" Alison asked.

"Yes," he said grudgingly. "She's interesting."

"Then she's worth the problems. Call up Equity tomorrow."

"Who's gonna pay for this? She doesn't have money for an Equity card."

"Brackman," Alison said, and the warning in her voice reached him.

"Never again," he muttered, and left the theater.

Alison turned back to the stage. Lillie Mae and the two boys were staring at her.

"I want to give you a job," Alison said, addressing Lillie Mae. "But you will have to sign a contract. Will you come here with your mother?"

"I dunno," Lillie Mae said, and then, indicating the boys, "what about them?"

"We'll see," Alison said evasively.

"We'll see now," Lillie Mae said stubbornly.

"I don't have a job for them."

Lillie Mae shrugged. "Will you take them home?"

"Of course. We'll take you all home. I want to meet your mother, I have to talk to her. As soon as possible."

Lillie Mae looked doubtful, but agreed. "It'll cost you," she warned.

"What does that mean?"

"She's an usher at the Paramount. You'll have to buy a ticket."

"I'll buy a ticket."

"For all of us."

"For all of you," Alison agreed.

The Paramount Theatre balcony conference was short and whispered.

"I want to use your daughter in a role in a play," Alison said.

"How much?" Lillie Mae Carter's mother asked.

"One twenty-five a week."

"She will get a hundred twenty-five dollars a week?" Mrs. Carter was making seventy-five. Somehow life was not fair.

"She will have to join a union," Alison continued, "and then rehearsals are every day now for eight hours. Once the show is open, she will perform eight times a week, and that means a late show on Saturday night at ten P.M. And a Sunday matinee and evening."

"She go to church on Sunday."

"Not all day, though."

"I dunno."

"I'm sorry, but I don't have time for you to think it over."

"I agree. It's okay," Mrs. Carter whispered hastily.

"You'll have to take care of her transportation, seeing that she gets to and from the theater," Alison said.

"What that mean? Lillie Mae take the subway."

"But it's midnight on Saturday when the show lets out."

"Don't worry 'bout it. I take care of Lillie Mae."

Alison nodded and started to leave.

"What about a contract? She need a contract," Mrs. Carter said flatly.

"There'll be a contract," Alison assured her.

"She won't work without no contract." Mrs. Carter was not educated but she was not dumb.

"If you go to the lawyer's office tomorrow at two the contract will be ready."

"I be working," Mrs. Carter said. "The lawyer better come here."

Which is how Brackman's lawyer, Ronald Tillich, Esq., found himself in the balcony of the Paramount Theatre—having paid his two-dollar-and-fifty-cent admission—watching Mrs. Carter go over her daughter's contract with the aid of her flashlight. Mrs. Carter found everything to her satisfaction, and by three o'clock that day Lillie Mae was learning what rehearsals were all about.

Chapter Eighteen

New York in August was steaming. The West Village was a sideshow. Roving through the heated night in tank tops and cutoffs, the homosexuals cruised from bar to bar. Air conditioning hummed out into the streets. The nineteenth-century four-story town houses, the gentle and the gargantuan, sweated and sweltered. *In the Jungle of Cities*, Alison thought. Another Brecht play. Everyone here was on the prowl. Taxis prowled the streets, pickups prowled, beggars and pretty boys. Police on patrol prowled. Animals, restless in the night, shadowed in moonlight or shaded in neon, it all became a kaleidoscope and a circus, and as Alison's days stretched into longer and longer nights of work and fewer hours of sleep, the whole experience of directing a play began taking on a dreamlike quality.

Jonas Brackman lived up to his word. He did not show his face in the theater until the technical rehearsal. He couldn't have picked a worse time to show up. It was the first chance Alison had to view the projections on the set and to see how Steven had lit them.

They were a lonely little band out there in the audience. The production heads, Brackman and two associates, and Alison.

She nodded to the stage manager, who gave the cue for the house lights to go down. In the dark Maurice played the overture. It seemed endless to Alison. Finally there was an end. All discord. Unpretty. Alison wondered whether disco-rock ears would take to Weill.

A light on Lillie Mae. But it wasn't Lillie Mae. The lipstick, the rouge—she resembled a black dwarfed Marlene Dietrich. And what was she wearing?

She began to sing. Monotonous. The song dragged on, one verse following another, lifeless. The pattern of light changed to a murky blue. Where was the first projection? Locked up in a safe? Thrown away? Discarded? Along with Alison's vision of a production.

"I can't see the projection," she shouted hoarsely.

"Oh, shit!" Steven whispered. He mumbled into the intercom system. The blue light dropped a point. Alison was vaguely aware of a ghostly image being projected.

"That's not any better," she said, "but let's go on."

They did. The first scene progressed tonelessly and tentatively. She heard a squeaking of seats behind her. Oh, God, Brackman, she thought, can't you oil the springs? She concentrated on the stage. Where were the projections? Where was the plan? What was going on? Nothing was going on. Empty dull black lifeless stage up there.

"What's gone wrong?" she asked Steven.

"The cylinder is stuck," he said, "and that's thrown the fucking light cues off."

"What do you mean?"

"I mean, at the moment, every light cue is going to be two cues off. If we're lucky."

"Can't we stop it?"

"Sure."

They did. It took a half hour to reprogram the cues. They started again. Alison noticed now that the projections were the wrong ones for the scenes.

"Now what?"

"We'll have to stop again."

And so it went.

The tech terminated. No other word for it, Alison thought as the houselights came up. Terminal illness here. She looked around, noticed that Brackman and group had already fled the theater. Well, to hell with them. She had other things to worry about.

The cast crept to the edge of the stage. They looked like whipped dogs, fear in their eyes. Except for Lillie Mae, who had the nerve to smile—with those vermilion lips. She sat down daintily on the stage so as not to dirty her pretty dress. Alison stared at her.

"Where did you get that dress?"

"My mama," Lillie Mae said proudly.

"And the lipstick? Who told you to put on lipstick?"

"Well, I am on stage. I never saw no one on stage without no lipstick on." Lillie Mae sensed disapproval.

Alison kept her voice under control. "Well, you are going to see one person here without any lipstick on, and without a nice new dress, and do you know *why*, Lillie Mae?"

"Why?"

"Because I am the director and I will tell you when to put lipstick on and when not to put it on. In this play you will not put it on. And I will tell you what you're going to wear. By any chance is your mother here?"

"Mama," Lillie Mae called out weakly. Mrs. Carter came on stage.

"Mrs. Carter," Alison said, "Lillie Mae does what I say here in this theater. Or she does not appear. Do you agree to that?"

A momentary blaze lit Mrs. Carter's eyes, followed by a pout, followed by a reluctant nod of agreement. Alison looked at the rest of the cast.

"I am going to ask for two volunteers to stay with me, the lighting designer, and the stage manager tonight. I want the rest of you to go home and get some rest. You deserve it." Hattie and Northern, who played Jenny and Macheath, volunteered to stay. The rest of the cast fled. "Tomorrow at noon," Alison called after them. "Rehearsal with orchestra. Don't worry. We'll have everything fixed."

They looked doubtful. Why not? Alison thought as she turned to Steven. He had a mess of curly red hair and the face of a puckish cherub. He wore rimless glasses. Tom Sawyer from the Yale School of Drama, she thought, what have you done to me?

"What happened?" she asked him.

He faced her. "I fucked up," he said simply.

She was too tired. She sat down in a seat and began to laugh helplessly. "What do we do now then?" she asked.

"We fix it."

"Really?" She couldn't believe it. "You mean it's possible to fix?"

"It's all posisble to fix. I didn't take into consideration the projections. That's one. And—" It was his turn to laugh. "I forgot we had a black cast."

"What does that mean?"

"You have to light differently for black faces. I just started going by the textbook. Now I gotta redo. We'll get it. Don't worry."

Alison looked at him in amazement.

"But," he cautioned, "we don't get it before morning. We'll just make it."

He was right.

Just before noon the actors strolled in, all bringing coffee containers and doughnuts to fortify themselves against the rigors of the day.

Then they heard the musicians rehearsing under Maurice's direction, and all thought of food vanished. Coffee forgotten, doughnuts uneaten, the actors were fascinated. They had never heard music like this, music that was biting and humorous and seductive all at the same time. Weill's harmonies supplied the dramatic comment; his rhythms were piquant, jazzy, the beat inexorable. Alison watched with fascination as the pieces began to fit together. Some of the actors started to sing along. One voice, then another. The glitter of the trumpet, the smoldering of the saxophone, curled around these voices. There was laughter and an anguish that slashed like steel.

Everyone was caught up in the excitement of the moment. Alison hated to cut it short, but the real rehearsal had to start. "From the top," she announced, but before the actors could take their places, a voice from the back of the theater broke in.

"I'm sorry to contradict Miss Carmichael," Brackman said, "but there will be no rehearsal this afternoon. I cannot cancel tomorrow's paid preview, so I shall be taking over the production as of tomorrow morning."

Having delivered his news he left, just like Messenger in the play. The Greeks used to kill messengers who brought bad tidings, Alison thought. She longed to do just that.

"Well." She looked at the cast. "Here I am, thrown out on the street."

"Aw, it ain't so bad on the street," Lillie Mae said.

Elvira Johnston, the heavy woman with the bass contralto voice who played Mrs. Peachum, boomed, "And I was just getting to *like* this."

"We oughta be takin' *this* to the streets," somebody mumbled.

"You mean, you would be willing to play this in the streets?" Alison asked impulsively. "Maurice, how about the musicians?"

"They've already been paid. They'll play anywhere."

"Washington Square, by the fountain," she said. "I just want some kind of performance. I'll see you all there in fifteen minutes."

She gave Steven instructions.

"This is save-your-ass time. Take the projections and keep them. They're mine. They do not belong to Brackman."

"Gotcha."

"See you very soon."

"Can't wait," he said, "to see your vision without your vision. No projections. None of that."

"I always wanted to play it this way," she said, and headed for Brackman's office.

He was sitting behind the desk, dressed in white. He was cool, his dark hair—what there was of it—neatly combed over the bald spot.

"Why did you do that?" she asked.

"Because you're through."

"You're really very happy, aren't you?"

"Not happy. Just practical."

"That was just a tech you saw. Not a performance. You never even gave me a chance to iron out the problems."

"You needn't lecture me about the difficulties of the theater. You, who just started."

"Then why don't you give me one performance to prove myself?"

"I've given you enough time. You're fired."

Alison was blazing. "You like this. You like sitting there in your ice-cream suit, telling me I'm finished. Well, I'm not."

"You are if I say you are. I'm barring you from the theater tomorrow."

"You certainly are within your rights," she said coldly. "I don't think there is anything more to discuss."

She left and walked across West 4th Street to the park.

It does not take much to attract a crowd in Washington Square. But it does take a great deal to hold their attention. Alison looked around warily. She saw Nixon's face in the group. It startled her. Then she realized it was one of the rubber masks sold in novelty stores. The cast was ready. Maurice had the orchestra in place. Alison jumped up and pointed to the kid wearing the Nixon mask.

"We invite you to enter the realm of thieves and murderers!" she cried out. "Our performance is a picnic, a celebration of all the lousy, fucked-up, fucked-over de-conned slum-dwellers of the world." Under her breath she said to the cast, "Give it to 'em! They'll get the point!" And then she sat back and watched them perform.

The overture began and the cast's instinct for street theater took over. When the hurdy-gurdy started up the familiar strains of "The Ballad of Mack the Knife," the crowd was all attention. Lillie Mae slid out. She eyed the crowd. She had worked them before. She wouldn't let them look at anyone else. Her voice pierced the park, literally stopping people in their tracks. Like the barker at a sideshow, she drew the crowd together, and once she had done that, she left it to the other actors to keep them together.

And they did. Suddenly they were talking to someone, about something. The scenes made sense. Mood changes were as smooth as the commercial breaks on television.

The crowd got it. Alison could see how quickly they were drawn into *Threepenny's* world. They cheered the "Barbara Song," in which Polly tells of how she couldn't say no to the wrong man, then were all but breathless when Low-Dive Jenny sang the bloodthirsty, vengeful "Pirate Jenny." They applauded wildly the viciously catty "Jealousy Duet," and then were silenced by the mighty cry of the poor in the second act finale. And when Macheath was reprieved at the very last moment, Alison feared she might have incited a riot.

Her vision had come true. This was street theater at its most powerful.

Following the performance, she faced a jubilant cast and began to play her own scene. She brushed the honey-colored hair away from her face and instructed her actors.

"I won't be there tomorrow. Brackman has locked me out. But that doesn't matter. This is the play I want you to present. Now you know what you can do to an audience. The only difference will be, yes, there will be lights, finally. And projections. You won't see them for the most part. They will be behind you. They'll be street scenes, pictures I have shot. Pay no attention to them. All they will do is help you do your job."

Then she smiled at them, shook her head, and kissed them all.

"You did it. Thank you. Thank you."

The group disbanded. Alison made her way toward the edge of the park, where she was stopped by a cyclist, very serious-looking, with horn-rimmed glasses and a modish mustache.

"I couldn't help overhearing," he began. "What did you mean, Brackman locked you out?"

Alison hesitated. The man showed all the signs of being from the press. Was he friend or foe? Hard to tell.

"There has been a disagreement." She shrugged. "I was just proving my point this afternoon."

"And did you?" the man inquired.

"You watched. You tell me."

The man nodded. Alison started to walk away and then turned.

"Oh, by the way," she called to him, "which paper are you with?"

"*The Post*," he called. "Am I that obvious?"

"Yes."

* * *

Alison was learning.

She arrived at the theater the following evening, just before curtain time, and was not surprised to find a photographer from *The Post* and a woman reporter.

"Are you going inside?" the reporter asked.

"I've been told not to," Alison said, smiling. Meanwhile the photographer was snapping away.

"Why?"

" 'Artistic differences' I think is the term."

"How do you feel about this?"

"I would like to be able to finish what I started, but it's not my theater—only my production."

The reporter thanked her and disappeared in the crowd. The photographer took a few more shots. Only when the last of the audience had entered the theater and the performance had begun did Alison head for the bar next door.

She only found out about the audience reaction secondhand, through Steven. He came looking for her at the first intermission. She was sitting in a wooden booth, staring at a glass of white wine.

"Hey," he said excitedly. "Where you been?"

"Right here," she said. They looked at each other. "Well?"

His face was solemn. "The lights are all right tonight."

"Good."

"The projections are working."

"So, you're here to tell me the audience doesn't like it. That it *still* doesn't work," she muttered, her shoulders slumping in defeat.

Steven looked at her levelly. "No, I'm not here to tell you that at all."

She raised her head.

"I'm here to tell you that there might be a riot in the theater."

"What do you mean?"

Steven could hold back no longer. "It's a sensation, Alison! It's causing a sensation. Yes, it's all working. By that I mean, it really does shock people. And entertain them. And move them. The projections of the parades

during the overture. Then, when Lillie Mae came on, I
swear the audience gasped. They just didn't expect a kid
to play the Street Singer. And they didn't expect her to be
good. She stopped the show before it had even started.
Then when Mack and Tiger Brown did "The Army Song"—I
mean, with all the feelings about Vietnam, the audience
began to go wild. There were boos and yells, and I thought
there was going to be a fuckin' demonstration right there."

Steven had sat down and, in his excitement, was
drinking her wine.

"Then it is working," she said.

He leaned against the back of the booth and started to
laugh softly. "Yeah, I think you could say that, Alison. Pity
you can't watch it."

She looked at him seriously. "Not until I'm asked
back."

She couldn't tell more than that there was a burst of
energy as the audience left the theater. Was it because
they were all vying for taxis? She listened for comments,
but heard none—none about the play. Brackman passed
without stopping. Only Steven stopped. She had difficulty
speaking.

"Well?"

He didn't tease her this time. "The response was
incredible. You did it. Really you did it."

She felt she was going to cry. He patted her hand and
said fondly, "I'm going home. I have a wife and a lovely
baby." He left her and crossed Sheridan Square, and she
started walking south, wondering what the next day would
bring.

She waited for Brackman's call. But when the phone
rang the next morning, it wasn't he. It was Myra Van
Steen.

"My dear," said that familiar throaty voice, "what
have you been up to down there in the murky Village?"

"Why, Myra?" Alison asked.

"Because it's all in *The Post*. You mean, no one has
called you yet? Well, that's not surprising. I always have
the earliest editions delivered to me. According to *The Post*,

you have some *succès de scandale*. A review on page twenty-eight. . . ."

"A review?" Alison echoed. No reviewers were scheduled to come until a week before the opening.

"A review—and a rave at that. Just to put your mind at rest—but then there's a story on page three and pictures of you. My dear, you do manage to get into the headlines. I am surprised Trevina's press agent hasn't called you to take all the credit for it."

"What about the review?" Alison asked impatiently.

"Well, what did you do? They talk about some genius waif—I presume that is not *you*—which they call inspired casting. They mention the brilliance of the concept. There's a lot of nonsense about eighteenth-century parallels, and you are called a twentieth-century Hogarth. As usual. The cast will be asking for raises immediately, that's how good *their* reviews are. All in all, "a masterly production of a masterpiece." There's your quote. You could run for five years on that. God knows, the last production did. Now, what about Brackman?"

"What about him?"

"Why am I telling you everything and you telling me nothing? In the story it says that he banned you from the theater and that he is going to take over the direction."

"It says all that?" Alison asked innocently.

"Yes, dear, it *does*," Myra said caustically.

"Well, then, I guess he is."

"But, Alison, you have him in what my Army friends have described as a most uncomfortable position."

"We'll see, Myra. I haven't received any word yet."

"My, my, we have come a long way in this little jungle, haven't we?" Myra laughed. "Well, if you need a good lawyer, one just arrived in town."

"Ben?"

"Yes, he's staying at the Sherry Netherland, which, of course, is where everyone stays who is trying to finance a production."

"Is Ben producing?"

"So I was told. But not by him. I'm sure you can reach him there . . . that is, if you have the guts to call him."

"I have the guts— What do you mean, if *I* have the guts?" Alison interrupted herself.

"Excuse me, dear. I have a call from Greece I must take. Talk to you in a day or so." And Myra clicked off.

The moment Alison replaced the receiver, the phone rang again. It was, of course, the press agent, crowing about the coverage "we" got. Alison let her rave on. No, she was not available for the talk shows. She was no longer the director. That didn't matter, the press agent insisted. If she were the director, she couldn't get on the shows. But since she'd been bounced, she was news.

"Oh, incidentally," the press agent added, "*The Times* and the *News* are coming tomorrow night, *The Village Voice*, *Manhattan Magazine*, and *The New Yorker* over the weekend."

"Oh, why don't they leave us alone? We're not ready," Alison wailed.

"We?"

"I mean, 'they.' The cast."

"Well, it doesn't matter to you. You're no longer the director, right?"

"Right," Alison said, but she sounded like a little girl who had been told she couldn't attend her own birthday party. She hung up.

At two o'clock she answered the twentieth call of the day. It was Steven.

"Have you heard the news?"

"Yes. We're a smash and we haven't even opened yet," she said sarcastically.

"No. I mean, what just happened. The cast struck."

"*What?*"

"They won't go on unless you're reinstated as director. That's what they told Brackman."

"When did this happen?"

"Just now. Just this moment. I had to get to a phone and call."

"Curioser and curioser."

"I'd cast you as the Cheshire Cat. Nothing left but the smile. I better get off." He hung up.

Two minutes later the phone rang again. Alison let it ring exactly five times before she picked it up.

"Hello?"

"Could you be in my office in five minutes?" The man's voice was cold. He didn't identify himself. He didn't have to.

"No," she said. "I couldn't."

"Why not?" Brackman asked, furious.

"Because I have nothing more to do with this production. That's what you told me when you fired me."

"Well, I was wrong."

"So you were wrong."

"So come back."

"No. You fired me."

"Well, I'm hiring you again."

"I don't come that easy."

"What do you want from me? A public apology? A hanging? You want me to put my head in Macheath's noose? What do you want?"

"Those all sound good."

"Then you'll come back."

"No. You hire and fire entirely too easily. And you don't care whom you hurt. And you rather like to hurt people, I suspect. No, it's all too easy for you."

She hung up.

Five minutes later the phone rang again.

"You win," Brackman said. "What are your terms?" It was the voice of a Jewish General Lee.

"Simple," Alison said. "A statement to the press that can express our artistic disagreements, but that recognizes my worth as a director."

"Granted."

"And . . ."

"Yes?"

"One production each season to be directed by a woman."

"There aren't enough talented ones around," he protested.

"Find them."

"All right. Granted."

"And . . ."

"Yes?"

"For one week you will play the Messenger who brings the pardon."

"I will not!" he shouted. "You're trying to make a fool out of me."

"One week," she reiterated.

"All right!" He capitulated. "One week."

"That should be enough," Alison said. "Now excuse me, I have work to do. Good-bye."

She hung up and wondered if she had let him off too easy.

The problem was that Alison was a perfectionist. After seeing the rehearsal that afternoon, with the projections, she decided she needed some new shots. She knew what she wanted. Harlem lights and Harlem nights, some of the storefront churches.

The cab driver was reluctant to take her to 125th Street. She got angry. He got sullen. She knew her rights.

"Okay. Okay. But roll up the windows," he growled.

"It's stifling, and you don't have any air conditioning," she protested.

"You can call the cops then. I don't go up there unless it's locked and the windows closed."

She reluctantly agreed to do as he asked.

One hundred twenty-fifth Street was ablaze with lights. The bloods were hanging out. Life in the summertime was lived on the stoop. A game of cards under the street lamp. Alison walked down Lenox Avenue, snapping away. Lost in concentration, she moved farther away from the lights and more in the shadows. On 123rd Street she saw a blue neon cross. She needed that; it was a Peachum touch. She moved down the street. Head bent, peering into the camera, she stopped. The blue neon cross came in focus.

Hands were suddenly on her. Muffling her mouth, her nose. She could smell garlic. Touch of steel at her throat. Was it a knife? The adrenaline exploded in her. Instinctively she started to cry out.

"Ssssst!" It was like the threat of the knife. Sharp. Short. She stopped herself. Someone tugged on the camera. She released it.

"Money!" the voice whispered behind her ear. She couldn't tell if it was a man's or a woman's voice. Just the demand of the whisper. The hands felt like man's hands. Rough. Strong. Another arm was around her. She thought she was drowning. They were forcing her down to her knees. She kept looking at the blue neon cross as though it were God and he could help her.

"Money!" came the voice again. She made a gesture with her arm. They found her change purse. There were some crumpled bills in there, some change. Not much. Maybe not enough. She heard the sound as they threw the purse away. There was a stifled curse. Then a whispered command.

"Off her!" She waited. How many times had she read of the knife in the back, under the ribs, the plunge into the heart, across the neck, the victim staggering away, dropping on the street? Another victim, that was what she was going to be. Fool that she was, fool that she had been, to be so arrogant as to come here in the first place. Fool that she was, and that might be a reason for dying.

But they released her as suddenly as they'd grabbed her, and she could hear them running away. She was in a heap on the sidewalk and she could feel how hot the pavement still was. Her arm hurt where they had held her. Her neck was going to be bruised. She was crying. She heard a voice.

"Whattya doin' up here? Who tol' you you could come?"

It was Lillie Mae and three boys behind her, but Lillie Mae was doing all the talking. Scolding. Furious.

"Who tol' you you could come up here alone? You ain' got no sense at all. You come here with a camera. Man, they would off you for a Mickey Mouse camera, you come up here with expensive equipment. Man, I'm disgusted with you! You all right?"

Alison nodded. Yes, she would be all right. They helped her to her feet. Walked her to the corner.

"How did you find me?" she asked Lillie Mae.

"I heard from Steven where you had gone. Once I was here, wasn't no problem askin' if anyone had seen you. Man, up here you stick out! You all right?"

"Yes," Alison said. "I'm all right. And yes, I was a fool to come up here. And I'm sorry, Lillie Mae, to have caused you trouble."

"It wasn't no *trouble*," Lillie Mae said.

"And I'm going to need cab fare," Alison added. That did it. She started to laugh.

"Man, you got no sense at all. You mean you don't hide your money? Where are your brains at? Give 'em the mug money and keep some hid. Well, don't worry. We get you some money."

And so Alison found herself in a cab, headed south, minus camera and money but with a much truer sense of what life in the streets was like. In retrospect she had always been aware that in some ways Lillie Mae was much older than she was.

There was no grand opening, no big announcement. And yet the limousines started coming downtown. The Beautiful People who inhabited the Hamptons dropped in. It is very easy in a city of seven million people for word to get around. Nothing goes unnoticed in the theater. After a first performance—it may be in the dreariest renovated loft—word gets out. In this case the word was good. Performances were sold out, and there was a line for ticket cancellations. The little theater was packed. Secretaries called up during the afternoon, demanding tickets for the Big Agents.

By the weekend the cast and crew decided they had a hit. It was time to *party*. They started at the bar next door, then went to Sardi's, where Jimmy, the omniscient maître d', was baffled. He searched the list. He hadn't heard of an opening-night party. But he had heard of them.

"Where else would you go to celebrate?" he said to them. He made room. The Andrew Sisters and John Travolta were in other parts of the main room. They started to cheer. The excitement was infectious. But even Sardi's wasn't enough. No place was big enough to contain their joy. They all found themselves at Northern's. He had a floor-through on the second story of a building at 77th and

Broadway and the music was turned on as loud as possible and everyone danced. Stomped. Kicked. Moved! More champagne. And Scotch. The night had turned scorching again but nobody cared. This was a celebration. It lasted until the cops showed up at five in the morning and asked them to cool it, please.

Chapter Nineteen

Alison read the reviews, called the general manager who confirmed that the box office was wrapping twenty thousand dollars a day—unheard of for an Off-Broadway show—and then she crashed.

She wanted to go *home*. But there was no home to go to. No refuge. No Daddy. She was about to call her mother in Boston when the phone rang.

It was Ben Sawyer.

"Congratulations," he said. Why was he so sure she would recognize his voice? she wondered. But she did.

"Thank you," she said. "I heard you were in town. From Myra."

"I saw your show. I liked it. A lot."

They were having trouble communicating.

"I can't talk to you over the phone," he said. "Can I come see you?"

"Oh, I don't know."

"It's time."

Was it? she thought. She wasn't sure. Suddenly she didn't know how she felt. Lonely, yes. Triumphant too. Bitter?

"Where are you now?" she asked.

"I'm right outside the theater. I thought maybe you'd be here."

"No. It's time for them to fly by themselves."

"They certainly did that."

"Yes," she said abruptly, "you're right. It is time. I'll

tell you what. I'll meet you at the bar around the corner.
The old one. It's a *bar* bar."

"Good."

He was sitting in a booth facing the door when she
arrived. His grin was so open, so cheery, that she dropped
her defenses.

"Oh, it *is* good to see you," she said. He hugged her.

"God, how I have missed you," he said. "I wanted to
call, and I didn't dare call, and then I started to call . . .
Well, enough of that."

He ordered the drinks and Alison took a look at him.
Too handsome for his own good, she decided. He could
persuade anybody to do anything. He had charm. And he
always looked like he'd just gotten off the courts or the
slopes or the course. Boyish. Fresh-faced.

He saluted her with a Scotch. "You did it. You made
the jump."

"From?" she asked.

"From photographer to director."

"Yes." She considered it. "Yes, I did."

"And beautifully."

She just nodded.

"I'm trying to make that leap too," he continued.
"You're looking at a producer. Or maybe a would-be producer. I've got the script. What I haven't got—yet—is the
money."

"And is that hard to get?"

"Well, it might be simple. With the right package,
people fall all over themselves to give money. I don't
know. That's why I'm here. I got some promises in L.A. If
I can get all the financing together, then I'm in business.
At the moment I'm merely out on a limb."

"That's all right," she said.

"You could direct the film," he said suddenly. She
stared at him. "You'd know just what to do with this
material."

"What's it about?"

"Skiing. Racing. The life, you know. You do your
time in Aspen and then in Zermatt, and then in Chile.
Wherever the races are. It's not such a jet-set life. But it is

a way of life. I know guys who have devoted their entire existence to skiing."

Alison smiled. "When I first met you, I thought you might be one of them. What's the title?"

"*The Ski Pro.* It's about a guy—my age maybe—single, credit rating poor, who started at fourteen and learned to beat all the other kids to the bottom. He never had a steady job. Never had a home. He can't stay long in one city. He has women, but not a woman. And all for one thing. To be able to ski. He would wait tables, set up pins in a bowling alley in order to afford the tickets, a place to sleep, food. The story is what happens when he finds himself an alternate on the Olympic team and then becoming the U.S. hope when one of the other skiers gets wiped out. It's about winning . . ."

". . . and it's also about taking chances," Alison murmured. Their eyes met.

"Exactly."

"And you thought of me," she said, puzzled.

"Yes, I did. I don't know if I can swing it. You're a woman. And you've never directed a film. But the moment I read the script, I thought of you and—" He stopped.

"And Kenny," she said, finishing it for him.

"Yes."

"Well, Kenny's bankable. How many bankables do you need?"

"I don't know." He grinned. "I won't know until I try. Could you work with Kenny?"

Alison leaned her head back against the wooded separation of the booths and considered that. Could she? she asked herself. Hard to know. She was certainly less trusting.

Maybe. It hadn't come to that though. This wasn't really an offer. It was a "could you."

"I think so," she answered finally. "You let me know what happens."

"I was looking at you," he said softly, "and you are so damn gorgeous."

"Time to go home," she said, and he laughed.

He walked her home, his arm around her, and she didn't mind. His arm was a comfort and it shut out the loneliness she was feeling.

"Is this where you live?" he asked when they got to the loft building.

"Yes."

"Can I come up?" They looked at each other. She knew if he came up, she would go to bed with him out of the loneliness and the need. And she didn't trust herself. Didn't trust him. If only he wasn't so damn careless, boyish, sexy.

"No. I'm leaving tomorrow for Labor Day."

"Oh," he said, disappointed. He had thought, Maybe. Their relationship was built on maybes.

He kissed her. That was a definite. His kiss took her breath away. It was a very assertive kiss, and she could feel him getting aroused as his body pressed against hers. She finally came up for air.

"I've got to go in," she said.

The careless grin returned. Undaunted. "You go in. But there's more where that came from."

"I'm sure. Call me after the weekend. See how you do on your packaging."

"Have a good time," he said.

What did he mean? she thought. Oh, yes, she had lied. She had told him she was leaving. She nodded and went inside the building.

Upstairs she called her mother. Her mother's first question was, "What's the matter?"

"I don't know," Alison said, laughing at her mother's intuition. "I've just been working too hard."

"I hear you have a hit," Phyllis said, startling Alison.

"Yes," she said. "A smash. And I want to come home."

"Oh. Well, I'm going up to the Atlantic House for the weekend."

"Oh." It was Alison's turn. It had not occurred to her that her mother might have a life of her own.

"Alison." Phyllis's voice was hesitant. "I'm not going to Maine alone."

"Oh."

"However, you come up. I'll see you get a room. It may not be in the Main House," she warned.

"I don't care. It can be in the shed. I just want to get away."

The room was over the shed. The management was most apologetic. But once Alison had seen the room, she couldn't have been more pleased. It had been built under the eaves. The walls sloped sharply and could just accommodate a four-poster bed. A commode of oak served as a dresser. A candlestick table, just big enough for a hurricane lamp, and a rocker, hardly larger than a child's, waited by the window. The window looked out over a field of blazing goldenrod to the rocks and breakers. Behind the window, on the other side, was a giant shady maple with a rope swing. Alison was overjoyed. She felt like a child again.

She found her mother among the row of white wicker rockers that faced the deceptively peaceful Atlantic. The porch, which must have been two hundred feet long, was called the Veranda, and beyond was a sun deck called the Bulge. The hotel was perfect for reading or card-playing, for gossip, for staring out at the sea or at the other guests. There was a game room equipped with card tables for bridge tournaments. There was a library containing more than two thousand books, most of them comfortable novels, which always smelled of rainy days and hot weather.

Beyond the porch lay the kept lawns, an enviable one-inch green carpet. There was room to play croquet. Or volleyball. And for the younger generation—the knobby-kneed twelve-year-olds—soccer.

Beyond the lawn was the small stretch of beach and beyond that, the always shockingly icy Atlantic, freezing to the toe even in the height of August. There were bathhouses left over from a more modest period, but still, even today, one dressed for dinner. It was not uncommon to see tuxedos, and never anything less than a jacket and tie for the gentlemen. Certainly never slacks or shorts for the ladies. The hotel was one of the last in its line. Four stories, white clapboard, one hundred and twenty-three years old, and a link in the lifeline of the well-to-do from Boston, Chicago, and Montreal. Alison had been there often as a child, and if she had any home left at all, the Atlantic House was it.

She ran toward her mother, hugged her, and was hugged back. Later she realized the warmth of their embrace. They had never done that when Jonathan Carmichael was alive, and Alison wondered why.

Her mother was tanned. She had just been playing tennis. She still sported the hairdo that all Smith girls wore during the early 1940s when one danced to Glenn Miller records, and half the world was fighting overseas. Her mother's hair, totally gray now, was most becoming. In short she was a knockout.

"Good heavens," Phyllis said, conversely, "what have you been doing to yourself? You look like a leftover in the lost and found. Doesn't the sun shine in New York?"

"I wouldn't know. I don't remember seeing daylight these past two months," Alison said. "Oh, gosh, I am glad to be here." *Oh, gosh?* she thought. Was that her?

"Do you like your room?" Phyllis asked.

"It is the most romantic room in the entire world."

"I know. When I saw it, I thought of giving you mine and taking that one. But I gather you need it more than I do. If you hurry, you can get in a swim before dinner. I'll meet you for a drink at the bar."

"The bar!" Alison exclaimed. "Since when was there a *bar* here?"

"Oh, I'm glad to say there have been some happy improvements. That is one of them. But one still dresses for dinner."

Alison grinned. "I'm glad one still does," she said, and went off for a swim.

She had forgotten the curative powers of the ocean. The cold water seemed to cleanse every pore, shake her briskly, give her renewed strength. She had planned on a dip, but found herself swimming the Australian crawl along the shoreline, feeling like a Camp Wyonegonic senior competing in the Olympics. Finally she stopped for breath and looked back. The setting sun was streaking the lawn a brilliant green, the hotel was already in shadow. Ancient Maine pines, also in shadow, lined the coast. The water before her was almost amethyst in the gathering darkness. The light from the bathhouse had just been turned on and was like a beacon calling one home. Alison swam back to the pier, dried herself off, and went to her room to change.

She dressed in pink and carried a white sweater for

the chilly Maine night. The lobby was filled with ladies attired in similar pastel colors, white sweaters draped over their shoulders. No stoles for Maine. That was left, perhaps, to more effete places like the Hamptons.

Her mother was sitting at a table in the lobby with a white-haired man with a mustache. Too handsome for his own good, Alison thought. Fine eyes, though. Phyllis introduced him as Stanley Warren.

"From Toronto," she added parenthetically. There was a moment's silence. The fact that Mr. Warren was from Toronto was far from being an icebreaker. Then, impulsively, Phyllis took Alison's hand and spoke rapidly.

"I'm awfully glad you phoned, because I was going to call you, and it's really much better up here and I wanted to tell you that I going to marry Stanley and move to Toronto." She stopped and reflected. "It's so hard to say that sort of thing over the phone."

"Could I have a drink, please?" Alison said weakly.

"Of course." Mr. Warren spoke up with alacrity. "What can I get you?"

"I want a martini, with practically no vermouth and a twist of lemon. Oh, please make it a double." Mr. Warren was glad to make his escape.

"I didn't know how to tell you," Phyllis said, "except to just tell you. So I did. I really thought you'd wonder, and maybe you'd worry, so . . ." She completed the thought with a sigh.

Alison smiled. "No, I'm glad you told me. I just wish I could have had *one* martini beforehand."

Phyllis settled back, relieved. "He's very nice. Don't you think so?"

"He's very handsome," Alison hedged. "I don't know that that's the same thing at all. Where did you meet him?"

"At the Myopia Hunt Club," her mother answered vaguely. "He was playing polo. He brought all his horses down from Canada."

"Oh, he must be rich, then."

"Yes, he must be. I mean, it does cost a lot of money to transport horses. And feed them. And keep them."

"I didn't know you still went to the Myopia."

When Jonathan was still alive, the Myopia had been *their* country club, and it was the epitome of an aristocratic playground. Rolling terrain, handsome golf course, with enough space for one to ride to the hounds. Like the Atlantic House the Myopia was one of the last of its kind. Perhaps because the United States was running out of space. Or aristocrats, Alison thought. She looked at her mother. She had considered her as Mother, Wife, Widow. Never as Woman. During the past two or three years, she had seen many women. Her mother was one of the best. She carried herself with poise, she smiled easily and spoke intelligently. How attractive she must be to men!

"What are you looking at?" Phyllis asked.

"You. The surroundings."

Phyllis leaned forward. "Don't you dare take any pictures here. We like it just the way it is. We don't want this place to be exposed or exploited. So just leave your camera where it is."

"I left it in New York, Mother," Alison said. "No. I was looking at you as a woman for the first time and thinking how attractive you are to men."

"I had to be," her mother said simply. "How else was I going to exist? I didn't know how to *do* anything. I played a passable game of tennis and spoke adequate French. So I had to have something. Had to develop it, that is. I learned how to make men comfortable."

Alison sighed. "I think I've learned just the opposite." But then she couldn't say more because Stanley Warren came back with perhaps the largest martini Alison had ever seen. The glass was chilled and the liquid was shining through the frost.

"Oh, my word," she said. "I am going to enjoy this weekend."

After they had finished their cocktails, the three of them walked into the dining room. They were given a table by the large window that looked out over the ocean. Some heavy clouds were rolling up from the south. Far out to sea they could see flickers of lightning from an approaching storm. The water took on a silver sheen, luminous in the last of the twilight. They ordered another round of drinks and watched in silence.

Alison ordered lobster stew and when it came, she gratefully looked at the giant pieces of lobster floating in the cream and butter. The real thing, she thought. No skimping. No waste either. She finished the entire portion and sat back to find both her mother and Mr. Warren watching her.

"Tell me something," Phyllis said. "Have you had anything to eat in the past two months?"

"I suppose so. All I remember is containers of coffee at the theater. And, once in a while, a sandwich brought in. I will never eat tuna fish again."

"Would you like more stew?" Phyllis asked.

"No, thank you," Alison said, and proceeded to attack the rare sirloin and corn on the cob. She had just started in on the blueberry pie when the storm struck. There was a murmur in the dining room as the wind picked up and raindrops fell heavily against the huge picture window.

"Oh, my," Phyllis said. "Isn't it beautiful? I love to watch the storms come in over the water. I'll miss that."

"No," Mr. Warren said. "You'll see. We have quite the same thing at the club on Lake Ontario." He turned to Alison. "I do hope you'll come visit us." But he was saying more than that. He was asking her to approve of him, to accept him as someone who would and could make her mother very happy, to realize that their union would never exclude her, only welcome her.

"I'd love to come. To the wedding, of course. When are you getting married?"

Phyllis brushed that aside. "In due time. Meanwhile we are registered for a bridge game tonight. Do you want to join us?"

"What, as a kibitzer?" Alison laughed. "Oh, no. You two have fun."

They got up from the table. Alison kissed her mother goodnight and went to her room under the eaves, where she could hear the rain falling on the roof and had the comfort of a good New England storm to remind her who she was and where she was from.

The following morning dawned clear and cloudless; a brilliant sun warmed the cove. The flower borders were a vivid parade of orange and yellow zinnias, petunias, the fluffy pale pink and deep magenta of phlox. Still summer.

And yet, beyond the fields to the west, the first maples were turning color, almost matching the zinnias. Autumn was at hand.

Labor Day has a tendency to be the most glorious weekend of the year, reminding one of all the summer pleasure, of picnics and leisurely sails, berry-picking and hotly contested tennis matches. There is also a snap in the air to remind the summer sailor to haul the boat out of the water, scrape off the barnacles, repair the pier. Soon it would be time to cut back the flowers, turn over the earth, shutter the hotels, and lock up the liquor closets till next year.

This weekend was no exception. The days were hot without the mugginess of August; the nights called for a fire. For two days Alison recaptured a time gone by. She played croquet, partnered by Mr. Warren, and they won. He was an excellent player with an almost British sense of strategy. He took command of the croquet field, and his aim was unerring when it came to hitting an opponent's ball.

"It's all that polo," Phyllis complained. But she beat her daughter at tennis 7–5, and was as pleased as a young girl winning her first match. The three of them went sailing, racing down the endless blue Atlantic, the pines and the rocky shore keeping watch. Here Alison was captain. She was at the tiller, Mr. Warren manned the mainsheet, and Phyllis moved from side to side as commanded.

It was a wonderful weekend, Alison thought, but it ended too quickly. On Sunday evening, while Mr. Warren was changing for dinner, Alison and her mother took their drinks out on the Bulge. It was the most beautiful time of day, all setting sun and sloping shadows. The wind had died. There was a comforting murmur of conversation. Everyone appeared radiant in this light; ruddy complexions, healthy, happy, white starch and pastels. Cocktails tasted better for being mixed with the Maine air. The residents of the hotel lingered over their drinks as they lingered over the season. It should not come to an end.

"I like him," Alison said. "I think you'll be happy."

"I'm so glad," Phyllis said. "I haven't known him very long and I haven't known him very well." She sipped her drink. "It will be an adventure. Think of it, an adventure! I look forward to it."

"What does he do?"

"I don't know exactly. He's involved with properties. Real estate, I think."

"I'll find out when I get back to New York."

"Don't." The sharpness in her mother's voice surprised Alison. "I will find out for myself all I need to know. And"—she hesitated—"there is the question of love. Alison, it may sound foolish, but I am not being a fool, honestly, I am not. I love this man." She paused again. "I love him the way I never loved your father. It may have come to me late in my life, but I am truly in love."

Alison felt more than a twinge of jealousy, and it wasn't loyalty to her father. It was pure envy. Her mother was happy with a man.

"I don't think you're a fool, Mother. But I wish I were more like you. I wish I were living this life again."

Phyllis's voice had an edge to it. "Nonsense. You're feeling a little sorry for yourself. I can understand that. You came up here looking like some malnourished ghost. But you wouldn't be happy with this life. You'd be restless, and then you'd have an affair or drink too much. You're a fighter and I guess you need the combat. I'm not a fighter. Your father wasn't. These people aren't. They let things go," she said bitterly. "They let the rest of the world take away the quality of their lives. They seek refuge here for a little while. They run to Florida, or the Antilles. They hide out."

Alison shook her head. "I don't like combat."

"I don't believe you," her mother said. "You're not like us, Alison. You do fight for what you want. And I gather you have just won. That, I would imagine, is always scary." She set her drink down and covered Alison's hand with her own. It was the most comforting, motherly gesture she had ever made.

"What you need now is an ally, darling. And I know you'll find him."

"Him?"

Her mother laughed. "Yes, I'm old-fashioned enough to think you need your man."

It was growing chilly. They got up to leave. Her mother had the last word.

"But thank God you gained your independence. I never had that."

By the time they began walking inside, the shadows had completely covered the perfectly manicured lawn. Night was covering the ocean.

Chapter Twenty

When she got back to Manhattan, Alison expected Ben to call. Waited for him to call even, although she would not admit it. She finally called his hotel to find he had checked out and left no forwarding address.

She telephoned Trevina.

"I am so glad you called," Trevina started right in. "I think it is disgusting that such destructiveness is allowed. You should pay it no attention."

"What are you talking about?" Alison asked.

"That man's review in *Gotham*. Everyone knows he is biased and arrogant. Besides, he is a friend of Brackman's."

"I didn't hear about any review," Alison said. "I was calling to find out where Ben is."

"He is in Europe. He will be back in a month's time. He sent you his love. He made a point of it."

"Oh," Alison said.

Nobody, it seemed, had a copy of *Gotham*, a magazine that was not as trendy as *New York* magazine and not as influential as *Women's Wear Daily*. The press agent had somehow mislaid her copy. Alison went to Nagy. He was distracted.

"Do you have a copy?"

"Probably. I just returned from France. I have not yet looked at my mail. You may find it under the Con Edison bills."

Alison searched. Nagy was right. It was lying under a mountain of envelopes.

"Don't you ever pay your bills?" she asked irritably.

"From time to time. But they are very nice. They never shut off the telephone or the gas and electric. And no one can evict me. It is nice, this co-op business." He had bought on West 91st Street in the heart of the Clean-Up-the-Neighborhood Section. Pots of geraniums graced every window. It was a neighborhood of purposeful pioneers.

Alison opened the magazine. The review was an absolute pan from beginning to end. And its end was directed to Alison herself.

> Ms. Carmichael has let no opportunity slip by to exploit the tribulations of child actors and talented black performers in a desperate and clumsy attempt to link the trendy to the trenchant.

She threw the magazine down.

Nagy looked up, startled. "What's the matter?"

"I can't believe it, but I have just been stabbed in the back."

He broke into mocking laughter. "You cannot believe that happens in the wonderful world of entertainment?"

"But to get back at me? After all it's Brackman's hit too!" she shouted.

"You have just received a low blow from Jan Barton. Actually he is a rather interesting, though silly, pedantic man. We once shared a room at the Tehran Film Festival." Nagy gave a careless European shrug.

"Son of a bitch!" Alison said. She wasn't listening to Nagy. She was already downtown, carrying machete and machine gun and slaughtering at will. She got up from her seat.

"When shall I see you?" Nagy asked. "I have tickets for your show tonight."

"Call me. I'll be home."

"You leave so soon? You just arrived."

"Call me tonight."

Clutching the magazine, she hailed a cab on Central Park West, and after a frenzy of passing red lights, strode into Brackman's office.

He did not seem surprised to see her.

"Back-stabbing bastard!" she yelled.

"Ah, a weekend in the country has revived your spirit," Brackman said from his desk. He did not rise and did not flinch. He stared at her.

She found herself wordless.

"I do not like being bested," he continued coldly. "I do not like to be humiliated, least of all by a woman—and an amateur theater-person at that. I do not take kindly to pressure. So this is a pay-back. Jan Barton's review will not make the slightest difference at the box office. But it has succeeded in its intent. It has brought you down here. And it has hurt you. I ask for nothing more."

Alison still felt at a loss for words. "You are a very sick man," was all she could manage.

"Successful," he corrected her.

"We shall not do business again."

"That's right. But I feel rather lucky. I have my hit. And my revenge."

The door didn't even close correctly when she slammed it on leaving. It was like a bad night in the theater, when the props didn't work.

Actually Barton's review did her more good than harm. Several critics came to her defense. There were many letters in the Sunday *Times*'s theater section, arguing that female directors were perhaps the last minority. Alison became, for perhaps a week, a cause célèbre. She represented the New Female Director. She suddenly found herself on The List. The List to invite. The List without which no premiere, party, benefit ball, tennis tournament, or supermarket opening was quite successful.

All doors were open now—save one. She was feted and dined. She attended screenings and art openings. But she was not asked to direct another play.

She badgered Nagy.

"What do I have to do to direct a play?"

"Buy a producer," was his answer. She threw the phone book at him.

"I have a hit!" she said. "But nobody wants to take a chance on me."

"Please don't mistake what I will tell you," Nagy said, suddenly serious. "It is obvious you have drive and talent. But you lack experience. I am not sure I would risk my production by hiring you."

"Because I'm a woman!"

"Because you are inexperienced. Get some experience and then see. And why not look around and see what the others are doing?"

"You don't learn from watching others."

"You learn from everything," he said with finality.

And so, under his guidance, she began to learn her craft. She haunted the Public Theater to see Papp's productions; she did a workshop at La Mama and tried her hand at Ionesco at the Manhattan Theatre Club; worked on *You Can't Take It with You* and *Three Men on a Horse*. She pestered Steven Lang to teach her the rudiments of lighting. She saw all the British imports on Broadway, all the smash-hit musicals. And the flops. Nagy was right. One could learn by watching.

Myra, whose concern with chic did not rule out a watchful eye and careful ear for gossip, finally came right out with it.

"Are you sleeping with Nagy?"

Alison looked astonished. Her reaction disappointed Myra.

"Well," she said, "so much for that theory. Alison, my darling, you seem to have reversed your life. I do remember a girl who threw over Culture and Career to follow her man across the Rockies to California. And now you are Cinderella who spends her time in basement and garret. Don't tell me Kenny Buck spoiled you for any other man. He couldn't have been *that* good." When Alison kept silent, she added, "Or *could* he?"

Alison wasn't sure.

By the end of October she had two offers. One, to direct a production of *Mother Courage* in Edmonton, Alberta. The second, to mount *Porgy and Bess* in Charleston, South Carolina. Either Brecht or Black—that was her niche, she thought. Still, it would be experience. She would have to make a decision soon.

Ben Sawyer returned from Europe. He had been in Paris and Frankfurt and Rome and London and had not been successful anywhere. He took her for a drink.

"I thought it was going to be easier than this," he said. "After all, I've known all these guys, gotten drunk with them, partied with them. But now, when it comes to a production—and this one isn't even all that ambitious—I get the feeling someone is behind the door telling everybody to watch out."

He shrugged. He looked tired. He needed a haircut. Alison took his hand.

"You'll get what you want. I just have a feeling about it."

"Yeah, thanks," he said, and a trace of his grin came back. "Well, I'm going to make one more pass at Hollywood. A couple of people to talk to. It's a last resort."

"You'll work it out." He needed encouragement as well as a haircut. Needed mothering too, Alison thought. "You look tired."

"It's jet lag. I din't have any sleep the last two days in Europe, and I just got off the plane and here I am." He looked around the cozy bar. "I like this place. What do they call this area?"

"SoHo."

"Nice," he said, eyeing the Victorian fixtures and the Art Deco figurines that had been found in a junk shop and were now "in." SoHo was in its infancy. Artists were renovating lofts and they got thirsty, so little bars like this one had sprung up on unlikely corners. New beginnings. New hopes. The atmosphere began to revive his confidence.

Outside it started to rain.

"Oh, Christ," he said, then quickly changed attitudes. "Might as well enjoy it." They sat at a table by the window and watched the rain swirl into the gutter. Had another drink, and then one more after that. Then he leaned over and kissed her. Caught her unawares. She responded.

"I think I love you," he murmured.

"I think it's jet lag," she said.

"I don't think so." He kissed her again. She welcomed the touch of his lips. It was a long, lazy, sensual kiss. The rain, the almost-empty bar, and the nearness of the two of them inspired a curious intimacy. The rain kept up.

"You can't go home tonight," she said finally. "And I have to. So stay at my place."

He slept on the couch. It wasn't planned that way. Afterward she felt she might have gone to bed with him, if only to answer Myra's question. But as it happened, Ben sat down on the couch while she was looking for bed linens, and when she turned around, she found him fast asleep, his hand over his cheek. A small boy's gesture. She covered him up and went to bed.

He was very apologetic the next morning. His masculinity forced the apology.

"I'm really sorry," he said. "That's never happened to me before."

"Nor to me." She giggled. "But I'm glad it did."

"I'm not. Maybe—"

She handed him a glass of orange juice. "No. We've got a lifetime ahead of us. If it's going to happen, then it will, when the time is right. But you've got a plane to catch and I'm meeting Nagy."

"Why?" There was a touch of jealousy in Ben's voice.

"Why? Because he's my mentor," she said, joking. "Every girl needs a mentor."

Ben left for the Coast and she left for her appointment with Nagy. On her way out the door she looked back. A rumpled blanket was the only sign that Ben had spent the night.

Myra Van Steen was relentless.

Two weeks later she was saying, "But it bothers me you aren't going to *bed* with anyone."

"I'm after something," Alison said, "and at the moment it doesn't involve a man. Not that way. Myra, do you like power?"

Myra looked around her stunning beige and white office. "It's an addiction," she said.

"It's rather nice to go to restaurants and be recognized."

"Indeed it is."

"To have the best table and the theater tickets, and the *first* first-class stateroom."

"Oh, yes, yes. My, I wish my life was half as fascinating as you make it sound."

"To be recognized as being good at what you do. To be able to do it. To have the chance to work at what you want to."

Myra closed her eyes and purred. "You make it sound better than sex."

"Well, is it?"

Myra opened one eye. "If memory serves . . ." She paused and thought it through. "No. But"—she held up a finger—"sex wouldn't be much fun without the power."

It was Alison's turn to smile. "I notice you didn't mention love."

"My dear, I have not been in love since . . . maybe the third grade. Daniel P. Elliot. He became a minister and father to nine children. No, I have never been in love."

"Well, I have," Alison said slowly. "I'm not sure I want that again in my life."

"All the better then. Settle for sex. Settle for something."

Alison shook her head. "No. I'm not going to settle, Myra. I'm going to go for what I want, and if I don't make it, to hell with it. At least I tried."

"And what is it you want?"

"I want to direct. I want to make films. I want to create."

"You don't want much, do you?" Myra said dryly.

"Not too much."

"You couldn't settle for being perhaps the world's best photo journalist? You really have to invade the Masculine Domain? Do you know how many women film directors there are?"

"I know two or three who are trying. No, more than that."

"And they certainly are world-famous and powerful and get the best seats, and shopgirls drop everything to wait on them," Myra said mockingly.

"All right. You're making me eat my words. No, they have to fight for everything they get. They do not travel first class. Not in this world, not yet. But they do have a challenge. And they do have a goal."

"And in the theater how many women directors are there? Oh, Alison, be sensible."

"No, Myra. I'm going to be like you." She paused. "And gamble everything."

The older woman's face turned serious for just a moment. "You don't know what you're risking in your life," she said.

"I'll take the chance."

The veneer was back. "Stop wasting my time. I gather you won't take any of these fabulous assignments?"

"I may have to later. God knows, last year I would have grabbed them!"

Yes, and next year you may come begging. At the moment you're being grand and independent. See you on the sixteenth?" It was a dismissal.

"What's that?"

"Anne-Marie Ellenfield's party. I *know* you were invited."

"Oh, *that*. . . ." Alison wrinkled her nose in distaste.

"Oh, come. After all, you never know what might happen."

Chapter Twenty-one

Cinderella almost decided not to go to the ball.

First of all, it was snowing. On the sixteenth of November a sudden snow. It was impossible to find a cab at 52nd Street and 11th Avenue at four-thirty in the afternoon, so Alison walked to the Broadway-IRT line and took the subway home. This did not put her in a party mood. Safe in her loft, alone with her plants, she looked in the mirror and sighed. It was already five-thirty. It would take at least two hours for her to pull herself together. She looked like a hard hat. She was wearing jeans and an L. L. Bean wool jacket and her hair, still wet from the snow, was clinging to her head.

After a shower she felt better. She picked out an evening gown—black velvet and strapless—put it on, and felt even better. She looked out the window. The snow was falling fast. The evening took on the aspects of an adventure. She got out her galoshes and ski parka, hiked up her skirts to avoid the snow, and set out.

On Houston Street she vied with a man for a single cruising cab. They both won. But instead of acting like typical New Yorkers, they decided to share.

The evening looked promising. Alison wondered what the Ellenfield party would be like. Lord knows, she had read enough about the residence—a pink brownstone on East 52nd Street. Billy Barnes, the decorator, has spared no expense, had in fact, gone slightly giddy when collaborating with the formidable Anne-Marie Ellenfield—whose husband *was* Ellenfield Communications. Alison had gleaned all this information from the gossip columns. Harry Ellenfield was depicted as a self-made man who had started out in radio; seen the light, as it were, of television before the war; and then had reaped postwar rewards many times over. He now owned ten newspapers, a losing baseball team, and an up-and-coming boxer, in addition to his television franchises.

Anyway, according to *Charm* Billy Barnes had suggested they paper the first-floor powder room with franchises, but Anne-Marie—who wanted a "fun" house—decided Billy was being just a teeny bit bitchy and nixed the idea. However, she did approve the giant polished tortoiseshells that hung on the wall across from the Jules Olitsky oil and completely overshadowed the Trova sculpture. For, in a sense, that did reflect their tastes. Harry hunted Big Game while she tracked down Artistic Adventures. Billy Barnes had noted that.

What Billy had missed was how carefully Anne-Marie had calculated opportunity. She had been married earlier and unfortunately to a man who had designs on her dresses and who committed suicide by combining alcohol with Antabuse, which made one throw up. He had strangled in his own vomit while Anne-Marie had been skiing in Sun Valley with a crowd of good friends, including the Kennedys. She had met Harry Ellenfield through Aristotle Onassis and courted him relentlessly. It had not been difficult. Harry gave in with barely a murmur. He needed Anne-Marie because she gave him social position, which meant that even an ambassadorship was possible. In the meantime wherever they went—their yacht moored in Fort Lauderdale; their ranch in Palm Springs, which had welcomed several Presidents and Frank Sinatra; their elegant home in Washington, D.C.—they felt the need to relax. To get with it. This pink brownstone was to be their fun house.

It was about as much fun as a Los Angeles funeral parlor.

Walls had been torn down and Chinese screens substituted. Byzantine tapestries served as rugs. Awnings hung inside, making the living room resemble the pro shop at a golf club. The main dining room contained three pinball machines and a jukebox circa 1936. ("Just before the too-garish period," *Charm* had reported.) They shared the space with a truly exquisite Sheraton dining table and chairs, and a work of art that was a real working miniature roller-coaster with lights that blinked on and off in different patterns. It was rumored that the art work alone had cost four hundred thousand dollars. The Ellenfields' *serious* collection remained in Washington.

Everyone came to Anne-Marie Ellenfield's parties. She had hired someone to make sure everyone came. She mixed a party as carefully as her chef prepared a salad. Her social secretary kept a careful list of who was "in" at the moment. For every top industrialist there was a stunning rock star; for every diplomat, a pornographer. Very few politicians—always, of course, excluding the Kennedys—ever made this list. Their positions were too unstable.

Doris Lilly, social reporter for *The New York Times*, was covering the party, as of course, was *Women's Wear Daily*. Otherwise, what was the point?

As Anne-Marie escorted Miss Lilly into the living room, Miss Lilly leaned forward to sniff the phlox. The flowers had no odor. They were artificial.

"Diane Love," Anne-Marie informed her, never failing to give credit. Doris Lilly glanced around at the arrangements of anemones, daisies, swamp roses, primroses, violets, rhododenron and began figuring the cost. At ten dollars a flower, that would amount to . . .

The theme of the evening, Anne-Marie continued, was *la vie bohème*. She had invited artists and writers, critics and filmmakers—"the people who make the arts hum." Therefore Myra Van Steen found herself facing the Bronfmans. She was *Charm;* they were Seagram's and patrons of the arts. Anne-Marie always picked carefully. Which was why Ben Sawyer disturbed her.

"Who *is* he?" she whispered to Myra.

"My escort," Myra said blithely.

"Yes, but who is he?" she insisted. "What does he do? Is he a gigolo? A reporter? Does he run a spy ring?"

"He's handsome enough to do any of those, isn't he?" Myra said, but Anne-Marie had no time for that.

"Yes, yes, but what does he *do*?"

"At the moment he is persuading your husband to invest in a film he's producing."

"Ah! He's a producer!" Anne-Marie was satisfied. She told Doris Lilly, who jotted it down in her notepad, putting a question mark next to the name. Maybe a somebody. Probably nobody, but very good-looking.

As a matter of fact, Miss Lilly thought, most of the guests were young and beautiful. Except for Myra Van Steen who didn't have to be—she was *distinguished*—and Harry Ellenfield, who looked out-of-keeping in his own house. He did not look like fun. Her eye caught another man, moving through the room as though he were the center of it. The power was with him. He was not quite as handsome as the maybe somebody–maybe nobody producer. Slightly shorter, sandy-haired, powerfully built. Funny, *he* looked at home in Harry Ellenfield's house.

At that moment an apparition appeared in the foyer. A bag lady—one of New York's crazies—had slipped through security and was going to cause a scene. Galoshes, a rather messy parka that had actually been used for skiing before designers had discovered the ski trade. Would this make news! Miss Lilly thought.

The bag lady threw back the hood to her parka, revealing one of the most stunning women Ms. Lilly had ever seen. Yes, this party might be interesting after all.

Snow and cold weather had brought out the best in Alison. The cold made the New England Yankee glow. She was laughing, giving her honey-colored hair a toss. Her skin was a vibrant pink. My God but she was *alive*, Miss Lilly noted. Anne-Marie stepped forward.

"I'm Anne-Marie Ellenfield," she said, extending her hand, wondering who this creature was.

"Alison Carmichael," she replied. "I'm sorry. I'm dripping all over your carpet."

Anne-Marie said, "I see. Here, let me get you some help with those—"

"Galoshes," Alison said. Anne-Marie looked for a chair. She needed more chairs. She made a note to consult Billy Barnes. Not enough chairs.

"Alison, you need some help?" she looked up to see Ben.

"You're back!" she said joyfully. "What are you doing *here*?"

"I came with Myra—"

"The matchmaker," Myra said, approaching them. "Darling, do you make a specialty of entrances? You certainly are expert at them."

Ben knelt to take off a boot.

"How are you, Ben? Still tired?" Alison asked mischievously.

"No, I caught up on my sleep," he answered rather uncomfortably.

Another voice intruded. Masculine, soft and purry with a Texas twang. "Looks like you could use some help," the voice said.

Alison looked in its direction. There stood a man, solid, sexy, whose nose was too wide and looked as though it had been broken once, whose grin was oh-so-friendly, whose eyes— She stopped right there. The eyes belonged to a man who was used to winning.

"I'm helping her," Ben told him.

"Well, let me help you help her," said the friendly Texan. Alison felt like Scarlett O'Hara among the Tarleton twins.

"Is this a put-on?" she asked the two of them.

"Partly," the Texan said. "My name's Sam Pendexter."

"Oh, this is Ben Sawyer." Alison was making introductions with one leg in midair.

"Could you give me your other foot?" Ben said between gritted teeth.

"Sorry, Ben. I must say I'm not used to all this service."

"You take to it nicely," Myra commented.

"You know, I should put more chairs in this room," Anne-Marie said. "There's no place to *sit*." She felt out-of-place at her own party and quickly decided she should supervise the three bartenders. Or do something hostessy. She did not like *not* being in control.

"Who's that?" Doris Lilly whispered discreetly to her.

"Alison Carmichael, the photographer," Anne-Marie

answered automatically, and then, with just a touch of pique, "Or director, take your pick."

"Well, she certainly perks up a party," Miss Lilly commented.

"Yes," Anne-Marie conceded. "Isn't she *fun!*" She decided she had made the right choice in inviting Alison.

What Myra had planned as a twosome quickly became a threesome. Ben and Alison became Ben and Alison and Sam. The problem, there, from Myra's point of view, was that the two men liked each other.

The new threesome went for a drink. Ben had Scotch, Alison white wine, and Sam bourbon. The wine was very cold and very imported and very good, and Alison was very glad she had decided to come. She started to compare the two men. Ben was taller. He was blonder. He was handsomer. Sam was more compact. He was not really handsome. He had—was it possible? Yes it was—a dimple in his chin. She looked at his hands, examined them. They were tough hands. She could imagine them balled into a fist. She looked at Ben's. Ben's hands were wrapped around his glass. They gave no indication. Ah, yes, Ben the lawyer, never showing what was really going on. How strong was Sam? she wondered. And then she really had to question herself. Why, when she had seen Ben only briefly in the past three years, was she forgetting his presence? Was she attracted to that soft West Texas accent she heard as Sam told them he had started off as a poor boy in Odessa, Texas, wearing other families' hand-me-downs?

"I have always been well-to-do," Alison said. "I come from Money."

"And I have always been the ne'er-do-well black sheep," Ben said. They had by then each had three drinks and were sitting on the Aubusson carpet. Anne-Marie usually didn't approve of sitting on the floor, but this night, well, it was turning out to be that kind of a night. People were doing what they wanted. Even the diplomats were talking. They tended, usually, to look into their glasses of soda—soda with just a touch of wine—and brood. Bankers, on the other hand, often thought they were the life of the party and played the piano and sang college songs. She wanted to avoid that tonight. Harry encouraged it, because he had attended Yale, and everyone knew "Boola-Boola."

"*I* went to the Sorbonne," Alison said.

"And I went to Berkeley." Ben laughed. "The Sorbonne of San Francisco."

Sam said nothing.

"Well?" Alison prodded.

"I didn't attend a college. I just about finished with high school, I got that diploma. Odessa High bids you good-bye," Sam said.

"Were you a hell-raiser?" Alison asked.

"No, ma'am." Sam thought it over. "I just was into other things." She noticed the look that passed between the two men.

"Like what?" she persisted.

"Well, tennis, for one thing. I was a pro for a couple of years, but I wasn't going to be Jimmy Connors, and besides, I had the feeling there was more money to be made."

"Then you were into money?" Ben asked.

"Yes, *sir*." Sam was emphatic. "I was certainly into money. I read up on Rockefeller and Hunt and Getty and Mellon. Those ol' boys started off no better than me—"

Alison excused the grammatical error. She was suddenly getting buzzed. No wonder. She hadn't eaten all day. Sam was continuing his history.

"—so I figured if I put together their best assets, I could make myself an empire." He said this very matter-of-factly. Ben and Alison looked at each other. Sam Pendexter was a breed apart.

"And did you? Have you?" Alison asked.

"I made a good start on it," he admitted. "I swore I'd be a millionaire before I was thirty." He took a drink. "And I am."

"Thirty?" Alison asked.

Sam looked slightly annoyed. "A millionaire," he said. "I got three years to go yet before I'm thirty. So you see, I'm ahead of schedule." He turned to Ben. "What do you do?"

"I'm producing a movie."

"By yourself?"

"So far. I'm looking for money."

"So am I," Sam confided.

"I thought you were a millionaire," Alison said quickly.

"Girl, how do you think I got to be one?" He turned to her. "I started out buying a piece of real estate for four thousand dollars. Borrowed three of that from the bank. Six months later I subdivided and sold it for forty thousand."

"There are no fields left," Alison said mournfully. The wine had gotten to her.

"Beg pardon, ma'am?" Sam said.

"There are no fields left. When I was a girl, there were lots of fields, hayfields with wild strawberries, and you could look a long way without seeing anything but land. Now, there are just houses and lawns, and right-of-ways. But there are no *fields* left."

Sam felt she was accusing him. Ben took a new tack. Here, perhaps, was a prospect.

"So you're in real estate?" he asked.

"And oil. Now Harry Ellenfield is after me to go into communications. And I'm after him to back me. I want to produce liquid coal."

"Coal?" Alison repeated. "Coal comes out of the ground and makes a mess."

"That's right. It does make a mess. That's what I want to experiment with. How to turn that lump of coal into a liquid. Home fuel. Gasoline. That would set OPEC on its ass— Excuse me, ma'am."

"But you're in oil. You'd put yourself out of business."

Sam laughed. "No, ma'am. Just diversify. That's what the ol' boys did. Diversify. Make investments."

The two men were sizing each other up. Alison stood up, feeling slightly dizzy. The men stood as well.

"Harry's investing in some movie deal. Wants me in on it with him," Sam said to Ben. "Is that you?"

"That's me," Ben said.

"Then you're getting the money!" Alison exclaimed.

Ben's eyes told her to cool it. "Maybe."

"Okay, tell me about this movie deal," Sam said. "Do you have a star? A director?"

"You ever hear of Kenny Buck?"

"Sure I heard of him. Seen one of two of his movies.
He's a pretty fair kind of actor. Sings too, right?"

"Right."

"And what's the movie about?"

"About a ski bum who gets on the Olympic team as
an alternate and finally becomes the U.S. hope when the
lead skier wipes out."

"Not bad. You got a director?"

Ben hedged for a moment, and then plunged in.
Looking straight at Alison he said, "I think so. It's a
package deal. Kenny Buck to star. Paul Masland to direct."

Alison thought she was going to be sick. It was Diane.
It was always Diane who stood in her way. Diane who was
putting together this package.

"Well, that sounds like a solid package. Masland's got
a real fine reputation," Sam said.

Alison stared at Ben. "Diane sure gets around," she
said.

"Beg pardon?" Sam said again. This woman confused
him.

"Alison's referring to Diane Landers, who put this
package together. Who probably will end up as co-
producer."

"I know who she is." Sam nodded. "Good agent.
Good-looking too."

"Oh, you two can go to hell!" Alison said suddenly.

"What did I say?" Sam asked Ben, but Alison gave
him the explanation.

"I wanted that job," she told him.

"But you're a photographer. Somebody told me you're
a photographer."

"I am. I'm also a director. I've got a show running.
Go see it!"

"No need to get mad at me."

"I'm not mad at you. I'm mad at—"

"Me," Ben said.

"Yes."

"I'm sorry," he said softly. "I had to go with the
money."

She shook the hair out of her eyes. "I know, I know."

"Hold on a minute here," Sam said to Alison. "You ever made a movie?"

"No. I've done commercials. I know how to use a camera. I'm a director."

The West Texas drawl came on a little stronger. "Hell, woman, it takes *balls* to be a director."

He was defending Ben! Alison looked at Sam, her eyes blazing. "No! It takes guts. And you men don't have a monopoly on that."

The two men reddened.

"What? Does it embarrass you that I'm being this straightforward? I'm asking Ben for this job."

"You're taking advantage of the fact that you're a woman," Sam said softly.

"Why are you defending him? You don't even know him. You don't know me. You don't know anything!"

His quiet voice kept her in check. "I got a feeling the three of us know each other real well. He's made a business deal the best way he knows how. And you're reacting like a woman. What makes you want to be a director anyway?"

"Because I'm better than Paul Masland!"

"Is she?" Sam asked Ben.

"Alison's good," Ben said, "but she's not bankable. And I'm not bankable. Kenny Buck is. And so is Masland."

"Well, there you have it," Sam said, spreading his hands out. "Let's all go and get some grub."

"I don't want any," Alison said.

"Yes, you do," Sam contradicted her. The two men escorted her to the buffet.

Anne-Marie Ellenfield breathed a sigh of relief. Their conversation had been too intense. It had become a centerpiece. All other conversations around them had paled beside these whispered statements and flashing looks. She was glad they were headed for the buffet.

The long table ran almost the length of the brownstone. On it were great chafing dishes containing Anne-Marie's own recipe for *bœuf bourguignon* and a spaghetti whose secret ingredient was the caraway seed in the butter dressing. Then there were dishes of scallops and shrimp in a champagne sauce. Piping hot rolls and homemade strawberry preserves imported from her California ranch.

From her vantage point on the stairs Anne-Marie viewed her world and found it perfect. Fifty ladies and gentlemen dressed to the nines (as they used to say when her uncle Seymour was producing movies) gathering around a festive board. Enough old silver for elegance, and enough neon and flashing lights for fun. That was a winning combination. Her eye caught Harry Ellenfield's. He gave her an approving nod; Anne-Marie, it said, you have done it again.

Nagy and Myra were surprised to find each other. They both looked in Alison's direction. Ben and Sam were heaping food on her plate.

Myra sighed. "Four days ago I was so worried about her. She told me she had no interest in men. *I* thought she was sleeping with you."

Nagy grinned. "Is that what worried you?"

"Partly. You're not serious about Alison," she said reproachfully.

"As a lover, no. Any way I can help her, yes."

"Well, look at those two. They look serious." She indicated Ben and Sam Pendexter.

"Is that why you brought Ben?"

"Yes. I didn't count on a dividend. And why are they getting along so well, the three of them?"

"A *ménage à trois* in the making."

"Oh, don't be so European."

"Europeans didn't perfect the hot tub," Nagy reminded her, and they moved on to the scallops. Myra was being helped to a portion when Nagy said under his breath, "Oh, no!"

"What's the matter?"

"I think our hostess is making an error."

Anne-Marie was escorting a slightly balding fuzzy-headed gentleman with gimlet eyes and narrow features down the line, introducing him to everyone. To each introduction his reaction was the same. A slightly ironic nod, formal and condescending at the same time.

"Who is he?" Myra asked Nagy.

"Barton."

"That man who gave Alison such an awful review?"

"Yes."

Alison was concentrating on her food. She hadn't eaten all day, and had been too involved in conversation to sample the hors d'oeuvres. She was making up for it now. A double portion of the spaghetti. Yes, and more salad, please. Behind her she heard mumbled introductions and paid them no attention until Anne-Marie addressed her.

"Alison Carmichael," Alison looked up to see a man standing before her with a quizzical, almost supercilious smile on his face. How disagreeable, she thought.

"This is Jan Barton, the critic," Anne-Marie said innocently, preparing to move on. The man gave a nod.

"*Who?*" Alison blurted out. She had not been listening.

"Barton, Miss Carmichael," the man said with all the self-assurance in the world.

Alison lifted the plate in her hand and, in an automatic reflex, dumped its contents over Barton's head. He stood there, spaghetti and salad dripping down over his ears, the smile frozen on his face. The crowd was stunned into silence. Barton did not lose his composure. He picked a lettuce leaf from his shoulder.

"Ah, Miss Carmichael," he said, "at last you have found something you can do. Perhaps you should take up pitching." And with that he continued down the line, passing Nagy.

Doris Lilly reached for her pad. This was not for the social column. This was front page, second section! Anne-Marie trailed behind Barton, picking up dropped strings of spaghetti and signaling for a servant to help.

What made it interesting, from Miss Lilly's point of view, was that neither adversary relinquished the field. Alison Carmichael was given another plate. Her two escorts filled it for her. The three sat down with Myra Van Steen and Nagy. Across the room Barton drank a glass of red wine; he made no reference to the incident. The party continued as though nothing had happened.

However, it had. Doris Lilly had already sneaked out to use the phone. Harry and Anne-Marie held a hurried conference and nervously decided it the most fun thing that had happened that year. They couldn't have been more pleased, they assured each other. Harry made a point of chatting with both sides; in fact, with everybody. He closed a deal with Sam Pendexter on a partnership for the liquid-coal deal, was minutely disappointed that Sam didn't want in on the movie deal. However, he concluded his deal with Ben Sawyer, smiled at Alison Carmichael, and complimented Jan Barton on his remarkable savoir-faire. Anne-Marie made a mental note to invite Alison Carmichael to more parties—after she had carefully screened the guest list.

The snow continued until midnight. The last guests left by one. By that time the late city edition of the *Times* was already out, with Ms. Lilly's story right where she wanted it. First page, second section.

Chapter Twenty-two

"Hello, this is Sam," the voice said over the phone.

"Sam *who*?" Alison said touchily. This was the fourteenth call of the morning.

"Don't tell me you were *that* bombed," the voice continued. "Sam Pendexter."

"I wasn't that bombed at all," Alison said.

"Buzzed, then."

"Not even that. Angry. I was angry. I had every right to be. I—"

"I didn't call to go over last night, although I do have to take back one thing I said." The voice sounded solemn. "I was wrong. It does take balls to smash a plate of spaghetti over the head of a critic." He laughed. "How about lunch?"

"I couldn't possibly."

"Of course, you could. If *I* could, you could."

"What makes you say that?"

"Because I canceled three meetings so I could have lunch with you." She remembered him very well. And as he spoke, the picture became even clearer. The hands, she thought. She remembered his hands the best. And then the eyes. In comparison she was trying to remember Ben, but Robert Redford kept getting in the way. This annoyed her.

"Do you know where I live?" she asked.

"Sure. I'm right across the street."

"How'd you find out where I live? How'd you find my number?"

"I called my office in Houston. They can find out anything for me. Shall I come up?"

"No," she said hastily, "I'll come down. There's a restaurant around the corner. It's called Sweet Agony. I'll meet you there in fifteen minutes."

"Sweet Agony? Did I get that correctly?"

"Yes, you did. Welcome to SoHo."

He was waiting with a Bloody Mary ready. She was really and truly grateful. She drank it fast and he ordered another.

"I'm becoming an alcoholic," she said.

"No. I'm an expert on that. Most of my family were alcoholics. Lone Star beer, mostly. But my three brothers drink nothing but Perrier now. They're not approving of their daddy."

"And were you?"

"I loved him. I miss him."

"Did you tell me he died?"

"You don't remember too much now, do you?"

"There's a cutoff point," she admitted.

"You remember who took you home?"

"No."

"We did. Ben and I."

"Oh. Ben."

"Now that's how I knew where you lived. But I did have to call Houston to get your number."

"Why didn't you call Ben?"

"I thought it was enough of a threesome. Alison"—it was the first time he had used her name—"you don't realize. I have come courting."

She hadn't realized it. She looked carefully to see whether he was joking. He was smiling, but he was not joking. She could tell from his eyes. His eyes warmed her. She liked looking into them.

"Exactly what do you mean by that?" she asked.

"Nothing fancy. I got myself an empire. I want a wife. I want you to be my wife."

"And live in Houston?"

"There are planes."

"I don't want to live in Houston."

"How do you know? You've never been there."

"I don't want to go there."

"Well, that is a problem, isn't it?"

"That's only one problem. I have a goal in mind."

"That's all right. I can help you with that."

What did he think? That she wanted to head up the P.T.A.? "What am I going to call you? Sam? Pendexter?"

"Then you do like me some."

"Yes," she said. "More than some. I find you very attractive. I imagine most women do."

He didn't stop smiling, his expression never changed, but he made no acknowledgment.

"Sam." She tried out the name. It wasn't bad. She could see calling him Sam for a long time. "I want a career."

"I said that's all right."

"You don't understand. It's not up to you to say it's all right. It's up to me. That's where our problem lies. It's my life and my career, and I'm not giving up that independence just to get married."

"Just?" He picked up on that.

"Well, that's another problem, isn't it? Yes, I guess that's what I meant. Marriage isn't very important to me now."

"Well, that's what we're going to work on. I'm going to make it so's you want to marry me. I know you want to sleep with me."

"How do you know that?"

"I knew that last night. Or thought I did. Then I thought maybe it was the sauce. But when I called this morning and you didn't want me to come up, then I knew."

"I'm not sure how well we're going to get along," Alison said doubtfully. She was feeling dizzy again and blamed it on the two drinks.

"We're going to get along just fine. Because we're both fighters. We tough it out."

"Did you find that out from your Houston office?"

"Partly from that, and partly from observation. And partly from just talking to you now. We'd make dandy adversaries. But better partners." He raised his glass in a toast. She found herself following his lead. *Oh, no,* she thought, *not so fast. Not again.* But she drank her drink and they ordered some food and sat there, surrounded by potted palms. A talented amateur with a Cuisinart was in the kitchen turning out good food, and Alison had no desire to move away from Sam Pendexter. Around two o'clock his hand was covering hers and it felt good, and by three he had kissed her. They were still in the restaurant, but practically alone. She gave herself up to his lips and could feel her resolve swaying. If only he just wanted to sleep with her, they could pop upstairs in a minute. But he was holding out for more. And being very persuasive about it.

"You're a swell kisser," she said to lighten things up.

"I love you," he said simply, and destroyed all her defenses.

"You can't tell that so quickly," she said.

He kissed her again and said very softly, "I can tell a lot about you. I can tell you've been hurt and I don't want that to happen to you again, and I can tell that you love me, if you'd let yourself, and I can tell you're scared, and I want you to get over that."

"You must have a line attached somewhere on your person to the Houston office," she said, and he smiled, but didn't kiss her again. He caressed her chin with his hand. Tough? she thought. The hands were gentle hands, loving hands. She did the unexpected. She kissed his hands.

"That's the sign I was waiting for," he said sweetly. "I think it's enough for today. I'll call you tomorrow. We'll do this again."

"You make it sound like breaking in a horse."

"It's probably the same. I was never on a horse in my life."

"But you're from Texas."

"I was poor. Poor people don't have horses. What would they feed them with?"

He left her by the entrance to her loft and walked off into the gathering dusk. The streetlights were coming on, and the grime and hard time of Manhattan were softening into a romantic gray. Alison decided she better do something about herself.

As it turned out, she didn't have to.

The phone was ringing when she entered the loft. It was Nagy.

"No, I was *not bombed*," she said firmly before he could say anything.

"I'm sorry you weren't. In any case, that is not why I called. I have an opportunity for you."

"What do you mean?"

"There is a festival in Paris set to run January through March. International theater. There will be examples from all over the world. Tom O'Horgan and the Becks will be there with the Living Theatre. I suggested you as a director and the response was very favorable. You would direct two American classics—one Wilder and one O'Neill—"

"Oh, my God!" she exclaimed.

"In French," he added.

"Oh my *God*!" she wailed. "That's like a sentence in purgatory."

"Wait. I'm not finished."

"Then I'm to play Joan of Arc at the stake, and they really burn me."

"No, no, it is not so bad as it sounds. It is a challenge. For the third play, you may choose your own author."

"Can I think it over?"

"Unfortunately no. They need to know tonight. It is already November. Rehearsals start in a week."

Alison closed her eyes. She wanted this. She wanted, had been waiting, fighting for such an opportunity, and now she felt trepidation. The thought of Sam flashed through her mind and made her decide. She needed some distance.

"Okay," she said. "When do I leave?"

"Tomorrow."

"Wait a minute," she protested. "What's the rush? Did somebody die?"

"Yes," he said bluntly. "You are the substitute."

"Okay," she said again. "Okay. What time does the flight leave?"

"Nine o'clock from Kennedy."

"At night?"

"In the morning."

Silence.

"So," he persisted, "I shall tell them yes?"

"Yes," Alison whispered, and hung up.

She had a lot of phoning to do. She sent her regrets to Edmonton, Alberta, and Charleston, South Carolina. No *Mother Courage*, no *Porgy and Bess*. She left a message for Myra. One for Trevina. Called the stage manager at the theater and left instructions. She was in the middle of packing when the phone rang.

Ben.

"I'm really sorry," he said.

"Don't be." She was tired of men feeling sorry for her.

"I wanted to find a better way to tell you but there wasn't any. You know I wouldn't do anything to hurt you."

Not if you could help it, she thought. She almost said it out loud, then held her tongue. Her silence put him on the defensive.

"I wanted you, okay? I still think you're the right person for this job, but I'm not dealing from a position of strength. I just want you to know I think you're terrific, *okay*?"

"Okay!" she yelled back at him. "It's all right, Ben. I got a job. I'm going to Paris to direct two plays for the festival."

"You're kidding!" He sounded genuinely gleeful. "That's wonderful!"

"Also terrifying," she added.

"You can do anything. When are you leaving?"

"Tomorrow morning."

"Oh. Then I can't see you. Look, I'll catch up with you in Europe. We're shooting in February." He stopped then and asked, almost like a little boy, "I *can* see you again, can't I?"

"Of course, you can. You can always reach me through Nagy. You have his number, don't you?"

"Yes. Well. Good luck."

"To both of us."

They hung up. Ben's call put her in mind of Sam

Pendexter. How was she going to get in touch with him? She couldn't meet him.

In desperation she called Houston, but his private number was indeed unlisted. She had no idea of his company's name. She ended up leaving a note at the entrance to her loft and one at Sweet Agony. All it said—for what more could she say without saying a lot more?—was *Gone to Paris. Career comes first, Empire later. Alison.* For a moment she hesitated. Should she sign it *Love, Alison? As ever?* No. *Alison* was best, she told herself—and noncommittal.

At nine the next morning she was on the plane with Nagy. She looked down at the receding coastline of America. And her thoughts turned to Paris.

Chapter Twenty-three

"Good-bye," Nagy said.

Alison was startled. "Where are you going?"

"Germany. To make a film. Didn't I tell you?"

"Of course, you didn't tell me. That's wonderful! But where can I get in touch with you?"

He gave her the address and phone number in West Berlin, then said, "And I want you to stay here. I will be gone three months. Not a day longer, if I know the Germans."

"But I can't stay here," she protested. Nagy's flat occupied an entire floor of one of the great Paris houses, and it carried with it an elegance of burnished parquet floors and creamy walls with six-part moldings, a series of little balconies opening off from the French windows that looked out on the broad expanse of Avenue Foch. Nagy's apartment had an elegance that would escape Anne-Marie Ellenfield completely.

"Oh, yes, you can." Nagy grinned at her wistful tone. "Besides, you'll be near your job."

Some job, she thought to herself. She was working in a national monument. the T.N.P.—The Théâtre National Populaire—was situated at the Place du Trocadéro, surrounded by the edifice of the Palais de Chaillot, the magnificence of the Avenue Kléber. One could look down the Avenue Raymond Poincaré and see the Place Victor Hugo. National monuments, national figures. Tradition! She had not really begun to work yet. She planned to cast the Wilder play after the weekend.

"I can't wait forever to say good-bye," Nagy said finally.

"I'm sorry," Alison said, "but I can't seem to find my mind anywhere."

"Look in the Place du Trocadéro among all the heroes." He kissed her on the cheek and was gone with his raincoat and two suitcases. Nagy traveled the world and he always traveled light.

Alison found herself alone in the midst of understated magnificence. It had never occurred to her that Nagy was rich, because he never came on with any pretense. He was still the fifteen-year-old Hungarian resistance fighter who had a tendency to look around corners and who took his love and his sex on the run, and probably always would. Never settle down, not Nagy.

But, in contrast, the furnishings of the drawing room, for example, were exquisite French antiques. The butler had already kindled the fire and brought in a breakfast tray with a croissant, steaming hot coffee, and wild plum jam, all on the most delicate Sèvres service. The napkin was the softest pale pink linen.

Deep in thought, Alison sat down by the fire and munched on the croissant. Somehow this elegance did not seem to be Paris. It wasn't the Paris she remembered from six years ago. She had deliberately avoided the Left Bank, the Sorbonne, any reminder of Alain, but memories came back to haunt her anyway. To walk down a street, to hear lovers laughing, to have that painfully buoyant language once more surrounding her, filled her with an emotion that was more pain than nostalgia, and yet she wouldn't have given up the pain of the memory for anything in the world.

However, there was a hauteur about the T.N.P. —revolutionary as its principles might be—and there was a rigid quality about this section of Paris, the Avenue Foch in particular, that went hand in hand with the formality of the French language.

So now what? Alison thought, a little American rebellion creeping in. What did she give them that wouldn't

crumble under all the historical tradition? Wilder and
O'Neill. Like a schoolgirl, she had been handed her assignments and like a schoolgirl, she thought rather guilt-
ily, she had taken the easy way out. Easy way! She laughed
at herself. *Our Town*. She would do *Our Town*. For that
she had the background, and, after all, she had done one
small scene from it for the West Coast workshop. For the
other—the O'Neill—she had decided on *Long Day's Journey into Night*, and only after she had made the decision
did she realize that, among other things, she had committed herself to two plays about New England. The ordinary
life of *Our Town* and the tortured, extraordinary life of the
Tyrone family in *Long Day's Journey*. She had seen only
one production of *Long Day's Journey*—the original, when
it was trying out for its Broadway opening. All she could
remember was a long monologue of Jason Robards's, which
perfectly represented the love-hate relationship between
brother and brother and mirrored the entire family's love-
hate relationship, which was the crux of the play. She had
never forgotten the burned-out passion of Jamie's monologue, the brilliance of Robard's performance.

How could she have understood it at the time? she
wondered. She had been a nine- or ten-year-old girl who
adored her father. Her parents could do no wrong; they
bore no relationship to the tortured characters on that
stage—until her father's suicide, which had stripped away
the brightness and sunnyness and light that had masked
his fears and loathing and desperation.

Now it was possible for her to understand the elder
James Tyrone's obsession with money, his miserliness.
She remembered the days in Los Angeles, the shoplifting,
the insecurity. And she could understand Mary Tyrone's
pain and grief, the sons' longing for one more half-
remembered happy family meal, and their loathing of the
drunken, raging, drug-filled nightmare that had become
their existence.

But who was to play this play? Alison wondered.
What kind of actors existed here in France? She suddenly
felt such trepidation that she had to get up and walk
around the room. She gazed out the window. The leaves
had all fallen from the trees, the famous avenue looked

bleak in the gray of Paris in November. The buildings across the way were forbidding.

The telephone rang.

She answered it, automatically, at the same time as the butler. A voice asked for Mademoiselle Carmichael. She said *"J'écoute"* and, with what she could sense was a sigh of relief, the voice on the other end introduced himself as Jean-Louis Barrault. Would it be possible for him and his wife—did Mademoiselle Carmichael know of her, Madeleine Renaud?—to make an appointment to investigate the possibility of their appearance in Mademoiselle Carmichael's production of O'Neill's masterpiece? How polite the French are, how accurate, how admirable, Alison thought. Hiding her excitement—after all, famous and experienced though they were, Monsieur Barrault and his wife might have no understanding of this play—she arranged for a meeting that afternoon.

They came to her. Alison felt honored, although a trifle embarrassed. It had been impossible to book the T.N.P. Rehearsals were timed to the minute. There was not a spare second of time or a spare foot of space. The apartment seemed the right location.

When she saw them, her heart sank. Madame Renaud was too *parisienne*, too chic, too self-controlled, Alison felt. She was right for boulevard comedy perhaps. And he, taller than she had thought, less wispy than when she had seen his film *Les Enfants du Paradis*, but still slight in stature. Only his voice suggested an actor's presence. Alison welcomed them, rang for tea. They sat, the three of them, rather stiffly discussing O'Neill and drinking tea, talking of rehearsal schedules, the difficulty of mounting any production. Alison kept wondering how to ask them to audition, how in all probability to refuse them, these *monstres sacrés de Paris*.

Monsieur Barrault was extremely direct. "Shall we read for you?"

"Oh," Alison breathed with relief, "would you?"

"But of course," he answered. "How else will we find out about one another?" He selected a section where Tyrone, the once-great actor, tells his son Edmond about performing Shakespeare. Barrault turned his back on Alison and began to speak. How different it sounded in French, she thought. How easy. Where was the passion? The despair?

And then Barrault turned around. His entire visage had been transformed. He was talking to his son, the words became too much for him, he stuttered from the still remembered glory, the long-gone power, the sad longings of a man who had chosen to devote his life to playing second-rate melodramas, for that was where the money lay.

Monsieur Barrault was transformed. He had linked his experience to that of O'Neill, to all aging actors. He was glorious.

Then, before Alison could speak, Madame Renaud began. Alison had forgotten about her. At the sound of her voice, she turned her head. She was shocked. Where was the stylish *parisienne*? Sad lines traced her face, the hairdo was all wisps and remnants, the expression was a mockery of a once-beautiful woman. The voice quavered between flights of morphine remembrance—remembrance of a fantasy existence, of a happy family. She chirruped in her cage, the maimed songbird, then expressed the terror of the bird let out of its cage with nowhere to go. The voice turned harsh; the eyes burned with a mad passion. And Alison knew she had found James and Mary Tyrone. Suddenly she realized these two brilliant actors had thought it all out, how to convince her. And they had, without question.

Finding a Jamie proved much more difficult. French actors, brilliant technicians, were used to playing the words, not what was unsaid. Most of the actors who auditioned could not understand Jamie's torment and his despair, his love for his brother, yet his anger at him. Quicksilver. She was looking for another Jason Robards.

When she found him, she thought she hadn't found him at all. He ambled in to the rehearsal—by now she had acquired rights and schedules at the T.N.P. right up to the opening nights of all three plays—and she checked her list for his name: Georges Martin. He looked all wrong.

He was not Robards-gaunt. She selected a short scene, one she could cut in the middle if necessary.

Martin began. All wrong. Too self-pitying. She was about to stop him when he stopped himself.

"May I start again?" he asked. She was about to refuse when something inside of her told her not to.

"Of course," she answered. This time his tone was bluff, hearty. Two drinks into the evening he became almost gross in his camaraderie. On the right track, she thought.

She gave him another scene. And then the monologue, the speech to his brother. Martin sighed, and it poured out of him—the tirade, the anger, the love, the tenderness, the final toughness. Nothing to touch there. Nothing for her to do but have him play it. She looked up. There were tears in his eyes. She found that suspect. She kept her own emotions under control.

"Would you try that again, please?"

The tears disappeared. The Frenchman was outraged. "The whole thing?" he asked in disbelief.

"Please."

He did not hide his temper, but he began again. He played it slighty differently this time. He did not try to repeat his performance, but let it grow. The anger was a little more violent—directed at her, of course—but the final result was the same. Devastating. Yes, and the tears were in the eyes again. For just a moment, and then Jamie became Georges Martin, the actor, again.

"Satisfied?" he called across the footlights.

"Yes," she said. "I've never seen an actor like you in France."

"That's because there isn't another actor like me in France," Martin said.

Oh, Alison thought, would there be trouble there? No matter. He was worth it.

"Would you like the role?"

He shrugged. "Of course. I did not come here to be rejected."

"Oh, and did you think you would?"

"Not for an instant." He gave it a second thought.

"Or, if I was, then I knew you were not the director for this play."

"Well, I am," Alison said firmly. "And I wish you would speak to the management about contracts."

"With pleasure." Martin bowed and was gone.

Edmund was easy. The boy had a pallor about him. Sensitive, brooding, he looked a little like O'Neill himself. A talented young actress was cast as the maid.

Amazingly enough, there were few problems with the O'Neill play. The set was an incredible replica of that famous dark dining-room parlor of the O'Neill house in New London. The actors practically blocked themselves. Once in a while, Alison would offer a suggestion. Every so often she would change a word in the French text, choosing one that was more appropriate to O'Neill's intent. But mainly it was a question of sitting back and watching brilliant actors and the depth of O'Neill's play. They instinctively discovered the pacing. There was no resistance to her suggestions. Monsieur Martin, whom she had thought might be troublesome, was a delight to work with, a totally creative actor. The four of them played ensemble as though they had been working together for their entire careers. O'Neill was no problem.

Mr. Wilder was nothing but.

First the translation was pedestrian, as opposed to Mr. Wilder's deliberate use of the commonplace. And the actors could not understand the inhabitants of Grover's Corners, New Hampshire. The small town life seemed incomprehensible to them. No respectable *petit bourgeois* fed chickens. There would be a servant for that.

George Gibbs's passion for baseball was, in the actors' view, merely another example of the mindlessness of the play. As the days progressed Grover's Corners resembled a village in Normandy, Wilder's characters grumbling peasants. The love scene at the soda fountain between George and Emily was maudlin; the scene in the cemetery at the end of the play unmoving.

Alison discovered director's panic. Mr. Wilder's play was supposedly universal. Anyone could understand it. Everyone could. Couldn't they? She had the play retranslated; she was lucky enough to find someone who understood

Wilder and who had her own sense of poetry. She was an actress as well as a writer, and ideal for Alison's purpose. The new translation helped a little.

The weather helped not at all. It was mid-December. The darkest gray Alison had ever walked under, the color of her own depression. On the Faubourg St. Honoré Christmas decorations had been strung, arcs of lights crisscrossing the street. The mood of the holiday season escaped Alison. She was having her problems with Frenchmen in New England. How had they solved it when they played Arthur Miller's *The Crucible* in France? Of course, they had made them all peasants. In desperation Alison was willing to turn the entire play into French. French surroundings. French attitudes. When she suggested it the next day, the cast encouraged her to.

"We do not know New Hampshire. Yes, set it in Normandy, or better still, closer to the Central," the actor playing Editor Webb advised.

"No, no, the Central is all wrong for the mood of this play. It should be closer to Switzerland," the Stage Manager said.

"Ah, well, that is because you are from there," Mrs. Gibbs said.

"Of course. In the Savoie we look at the stars. We have graveyards. At least I know where I am."

Alison seized the opportunity.

"Tell me about your village," she said to the Stage Manager.

"My village?" he said, sitting down and thinking. "My village is very small. It is on the route to Geneva, you know just before you reach Annecy. It is high in the mountains, one must walk great distances. There are cows. Grazing. Some farming."

Alison breathed a sigh of relief. "Now keep that image in mind and tell me about Grover's Corners."

The Stage Manager began. The voice grew stentorian. He was making pronouncements.

"No, no," Alison said. "The same way you talk about your village."

He started again.

"Let me see it," she said. "Now, where is the Gibbs house? What does Main Street look like? The man who delivers milk has a horse. What color is the horse? What is the rattle of the milk bottles? Mrs. Gibbs, what color is your apron? Was it your mother's?"

Finally she had them play baseball. All of them, the women too. They were not rebellious, but they were totally confused. Alison could think of no other way to loosen them up. Georges Wilson, the rather grand man who ran the T.N.P., looked in on that particular rehearsal and left, his eyebrows two inches higher than they had been.

New Year's approached. Again Alison was reminded that when one was involved in the theater, there was no outside world. Wars came and went, unobserved by actors. Governments rose and fell, revolutions occurred, and no one took any notice. In this case it was the beginning of a new year, 1974.

All around her, as she walked home through the dismal night, the French were having the traditional *réveillon*, the New Year's Eve celebration which was much more festive than Christmas, which was, after all, family.

She was totally alone in her apartment. She had given the butler the night off. She lit the fire and opened a bottle of champagne. Then she watched out the window as the drizzle turned to snow—the first snow of this abominable season, Alison mused. Across the way lights were on. She could see people dancing. Limousines and taxis pulled up to the entrances. Laughing couples entered and left. Alison sipped her champagne and watched them, and began to think of all the people she knew. Where were they? Her mother was in Toronto. Myra? Ben? Ben and Kenny. Weren't they supposed to be in Europe? Nagy? She hadn't heard a word from him since he'd left. But that was his way. He was totally involved in your life, and then not at all.

So 1973 slipped into 1974.

Nothing went right with *Our Town*. Even the timing was off. It followed by three days the famed Berliner

Ensemble's production of Brecht's *The Resistible Rise of Arturo Ui,* which was a total triumph. The Chicago thug representing Hitler, the great banners unfurling from the rafters, made for exciting theater, and the Parisians roared their approval. The reviews were ecstatic. Deservedly so, Alison thought as she watched the dreary runthrough of *Our Town.* The play looked lost.

Outside the rain had partially washed the snow away. Little Alps remained on street corners. As Alison walked back to Nagy's apartment the rain turned to snow again. Would the sun ever shine? she wondered. Would she ever see the moon or stars again? Clouds hung over the city, and all the Christmas lights looked despairing. Why didn't they take them down? The holiday season was over.

She was feverish. Her temperature was a hundred and one. She made herself some tea and went to bed. She would be better in the morning.

If anything, she was worse. Her throat ached and her head throbbed, but she attended the last general rehearsal anyway. She might as well have stayed in bed, she thought as she watched the actors struggle with the simplicity of Mr. Wilder's work and the technicians struggle with the lighting cues. An assistant brought tea. The French were very kind in that way, she thought. They worried whether the tea was the right temperature. Alison wanted to weep. Her throat was raw. Finally she could stand it no longer.

"Stop!" she cried out in English, starting for the stage. Startled, the actors stood immobilized. One did not interrupt a dress rehearsal.

"This is all wrong, all wrong," she said, and then realizing the actors were baffled because she was speaking English, she switched to French.

"You are making everything complicated. This play is about living and dying in a small town, and that small town is part of the whole structure of the cosmos. But you cannot play the cosmos. You can only play the small town."

"But one must do *something,*" the actress playing Emily Webb said. She had already starred in two movies and was to work for Vadim the following summer.

"Do nothing!" Alison commanded them. "If you fail,

you fail. No. *I* fail. But do nothing. Make no moments. Let them happen. They will if you let them." She went back to her seat. She was shivering. Her bones ached.

"We will start where we left off," she said. "And just say the words. Nothing more."

She watched. Oh, it was so difficult for them. They were used to all the fireworks, the artifice of classical French theater, Alison thought. Here they were lost. Gestures left over from Racine appeared in the middle of a New England springtime. Declamations that could have sprung from the pen of Corneille bowled over poor Thornton Wilder. But the actors persisted. They struggled. But they did not believe. They did not believe in Mr. Wilder's play.

Until, curiously enough, the wedding scene at the end of the second act. The Gibbs and Webb households swing into full preparation for the ceremony. George Gibbs has a talk with his father. He doesn't want to get married. He wants to be free. On a separate part of the stage, Emily, petrified, asks her mother, "What will we say to each other in thirty years over the breakfast table?"

Something started to happen. Alison forgot her throat. Emily Webb was no longer acting for Roger Vadim—who, she knew, would be attending the premiere. The actors were beginning to understand. Perhaps it was their fatigue, their own terror of this unknown land, but the connections began to appear; the characters took shape. It was after midnight when the Stage Manager finally put the town of Grover's Corners to bed under stars that had been shining for a billion years and would, give or take a catastrophe, shine for a billion more. He spoke the final line of the play. "You get a good rest, too. Good night."

Alison found her strength again for a moment and approached the weary actors.

"Bravo," she whispered. "Risk it. Take the chance. Do nothing. Let it happen. If they don't understand, they don't understand. But you will have been true to Mr. Wilder. Good night."

The premiere was a gala. Alison, still pale from her illness, watched the audience assemble. Every jewel in

France must have been worn that night—great diamond diadems, necklaces of emeralds, ropes of pearls, adorning the most jaded faces she had ever seen. Ladies' wrinkled faces. The grand disdain of the old gentlemen. Alison's fleeting thought was of Alain and his desire to shatter precisely this group. The aristocracy. The *tout-Paris* that seemed to possess the patent on glamour. It was also the *tout-Paris* that had bravoed the Berliner Ensemble's performance of Brecht a few nights earlier.

Purely out of instinct, Alison had drawn her hair back. She looked totally American, almost severe, in contrast to the audience. She wore no makeup, no jewelry.

As she was standing there she thought she must be hallucinating. Diane Landers was approaching her, all jewels, all smile, still the gypsy she-cat. Dressed in clinging black velvet, she was devastating.

"Surprise!" she greeted Alison. "I knew Vadim was coming. I asked him to get two extra tickets. Fortunately it was not all that difficult. Have you seen the Brecht? Absolutely incredible! I could not speak for two hours afterward."

Alison was sure she was going to faint. Why now, why this? Openings were tough enough. She did not need Diane Landers.

"My God, you look worn out. Are you all right? French critics can be tough."

Enough.

"Yes, I'm fine, Diane. It's just the shock of seeing you. I didn't expect you for another month."

"We had some preproduction work, so Ben and I flew over, thought we'd combine it with a holiday."

"Is he here?"

"Of course, he's here. He was just thanking Vadim for the tickets. Have you met Vadim, by the way? Well, you must."

Ben showed just in time. Welcome American face. Welcome grin. Nothing could be too bad so long as happy-go-lucky, boyish Ben was around for support. He kissed her on both cheeks—which was only proper—then gave her a hug he really meant.

"I missed you," he said. "I'm glad we got here in time. What are you doing after? Can we go out?"

"Don't start with the plans so fast," Diane said sharply. "Look at her. Poor baby. She looks exhausted." Diane was positively cooing with conciliation.

The houselights flickered. They took their seats.

The play began. The audience was cold. They were judging everything and finding it wanting, Alison felt.

She could not fault the actors. They were performing as directed. But the audience was not buying.

At intermission she glanced at Ben's face, saw the pain there. The grin almost covered it up.

"I hate opening nights," he said.

"Do you?" Diane caroled. "I adore them. You see everyone. Oh, Alison, do you know the critic from *Le Figaro*? He's just over there. Do you want an introduction? No? Well, perhaps it's just as well. Excuse me. I just want a word with him."

"It'll be okay," Ben said, and Alison tried to believe him. For a moment he put his arm around her, and she thought, yes, it would be all right, but then it was time for the second act. And Alison knew it would not.

In the third act, as Emily Webb was bidding good-bye to all things on earth, her good-bye to Grover's Corners and her mother's sunflowers and hot baths, there were scattered titters from the audience.

It suddenly struck Alison that she had been a fool. The words sounded ridiculous in French. The Berliner Ensemble had played in German. German actors performing a German work in their native language. And that had been accepted. But this—this was a hybrid. It was not American; it was not Wilder. It was some strange combination she and the actors had struggled with—and not succeeded. What a fool she had been to allow this to happen.

The audience filed out of the theater; the management passed her with a nod. A failure. Alison was tasting the acid of defeat.

Diane came up. Floating. Gloating. Ben was a pale figure behind her. Sorrowful. *Do not feel sorry for me*, Alison thought. She couldn't bear that.

"You want to go someplace?" he asked.

"Ben, you know we can't!" Diane said impatiently, and then parenthetically, to Alison. "We promised Vadim--"

Alison cut her short. "I quite understand. No, I want to go home anyway. My throat's feeling lousy."

"Can we drop you?" Ben asked, concerned.

"No."

"Tough it out," he whispered. She nodded and they left. The theater was empty. Discarded programs littered the carpet.

She went backstage to praise the actors, tried with no success to restore their confidence.

Then she walked home again. This time it was not raining.

The rain came again—in the form of abuse. The critics were merciless, not only with Alison. Quite often, she was not even considered worthy of mention. But Mr. Wilder was crucified. "This simplistic collection of homilies," "watered-down Brecht," "One night we are given Brechtian brandy; the next, skim milk. Is this truly one of America's great playwrights?"

The management called Alison. They were canceling her third play—which she hadn't even chosen yet—"due to the overwhelming demand for tickets to *Arturo Ui.*" Alison accepted this cynically. She knew the only reason they were not also canceling *Long Day's Journey* was because of the potency of the Barrault-Renaud combination.

She had the day off. Tomorrow would come the final rehearsals for the O'Neill. Meanwhile she had time to breathe. She took a walk, in no particular direction. The skies had cleared for the first time in a month. Gray clouds raced across the Parisian cityscape, borne on a western wind. And behind the clouds was a pale-blue winter sky. And the sun. The city glistened from the light. Alison marched briskly down the Champs-Élysées to the Place de la Concorde, then along the right bank of the Seine. She was looking at the buildings, the expanse of the boulevard, the river. She could not deny herself. Her eyes sought the opposite bank. The Left Bank. Across the Seine, past the Île Saint-Louis, past Notre-Dame to the

Rue d'Arcole, until she was back where she had thought
she never wanted to be. The Boulevard St.-Michel—the
Boul' Mich'—was in front of her. To her left the Sorbonne. She wandered the twisted little alleyways of this
most ancient arrondisement in Paris. The Latin Quarter,
the sounds of the police whistles, the sirens, the shouts,
the cries of revolution, drowned out the present. Alison
passed the little shop where she had bought flowers. Passed
the School of Photography. Alain. Suddenly he was everywhere. In the wan sunlight students sat at sidewalk cafés,
sheltered by the glass, bundled in mufflers, warmed by
their hopes and arguments. They sat as though nothing
had happened. As though '68 had been forgotten. Perhaps
it had been. Was that another generation? The end of an
era? she asked herself.

Alison could see Alain, in the corner with a circle of
friends. The boy smoked the way Alain had smoked. There,
across the way, the curly black hair. That was Alain. She
heard a voice. She turned, sure that he would be running
up to her. She closed her eyes.

*The feet on the landing, the sounds of fleeing. The
police. The knock at the door. And even in his frantic
flight he filled her room with vitality.* Near the Odéon,
she stopped. She sat down at a café, ordered *un filtre*, and
let the sun warm her as she drank the coffee.

A most curious thing was happening to her. She was
becoming unfrozen. Tears filled her eyes, tears of mourning for a love, her first love. She had never said a proper
good-bye. She was doing so now. And her heart began to
melt. Her own feelings were no longer under control. She
did not trust herself to get up from the table and walk.

She sat in the café and let it happen. She remembered the girl she had once been, the lover she had once
been, the young blond breathless American. And she allowed herself to remember Alain and the *chaleur* of his
passion for life.

"*My God,*" he was saying to her, "*is this what you
have become? I would never have stayed with you, droop-
ing like this. You live and you fight, and you love, and you
may lose, but you fight again. That is how it goes. If you
don't like it, go back to wherever and rock on the porch.*

But spare me your tears of self-pity. I could have told you about French decadence. I could have told you—I did tell you—about the petit bourgeois. They destroyed me with a bullet. If you let them destroy you, I will never forgive you."

She sat in the afternoon sunshine for a few more minutes, then called for the check, paid it, and strode down the street, back to her job.

She did not look back.

When she returned to Nagy's, the butler informed her Ben Sawyer had called and left a message. He and Miss Landers were leaving for Austria that day and could be reached at—

Alison did not care to know.

She opened a bottle of champagne and started to drink. The more she drank, the more depressed she got. She was opening another bottle when the phone rang.

Who would be calling? Everyone was so *busy* with his own life. Maybe it was a call for Nagy. She picked up the receiver and said, *"Allò, j'écoute."*

"What in hell does that mean?" said a wonderfully familiar voice with that Texas twang.

"Oh, it can't be you. Oh, Sam, it's so good to hear your voice."

"Well, then, it was worth the call."

"Where are you, are you here?"

"Hell, I'm in Houston."

"It's snowing here and everyone is having a good time except me, and I'm miserable."

"Well, the sun is shining in Houston. It's a lovely afternoon. I'm taking off to play tennis, and then tonight I'm going to have a hell of a time."

"I never thought I'd say it, but I wish I were in Houston."

He laughed. "You could learn to like Houston."

"I'm learning to hate Paris."

"Oh, too bad. I'm coming over. Thought I'd drop by and see you on my way to Geneva."

"Oh, when? When are you coming?" She sounded too eager.

"God, you do sound in a bad way. I'll be there on the fifteenth."

"The fifteenth," she repeated. "I hope I'll be alive then."

"I don't want to hear any of that bullshit. I called to tell you that I love you—and that I did get your note."

"My note."

"You were kind enough to leave a note when you stood me up that day."

"Oh, Sam, I'm sorry. Will you forgive me?"

"I'm calling you, aren't I?"

"Yes." She could picture him. That was curious. Usually she couldn't keep a picture of a person in her mind, but with Sam it was different. And she remembered his lips and the way he kissed her.

"Sam, I think I love you," she said. "But maybe it's the champagne talking."

"Then drink another bottle."

Chapter Twenty-four

Where did her strength come from? everybody wondered. Hadn't she read the papers? Or was she hiding her feelings?

Alison threw herself into the final rehearsals of the O'Neill play with a concentration that was astonishing. The French were always a bit careful with their passions. Now, she found that nothing was enough. *Let it be big*, she kept saying. They could cut it down to size if necessary. They had all been too careful. *She* had been too careful. O'Neill had never been a careful writer.

What she was sensing was life, there on that stage. Unlike the Wilder production, this play and these players were already throbbing with an intensity. She stormed at the actors. They fought back. Argued. But it was all with a unity of purpose. Each one of them felt the enormous anguish that was the power of this play.

After the final dress rehearsal Alison looked around the dark auditorium. There was not a sound. The lighting designer was crouched over his board. The costumer was huddled in her seat. The three assistants—ordered to spy on the production, Alison was sure—rose and walked out in silence. Silence on stage. The players were motionless. Silence in the darkness of the auditorium.

Alison was terribly unsure of herself and her feelings. She walked a bit unsteadily toward the stage. Monsieur Barrault was sitting in the wicker chair. Madame Renaud was still standing near the landing where she had spoken her last line. The other two men hung back in the shadows.

Alison started to speak to them, but found she could not. No words would come out of her throat. She shook her head helplessly. Monsieur Barrault smiled at her.

"We did this one for you," he said.

She nodded, fighting the tears.

"Because you did not give up, and because you gave us the strength."

"It will never be this good again," Madame Renaud said regretfully from the staircase. And then they began to applaud Alison. The five actors. And behind her, the lighting, scene, and costume designers. She turned around. She could not move from the spot. Monsieur Barrault jumped down from the stage and put his arm around her shoulders, and then they were all kissing her, embracing her. They were the family now, united perhaps against a hostile world. Together. She was one of them.

A half hour later, she prepared to walk out the stage entrance. *À demain,* they called after her.

A limousine was purring at the curb. As she walked past it she heard someone whistle. Ignoring him, she walked on, but then it occurred to her that Frenchmen didn't whistle at women. American men did. She turned around quickly to find that her admirer was halfway out of the limo to follow her, his joke having backfired.

"Sam!" she cried out in joy, then said, "But this isn't the fifteenth!"

"I came a couple of days early."

She was so glad to see him she kissed him fully, welcoming him. He finally broke away, breathless. "You don't act like you're in so much trouble," he said.

"I'll tell you all about it."

"Could you do it in the limo? I've been waiting here an hour for you, and then you pass me by. Come on, get in. At least it's warm in there. Are you hungry? I'm starved."

There was a little place on the Rue du Berri, where most of the newsmen went. It served hamburgers, a good red wine, and an especially hot chili. Sam was delighted.

"Paris can freeze your bones," he complained happily as he ordered the chili.

"Where are you staying?" she asked.

"The Ritz," he said casually.

"And they don't have heat at the Ritz?"

"Oh, I wouldn't complain about that hotel. They got everything you ask for. It's when you go outside. But hey, I feel warmer now."

So did she. His grin warmed her. His openness. He reached for her hands and held them while she told him about her last six weeks in Paris, the problems she had endured, the critical whiplashing.

The grin faded and his eyes showed concern. "That's no life for a woman," he chided her.

"Oh, don't start!" Alison protested lightly. "You just want me in Houston making barbecue sauce."

"I got servants for that," he said seriously. "You'd never have to be in the kitchen. You could have lunch with the girls, and join the tennis club, and go with me—most of the time. Honey, I go all around the world."

"So do I. And look, here we are, in Paris, having an argument."

He regarded her carefully. "I just can't see us being in different parts of the world all the time."

"You're really serious," she said, surprised.

"Oh, yes. About you, I am very serious."

"Oh," she said, and couldn't think of anything else to say. There were many areas where she and Sam differed. But she liked that. She ate her hamburger in silence, and then realized it was almost two o'clock in the morning and she was dropping with fatigue.

"Sam, take me home, will you? I have an opening tomorrow and I'm really tired."

"Sure," he said. "Can I get a ticket for the show?"

"Why don't you stand in the back with me?" she suggested.

"You're not going to sit down for your own show!" He seemed startled.

"Not possibly. I get too nervous."

"Okay, wherever you are, that's where I'll be."

"And listen, if I'm crazy, just bear with me. Remember it's an opening night."

He repeated, "That's no life for a woman."

"Oh, shut up and take me home," she said fondly.

The Avenue Foch impressed Sam. "You live around here?" he asked.

"Right here, the next corner. And one block further down you can find Maria Callas."

"Hot damn!" he said. "This is very heavy territory."

"Okay," she said, "you can stop the little-boy act any time now. I'm on to you."

"What do you mean?" he asked innocently.

"I mean, country boy, that you know most of the industrialists on this little avenue, so don't put me on. You're just surprised that the likes of me is allowed in here, right? Well, it's Nagy's apartment."

She could see the tension come into his face.

"Don't worry. Nagy is somewhere in Germany making a movie."

The limousine had stopped at the corner, but Sam signaled the driver to wait. He stretched his legs and looked at Alison.

"You're right. There's a lot of the country boy left in me. I'm a very simple guy when it comes to women. They're mine or they're not. I don't share."

"If it comes to that," Alison said, "you won't have to. But it hasn't come to that."

"Not yet," he said, then changed the subject. "You know how long it took me to get used to limousines? About five seconds. The first one I ever had, that was four years ago, the accountant came in and said, 'Okay, you made it, the first million.' I'd sworn that I was going to do it. I couldn't buy my own limousine that day, but I rented one, and the driver opened the door and I sank back into all that plush. I like being rich!" he said suddenly. And he kissed her exuberantly. Alison had to fight down her desire for him.

"My God," she said, breaking away. "I feel like I'm back in high school necking in the backseat."

That made him laugh. He signaled the driver to open

the door, then escorted her to her apartment and said good night.

She left her clothes scattered in a path to the bed, climbed in, and fell asleep immediately.

The premiere the following night saw the same faces, the same jewels—or jewelry that was interchangeable—but somehow the faces didn't seem so forbidding to Alison. Perhaps because Sam was beside her.

"I thought you were going to be jittery," he said to her, almost reproachfully, as though he had been deprived of some amusement.

"I thought so too."

He busied himself casing the audience. "Whew, look at that emerald necklace. It's almost as fancy as Houston. Women are prettier in Texas though. And the New York furs are better."

Alison laughed. "I appreciate you putting this all in perspective for me."

"Anytime, ma'am," he said, spreading the accent a bit too thick. "Now, what is this play you're about to show me?"

"Just watch."

The theater darkened, the stage lights came up on the interior of the Tyrone house in New London, Connecticut, and the play began. It opened slowly, an ordinary day, ordinary people—a maid, a father who was a touch on the stingy side, a mother who was lovely and vague, and two brothers. The Parisian audience was silent, viewing the scene with curiosity. What were Barrault and Renaud doing up there on that stage? How tattered they looked as James and Mary Tyrone. She was always sticking pins in her hair; he was so mercurial. It was hard to recognize this famous French theatrical team. They were not as they had been.

And that was the way they worked their magic. Very subtly they forced the audience to look at the characters they were creating and forget the Barraults, forced them to concentrate on the struggles of this play, the undercurrents of tension. The play shifted into second gear as the day wore on and the subterfuges wore out. And the members of the Tyrone family got at one another's throats.

The French were caught unawares. They were not used to such naked emotion—certainly not from the Barraults. And who was this Georges Martin with his boozy face and false-happy eyes, fingers constantly drumming, who summoned up tension even in his silence as he watched his younger brother become the man he was unable to be?

The auditorium was totally silent, the silence of complete absorption. The play gripped the Parisians, startled them, shocked them. From moment to moment, from shattering climax to anguished revelation, the performers gave great moments to theatrical history. And the audience realized, as the play reached its last despairing note, what they had been watching. Mary Tyrone, cradling the wedding gown of so long ago, sat downstage right, locked in memory and morphine as the shadow of O'Neill's recall darkened the stage and surrounded them in black, as deep as death itself.

The silence continued in the darkness. And then the stage became an ordinary stage again, the lights came up, the spell had to be broken, and the audience stood. Not applauding, not at first. Just standing in salute, in honor. The five actors walked downstage to bow and the waves of applause began, swelled. Voices cried out in approval.

"Jesus," Alison heard behind her. It was Sam. She had forgotten about him, forgotten everything except the power of the moment. Now his arms were around her. He was embracing her with joy. And with respect. She could feel that and see it in the tears in his eyes.

"I didn't know . . ." he began. "I didn't realize." His tears overflowed. He was crying. She held him. He did not know how to handle the conflicting emotion he was feeling.

"It's all right," she said, trying to comfort him. "It's all right, Sam."

And then they were swept up in the pandemonium of the moment. The French are not easily moved; they value the intellect much too much for that. But, on the rare occasions they are, they go mad.

The stage lights went down. The actors disappeared from the stage and yet the applause continued, grew in strength, developed a rhythm.

Monsieur Barrault and Madame Renaud finally returned. The bravos were deafening. They stood there, immobile, accepting the homage, and then Monsieur Barrault raised his hands for silence. His hand was a command.

"I thank you—we both—we all thank you." He included the entire family of this production. "However, we would never have been able to offer you the power and passion of Monsieur O'Neill's masterpiece if it were not for one person. An extraordinary artist, an extraordinary woman. It has been an honor to work with her. Our director—Alison Carmichael."

His arm shot out, again a command, and all faces turned toward her. The jaded Parisians turned their wrinkled faces, their mascaraed eyes, and their enthusiasm became an almost religious fervor.

"My God, they think you're Marie Antoinette!" Sam whispered.

"Yes, and look what happened to her," Alison whispered back.

But she took her moment, accepted their applause— smiling and nodding, still not forgetting the response to the other premiere. It was all one, she realized as the applause continued. It was as much the rejection as the total acceptance. Get used to it, she said to herself. She'd probably have plenty of both.

Backstage was a festival of kisses, embraces, hand-shakes, multilingual congratulations. Georges Wilson, who directed the T.N.P., smiled cordially and kissed her on both cheeks. He would have given her the Legion of Honor if he could have. There were promises of extending the run, of moving it to one of the commercial theaters on the boulevards. Monsieur Barrault and Madame Renaud, sweaty actors underneath the makeup and greatness, still performers who had to work and who perspired under the hot lights and the glare of the audience, embraced her and laughed and cried. Georges Martin did a touching thing.

He kissed her gently and gave her a poem he had written. Then he vanished. She could not even approach the young boy who played Edmund, his dressing room was so crowded. She satisfied herself with a congratulatory wave to him, then she and Sam left the theater.

Thank God for limousines. Sam's would take them anywhere they wanted to go. And where did they want to go?

"To the Ritz," Alison said. Sam looked at her in delighted surprise.

"You mean it?"

"I mean it."

"It's not just the heat of the moment?"

"Partly," she said. Was he going to question her about everything? she wondered. Sam directed the driver and immediately they were passing the brilliant lights of Paris, circling the Place de la Concorde, approaching the Place Vendôme. Of course, it was the heat of the moment, Alison thought, and why shouldn't it be? Everything was brighter and more alive, the passersby more romantic, all of it out of a movie. Gene Kelly should come dancing down the street. But he didn't have to. She could do that. With Sam. They could both dance and celebrate. Like the shop windows that still displayed the most expensive wares in the world, Alison's world glittered. Nothing could shatter it. In the Ritz Bar Sam ordered champagne, but the management refused to let them pay for it. Compliments of the hotel. They had heard of mademoiselle's triumph. Alison was sorry they hadn't ordered two bottles.

They drank, were toasted. She felt Sam close to her and enjoyed the feeling. "I want to see your room," she whispered.

"*See* my room?" He laughed out loud. "You mean, you want to see if the accommodations are adequate?"

"Something like that."

They left the bar, took the elevator to the fourth floor. The apartment was breathtaking. It looked out on the noble expanse of the Place Vendôme. The bed, she noticed, was brass. As was the fire fender.

"Could we have a fire?" she asked Sam.

"Sure. And more champagne."

"Yes. That is definitely necessary." Sam rang for the porter, who lit the fire. The champagne was brought and some delicious sandwiches with ham pressed and rolled on bread. Delicious. Alison wolfed them down.

"More?" Sam asked.

She shook her head. "No. More champagne though."

He poured the champagne into her glass and they gazed for a minute at the fire, then she looked at him. "Oh, I am so glad we are us, and that we're here. Isn't it fun?"

"More than fun," he breathed. "More than I ever dreamed of."

"What do you like best? The room? The sandwiches? That wonderful fender by the fireplace? The champagne? What?"

"You," he said. She had hoped he would say that.

He was sitting on the couch. She threw herself on him, spilling the champagne.

He laughed and kissed her. But a kiss was not enough for her. She wanted more. She wanted everything. She wanted him to make love to her, and she wanted this moment not to end, and she wanted the next moment to come crowding in. She stripped him naked, shocking them both. He undressed her much more slowly before the fire. She was more abandoned than he. He was controlled, no less filled with desire, but controlled. He marveled at her body in the firelight, kissed the gold of her hair, covered her breasts first with his hands, then his lips, adored her body with his own, and then entered her. It was the most natural thing in the world. She accepted him, grateful for the wonderful virility of him, and he proved to be a most extraordinary lover, anticipating every single one of her desires as if he knew her mind better than she did.

Somehow, during the night, they found the bed and made love again in the soft luxury of sheets. He discovered her skin was as smooth as the sheets, she discovered his body was as warm and enveloping as a comforter. But hard-muscled. He used his body as an instrument of pleasure. To pleasure her. This had never happened to Alison, not quite so completely, a man both eager and able to pleasure her, never tiring. Sometime around three o'clock

they rang for more champagne, but they were back to
making love when the waiter entered with the bottle. He
retreated discreetly. After all, this was the most expensive
hotel in the world and he was used to such things.

Alison was not. In the morning she had both a tremendous thirst and a big hangover. She needed a shower
desperately. She stumbled blindly toward the bathroom.
It was immense. She was not sure whether she could
make it all the way to the shower, across the vast expanse
of tiles. She did. She closed the door and steamed herself,
letting the hot water pour over her. She soaped herself,
then braced for the cold shower. It was stinging, a reminder of New England and early morning dips in the
lake. When she emerged half an hour later, she found
Sam waiting.

Without saying a word, he picked her up and carried
her back into the shower she had just vacated and made
love to her again. She found herself totally celebrating her
sexuality. It was not to be denied, any more than Sam
himself was. Standing with the water pouring over them,
she responded again and again to the insistent maleness of
him.

An hour later they were back in bed wrapped snugly
in Ritz terry-cloth bathrobes that had been especially
warmed, drinking champagne and orange juice, and watching the sun dance over the elegantly striped bedroom
wallpaper.

"Let's go to Lugano," Sam said impulsively. "You
need a vacation. You earned it. Let's take it."

"Lugano?" she repeated. She wasn't even sure where
it was.

"Get out of Paris this time of year," he advised, and
she laughed. A week ago nothing would have been better;
today she was not so sure. She was in demand right now.
But so was he.

"A weekend," he said. "Today is Thursday. A weekend and then you come back to Paris and I go to Geneva.
That ought to suit your independence."

His grin was infectious and seductive. And persuasive. It was easy to see how he had charmed his way into a
fortune. It was less easy to see how he had fought to get

there. He had been careful never to show her that side of his nature.

"I'll have the concierge arrange everything," he added.

"What will I need in wherever it is?" she asked.

"A toothbrush and a pair of heavy shoes. The rest we'll pick up when we get there."

She shrugged in wonderment and proceeded to dress.

Sam's chauffeur drove her to Nagy's apartment, where she packed for the weekend, then returned to the Ritz. Sam was all ready. The limousine got them to Orly in plenty of time for the next flight to Zurich. On the way they stopped at a newsstand, and Alison picked up the papers that carried the first reviews.

Once in flight, with absolutely no sense of modesty, she translated them word by word to Sam, savoring every glowing tribute. The Alps lay beneath them, unobserved.

Chapter Twenty-five

The Splendide Royale was a hotel not easily forgotten.

Splendid it was, and in the past it had sheltered royalty. It was one of the last symbols of the Belle Époque. Their room was furnished in a Venetian style that resembled the salon of an ancient opera singer. Brocade walls and armchairs of red velvet, lamps dripping with silk fringe, and gilt, gilt everywhere, even on the little tables that were good for one ashtray or a calling card.

The service was inspired. That evening, as the Alps were swallowing up the last of the day's sun, martinis arrived on a silver salver. They sipped them on the balcony while Alison looked out in wonder.

It was January, but roses were blooming, their odor rising in the evening air. She could see palm trees and Italian cypress, sweet borders of marigolds and azaleas and the aquamarine of Lake Como. As evening descended a diadem of lights across the lake sparkled like a floating tiara. The air was fresh, the climate mild. She was in Eden.

Sam could hardly suppress his delight at being able to show her one of his favorite places in the world.

"Tomorrow we'll see the town, pick up a few things. Do you hike?"

He stopped himself. "Alison, I don't know anything about you. What you like, what you don't like."

"You know a few things."

He blushed. That pleased her. "I mean, like hiking. Outdoor things."

"I love them. Well, don't we fit together *nice*!" he exclaimed. "I don't think I could love a girl that didn't walk some."

"We'll do everything," she promised, and looked out at the evening again. "I can't believe it's so warm. It's spring."

"It's because of the Alps. They protect the valley here, so it's semitropical. It's my own discovery." He gave her his grin.

They ate dinner in the grand dining room while a string quartet played last century's music. The music was like the furniture—dripping with fringe. Alison was starved. She ate two helpings of the pâté, and then veal piccata. Sam had a chateaubriand and a salad, and they shared a bottle of red wine. He watched her gorge herself. Suddenly she put her fork down.

"How did you find this place?" she asked.

"A client brought me here." She was glad he wasn't all that familiar with the great resorts of Europe. It kind of spoiled the poor-boy image. "She didn't like Saint-Tropez and she didn't ski, so this was it."

The shock of jealousy startled Alison. Possessive, so soon? "An American?" she managed to say.

"No. Kraut."

"I think the war's been over long enough; we can call them Germans."

Sam shrugged. "That's what she called herself—kraut. So that's what I called her. You're mad," he said happily.

"Not a bit," she said.

"And now you're lying," he said, even happier.

"Okay," she said, spilling it out. "Is this your private pad? You take all your chicks here and have a good time balling them?" He didn't like her language. She coarsened it purposely. "And do they give you good head?"

"Cut it out—"

"You couldn't wait to get me out of Paris."

"You couldn't wait to get out," he countered.

"Well, I thought this place was some place original with you. What do you have? A standing reservation?"

Then she saw the other side of him.

"Cut it out right now." The voice was ice.

She was silenced. She listened.

"I told you I loved you. I was with a woman here once. I loved this place. It was peaceful. It was a great place to make love. I wanted to bring you here because I love you. I don't want you to spoil it. There's no other woman in my life. So don't carry this any further."

She sulked through coffee and he refused to take his eyes off her. When she was through with her coffee, she lifted her eyes and they met his. Suddenly she had to have him again, right off. She could not wait.

"Let's go," he said, his good humor restored.

The room smelled of the night, of roses and azaleas. After they had made love, they lay naked in the dark and he described her body to her, how her legs felt wrapped around him, how delicate the length of her neck was, how exquisite the odor of her breasts, the slight rounding of her belly. They slept in each other's arms all night.

The following morning they ate on the balcony, a breakfast of freshly squeezed orange juice, heaps of hot chocolate with whipped cream on top, croissants with an array of preserves—fresh raspberry with seeds that stuck to the teeth, sweet strawberry, blackberry, gooseberry, and orange marmalade.

In the distance the morning mist was just lifting off the lake. The scene was enchanting.

"This is the Swiss part," Sam explained. "After breakfast we'll go to the town for a taste of Italy."

Whatever he said was all right with her. She felt compliant and complacent.

They walked to the Piazza Reforma and shopped, buying some hiking gear and a tennis racquet for her. Sam paid for everything, but never without questioning the price and examining the bill to see that the figures were correct.

"You'll need a dress," he told her. They bought one at the Dior boutique. Then they dropped in to a café for cappuccino and to watch the pedestrians watching them.

When they returned to the hotel, she asked if he played tennis still.

"Some, he said noncommittally, and she challenged him to a game.

The hotel courts were splendid. The pro lent Sam a racquet and Alison began to rally with him. She was just good enough to know how much better he was than she. He kept himself in check, allowing her to make a few points. She wasn't a bad tennis player, she was a better-than-average club player. But Sam was in a different league. She could tell by the way he served. He tried to keep it gentle. Hard enough not to offend her, but not so powerful as to overwhelm her. Only once when she hit a surprise shot to his backhand did he automatically unleash the power and whip a shot cross-court for a clean winner that both awed and dismayed her.

By this time the pro, bored with the gentility surrounding him, was watching with interest. He and Sam agreed to play a set, and Alison sat down to observe.

The pro was younger than Sam, probably in better shape, Alison thought. Obviously used to playing more tennis. He won the first three games easily. But then Alison caught the glint in Sam's eye. The calculations of tennis came into play. The rallies got longer, the chances taken grew more startling. A backhand volley from Sam surprised the pro. The two men were sweating in the pleasant springlike air. The game was intense. They reached five-all. Then a tie-breaker. The pro got lucky and won with a shot that touched the net and dropped onto Sam's side. Sam shook his head. He didn't like to lose, Alison could see that. There was no warmth in his smile as he shook hands with the pro.

But, upstairs, he stripped off his clothes and she heard him singing in the shower.

"I didn't think you were such a good sport," she shouted over the noise of running water. He came out, hair streaming.

"I'm not," he said, standing naked in front of her. "But he's got to stay there on that damn court. And I got you." With that he swept her into the shower with him.

*   *   *

They were not adult. They did not behave. They were bad children sometimes. They couldn't keep their hands off each other. They skipped meals and made love, ordered from room service in the middle of the night. And made love. The following day they hiked up Monte San Salvatore, packing with them some grub—raisins and crunchy carbohydrates for energy—a bottle of red wine, and some cheese. Alison had no trouble keeping up with Sam. As they made the ascent they could view the Matterhorn, its majestic spire to the north of them. To the south was Italy, the plains of Lombardy. It was like standing at the apex of history, Alison thought. Huns to the north, Gauls to the west, Romans to the south. Everything had happened here, on this spot. Kingdoms and countries had swapped treaties and borders and bloodshed, and the vengeance was still remembered. Toward the Austrian border it became more difficult to speak Italian. It was the region known as Alto Adige, but the people stuck to their *Muttersprache*—German. And even there they found a meadow where they could strip off their clothes and make love, until they were interrupted by a young German couple who, horrified and embarrassed, excused themselves halfway down the mountain. Sam just laughed. They returned to their lovemaking and afterward fell asleep in the sun over the bottle of wine. That night, though, their sunburns demanded salves and ointments, and they made love gingerly, tenderly. And laughed. Alison Carmichael had never been so happy in the twenty-five years of her life.

Chapter Twenty-six

Sam was full of surprises. On Sunday morning they were awakened by church bells echoing through the valley. The sound drew them to the balcony, where sunlight dazzled their eyes.

"Do you want to go to church?" he asked. She looked at him to see whether he was being serious. He was.

"I'm Congregationalist," she informed him, not knowing what else to say.

"They won't burn you at the stake for going inside," he said.

"Are you Catholic?"

"My mother was. I was brought up a Catholic." He was already slipping into his pants. She dressed, dimly remembering that she should cover her head. On the way to Santa Maria degli Angeli he bought her a Gucci scarf decorated with graceful wild flowers. She tied it under her chin. They walked through the piazza, and he looked at her in the golden morning sunlight. He drew her aside and kissed her.

"You look like Brigitte Bardot," he joked. She wasn't sure she liked the comparison. Brigitte Bardot was *old*, Alison thought.

"Is that a compliment?" she asked.

"You betcha," he said quite emphatically, and they continued on their way to mass, the salty Texan and the beautiful New Englander, neither of whom bore any resemblance to Swiss or Italian peasants.

They are museums for most of the week, but on Sunday the Catholic churches of Europe are packed with aristocrat and peasant, the pious and the obligational devotee. The old Italian women dressed completely in black.

Alison gasped when she saw the interior of the church. The walls were decorated with frescoes depicting the Crucifixion, the Last Supper, and other scenes in a mixture of greens, golds, browns, oranges, violets. Like most works of the Middle Ages, weeping maidens and suffering saints crowded knights on horseback, while hordes of angels watched from a medieval sky. Alison was transfixed by the glory of the church, the acrid power of the organ, the sweetness of the boys' choir. Like the view from Monte San Salvatore, the ritual of the mass seemed to encompass all of European history, music, and art. The mass was still sung in Latin. Sam was at ease here. He knew when to kneel, when to rise. She followed his lead, feeling slightly uncomfortable. The ceremony seemed so natural to him, she wondered whether he was still a religious man. In fact, what kind of man he was altogether.

She asked him later, outside, the incense and the magical music left behind in the splendor of the church. They were strolling with the crowd, lazily passing through the town.

"I believe in experiencing everything," he said lightly. "I guess I believe in God. Like most of us, I don't think about it much, probably won't until it's too late. No, I tell you what it was. I follow impulses. This morning we were together, and the morning was like no other morning I have ever witnessed on this earth, and I felt like thanking *somebody*, so I thought of going to church."

His feelings never embarrassed him. And he never seemed to hide them. She envied his capacity for openness.

"Were you praying?" she asked uncertainly.

"I was talking some and listening some. And taking in the music. It was an *experience*," he insisted. "I wouldn't have missed it. Would you?"

She would not.

They were lying in the meadow that afternoon—clothed this time—the white Alps, spires against a cloudless sky, in the background. She traced figures on his back, happy to touch him.

"Tell me about your mother," she murmured. He did not change position, but something in him tightened. She could feel it in her fingers.

"She wasn't meant for the life she led," he said. "I remember her mostly either sewing or looking out the window. There wasn't a thing to look at out the window in Odessa. As a kid, I wondered what she was staring at. She had come from better things than my dad. He was pure West Texas. Not one of your good ol' boys either. He was a dirt farmer. She had come from back east, New Orleans or somewhere."

His voice was as far removed as the Alps, but he kept talking, telling her everything. "It used to bother him. My mother would go to church on Sundays when there was no one but Mexicans and her. The announcements were even in Spanish. But she went to church every Sunday, and on Holy Days of Obligation." He sounded as though he were falling asleep, yet the voice continued, telling of a lone sad woman stuck in the West Texas flatlands, so far from this meadow and this lake and the breathtaking Alps.

"She left when I was ten. She left and never came back." Sam was not facing her and she dared not look at his face. "Michael was eight and Daniel six and my father and I learned how to cook that day. He never mentioned her and when we asked he just said she had gone away. After a while we gave up asking." He was silent. She could hear salon music drifting up from the hotel far away. Sunday tea was being served. She could only wonder at the wide expanse of the world; how much experience it encompassed.

Sam turned to her. "That play, the O'Neill, the mother brought up by the sisters, ready to go into the convent. What did she say at the end? 'Then I fell in love with James Tyrone, and was so happy for a time,' and holding that dress. That was Mama, staring out the window, caught in a life she never wanted." He kept on looking at Alison. "The play moved me, Alison. It was like my family in some ways."

"I didn't mean to ask you so much," Alison began, but he silenced her.

"No, why shouldn't you know? It's why I don't want to let you go." He kissed her—a long, slow, burning embrace. "I want to hold on to you forever," he said, and Alison once again felt herself caught between desire and independence.

The phone was ringing when they entered their room. Sam answered it, then handed it to Alison without a word.

The international operator asked if she was Alison Carmichael, said, "One moment, please," and then Ben Sawyer came on the line.

"Alison, I've got an emergency here," he said.

She was startled to hear his voice. How had he tracked her down in Lugano?

"Where's 'here'?" she asked.

"Kitzbühel."

"Where's that?"

"Austria. The Tyrol. What difference does it make?" he said impatiently.

"Ben, I assume you are calling me for help, and I wanted to know where you were."

"Well, I'm in the goddamn Schlosshotel Münichau in Kitzbühel and I've got a movie that's falling apart."

"Why?"

"Paul Masland, mostly. I flew to Paris to see the rushes, and they're impossible. I don't know what he's on, but prints don't match. I don't even know what he's shooting, because the performances are all incoherent."

"You think it's drugs? What about Kenny?"

"Well, I think he's clean, if that's what you mean. But he's lost and he doesn't know what he's doing, and now he's getting hostile and refusing to shoot retakes."

"And where is Diane?" Alison asked coolly.

"In the middle. Where else?" Ben replied. Alison looked up then, just in time to catch Sam's expression. It changed immediately; he gave her a bland smile, and walked out the door with a wave. She didn't have time to worry about him at the moment.

"What do you want from me?" she asked Ben.

"I want you to take over the direction of the film."

"How does Diane feel about that?"

"She realizes we've got a mess on our hands."

"No, what I meant was, how does she feel about me?"

"It's not her decision. It's mine," Ben said, evading the question.

"Is it?"

Why was it she could bring no warmth to the conversation, no encouragement even? It was as though she were talking to a stranger, the way she was protecting herself. Evidently Ben sensed this. He quoted her terms, how much salary she would get, how many points on the picture, the amount after the negative costs were paid off. She listened. The terms were fair. She had only one question for him.

"Who has the final cut?" This was a right reserved for only a few top directors. Otherwise the producer or the studio reserved the right to make that last great decision that had saved hundreds of movies, and destroyed as many.

"I can't give you that," Ben said.

"Who has it?" Alison insisted.

"Masland."

"But you're getting rid of him. Does that mean Diane gets it?" She found it hard to believe that Ben had worked himself into such a mess. He must have been desperate for money. Obviously he was desperate *now*.

"Work on it," she advised him, then added, "Where can I see the rushes? Are they still in Paris?"

He gave her the address of the projection room in Paris—as well as his phone number at the hotel in Kitzbühel. She jotted them down on a piece of paper.

"Arrange for a viewing on Monday morning. I'll call you Monday night."

"Okay, Alison," he said. He did not sound as carefree as when she had last been with him. Producing a film, producing anything, could be a humbling experience. She hated to do this, but she had found out by experience she had to.

"And Ben," she said before hanging up, "I want that final cut."

She sat still for a minute, then went out on the balcony and stared at the magnificent Alps. She was still resentful of the way Ben had treated her, using Masland as part of the package deal for director of the movie, and part of her was gloating a little that he was now having such problems. But after all, this was Ben, who was a friend, who had helped her out. He needed her now.

More than that—and her excitement was starting to grow—she was being given the chance to direct a movie, one that already tantalized her from the brief things Ben had said about it. Could she really pass up this opportunity out of bitterness and hurt pride?

But what about Sam? She shook her head decisively. Sam didn't own her, although she sometimes felt he wanted to, and she'd already told him she was determined to build a career for herself. There would be time for them to work things out when she filming was finished.

She found Sam in the bar.

"How is Ben?" he asked.

"In trouble," she said. "I've got to go back to Paris tonight."

"I thought as much. You want a drink?"

"Not if you don't." She didn't know how to handle his attitude.

"Well, I do. So you have one with me."

It came to her then. The only way to deal with Sam was directly.

"I came here for the weekend with you. I think I love you. But I also have my own life, and a career. Besides, I thought you liked Ben."

"I *like* the son of a bitch," he conceded. "What I don't like is the way you can get on the phone and forget all about me."

What he said was true, Alison realized.

"What can I do about that?" she said. "Are you telling me that if you had taken a business call, you wouldn't have forgotten about me?"

"The point was, I arranged not to take any calls."

"Then your business is in better shape than mine is."

"Obviously," he said, and the way he said it was like a slap in the face. It brought tears to her eyes.

"I thought you loved me."

"I do," he insisted.

"No. I think you want to possess me. And I can't handle that."

"I do want to possess you," he said thickly. He didn't understand the difference. His eyes turned stubborn with passion, hard with masculine determination. She couldn't argue with him and she couldn't deal with this. She rose from her seat.

"I'm going to pack," she said, "and make the reservations."

"Don't bother. I'll take care of the reservations. You want the evening flight to Paris?"

"If you please."

"I'm going to Geneva in the morning."

They were ending badly, and she didn't want that. She thought about them while she packed. Wasn't it possible to be lovers and friends? Was it necessary to possess each other's lives? And then it occurred to her that she might not love him if he didn't—as opposed to Kenny Buck—need her so completely.

At the airport, before she boarded the plane, they exchanged phone numbers. She knew his company's number, but now he gave her a list of private numbers that confused her. It was as though he were trying to make up for his former coldness.

"I feel quite poor," she said. "I can only give you Nagy's number in Paris. You know my number in New York. Oh, and it's possible I might be here"—she wrote down the number of the hotel in Kitzbühel that Ben had given her—"but I don't know if, or for how long," she finished lamely.

"Thank you, ma'am," he said dryly. "Just don't end up like most of the bachelors I know. No place of their own, and suitcases and belongings scattered all over the world."

Was he being sarcastic, she wondered, using the word *bachelor*? His eyes gave no hint, and she decided that she had been very wrong about him. He only let you see what he wanted you to see, and there was a great deal that he kept to himself.

"How long will you be in Geneva?" she asked, to make conversation.

"Until my business is finished," he said, but did not elaborate.

"Are you saying good-bye to me?"

"More the other way around."

"Did you expect me to go to Geneva with you?"

"It's a beautiful city."

"Sam." She shook her head sadly. "Maybe we shouldn't see each other until we've straightened this out about our lives."

He nodded, apparently in agreement. Then, abruptly, he got up.

"I won't say good-bye. It hurts too much," he said. He left her and was immediately swallowed up in the international bustle of Zurich's shiny airport.

Chapter Twenty-seven

Nagy was in the apartment when she returned late that night. She threw her arms around him.

"I've only been in Germany, not around the world," he said, laughing.

"I've missed you."

He nodded at the stack of newspapers he had saved for her. "So I see. You obviously needed my help."

She looked at him apprehensively. "Are they bad, the notices?"

"Only one. *L'Humanité*. But O'Neill doesn't fit in with any party line. Don't worry. However, the T.N.P. has called up six times since I arrived, which was Friday night. They are upset because you left." He walked toward the phone and started to sort out the pieces of paper. "They want to extend the run. They would like a third piece to replace the Wilder." He read more. "Oh, and they would like to give a party in your honor. The press, of course, would be invited."

Alison sat down in one of the chairs. She relaxed in triumph. "Oh, would they? In my honor? Too late, I think."

Nagy looked amused. "Where have you been, my darling? You are slightly tanned and very rested, and you look enormously self-satisfied."

"I was away for the weekend. With Sam Pendexter."

Nagy's eyebrows lifted in surprise. "How interesting."

"I spent the weekend with him and I never thought

once about Paris and the productions and I think I'm in love with him, which is a horrible problem because he is jealous. Nagy, he's jealous of my life and my career." She stopped, out of breath.

"Obviously I came back just in time," he said. "Did you part on bad terms?"

"Not bad, exactly. Well, yes, I guess we did. I said we shouldn't see each other until we've resolved this problem." Suddenly she looked like a little schoolgirl in the big chair. She leaned forward. "Oh, Nagy, I do love him so. He's an incredible man."

"You're leaving out something." Nagy looked at her perceptively.

"Ben. I'm leaving out Ben. And Kenny." She began to laugh. "I sound like the town pump!" she exclaimed. He didn't understand the reference. "It's a term for the girl in town who's most easily had by everybody," she explained. "Now, Ben called from Austria, I don't know how he got the number," she added as an aside.

"The box-office man at the T.N.P. is an old friend of mine." Nagy shrugged. "Hungarian. He told me you had picked up a *laisser-passer* for an American man, and I assumed that was Sam. I then started calling the hotels, luckily starting with the Ritz. The concierge·there is an old friend of mine. Has a Hungarian mother."

"Do you Hungarians always stick together?"

"Only when absolutely necessary," he said wryly.

"So you knew! All this time I've been talking! You knew exactly where I'd been." She stopped for a moment and looked at him. "I suppose you have a chef at the Splendide Royale who also has a Hungarian mother."

Nagy was shocked. "Do you think I would spy on you! You have no faith in your friends."

"I have no faith in you!" she said, and then immediately contradicted herself. "Oh, Nagy, I do need your help. This may sound crazy to you, but Ben has asked me to take over the direction of his movie."

Nagy, wise in the vagaries of filmmaking, merely smiled. "Masland was living a little too 'high'?" he asked.

"Evidently. You would have been very proud of me. I

asked for all the right terms. Diane is in there somewhere, either protecting her clients or trying to be a producer. . . ."

"I only know one position of Diane's," Nagy recalled, "and she was very successful at that."

Alison ignored that. "I'm supposed to go look at the rushes tomorrow morning to see if there's anything to salvage. Frankly I don't know what I'm doing."

"I'm glad you're so honest. Be less so when you talk to movie people. You must always know exactly what you're doing. And then you go get help from the crew. Make friends with the cameraman, the editor, and make sure you take enough 'cover' shots. You'll do fine."

Alison was a little more cautious than that. "Come with me tomorrow. Maybe there's nothing I can do. You can tell me."

"I'll come with you, but believe me, you will know what the film is like. How much has been shot?"

"Evidently most of the action shots, the skiing. And—well, we'll see tomorrow, won't we?"

Nagy nodded. "Yes. We'll see."

The screening room was off the Champs-Élysées. Everything had been prepared for a viewing. The copies of the script were in a manila envelope, pads and pencils had been set out for note-taking. The staff obviously concluded, when they saw Nagy, that he had ordered the viewing and became superefficient. Nagy introduced them to Alison, and left it up to her to set them straight.

She did.

The room darkened, and the numbers began to roll on the screen. Nagy lit a cigarette. The first day's work had been a love scene between Kenny and a young blond woman. They were in bed evidently, but it was too dark to see more than shadows and a vague movement of bodies. Alison watched in silence for a moment. Her first instinct was to order the film stopped and to leave. Then she thought perhaps it was some kind of monstrous joke that either Ben—could Ben possibly be so sordid?—or perhaps Diane—who certainly had that kind of intelligence—had ordered played on her.

"Westerling's work," Nagy commented. "He always

shoots as though he had been brought up in a dungeon. One can see nothing. In this case perhaps it's just as well."

The next day's rushes were exterior shots of the preparation for a downhill competition. All the young men were shown at the top of the mountain, snapping on their goggles, adjusting helmets, crouching, eyeing one another and the course down the mountain. The scenery was breathtaking. The scene had tension.

"*Not* Westerling," Nagy said, puzzled. "Seems more like Jimmy Smith. Now *he* is first-class."

A moment later Kenny Buck's face appeared on the screen, first in a medium shot, and then in a close-up. And Alison decided then and there that she should do the film. There was a weariness on his face that touched her. Kenny's look had always been fascinating, but there had been such confidence, such power, that nothing else ever showed. Now, evidently, life had caught up with him too. When she had first learned of the project, the idea of Kenny playing a ski bum with one last chance for glory had seemed money-motivated. But now, viewing the rushes, she realized that Ben had made an inspired choice. Kenny was absolutely right.

However, during the course of the screening, Alison could detect a change in Kenny's performance. It was as though he had withdrawn from the production. Often, in shots angled to focus on him, he seemed to dissolve into the background. She could not understand why. And the film work itself was a jumble. Ben had been correct. Shots did not match up with one another. Take after take missed the right moment, the right reaction.

They came to the end, the lights were brought up. Nagy stubbed out his fifth cigarette in the ashtray. He and Alison looked at each other.

"See if Jimmy Smith is still the director of photography on this film," he said. "If so, do it. If not, forget it. Westerling is impossible. I don't know whose work the middle section is, but it is no one who can help you. Or the film editor."

"Kenny could be good," Alison said, wanting to check her own reaction.

"He could be wonderful. He could even be an actor,"

Nagy said. "Something happens to him in the middle of this mess. He disappears."

"Can you come along?" she asked.

"To hold your hand? No, my darling, I must return to Somewhere in Germany. Maybe I never leave Somewhere in Germany. Oh, God, when are they going to get tired of shooting these East-West spy pictures?"

"Then if I do this, I have to do it all alone."

"Alison, I told you. You get your right cameraman. And you make a friend of him. He will always tell you, 'No this shot will not work, why not try it this way?' If you're smart, you listen to him. And you find out how to make a movie. You're good at this thing. You pick up fast. You will learn." He lit a cigarette and squinted. "What can you lose? If it doesn't work, they blame the other director. If it does work, you get the credit. And you learn. Just thank your stars you are not shooting *The Blue Bird* in Russia. I hear they all get scurvy. No green vegetables. The tapwater runs brown. You only drink vodka. At least where you're going"—he had already made up his mind she was—"you will have a good time. And if you're lucky, you'll have a good film."

Alison said nothing for a few minutes, then asked for a telephone and called Ben in Kitzbühel. He answered with a dull "Hello."

"Who is your director of photography?" she asked him.

"Jimmy Smith," he said, "but he's leaving."

"Tell him to stay," she ordered.

"You tell him. He's here."

Alison passed the phone to Nagy. "You know Jimmy Smith? You talk to him."

Nagy took the phone, sighing. "After all I do for you, you should at least go to bed with me."

"We would giggle too much," she said.

"What's wrong with that?" he retorted, then switched tones and became the important filmmaker.

"Hello, Jimmy. It's Nagy here. What are you doing down there in the Alps? Has the altitude gotten to you?"

He listened, making sympathetic sounds and managing to light another cigarette at the same time. Then he began to talk again. "Yes, I can see all of what you say is true. We have just finished the rushes. It is chaos. But I am with Alison. Do you know her? No? Well, you will get to know her. She is smart. You will get on well together—"

There was an explosion of sound on the other end of the phone that even Alison could hear. Nagy went on as though nothing had happened. "She is very talented, she will listen, take suggestions." More words from the other end, all negative.

"I have taught her myself. I would use her. You have the makings of a first-class film. Your work is first-rate. Now, trust me!"

This time there was no argument from the other end.

"What you will do is meet with Alison, you will spend three days together and decide what is needed and then you will do it and have a marvelous success. Will you do that? Good. She is flying down this afternoon. Now pass me to Ben."

His look to Alison said, This was nothing. You see how simple it is? But she knew he was basking in her admiration.

"Hello, Ben. You have worked out the terms, yes, for Alison? I would not want her to make a trip for nothing. Yeah, sure, I know there are lawyers. You are a lawyer. I want *you* to protect Alison. And by the way, what is wrong with Kenny? Is it something Alison can fix?"

He listened for a moment and then handed Alison the phone. "It's very simple," he said. "Besides the director, what's wrong with the film is they're having a party down there."

"What about final cut?" Alison asked Ben.

"It's yours," he said. "I talked to Diane."

"What is her involvement?"

"She's an investor," he said carefully.

"Is she also a producer?"

"We are partners," he admitted.

"Then I want everything in writing, all the agreements, by the time I get there."

"You'll have them."

They hung up and she turned to Nagy. "What am I getting into?"

The familiar crinkle edged Nagy's eyes. "It sounds extremely interesting. Phone me in Berlin."

Austria. The Tyrol. Chalets and snow and horse-drawn sleighs with bells jingling. Skiers everywhere. It took Alison time to adjust. There'd been Paris—a world she had conquered, at least for the moment. Lugano, which had been like eternal spring. And now Winter Carnival.

The hotel lay two miles out of town. It had been called a *Schloss,* a castle, but she hadn't expected a real one—a hunting castle with towers and turrets and great walls. Beyond the spires loomed the Alps, greater, grander peaks.

Before leaving Paris she and Nagy had run through all the dailies one more time, making copious notes on what would and would not be usable, so Alison felt more than a little prepared for her meeting with the crew. But she still approached the Schlosshotel Münichau with trepidation.

No one had met her at the station—not that she had expected them to. With this kind of chaos she could imagine the frantic calls to New York and Beverly Hills, the appeal to money men in Brazil and Zurich. And since the production had been halted for several days, she could picture the international crew, the grips, the lighting men, cameramen, script girl, costumer, supporting players, Kenny even, sitting in the gloom of the restored Knight's Hall, staring into their beers.

She hadn't expected a house party, even though she had been warned. The lobby was jumping. Blue jeans and cowboys boots were everywhere. Swell-looking sportswear from Olympia and Cacharel. Après-ski, the latest and most expensive. A roaring fire and a live trio. Drinks. Laughter. A poker game.

She thought she was in the wrong place. Where was the chaos? The disaster? All around her, as it turned out.

The film crew had taken over the entire hotel, and the management was not happy with the results. They were used to the sexual cavorting. Winter sports and filming seemed to produce the same results. Lots of appetite for everything. Food, drink, and sex.

But this group made it impossible to keep track of the

number of registered guests and the number of *their* guests. Young men, young girls, poodles, and pomeranians drifted in and out of the hotel, and tended to nap on the furniture in the lobby. They kept the chambermaids very busy. The desk clerk. The manager.

And now the latest character to appear carried nothing but a rather battered bag from the Bottega Veneta and an overnight bag from Vuitton. The label-conscious desk clerk recognized her immediately as being the real thing. But what was she? *Whose* was she?

"Madam," he said tentatively. "May I be of assistance?"

"I have a reservation. Alison Carmichael." The clerk looked doubtful. Alison prodded him. "Made, I believe, by Mr. Sawyer."

Ah, Mr. Sawyer, one of the sane ones, the desk clerk thought. He became much more helpful and found a bellboy to carry Miss Carmichael's luggage to her room. If she would be so good as to follow the boy . . .

"Where is Mr. Sawyer?" Alison asked.

"Apartment Twelve. It is down the hall from your apartment."

"Thank you," she said, gracing him with a smile, and proceeded up the stairs to the first floor.

Several doors were open. This was a college house party, she decided as she glimpsed a lot of bed-sitting, groups of people collected in rooms. The acrid odor of marijuana reached her nostrils. She walked on, found her apartment, gave the boy a tip. He was a blond peasant boy, quite good-looking. It occurred to her that he quite possibly had been involved in more action than would come his way for the rest of his life.

She changed into a pair of jeans and a white wool sweater. She combed her hair until it curled naturally around her face. She looked supreme, glowing. A triumph in Paris, a lover in Lugano, and now the offer of a movie could do that.

Ben Sawyer was in his apartment with Diane; Kenny, fast asleep on the white sofa; and an emaciated man with fashionably long hair, a graying goatee, and wearing the slightly offbeat outfit that was now de rigueur. Faded jeans, faded denim cowboy shirt. He was inhaling with a rolled-up piece of paper the little white powder that was piled on the cocktail table. That, Alison thought, must be Paul Masland.

It was quite obvious what the problem was. Masland and cocaine. Not uncommon, this problem, but a bother. It gave every taker such grandiose ideas, and then proceeded to make them paranoid and irritable.

Masland's greeting was unexpectedly euphoric for a director who had just been fired. He finished his snort and gave her an expansive "Hi! Welcome to the club!" His mood was not matched by Diane and Ben. Kenny had nothing to say; he was out cold.

"What's going on here?" Alison demanded of Ben, but Masland gave the answer.

"It's a groove. Hell of a party."

"What are you doing here?" she asked him.

"You want a hit?"

"No, I don't. Ben. Diane. Explain this to me."

"I'm Paul Masland," the crouched figure continued.

"I know who you are."

"You want to go to my place?"

"I'm Alison Carmichael."

"Glad to know you, Alison," he said affably. She looked at Ben and Diane. Hadn't they told him?

"I'm replacing you," she said.

"Yeah, I know. You'll do a hell of a job, a hell of a job. Sure you don't want to come to my place?"

"No. Listen, Mr. Masland. I need to speak to these people alone."

"Don't mind me. I don't hold any grudges. Hey, I blew it. But I start work next week on a new horror film. A beauty. Classic. You'll love it."

Alison lost her temper. "Get this together," she shouted. "You, Diane, get him out! Ben, I want our male star here awake. Where is Jimmy Smith? I am not about to play housemother in this overblown chalet."

"Good luck!" Masland said as he left with Diane.

Alison looked at Ben. "How could you let this happen?"

"It got out of hand," he said. "I had to go back to the Coast for a couple of days, and when I returned, well, I found our own little Mardi Gras."

"Who are all these people?"

"If you think I know the names of most of them, you're crazy. I don't even know their nationalities."

"How long has this been going on?"

"I came back Tuesday. I saw the dailies on Wednesday and located you on Sunday."

"And tried to get how many directors before you found me?"

"A lot," he answered honestly. "But then the problem didn't seem to be Masland. It was Kenny. He's on a little of everything now. For the first couple of weeks Masland was his buddy. They were like soldiers on leave. And then Kenny felt things weren't going the way they should. Your Kenny is fairly intuitive."

"One, he's not my Kenny, and two, it's the Indian in him."

"Diane suggested you."

That shocked Alison.

"I thought that might set you back a bit. Frankly I didn't know how you felt about him. I knew how you felt about her. I wasn't sure how you felt about me."

"A little to the right of throwing a plate of spaghetti," she said. The old smile returned, thank God. She thought, let's just get at the work and forget all the rest of this. It's too messy, and it's too long ago.

"And you didn't hear about any of this on the Coast. Weren't you in touch with Diane?"

"She covered it up."

"Some partner."

"It's her money too," he said defensively.

"Yeah, and her star and her director. Well, do you have the papers? And Jimmy Smith? What are you going to do with Sleeping Box-Office there?" She indicated Kenny.

"He had a bad night."

"Everyone did," she retorted.

Ben went to find Jimmy Smith, and Alison looked at Kenny. She was having second thoughts. Maybe this was a mistake. She stared at his sleeping face. It still aroused her. It brought back many memories. She had loved to watch him as he slept, because it was the only time she had felt in control. And in some way she had wanted that control, she realized now. She had wanted to direct him. She walked over to him. His hair was long and uncombed, jet-black, his face covered by a stray lock. With one finger she brushed it away from his face. He stirred in his sleep, then, abruptly, his eyes opened, focused, and he saw her.

"You came," he said slowly, happily, and went back to sleep like a small child who had seen Santa Claus.

Jimmy Smith was a Californian. He also wore the jeans, the cowboy boots, a sheepskin coat. On him, they looked right. He had grown up on a ranch, spent every Saturday night at the movies, and finally at fifteen, hitch-hiked out of that little dried-up town on the other side of the desert to Los Angeles. It had been hard getting into the movies, but he had made a pest of himself and finally got on the lot. Once there, he saw to it he kept busy, kept his eyes open, made friends, found the opportunity to make a little experimental movie. And was discovered. Now, for the past five years, he had been hot. He had the sense of style the way Nestor and Bowman had theirs.

At the beginning his meeting with Alison did not go well.

"I told Ben to get that Swedish guy," Smith said. "He's beautiful. He can give you everything you want."

"He's busy," Ben said.

Jimmy Smith spread his long legs out on the bed. "Well, postone then. It can't be more than a couple of weeks."

"We don't have a couple of weeks," Diane reminded him.

"I know. You told me that already," he said to her, and the tone in his voice changed.

He'd been sleeping with her, Alison thought, and she'd already given him one too many orders. It was time to step in.

"I understand you don't like working with a woman."

"Working *under* a woman," he corrected her. Diane rose. Alison felt she could detect the slightest flush under all that makeup.

"Let's see how you like working *with* one," she suggested. "I made my notes before leaving Paris."

"I made some here, too, as we went along."

"Well, let's compare them."

No man was going to resist that smile. She became so feminine, so blond and aboveboard. There was no way he was going to fight her.

They went to the bar at Knight's Hall and sat under a banner that had hung there since the days of the Third Crusade. He drank Scotch, straight, and she ordered a half bottle of white wine. They went to work.

They had no disagreement. What Jimmy had suspected in the shooting, Alison corroborated in the viewing. The same scenes. The same amount of work to be done.

"You've got to help me," she pleaded, taking Nagy's advice. "I don't know what a motion picture camera is capable of. If I make a fool of myself out there, I'm going to blame it all on you."

He smiled, accepting her flattery as his due, then looked at her seriously. "I'll help you any way you need, but you're gonna have to handle Kenny by yourself. There's no way I can help you there."

"I saw one scene," she said. "At the top of the mountain, just before the competition. I liked that."

"Yeah. Ol' Kenny had tied one on the night before. He was dragging ass."

"Well, maybe that's what he needs."

"Whatever it is, you gotta supply it. I can't."

"That's a deal. Don't run out on me now."

"I wouldn't do that. If I say I'll stay, I'll stay."

"Then say you'll stay."

"I thought I made that clear."

"I just wanted to hear you say it," she confessed, "because I have a tough couple of months ahead of me." They shook hands under the banner of Ethridge the Courageous.

That evening, after dinner, Alison called a meeting with Ben, Diane, Jimmy, and Kenny Buck. Kenny chose to attend with a small dark-haired beauty who hung placidly on his arm.

"Who is she?" Alison asked.

"I don't know. I don't even know what language she speaks, but she sure is sweet."

"Out!" Alison ordered. Kenny looked at her, mildly amused, then shrugged and handed the girl the key to his hotel room. "Later. *Später,*" he said. The little brunette nodded and docilely left the room.

"Kenny. You first, because you are the most important. No more cocaine." She could sense him tense. He had never liked orders, unless he was giving them. "And get rid of the girls, the hangers-on. You got work to do."

"She don't hurt nothing. None of them hurt nothing."

"Don't come on dumb with me, Kenny. Never do that to me, cause I know you so well," she warned him. He fluctuated between resentment and amusement. And maybe a little respect. That was hard for her to judge. At any rate amusement won out.

"Then you want me straight all the time," he said.

"That's right. Straight, and sober. And ready for work. You agree?"

He looked to Diane for confirmation. She hardly moved her head, but he saw her nod.

"You're it, Alison. I take orders from you for the moment."

"That's right, Kenny. From me, and from me only." She then looked at Ben and Diane. "See that all these extras, whoever they are, get out of here. It's impossible to have this February Frolic and also make a movie. Who are the paid personnel and who are the freebies?"

Ben gave her a list. She handed it to Diane. "Here, you get rid of the unwanted. You've had experience in that department."

Everyone was smiling, it seemed. No matter what Alison had to say, they smiled. Kenny smiled. Diane. Everyone except Jimmy Smith. No, she saw he was smiling too. Why? At the change in attitude? Ben's smile was one of relief. Nagy's words came back to her. *You must always know exactly what you're doing.*

"Now, day after tomorrow I want to begin shooting. Will the weather hold so that Jimmy and I can go over continuity?"

"We're in for a week of good weather, so I'm told,"

Ben said. "Nice to have a little luck for a change. Maybe you brought it with you, Alison."

"Oh, perhaps, Ben," she said with a trace of irritation in her voice. "And perhaps it isn't a question of luck."

As it happened, a storm delayed the shooting of exteriors, so two days after she arrived, Alison was forced to do an interior. The first scene on her list was the love scene between Kenny and the little snow bunny, Julia Craven, who turned out to be a very nice girl and a straight-ahead actress.

The setup was for seven in the morning. The hotel staff had suddenly become terribly efficient. There was coffee, Austrian pastry. The entire crew devoured fluffy baked goods with long German names and drank the steaming coffee with gusto. And then sat around to watch.

The new girl on the job. What would she be like? Alison knew that's what they were thinking. She conferred with Jimmy.

"I want to start from overhead," she said, "and then come in on them. Then shoot it from behind the bars of the headboard. Can you get a hand-held camera and just follow me?"

"We'll try it, see if it works," Jimmy said noncommitally, then whispered, "They won't know. Try anything."

"Is the lighting okay? I mean, the last time it was like the dead of night."

The plot of the episode was familiar to Alison. Kenny's character, the Ski Pro, had been in training for nearly a month. In two days the Olympic event, the first run, would be covered, and in this scene he was falling back on what he knew best: how to drink and how to seduce a woman. Snow Bunny had come to his room because Jean-Claude Killy and Stein Eriksen were not available. The dialogue was rudimentary:

SNOW BUNNY: Do you really know Killy?
SKI PRO: I've met him.
SNOW BUNNY: What's he like?
SKI PRO: He's French.
SNOW BUNNY: Are you anybody?

SKI PRO: I was once.

SNOW BUNNY: And now . . .

SKI PRO: That's what I want to see—if I still am anybody. Any more questions, or can we go to bed?

SNOW BUNNY: Oh, sure, we can go to bed. But I just like to know whether I'm sleeping with a somebody or not. It's hard to tell. You're all so tanned.

SKI PRO: (Stripping her) I got a tan that don't fade.

SNOW BUNNY: Oh. That must save you a lot of money.

SKI PRO: (Taking her to bed) It almost makes me a somebody.

FOCUS ON THEIR LOVEMAKING

Kenny and Julie sat and listened while Alison explained what she wanted.

"Don't play it sexy, Julie. To you it's like chewing gum. You just pop another piece in your mouth." That brought a laugh or two.

She looked at Kenny. "I don't know what to say to you yet. Let's just rehearse the scene."

She was fine, Julie the snow bunny. She was funny and very matter-of-fact. At first Kenny tried to top her, making the lines funny. They just turned out smart-ass. Alison took him aside.

"Don't try to be funny. It won't work. Just get her into the bed. She's some kind of lifeline for you. The fact is, you're scared and you got a race in two days and the best way to forget about it is to fuck. Use her. She's using you."

Kenny glanced at her. She stared right back at him. "Isn't that what this scene is about?" she asked quietly. He nodded.

They ran the scene again. It was much better. Alison could see she would have to be careful with Kenny. He was walking a fine line at the moment. She recognized the case of nerves. Well, why not? It was only his career on the line.

Before she ordered the cameras to roll, she whispered to Kenny, "I saw what you could do. On film. In Paris. You will be wonderful here. I'll see to that." And he gave her the same look of wonder that he'd given her when she first arrived at the hotel.

He was quite good, until he and Julie were in the bed. He started to kiss her hungrily. Poor Snow Bunny. This gave her nothing to do but writhe and simulate some kind of pornographic movie. Alison moved in closer and began to issue directions to the two of them.

"Touch the top of her lip with your tongue, Kenny . . . How does it taste? Julie, do you like what he's doing? Does it tickle? Do you want to laugh? Do it. Kenny, what does that do to you? When is the last time you laughed? Do you like it? Good! Then hold off. Let your lips brush each other's. Do not touch. Imagine what it will be like to touch each other. Kiss her eyelids. No, as gently as a butterfly. Now! Gently . . . gently. . . . Kiss her fully."

Ben met Alison in the corridor late that night. He took hold of her arm.

"I want to thank you, Alison."

"Oh, Ben. It's work. You're paying me to do this. And I love doing it. You don't need to thank me."

"But I do. And I want to."

She found herself in his arms, glad to be there. It was late and she was confused. She wasn't sure she saw him clearly. Was it him? Was it Sam? She needed a man's arms around her, that was certain. She welcomed Ben's.

"You want a drink?" he asked her softly.

"I don't know."

"That means yes."

"I'm too tired to go back to the bar."

"I've got a bottle."

In his room he poured some Scotch and she drank it neat.

"No ice?" he asked.

"Too much bother," she said.

"No bother at all." He grinned, went to the window, picked an icicle off the eave, and broke it in two.

"Thanks," she said. They sat beside each other on the

couch. She was overly aware of his proximity. He was staring at her. She felt the attraction. Always had. He was what all those Andover boys never turned out to be: Dashing. Fun. If not too reliable. But then, nobody had ever been that reliable. She drank more Scotch. He moved in, set down her drink, kissed her. At first she just let him, but then began to respond on her own. She hadn't thought she was lonely. Maybe it was seeing Kenny making love to the little snow bunny. Where was Sam now? She couldn't concentrate.

"I'm very attracted to you tonight," she said to Ben. "Does this always happen on location?"

"Beats me. This is my first time," he said, and they both laughed. On-location virgins, the two of them, Alison thought. And then she felt his hands discovering her breasts, and she wanted to make love with him. Her bed was lonely. She was lonely.

The phone rang. He groaned, did not answer it. It persisted, annoyingly, until he did. It was Diane, of course, with a financial problem, telling him he had to go to Paris on the morning plane. By the time he hung up, the magic was gone. Alison was just plain tired. She drained her glass and got up.

"Don't go," he said, but she shook her head.

"Bad timing."

He held her. "Stay," he said. It was almost a command. He followed it with a demanding kiss. She didn't want that now. She just wanted sleep. She shook her head again. They looked at each other.

"Guess you're right," he said, that life-saving grin on his face. "Bad timing."

"Good night," she said sleepily. "Enjoy Paris."

Chapter Twenty-eight

It was a mad four weeks for Alison, but also perhaps the most exciting she had ever known.

Actors had told her how boring moviemaking was. She didn't have time to be bored. Impatient, yes. The resetting of lights—indeed, all the mechanical processes that went with film—seemed to take forever. If she had been better briefed, she might have found the preparations intolerable. But as it was, she welcomed the opportunity to plan the next scene, the next setup, the next shoot, the next day's schedule. If she had a speciality, it was shooting the two shots, the medium shots, the relationships. She discovered the linkage between actor and character and exploited it to the fullest. Her ability to create excited her. For an action film, there were many levels of feeling. The Ski Pro's desire for victory, his self-loathing, his womanizing, his loneliness, his competitiveness with the other younger members of the Olympic team. He was a man who had never faced the future and suddenly found himself growing older—with no future to face. He had sacrificed everything for his desire to ski. And that was what Alison had to express. She had to capture the almost sexual euphoria of sweeping through parallel turns, body flowing, knees driven forward, leaning down with the snow spraying glittering arcs off the edges of the skis. Skiers called it a rush. Alison, amateur skier that she was, could understand that. But how to capture it on film? That was where Jimmy and Kenny both came to her rescue. Jimmy could station cameras all along the course. He was a magician. He found a way to capture every facet of the excitement and challenge of a downhill run.

And Kenny.

Kenny insisted on performing all the runs himself. He argued that the stuntman was not the same thing. Alison was after reality, and Kenny was going to give it to her. He was tireless. Each run seemed to give him more energy. He, like the character, knew the "rush."

Although he would not admit it to himself, it was the only way to stay off coke. He needed the substitute. He never complained. He performed like an athlete in training. The film was his own Olympics, to prove that he was more than a remnant of the sixties. He was holding on to his perch in the seventies by his fingertips. He realized that the fan clubs were diminishing, that the publicity agents had to work harder to get his picture in the media.

Alison watched him change almost by the minute. The constant skiing trimmed his body down, burned the waste off him; he became leaner. It accentuated his jawbone, the cheekbones. The Indian in him came to the fore. Only now there were lines; the face was weathered. The eyes had seen too much. Only in skiing, only in the wild sunny brilliance of the Alpine *piste* did the sparkle return, that incredible youthful vitality that she had first known.

She exploited every second of this—as he had exploited her. She exhausted him, and he came back for more. She ordered retake after retake until she was satisfied. He never complained. He welcomed the opportunity to channel all that energy into some pursuit that would let him sleep nights.

And he did sleep—without the Seconal or the Placidyl. He dropped off at eight o'clock, was up at five the next morning, and out on the slopes by seven to catch the early-morning alpine light.

They all slept like exhausted soldiers and woke refreshed, ready to do battle with creativity once more. Again Alison sensed the feeling of family—the company whose members are all working together; who, for the few brief weeks they are assembled, become one another's comrades. And it didn't hurt that Diane had left for Paris. Kenny relaxed. After the day's shooting, like skiers they all gathered around the fire in their medieval castle, drank a few beers, told a few stories, reminisced about Hollywood, gossiped, then ate together at one long table in the Great Hall. The food was hearty and plentiful. Great mounds of roast potatoes, schnitzel, boiled beef, carts of pastries. They gorged themselves. With all the exercise on the slopes, there was no chance of gaining weight. At the end of two weeks the crew looked like a goddamn health club, Alison mused. The sallow Parisians were bursting with some inner peasant vitality; the Americans had lost that laid-back Hollywood exhaustion.

They were happy. Too happy maybe. Alison was crazy to see the rushes. Ben and Diane had insisted that they be processed in Paris. In some kind of dumb move they wanted to fly Alison to Paris to view them.

Diane returned with a totally new series of ensembles from the Givenchy collection, modeled them, and was disappointed that nobody seemed to care. She, too, was aware of the change in the company—and in Kenny.

The moment she saw Alison her first night back she said, "I've looked at the rushes. They're fabulous!"

"Really?" Alison said.

"Would I lie to you?" Her reply was less then reassuring to Alison. Later that night she approached Ben.

"Why can't we rent the little theater here, anyplace that has a projector? Why must I go to Paris? I have no time."

Ben, who was now as immersed as anyone in the action side of the film, shook his head.

"Dumb. Maybe one-hundred-grand dumb. That's what I've been. Sure, we'll fly the dailies in. We'll find a place. Hey, maybe we'll even charge admission. It'll make up for the fact we're over budget."

They were, in fact, quite over budget. Having allotted so much time and money to ensure privacy on two of the downhill slopes and having rented the hotel—for a fortune—they were now running close to the edge. It was high season in Kitzbühel. Fortunately they were two miles from the village, but of course, word had gotten around that a movie was being made, and they found it necessary to set up ropes and barriers to keep away the curious.

It didn't hurt Kenny's ego to be pointed out. The only difference—which he detected—was that three years ago his fans would have broken down any barriers to get to their idol. Now they were simply satisfied with pointing him out, another feature of their European junket for Americans. But it all helped.

The night the collection of dailies were flown in— Alison had to laugh; there were almost two weeks worth of *dailies*—she ordered that no one but her, Jimmy Smith, and Ben were allowed to view the film. Kenny pouted.

"No," she said. "I don't want you to know anything."

They waited in the little village cinema for the projectionist to arrange the reels. Then the lights darkened and they sat and waited for magic to appear on the screen. They had worked so hard. Alison looked at Jimmy. Veteran though he was, his excitement was showing. Alison feared she might throw up. The thought flashed through her mind of that day in Paris years ago, the breathless excitement of running through the streets, the anticipation of seeing the results of her first work.

Watching dailies is not like watching any movie. There is no score; no continuity. Only the endless number of printed takes. You look for the moment, again the right moment, hope for enough of them to build a character, a conflict, a mood, a story. It must all be there. Alison watched, hardly daring to breathe.

The first reel consisted mostly of the action shots. She gasped at the color. The film seemed to spring out from the screen. She clutched Jimmy Smith's hand. "Oh, you bastard, you really did it. Look! Look!"

Ben was just muttering happily, "Sweet Jesus, Jesus, sweet Jesus." Jimmy Smith was chuckling. Better than they had expected. Better than they had ever dreamed of! And Kenny. That desperate sunburned visage filled the screen. Like all good screen actors, he seemed to be doing nothing, but you knew exactly what he was thinking. He *was* the Ski Pro, hurtling toward the bottom of the mountain, straining every muscle to beat the next man's time.

Alison had seen that look on another face. Illie Nastase
going for the title at Wimbledon a year or so back. The
ferocity in the face was identical.

The projectionist stopped to change reels and already
Jimmy and Alison were huddled together, discussing selection with Ben.

"Get Huttner for an editor," Jimmy told Ben. "He'll
cut this film like a bitch. Christ, even I could cut what I've
seen so far."

The second reel began to unroll. It was the love
scene. The first printed take that Alison had liked so much
at the time fell flat; Julie was pushing too much. Kenny,
however, seemed better than he had in reality. Ah-ha,
Alison thought, she was going to have to be very careful
with this one. He took to the camera like a natural and the
camera loved him. The second take appeared; Julie was
more real this time, therefore both funnier and more
vulnerable. Was the chemistry there between the two of
them? Kenny gave his snow bunny a look; it sizzled. The
sensuality and the weariness combined to give the scene a
loneliness that was lovely to watch. The two actors played
well together. As man and woman, they were inevitable.
They had to reach the bed. Once they were there, Alison
saw her own magic take hold. The way she had coached
Kenny to make love paid off. Each caress of his hands
seemed both tender and doomed; his thirst for her lips
came across as a thirst that could never be quenched.
Their lovemaking was forcefully tangible. The last shot on
that reel was of the morning after, the Ski Pro gazing at
the dawn. Alison had gambled on one take.

On screen, the Ski Pro rolled away from his sleeping
partner. Alison had placed him so that there was a key
light on his eyes to pick up the least flicker of emotion.
The camera focused on his face. Strong, sad eyes viewed
the light of yet another morning. Alison had whispered to
him at that moment, and his reaction had been to close his
eyes for a second, to shut out the world and the pain and
the knowledge that he was growing older. Then his eyes
opened again and blazed with the old fury, the determination of a man getting ready for a challenge.

"Cut it right there," Jimmy said softly. He put his hand on Alison's. It was a gesture of congratulation.

Ben whistled. "Well if that ain't a kick in the head." He sat for a moment, then jumped up. "Who'd you say should be film editor?" he asked Jimmy.

"Huttner."

"How do I reach him?"

"I'll get you his number. Better still, I'll talk to him myself."

"Call on my phone. Or charge it to me."

"You bet your ass I will. It'll take some convincing. He likes his ranch too much. Where will you do this anyway?"

"Oh, I think we should cut it on the Coast, don't you, Alison?"

"I'm becoming a gypsy at heart. You can cut it in Timbuktu if you get me a good editor," Alison said.

"He's the best," Jimmy assured her. "For this kind of movie he's the best."

The third reel was ready and they sat down again to watch, but their minds, all three of them, were already four weeks ahead of schedule.

After that night's viewing Alison, Ben, and Jimmy formed a team. Kenny agreed that he should never see the rushes. He trusted Alison. Diane fumed, but there was nothing she could do about it.

She did confront Alison once.

"Listen," she said, "I am one of the producers, and I feel I should be in on every decision."

"I work best when people stay out of my way," Alison said firmly.

"Well, you have Ben with you."

"Ben isn't in my way."

"I know a lot about the movie business," Diane said rather loudly.

"Diane. I know exactly how much you know about everything. I agreed to do this on my terms. If that's not satisfactory, I'll leave."

Diane turned away. It was a small victory for Alison, but it made her feel good. From then on Diane always greeted her with a ravishing smile and a "Hello, darling!" that reeked of Palm Springs.

The weeks passed swiftly. They all worked with a kind of energy that left them tired but elated at the end of the day. It was like most of the best work—demanding of concentration but seemingly effortless.

Ben flew to Paris with a selection of the dailies, not even a rough cut, and on the basis of two viewings made three international distributor deals. Word had gotten out, somehow, that this was a hot one.

It also didn't hurt that the 1976 Winter Olympics were scheduled for Innsbruck. The film would be released in time to cash in on the public's interest.

As Alison was shooting she had only one problem. The ending, according to the script, called for a celebration of the Ski Pro's victory, which was described almost in locker-room terms: champagne being poured over his head, a mob scene at the bottom of the slope, the banner of the finish line. The camera would draw away for a long shot, which would show the fans, the racers, the Ski Pro swept up in the crowd.

Alison shot it as written, taking two days to line up extras. No problem there; news of the film had traveled across Europe. Ben hired some name skiers. The scene was shot from four angles. A helicopter gave them a distance shot. But something disturbed Alison. The scene was not faithful to the Ski Pro. He went his own solitary way. He was not a locker-room hero. Whatever he had accomplished, his once-in-a-lifetime win was just that: once in a lifetime. But what kept driving him was skiing itself. She could picture him taking a last run, the crowds gone, the sunlight disappearing, in shadow and in blazing sunset, hidden by the dark pines and streaking across a slope, flying like an eagle. That was how the film should end. She knew it in her bones.

She could talk to only one person about it. Kenny.

She stood over his table by the bar. He gestured for her to sit down.

"I want to ask you something," she said. The filming was almost over. They were like lovers leaving each other again. She could feel the strain.

He smiled. "Whatever it is, I say yes."

"No, listen first. You may not say yes so fast. I want to know your feelings. Remember the race at North Conway the day we met?"

He nodded absently. It was such a small part of an action-packed life, he could remember it only dimly.

"Do you remember who won? The instructors or the townies?"

"The instructors." He recalled that much.

"And what would the winners do? Go off and celebrate?"

"Hell, no. They'd take another run down the mountain."

She slapped the table. "I knew it. I knew I was right," and she described her idea for the ending. Kenny listened and nodded.

"You're right. Shoot it that way. I'll do it for you."

She thanked him and started to get up. He held her hand. She didn't want him to do that; she still liked it much too much if he touched her. But Kenny Buck was still Kenny Buck.

"Am I really any good?" he asked.

She could assure him of that.

Alison wanted to shoot in the late afternoon, when the mountain would be striped with shadows. The Ski Pro would weave in and out of the shadows and at the last moment ski over one of the little hillocks called a mogul. Jimmy would be stationed underneath it to catch the Ski Pro in midjump, freeze frame, and leave him high in his celebration, thus ending the movie.

They planned the sequence very carefully. Jimmy marked the route and stationed cameras along it. They rented the helicopter for one more day's work. Kenny made the run three times during the day to make sure he knew the terrain.

On the last run he asked if they might move it along a bit, because the slope was beginning to ice up. Alison pushed as hard as she could, but she was waiting for that moment of light. She had seen it so often during the last few weeks of shooting. It was the golden time, when the snow peaks took on the cast of pink-gold, and Kenny's face turned the color of gold. Throughout the film she had settled for nothing but the best. For this last shot she resolved to hold out for what she wanted. Kenny was nervous. Jimmy shot her quizzical glances. There would be time for only one shot, for in ten minutes the sun would sink behind the peaks, and the slopes would be encased in darkness.

Finally she nodded. It was time. Jimmy spoke into his communications system. Alison could see Kenny adjust his equipment, dig his poles into the snow, and start the descent. She could hear the whirr of the helicopter as it followed him. She followed him, too, with her eyes. As planned, he curved over and down the swells in the slope, graceful as a sea gull, soaring on air. It was like flight; his movements were buoyed up as though an energy from the mountain were lifting him. As he neared them, he was no longer just a figure. She could see his face and the tension in it. He had been right. It was difficult skiing. The powder of midday was freezing together. He approached the mogul. She watched Jimmy swing into action.

Abruptly Kenny appeared over the top of the mogul, ski poles high, leaping over Jimmy's head. It took her breath away.

He landed behind them, down slope. Then she heard a ripping sound and turned to see Kenny tumble, somersault, his skis flying into the darkening sky. She cried out. He rolled a few feet and lay still.

She and Jimmy were running to him. He was motionless. Move! Move! she shouted silently, commanding him to be alive. When they reached the body, Jimmy knelt, felt for a pulse, found it.

"He's alive," he said.

"Of course, he's alive," she screamed. "Of course, he is. Why shouldn't he be?"

Jimmy looked at her for a moment, then said, "Cover him with your jacket. I'll go back to the communications system. Lucky we have the helicopter."

"Can it land here?"

"Hope so. He should be taken to a hospital as soon as possible."

Alison unzipped her down parka and covered Kenny's body with it. She dared not touch him. She looked uneasily at his face, dark against the ice. The sun disappeared. They were almost in total darkness. Could a helicopter see them?

Why hadn't she had the Ski Patrol up there? she railed at herself. They had always used the Ski Patrol before. She knelt over him to cover his face from the wind. She kept her gloves over his ears and prayed for help to come.

She had to be so perfect. If she had allowed them to shoot when Kenny had wanted them to, this would never have happened. She had only herself to blame. But he must not die. She whispered in his ear, told him to keep fighting, to live, to live. The best part of his life lay before him. She talked to him, alone there on the mountain, lover to lover. Whatever had happened between them, he had been her lover. And she his. They had shared their lives for a time. She watched for signs of breathing. As long as he kept breathing, she told herself, everything would turn out all right. Everything had to be all right.

When the helicopter arrived, it circled for a minute, then disappeared. She screamed at it. Where were they going? Where was Jimmy? Where had everyone disappeared to?

Then the helicopter returned, dropping a flare that lit up the mountain like a fireworks display. In the glare the helicopter's skis touched ground, settled, the huge blades slicing the night, filling the night with its sound.

She saw with relief there was a stretcher. And then she realized this was another helicopter and these were medics. He would be safe. They crouched over Kenny, talking swiftly to each other in German. She could guess from the tension in their voices that Kenny was alive, in danger, but alive. She was counting on that. They gently lifted his body onto the stretcher. His arm hung down. It looked so lifeless she wanted to put it in place, but she didn't dare touch him. She stood there, immobilized. She might have stayed on that mountain all night, but one of the medics nodded to her. *"Komm,"* he ordered, and she obeyed. There was enough room for all of them in the helicopter. In a minute they were up and away from the mountain, flying through the pass, toward the village. The

lights below her, the darkness of the Schwarzsee. Soon
there would be a hospital, and doctors and starched uniforms,
and everything would be all right. Alison had a child's
faith in the efficiency of white starched uniforms. They
were as good as a promise.

Kenny Buck had broken his leg and his collarbone.
He had narrowly avoided a spinal injury that might have
paralyzed him for life. But he was alive. He would re-
cover. Alison spent the night at the hospital and returned
to the hotel at dawn.

Ben, out of character, was furious. What if Kenny had
been killed? How could she take such a chance without
consulting him? It was only the second time Ben had ever
been angry at her. Perversely she found him more interesting when he was directing his fury at her.

She had nothing to say; she was helpless. She let
him lash out at her with his caustic comments.

"I have to sleep," she said at last, and left the room.
As she was walking out the door she thought she heard
Diane say to Ben, "What does it matter, so long as the
footage is in the can?" But she must have been mistaken.
Diane must have been talking about something else.

For two days she was not allowed to see Kenny.
When she finally did, it was between injections of morphine. He was in intense pain. This worried her, but she
knew that the hospital was used to such injuries. They
might not be able to perform brain surgery, but broken
bones were a cinch.

This was her one chance to see him. She had to leave
for the United States early in the morning to begin work
with the film editor. She had begged the doctors to let her
visit him, if only for ten minutes.

He smiled when she came in. She began to cry. She
hadn't meant to, hadn't wanted to. If only he hadn't *smiled*,
she told herself. If only he had been mean and rotten the
way he was other times, she could have handled it.

"I'm so sorry," she sobbed. He began to laugh, then
groaned in pain.

"Don't make me laugh," he said. "It really hurts too much."

"Oh, it's terrible," she said. "You're treating it like a joke. Kenny, you were right. We should have shot when the conditions were better."

"Hey." He stopped her. "I only asked you for one thing, remember? It was all that time ago, that night in Cambridge. When I came in, I said, 'You're going to make me famous.' And you have." She was silent. "Haven't you?" he added. "You did get all the footage, didn't you?" She looked at him in amazement and nodded. He relaxed. "Tell that lady out there that I need another shot. The pain is coming back."

Alison did just that. Ben was waiting outside. "It's going to be all right, Alison. You'll see."

"Why do I feel so sorry for him, Ben?"

"For Christ's sake, I don't know." He managed a smile. "Come on, we got a plane waiting and a film to cut."

On the plane she sat with Ben and they talked about everything, and finally they talked about the film.

"My instincts were right," he said.

"About what?"

"About you. I knew you could do this movie. And about Kenny. I knew it was right for him. I'm going to have a bottle of wine just to congratulate myself. Will you join me?"

They toasted each other over the Atlantic, made some crazy plans for future projects as they were passing over the North Pole, and held each other's hand all the way from Canada to Los Angeles.

Somewhere over the desert he confided to her, "You know, I wanted to make this film more than anything else I've ever done. And I wouldn't let anything get in my way. And now, you know what I want to do? I want to make the next one. And the one after that."

He dozed for a while and Alison watched America come into focus as they made their descent toward Los Angeles.

*   *   *

Two days later she cabled Kenny. She had seen the footage with Ben and Diane. It was magnificent.

Her wire read: YOU DIDN'T BREAK A NECK FOR NOTHING. LOVE, ALISON.

It caused one nurse who understood English some anxiety. No one had told her about any broken neck. She looked at Kenny Buck's chart to confirm this. But she only confirmed what her mother had told her as a child: Americans were crazy.

Chapter Twenty-nine

Alison knew she was in L.A., but the only time she saw anything of the city was in the early morning when she drove to the editing room on the studio lot on Gower, and at night when she had dinner with Jimmy Smith or Huttner.

The only thing the film editor and Alison had in common was that they both came from New England. Huttner had fled Vermont and punched cattle and worked on the railroad, then had finally landed in Los Angeles, where, after ten years—like Jimmy—he had found his way into the film industry. He was a typical taciturn New Englander. No wasted words. When they'd first met, she had said, "Glad to meet you," and he had said, "Yup." She had said, "Did you like it?" and he had said, "Yup." On that basis they'd agreed to work together.

As Jimmy had predicted, cutting this film was a dream. It turned out to be enjoyable for Huttner and fascinating for Alison. He could cut from take to take, giving Alison the pace she required, and magically make others' emotions appear on the screen. His own personal feelings never surfaced. He left them at his ranch in the San Joaquin Valley.

"What about the music?" she asked after a week's frenzied work. "I forgot about the music."

Huttner did not look from his Moviola. "You'd be lucky to get Bill Conti."

"Where is he?"

"Wait two days. Show him a rough cut. I'll get it together."

Conti came and was conquered. He had four weeks to write the score if they could be sure of their schedule. Huttner gave his word. It was good enough.

Running away with herself, Alison said, "Now, what I want for music is—"

Conti, at the piano, cut her off. "Before you tell me what you want, let me show you what I got from what I saw." He began to improvise a little melody that was wistful and a bit lonely, then he added rhythm to it. The harmony became fuller, more complicated. He never lost sight of the Ski Pro, though, that lonely figure.

Alison was properly chastened. "Okay," she said. "My movies speak louder than my words."

Alison had rented a house in the Hollywood Hills with an elaborate alarm system, which she had difficulty managing. Several times she left one of the windows or the garage doors open, and three minutes later found herself staring into the goggles of the Los Angeles Police Department. With great thoroughness they showed her the system, the combination of numbered buttons she had to push, the way to check the system when she was leaving. She nodded assent to all these procedures and was visited at least twice a week by squad cars.

One night after she'd been in L.A. for two weeks, she was in her peignoir getting ready for bed when the doorbell rang. She panicked. Nobody knew she was here. Worse than that, she was not sure how to open the door without summoning the police. There had to be a way. She shouted, "Who is it?" and when a voice answered "Sam!" she forgot about everything and flung open the door, setting off the alarm.

"What in Christ—" he began.

"Oh, oh, oh, oh, I did it again."

"Can't you shut this thing off?"

"No. The cops have to come. Oh, Sam, say it was your fault," she begged him. "They've been here four times now and they're going to think I'm some kind of idiot."

"You are!" he yelled over the noise. "Give me a kiss."

They were still at it when the patrol car drove up.

She was used to them by now, knew them by name. This was the younger one, Officer Michael Selby, incredibly patient.

"Miss Carmichael," he said.

"Michael, I'm sorry, but actually it was *his* fault."

Michael looked at Sam Pendexter, sized him up, and turned back to Alison. "Miss Carmichael, there is no need to lie about this. We all have our blocks."

"Oh, no," she protested, "it really wasn't a block. I know the combination, Michael, I swear it, but this is a friend of mine, and I hadn't seen him in so long . . ."

Michael's smile was understanding. He addressed Sam.

"Sir, if you would just take a minute to listen, I could show you how this system works, and then, at your leisure, you might instruct her." Sam agreed and Officer Selby began his lecture-demonstration.

Fifteen minutes later Sam and Alison were alone, inside the house. Alison was both elated and uncomfortable. Strange house, strange man. She suddenly felt quite girlish and insecure. She hated that part of her who used to quake at dancing school, hoping yet fearing that some eleven-year-old with shiny black shoes would ask her to dance.

"Is your chauffeur waiting outside?" she asked, just to break the silence. Sam seemed perfectly at ease, which infuriated her.

"No, I drove myself. I like to drive in California."

"Well, you do pop up at the most unexpected times."

"My God, but you can be a Yankee spinster when you want to be."

"It's just that I had no idea you were anywhere around."

"Did you think about me at all?"

"Think about you? Yes!" she blurted out.

"What did you think about?"

"I thought about wanting to forget you," she confessed.

"Why?" He had somehow maneuvered them into the strange living room that belonged to somebody else, with somebody else's books on the shelves and their own bar and bar glasses.

"Do you want a drink?" she asked.

"The usual."

"Oh," she said, and for the life of her could not remember what he drank. She reached for the bourbon bottle.

"You did remember. . . ." He smiled.

"Stop testing me," she said. "Listen. I don't know where anything is. Soda or any of that. You find it."

"Why, darlin', you forget. I take it neat," he teased.

"Oh—oh, yes." She left the drink on the bar for him to get up and get it. He did not. He sat comfortably where he was. She had chosen the wrong moment to be so ungiving. She had offered him a drink. He was waiting for her to give it to him. The momentary pause amused him. Everything she did seemed to amuse him, as though he were watching a cute puppy just learning to play. It was degrading.

She brought him the drink and when he took it from her, their hands touched. His hands, she thought, had never lost their authority, not once. Not once, she was sure, had this man dropped anything or hit his finger with a hammer. Maddening!

"Thank you," he said. "Aren't you going to join me?"

"No, I have to be up early to work," she murmured absently. She had to stop thinking about his hands.

"What are you thinking about?" he asked.

"Nothing." Did he know she was thinking about his hands? She had trouble looking at him. His direct gaze always aroused her and she did not want to be aroused. She was working, and she had difficult choices to make.

"Are you going to tell me why you're in Los Angeles?"

"Of course." He adopted the same familiar tone. "I am in Los Angeles on business. It will take me approximately three days to complete, and then I shall fly to Birmingham, Alabama. Have you ever been to Birmingham, Alabama, Miss Alison? No, I can tell from the look on your face that you have never visited Birmingham. Well, Birmingham resembles Houston in that it is an up-and-coming, aggressive city, although farther east and rather smaller, but there are many fine restaurants and hotels and pleasant places to visit. Guided tours even."

She looked at him then, but that penetrating gaze of his made her turn away.

"Now that we are through with the small talk," he concluded, "I only have one thing to ask you. Where are we, the two of us? Are you in love with me? 'Cause I sure as hell do love you."

Her "Yes" came out so small that he could hardly hear her. "Speak up," he said, sounding to Alison like Miss Flagg in the eighth grade. "I can hardly hear you."

"Yes," she said, more strongly.

"Good, because I have missed you in Geneva, Amsterdam, Tangier, Chicago, Pittsburgh—and mostly in Houston, Texas."

"You've been a lot of places" was all she could think of to say, but that also amused him, and then he did rise and kissed her. It was the one thing she had hoped he would not do, but when he did, she lost all qualms. Sam Pendexter was the only man who could excite and protect her at the same time. He was kissing her and his breath was sweet. Even the liquor tasted pure and sweet—and, oh, God, she was anticipating going to bed with him again. She could already see the two of them in her bed—had she made it that morning? Had she picked up the stockings? Was he trying to seduce her?

"Are you trying to get me to go to Houston?" she asked between kisses.

"Oh, yes, ma'am. Among other things, I am trying to get you to Houston."

"Well, I am not going to live in Houston," she said, even though she was breathing hard.

"I didn't say live there forever, I said, come for a visit." He was panting, too, she was satisfied to hear.

"Well, maybe a visit, when I have time," she conceded.

"We really could discuss this on another occasion."

"I have a bedroom over there." She pointed vaguely, but he had pulled her down on the couch and his gaze never wavered. Never did he take his eyes from hers.

"I don't think we need a bedroom, do you?" he asked. She shook her head and he began to shed his clothes and unfasten the belt to her peignoir and still his eyes were on hers.

His pupils were so small and black, his irises almost hazel. She was fascinated by his eyes. They were both now totally naked. His hands busied themselves with her body in a thousand ways and he was watching to see how everything affected her. He was silent, performing and watching. She had never felt so intimate with a man. His eyes grew clearer with passion. She opened herself to him and his body entered hers. He was not smiling now, he was doing nothing but concentrating on her and her pleasure. As the strokes of his body began to build in rhythm she closed her eyes, but then forced them open to look into his again. Now she did not waver. They made love slowly and with great absorption and their eyes never left each other, not even in the moment of rising ecstasy when she wanted to fling her arms around his neck. He was keeping his body slightly aloof from hers, caressing her, making love to her, teasing her, pleasuring her. Total concentration on what she was feeling. His thrusts were more forceful now. The eyes more demanding. His body was the master, but she was the most willing mistress. The moment of climax came; it flooded through both of them and still their gazes never wavered. It was stronger than ever, more complete. She thought she might faint dead away, and then she covered his neck with kisses and sniffed him and smelled him and found she wanted more and began to move under him, to make demands, and even *that* amused him. He made a sign and moved so that he was underneath her. She was riding him, and he said as he might to a bronco, "Go! Go on, darlin'. Go!" She went wild. She felt released from everything. Capable of any kind of behavior. No shame, only wonder, and when she had finally exhausted herself on his body, he said gently, "I think we both might make use of the bedroom now, what say?" She let him carry her in and no, the bed hadn't been made, and her clothes were strewn all around the floor and he didn't care, he didn't even look at them. They both fell on the bed, he covered them with the comforter, and they cradled each other. She was dozing off in the strength of his arms when a thought occurred to her.

"Are you intent on making another merger, Sam?"

"Not tonight, Alison."

"I didn't mean us. I meant *you*. You know"—she raised herself on one elbow—"you never really tell me what you do. I get this vague picture of conglomerates and cartels and a kind of poor country boy who knows his way around Geneva and Amsterdam and probably Singapore. Are you with the CIA?"

"You blew my cover," he murmured sleepily. He needed some rest. He was satisfied. She was back in his life again, not totally on his terms, but not totally on *hers* either.

"Are you? Or the FBI? Honestly, Sam, I mean it. I don't want to get mixed up in any funny business."

He did laugh at that. "You're trying to take over the entertainment industry, and you talk to me about funny business."

"Oh, you know what I mean. You talk about liquid coal and experimenting with it, and you probably have ten different interests. . . ." She was fishing but he didn't bite. He kept silent in the dark. "Don't you?"

"Two, right now. One of them is sleep."

"You *are* with the CIA," she said positively.

He didn't deny it. He only asked her, "How does it feel to sleep with an undercover agent?"

"I like that part of it," she murmured, feeling sleepy herself now. "Only when it comes time for you to unmask yourself, or whatever you do—"

"You'll be the first to know. Tomorrow, I'm really going to have to set you straight about business. Just a couple of things. One, why don't you have a telephone? And two, why don't you have a service"

"I'm using the phone that's here."

"But who knows the number, in case anyone wants to reach you?"

"I'll give you the number."

"It's not just me, babe. You got business to take care of. You got an assistant?"

"No."

"I got to straighten you out—tomorrow."

*   *   *

But he never had a chance to. The following day he was called back to Houston on business. He sent her a telegram, it was the only way he could reach her. All it said was HAD TO GO. COMING BACK FOR YOU. SAM, but there was more love in that telegram than any sonnet she could think of. She went back to work, but did decide to heed his advice and take care of a little business. She went so far as to leave her home number and the number at the studio with one of Mr. Pendexter's many secretaries, none of whom would give her the slightest clue as to his whereabouts.

Concentrate on this film, she told herself. That was the main thing. Conti saw the rough cut, and in two weeks came back with half the score. He played it on tape with electronic approximations of the instruments. Alison was overjoyed. Conti was a little shy.

"Would you hurry the editing process a bit?" he asked. "I'm supposed to be in Greece in three weeks."

Alison did not ask him why. She refused to ask about anyone's schedules in that city of breakfast conferences and intercontinental deadlines. She just kept working with Huttner and watched the film take shape before her eyes. She spent five minutes with Conti and the click track and left. The amount of complications, the mathematical calculations to time each segment of the music exactly to the frame of the film left her in awe. These were the *techniques*. Then she returned. This was also part of the business. She should know about it. Conti was only too glad to explain as he went along. After three days she had a grasp of the fundamentals. At least she knew how much she didn't know.

At the end of the three weeks she had a film she was ready to show to Ben and Diane and whomever they were associated with. She had never bothered to find out about their distribution deals or financial machinations. She never considered those things any of her business.

In the projection room were a few secretaries, Ben, Diane, Jimmy Smith, Conti (who had delayed his trip two days), Huttner and his wife, and several studio executives.

The film began.

"Credits to come," Ben whispered to Alison. "They'll

be on for the first preview in Seattle. But we have to deal with everyone's contract as to length of time on screen for billing, all that. Don't worry."

Alison nodded nervously. *That* wasn't a worry. Now, what the film was like, out of the Moviola and up on the screen, *was* a worry. The screen seemed immense to her.

The pace was fast from the very beginning. The film started with the sound of skis against snow, that seductive siren of the Ski Pro. When Conti's music entered, it was all the more effective.

The first two or three scenes merely established the Ski Pro's locale; the mundane job he worked at to keep skiing; the women who supported him occasionally; the vague ennui of time; and the chance encounter and the opportunity to substitute on the Olympic team.

By then the combination of a good script, Alison's direction, Kenny's performance, and the technical aspects had worked its magic. The viewers, tough and ungiving as they were, were caught up in the story. When the Ski Pro finally won the race, they cheered. Alison looked at Ben. He shrugged happily and smiled his most relaxed smile. Everything was going to be all right.

The last scene caught them unawares. The solitude of the skier taking one more silent run through the gold and dusk at the end of the day changed their feelings. When the movie ended with the freeze frame of Kenny's exultant jump, there were clearings of throats and murmurings. Alison sensed something was wrong. She knew she had led them in the wrong direction, or rather, changed direction on them. They had been so carried away by the championship that they did not care to know about the Ski Pro's future.

The lights came up. Congratulations were forthcoming. Good directing job. Fine performances. The secretaries —or whatever they were—did not know which side of the fence to stay on, so they crept out. Finally Alison, Ben, Diane, Jimmy, and Conti were left alone in the projection room.

"Are you finished?" the projectionist asked.

"Yes, thanks, Harry," Ben called to him. "We just want to use the room for a few more minutes."

"No problem. The next viewing isn't scheduled for two hours."

Diane turned on Alison. "You're not going to leave it like this." She did not phrase it as a question.

Alison looked at her. "What is it that disturbs you?"

"Disturbs *me*? Everyone! What a downer that ending is. You heard them. They were cheering, then you blew it."

Alison turned to Ben for corroboration. "I do have final cut, don't I?"

Ben nodded. "Yes, but I think you ought to consider what Diane's saying."

"I *am* considering it. I just want it clear who is in charge here."

Diane rose from her seat. "Look, I'm saying, change that ending."

"I never did take orders from you very well, Diane," Alison said coolly.

"I don't give a shit how well you take them. Just take them."

"Okay, ladies." Ben sighed. "We'll settle this tomorrow."

"No. *Now!*" Alison and Diane said simultaneously. "Not tomorrow," Diane added. "Right now."

"I have final cut on this film," Alison said firmly. Diane opened her mouth, but Bill Conti made a suggestion.

"I don't want to get in the way here. I find Alison's ending very moving, very much in character—"

"It's a downer!" Diane cut him off.

"It doesn't have to be. The sequence is shot beautifully. The idea of his taking one more run down the slope is emotionally correct, but the problem is I can't make out what he's thinking."

"Thinking?" Diane snorted. "He's thinking, Why did they shoot this dumb shot?"

"Look you, shut up!" Alison shouted, amazed at her own courage. She turned back to Conti. "I made a mistake, didn't I? I had him contemplating the future and how barren it was."

"Yeah . . ." Conti said. "And that does bring it down. Man, he's just won, he needs to be by himself to taste what victory is." In his excitement Conti got out of his chair. "He's celebrating."

"We can't reshoot," Ben cautioned.

"No need to," Conti said. "Just score it. I know what's needed." He turned his attention to Alison, collaborator to collaborator. "I can get it for you, I can hear it in my head now. I'll have it for you before you leave. Recorded, mixed, everything."

"You'd do that for me?"

"No." Conti smiled. "I'd do it because it's a great fuckin' picture."

He was as good as his word.

A second screening was ordered with the rescored ending. It was a triumph. Even Diane managed a smile— and a comment. "Thank God for Conti."

Alison ignored Diane. Conti had been right. The music carried the elation all the way to the end of the film, and that was all that mattered.

Ben gave her a hug. Ecstatic.

"We did it. We did it. Alison, you're a genius." He gave her a victor's kiss, as though *he* had just won an Olympic medal.

There was one disturbing moment. On her way out, Alison heard someone say, "Lucky they got Kenny Buck when they did. I hear he's a walking drugstore now. Name it, he's on it."

She thought of the morphine they were giving him in Kitzbühel for the pain.

A roomful of roses. She had never seen the like. From Ben. Such extravagance. The card read, *Gratitude and love, Ben*.

She was standing in the middle of the room when Sam phoned her.

"CIA reporting in."

"You're back!"

"I told you I'd be back for you."

"I'm glad. This is like living a James Bond thriller."

"Oh, I may be good, but I'm not that good," he said modestly.

"How did you get here?"

"In my Learjet."

At that moment an operator interrupted to say tha
there was an emergency call for Alison Carmichael from
Trevya—

"Trevina," Alison automatically corrected her. "Yes
I'll take it. Sam, call me back in five minutes. Better still
come on over."

He hung up. She waited for Trevina's voice.

"Alison, darling, I have some very bad news. Myra
has suffered a stroke. She's at New York Hospital, and
know she would like to see you."

"What do you mean? She's going to be all right, isn'
she?"

"No," Trevina said sadly. "No, I don't believe she wil
be. She has been totally paralyzed. Alison, if you can make
it, you should come."

"Right away," Alison said. "Where are you?"

"At the hospital. You know I never trust anyone to de
anything right!"

Alison hung up, threw a few things into a suitcase
and met Sam at the door. He glanced around the roomfu
of roses.

"Who died?" he asked, then seeing Alison's expres
sion, stopped. "What is it?"

"It's Myra. She's had a stroke. I think she's dying."
And then the full realization hit her. "Oh, Sam, I hate
death. I don't want her to die. I don't want her to."

Sam took over. He made a call. Three minutes later
he returned and they drove to the airport where his je
was fueled and ready for takeoff.

It was night when they saw the brilliant diamond o
Manhattan and made a landing. A half hour later Alison
and Sam were at the hospital. But they were too late.

Myra Van Steen had left her life as she had lived
it—with style. Just a wink to Trevina as a gesture o
farewell. And then she had let go.

Chapter Thirty

Myra had always wanted a fun funeral—and she got it. In her will she had arranged for a party to be held at the Colony Club, complete with the trio that had played in the Blue Angel when it was the Blue Angel, and an open bar. Her instructions were explicit. She wanted Alison to photograph the whole affair. And she wanted the story published in her magazine.

She had planned this party for a long time. It turned out to be a dandy.

Sant'Angelo flew in. So did Givenchy. Cardin chartered a plane from the French Antilles. Nagy arrived from Berlin. Monsieur Marc and Kenneth and Pauline Trigère and Rex Reed and most of the casts of Broadway shows showed up. Matrons and mobsters, fresh young things and not-so-well-preserved harridans, wispy men and overbearing women, models and missionaries all mingled.

Myra's variety of friends was awesome. They had loved her, and now they gathered to celebrate her life. They drank Dom Pérignon and nibbled on the dazzling array of tea sandwiches, watercress, and caviar. A rock group that Myra had nurtured to notoriety played a stomp-down set, and everybody danced. The jazz trio played impeccable Cole Porter and Dietz and Schwartz and Irving Berlin, all those tunes that had graced the thirties. And everybody danced. Pearl Bailey sang. Everyone applauded. Lauren Bacall and Ethel Merman performed a very woozy version of "Friendship." Everybody loved it.

Everybody laughed. For a while it was like being back on ship and being young and carefree again, suspended in time. All problems seemed manageable. When the theater folk left for what turned out to be rather bubbly performances, the nightclub set was just warming up. More champagne was brought and Trevina, in a fit of inspiration, ordered Chinese takeout for one hundred from Uncle Tai's on Third Avenue. The spring evening grew late as, very mellow and stepping lightly, the last group wove down Park Avenue, singing and looking up with champagne eyes at the new silver moon that Myra must have ordered for the occasion.

Somebody called the police, who came expecting a riot but found only revelers. They told them to disband, and disband they did, in a flurry of taxis and limousines, waving farewells and dropping feathery kisses on one another's cheeks.

"Hell of a funeral! Hell of a funeral!" Sam told the world, drunkenly.

It certainly was the send-off Myra had in mind.

But the next day was different. Alison found herself alone in her New York loft. Sam had flown to Houston. She kept having the urge to phone Myra, and then would remember Myra was gone. So she watered her plants and looked at the stack of mail that had accumulated, but she did not open it.

The phone rang. She answered it listlessly.

"I came down to see you," her mother said. "I read in the paper about your friend's death, and I thought maybe—"

"Oh, yes, yes. Come over. Where are you? Grab a cab. I can't wait to see you."

Phyllis Carmichael had changed, and all of it for the better. Some things, of course, would never change. The hairdo, for one. No, it was her presence that had changed. She walked with more authority, had more bounce to her. A kind of resilience. She exuded a warmth that Alison had never noticed. Or perhaps it hadn't been there before.

They had tea.

"I think I was jealous of Myra—a little," her mother confessed. "You obviously liked each other so much. The two of you had so much to talk about. And we—you and I—never seemed to."

"Maybe we never had the chance." Alison sipped her tea slowly. "Do you think about the past much? About Daddy?"

"No." Phyllis set the cup down abruptly. "I do not think much about your father. There was a time when I did. I discovered I was terribly angry at him. I felt he had abandoned me. I have never given up. You have never given up. He gave up. I have not forgiven him for that. But now I have made a new life, found someone who loves me, and whom I love. What about you?"

Alison had to smile.

"I'm not nearly so sure. I'm glad you don't think about Daddy. I don't think about him much either. Sometimes I think about the way life *used* to be, and then I remember him and I remember the good times and it's all because I want to be a little girl again. And can't. But it's only when death intrudes, like now, that I think about—well, then, I think about *all* of us." Tears suddenly sprang to her eyes.

"We don't write much," her mother said. "We're not a writing sort of family. But, darling, we are a family. You and I. We do have each other."

"Oh, Mother," Alison suddenly cried out, and they were in each other's arms. They hadn't held each other since Alison was a child.

Over dinner that night Alison asked her mother if she was planning to remarry. "I don't think so," Phyllis said. "I like things just the way they are. How do you feel about marriage?"

Alison sighed. "Oh, I don't know. Most women see it as a refuge, I guess. I see it as a trap. And yet, I think I'm in love."

"Think?" Her mother looked at her questioningly.

"I would be if I *let* myself," Alison said. The phone interrupted them.

It was Ben calling from Seattle. Excited.

"I'm sorry you couldn't make the preview," he said. "But I know what you've been through. All I can say is, the. reaction was terrific. The plan now is to enter the film in the New York Festival in September."

"You're kidding," Alison shouted in disbelief.

"And give it a couple of shots in New York and L.A. to make it eligible for the Oscars, then release it in time for the Winter Olympics in Innsbruck."

"Wait. Tell me again. Slowly. I can't grasp all of this. First you mean, they liked it? The movie? The audience, that is." She was incoherent.

"Loved it, loved it, loved it."

"That's three loves."

"And four stars. Hey, Alison, this is going to be a big one. It just takes careful handling. No overhype. Gently, gently with it. Surprise the critics."

"Have you talked to Kenny?"

"Diane has. He's somewhere in the Caribbean."

"Oh?"

"With David Sampson. And a lot of New Wave. He seems to be living life on high." The phrase rang in her head and then was forgotten in a swirl of words—Ben painting rosy futures, more films, more successes, wasn't it wonderful. His other phone rang and Alison was left holding a dead receiver.

Her first impulse was to dial Myra and tell her the news. And then she remembered. Of course. She couldn't.

She turned to her mother. "I just directed my first movie, Mother. And I think it's going to be a big hit."

Phyllis Carmichael looked at her daughter's shining face.

"I think you're all right again, darling. So I'll take the morning plane back to Toronto." And Alison realized this was true.

The following day she developed the film which she called "Myra's Last Soiree." *Charm* sent a messenger to pick up the prints. Sam called from Houston to tell her he loved her. She found a letter in the mail from Myra's attorney, arranging a meeting for the next day at 3 P.M. She called to say she would attend.

And then she attacked the pile of mail.

Here was the first sign of success. Great stacks of scripts had been sent, with notes attached; some casual, some grandly formal from the offices of big-time producers. One came with a cassette attached. It was in a dirty manila envelope and had Alison's name printed rather laboriously on the front. Inside was a note that read:

Dear Miss Carmichael,
    I want to do this. I want you to do this too. I hope you want to.

Your friend,
Lillie Mae

Lillie Mae, her little Street Singer. There was something so direct about the note that Alison opened the script immediately, and immediately became absorbed in it.

The story was about two teenagers who meet in Central Park and spend a perfect day together. The girl is black, from Harlem, the boy a Puerto Rican emigrant, from New Jersey. He's in town for an outdoor rock concert to be presented in the park that evening. She teaches him about the city and her park. He shows her all the things she has overlooked. Gradually their surface antagonism turns to respect. There is a theft and a bicycle chase involving half the joggers and cyclists in New York. In the end he must take the last bus back to New Jersey. She gives him a shy kiss. They promise to meet again. And the day is over.

Alison was totally captivated by the story, by the imaginative use of the park as a symbol for society—Central Park, bordered by wealthy Fifth Avenue on the east, Harlem on the north, a transient ethnic community on the west, and a row of grand hotels on the south. On weekends, the park returned to the people. No motor traffic allowed. It blossomed with string quartets, skiffle bands, magicians, vendors, lovers, bikers, roller skaters, baseball games, fiestas, barbecues, martini pitchers, races, competitions, games, and evening concerts.

She wondered what the music was like. She wondered who the writers were. The script fairly burst with youth and enthusiasm. She slipped the cassette into her tape deck, but the phone rang again. It was *Charm*. A problem with the layout. Alison sighed, put the cassette back on the pile of manuscripts, and left the loft.

At the lawyer's office the following day she was surprised and pleased to see Trevina. The lawyer came right to the point.

"Miss Van Steen, as you know, was a working woman and—I must add—an enormous success in every aspect of her life. But she had one failing. She never took vacations. She always postponed them. Therefore, she made it a part of her will that she wished the two of you—and any guests that you might invite—to spend two weeks in her estate in Guadeloupe."

Alison was shocked into silence; Trevina burst into tears.

"I *told* her to take a holiday," Trevina said. "I said that I would go with her, but no, she has this to do and that to do, and this article to finish, and now it is too late. No, I do not want to go," she finished angrily.

Alison turned to her. "Myra lived exactly as she wished," she said gently. "Don't disappoint her."

Trevina made a little European gesture of impatience. "Ah, I will go. Perhaps Nagy will go with me, but, Alison, I tell you, I am so angry with Myra. She would never listen to me."

"Well, listen to her then. Maybe she's saying she doesn't want what happened to her to happen to us."

"Perhaps," Trevina said as they left the lawyer's office. "But would it not have been more fun with Myra there?"

When Sam came back to town, the four of them—Trevina, Nagy, Alison, and Sam—planned the trip. They left on the morning of May tenth and arrived in Guadeloupe in time for tea.

Alison and Trevina were like schoolgirls, enchanted by the countryside—which was so like Normandy—the farmlands and little huts whose roofs were tin and not slate. But still, the yoke of oxen plowed the fields and the women walked behind, sowing seeds. Alison wanted to unpack her camera right then and there.

"Wait," Sam said with a grin. "Plenty of time for that. Let's get settled first."

Myra Van Steen's estate lay halfway up a volcanic mountain; the vista was breathtaking. Far below them the Caribbean sparkled. Mountains and rain forests stretched to either side. Still farther down, a twisty mountain path away, was a small fringe of beach, shaded by coconut palms. On the plantation banana trees, coconuts, and pineapples mingled with lemon and orange groves. The estate house itself seemed made of air. Breezes wafted throughout it. Enormous verandas curved around the sides. A dining room opened to the stars. The bedrooms were cool and shaded with blinds that were kept closed during the day and opened at night to let in the perfumed air.

A housekeeper, Marie-Claire, and chef, Lucien, were there to take care of their every need, starting off by preparing a langouste with a mélange of tropical fruits and serving, from Myra's copious wine cellar, a Montrachet that sparkled in the crystal glass under the candlelight.

"In all the years I was acquainted with Myra, I never knew she had this Caribbean paradise," Nagy said with amazement. "What did she do with it?"

"Lent it to friends," Trevina replied.

"I wish I had known. All the times I could have used it," he grumbled. Trevina smiled at him. Her eyes reflected the sparkle of the wine. She had drawn her hair straight back and knotted it in a bun. Alison sensed a growing attraction between Nagy and Trevina.

There were five bedrooms in the main house. Four had been prepared for occupancy, but Sam and Alison slept in the same room. Mosquito netting formed a filmy canopy over their heads. White wicker furniture and cool lime-green colors.

Nagy and Trevina slept in separate rooms, equally opulent and equally tasteful, for two nights. By that time Trevina had cavorted in the warm emerald Caribbean waters and her skin had darkened to a Mediterranean brown. She had unfastened her hair and let it flow around her shoulders, and Nagy had kissed her lightly once at breakfast, more experimentally during a long lazy lunch, and finally passionately and completely on the scary curving road back to the estate, following an evening on the town in Pointe-à-Pitre.

Then he slept in Trevina's room; Marie-Claire and Lucien were decidedly approving at breakfast the next morning.

For a week none of them thought of anything but the pleasures of the flesh and the glory of the island. There were wonderful morning breakfasts on the terrace, with the Caribbean below them saying, *Take your time, I'll wait for you*, and then descents to the beach with picnic hampers and chilled bottles of wine. The Caribbean caressed them, relaxed their tensions, restored their vitality, and at the same time left them somnolent. They would lunch under the shade of the coconut palms and sometimes sleep on the beach, eventually drifting back to the beautiful pure-white alabaster palace that was Myra's gift to them.

One day they rented a twenty-foot sloop and spent the entire day running at close haul, the boat pitched at an angle that caused Trevina to scream, Nagy to keep his arms around her, and Alison to shout with exultation. Sam and Alison were each surprised to find out that the other sailed.

"You're a poor boy from West Texas," she protested.

"I did pick up some things along the way up," he reminded her. "And you know Houston is just that close to Galveston. You do know where Galveston is, don't you?"

"No."

"On the Gulf. The Gulf of Mexico, which is actually the Caribbean, so if you want to look at it in neighborly terms, we're sailing right off the shores of Texas. Coming about!"

He was at the tiller and handling the main sheet at the same time. The boom swung around and they began a long tack back to the tiny marina that again could have been a little fishing village in the South of France—a tricolor flag was flying in the square. Except that the citizens had black faces instead of white. But they were French and proud of it. There were signs, graffiti scribbled on the walls, slogans. It reminded Alison of Paris. GUADELOUPE LIBRE! INDÉPENDANCE!

Yes, she thought. Exactly like Paris.

*   *   *

On Sunday, while they were at the beach, the two men walked away from the women, beachcombing.

Trevina watched them go, unaware that Alison was watching her.

"How lovely," she murmured.

"What?" Alison asked.

"Men," Trevina replied. "Look at them. How well they walk."

"Yes," Alison teased. "I suppose they were meant to do that, walk."

"Yes, but how well they look. I marvel at men."

Alison propped herself up on one elbow.

"You have changed, Trevina."

"I know, I know. Gone native. Wild. Put a gardenia in my hair, and I will be in island movies for the rest of my life."

"Is it Nagy?"

"No. Yes, of course it is Nagy," she amended, "but it is really Myra."

"What do you mean?"

"I mean that I realized the depth of the gift she was giving us—giving me. I was always so busy and I had no time for men, and most of the men I knew were homosexual or old or boring or all three. I liked the homosexuals because they were fun and very nice to me, and witty and smart and all the rest. But sexually I was always on the outside. With the old ones"—she shrugged—"they were kind and often loving, but they meant nothing to me."

She looked out at the sea. "Nothing meant anything to me but my work. I envied you. You always had men. Not any men—fascinating men. I wondered—no, I know, you are very beautiful—but I wondered, what did you do?"

"Well, what did you do with Nagy?"

"Let him know that I wanted him." Trevina laughed. "It was very simple. But my life, your life, we live such a short time, no matter how long we live. It is silly to fall into a rage because a pattern does not fit, an order is delayed."

"And Myra?"

"She chose her life. She chose not to marry. She chose a career. And she allowed that career to dominate her life. Do you know how many visits she made to this wonderful place? Only four in her entire life." She turned over and let the sun warm her back. "I do not intend to let that happen to me." She paused, watching Alison as she gazed after the two disappearing men. "And what about you?"

"I don't know." Alison shook her head. "I love a man and I love what I'm doing, and I couldn't do what I'm doing where he lives. I can't ask him to change his life."

"Why not?"

"Because he wouldn't do it."

Trevina chuckled. "You know this is the first time I have ever indulged in girl talk. I never had the time. It's fun. For instance, I thought you were in love with Ben Sawyer."

"So did I. Sometimes I still think I am."

"He is very handsome."

"But I don't like his hands. Did you notice Sam's hands?"

"I have noticed many things about Sam—he is delicious—but his hands, no."

"Sam is a fighter. He has the strongest hands I've ever seen."

"Ah, then you are in love with Sam." Trevina was probing.

"But I don't want to live in Houston," Alison cried.

Trevina just laughed. "There are airplanes."

"I don't want to always be on an airplane, or meeting him between flights."

"Then you would rather be like Myra? She was always on planes, too, but not meeting anyone. Not any man she loved. Alison, you and I have been friends for more than five years now. I have seen you be careless. Only the rich are so careless. You were careless first about a career. You tossed it away as though it would come back any day. And after that you have been careless with men. Really, you have had some of the most incredible men falling in love with you."

"I guess I want it all," Alison said, not really thinking about what she was saying.

"Ah, well, then take it all," Trevina said very seriously, adding, "if you can."

That evening, after dinner, Alison was rummaging through her bag when she came across the cassette Lillie Mae had sent her.

"What is that?" Sam asked.

"This adorable girl," Alison started to explain, "sent me a script for a musical. This, evidently, is the music. I was going to listen to it before we left, but never got around to it."

"I wonder what it sounds like."

"I'll listen to it when I get back."

"Then why did you bring it?"

She just looked at him.

"Let's listen," he suggested.

"You sure you want to?"

He insisted. Nagy and Trevina joined them and Alison placed the cassette on the player.

At first they thought it was the freshness of the evening, the luxury of living in this house, the fun they were having. The music was intoxicating. It sounded like it should be played at a fiesta. It had already been scored for guitar, flute, and keyboard. The first time through, they listened only to the music. There were several plaintive ballads, a rather goofy march, chase music, one really haunting love song, and three or four songs that Nagy kept describing as "fresh."

"Oh, they are lovely," Trevina said. "They make me not want to sit still. Let's hear them again."

So they did, and this time they listened to the lyrics. The lyrics belonged to the very young, which was only right, since this was a story of first love and the giddy adolescent joy of discovery.

"It is very beautiful," Trevina said at the end. "It is enchanting. What is the script like?"

Alison described the story, the different locales. Sam had remained silent, she noticed, but intent.

"Are you planning this for the stage?" he asked finally.

"I wasn't planning anything," Alison said, "but, yes, I suppose it was written for the stage."

"All those different locales," he said.

"Well, it's all Central Park. It would have to be representational. Scenic designers come up with miracles."

"Still, it's a pity not to *see* all of it," Sam persisted.

"What are you suggesting? A film?"

"Yes."

"I never thought of it. Oh, the studios won't hear of it. Movie musicals never make money. Except David Sampson's. And an original at that. Out of the question."

"Not necessarily." Sam was ruminating. "The music has the beat, but it's also charming. The story is about kids, but it's not limited to kids. It has action. There is the theft and the bicycle chase. They could be very funny. This is a story that kicks up its heels. It's time for something like that."

"Then you're serious?" Alison said.

"Yes, I'm serious, but I'm also on the enchanted isle of Guadeloupe. Let's think about it in the morning." He noticed the look on her face. "What the matter?"

"I should offer it to Ben first. I feel I owe him."

"Owe him? Hell!" Suddenly his Texas was up. "You don't owe him diddly-squat!"

"Diddly-squat?" Nagy looked at Trevina.

"A Texas locution," she told him. He approved.

Sam had his fierce look on. He was glaring at Alison.

"Oh, Sam, what is it? I just have some sense of loyalty."

"And no more business sense than a newborn puppy. You trust everybody."

She wasn't satisfied. "I don't understand. What does this have to do with you, except that you want to protect me?"

"I just might be interested."

"In making a movie?" She was incredulous.

"I might."

"As what? Producer?" All three of them were looking at him.

"I might," he repeated defensively. "It isn't any kind of crime, is it, to be interested?"

"No crime. Wonderful!" Nagy said enthusiastically. "Wonderful, Sam."

"Would you be?" Alison still sounded doubtful.

"What?"

"Interested?"

"I told you it once. Yes, I might."

Alison turned to Nagy and Trevina. "I don't know what to make of this man. Sometimes I think he's a CIA agent. I told him so. And then I think he's some kind of international hustler. Now he talks about movies. Do you know anything about the business?" This last was to him.

"Business is business," Sam said, with maybe thirty million dollars to back him up. "And I've been asking around."

"You're a mystery, Sam," she said fondly, but he was outraged.

"No mystery at all. I hear a property. I know this woman, even in the biblical sense, who is one hell of a director. I see a way of making some money and having some fun!"

"And being together," Trevina quietly reminded Alison.

"Yeah. And being together," Sam said.

Nagy's voice now took on the serious edge he used only when he was playing poker and making films. "You have real money contacts?"

"Hell, yes!" Sam fired back.

"For films?" Nagy was wondering why he hadn't tapped this source himself.

"For films. Tax shelters. I'm in the oil business, you remember *that*? Christ, all of a sudden I'm auditioning. And *I* got all the money." He was so outraged they all burst out laughing.

"If you have all the money, and the *Ski Pro* is a hot property"—Nagy was playing the cinema chess game— "then you could use the impetus of Alison as director to make a package. You wouldn't want to put up all the money yourself, would you?" he asked uncertainly. He was, after all, dealing with an exceedingly idiosyncratic Texas empire builder.

"Hell, no." Sam snorted. "That was Lesson One my

daddy taught me. Lesson Two was, Hold on to your property."

Nagy cocked his head. "You would want to hold on to the negative?"

"You got it."

Nagy was doubtful. "The major studios don't like that."

"Why should they? If you got a grocery store, you don't want another grocery store competing with you on the same street. Incidentally I should say, from all the asking I've been doing and all these executives I've been meeting, making movies is just like peddling Ex-Lax. Push the product and wait for the results. Darlin'," he confided to Alison, "there ain't much what you'd call 'heart' to this movie business. But that's what I would want. To hold on to the negative."

"Then why would a major studio agree?" Alison asked.

"Greed. We all got that in us. *They'd* come in if the banks came in, and I got a few favors owed me by a bank. So the bank would put up five million, on my say so, and Alison's being that new hotshot director. I'd pull a little bullshit there—excuse me, darlin'—but it takes a lot of bullshit to get banks and movie companies all hot for you—"

"Is that related to diddly-squat?" Trevina asked mischievously.

"Bullshit is diddly-squat's great grand-daddy" was Sam's definition. "*Then,* I would get foreign tax-shelter money, and then go to the studio for the rest. We'd work out a distribution deal." It sounded so simple.

Alison was silent during all this business talk. She saw great empires soaring from Lillie Mae's little script, and that made her nervous. Empires had been known to collapse. Jonathan Carmichael's had, for one.

"What do you think, darling?" Sam wasn't really asking her.

"I'd have to ask Lillie Mae," she began.

He grinned. "You do that, Alison. You ask Lillie Mae whether she'd like to be in a moving picture, whether she would give her permission, and then you ask her to ask whomever wrote the script and whomever wrote those good ol' fresh songs, as Nagy calls them, and then you get back to me and we'll get the lawyers in on this and get *moving*."

"Does that mean we'll have to leave here right away?" Alison asked plaintively.

"Not so long as there is telephone communication between here and the world. Alison." He shot her a look she both loved and hated. "You are one of the most perverse creatures it has been my pleasure to know. Now, do you wish to proceed with this little venture? Or should I go scuba diving tomorrow?"

"Let's go ahead," she said after a moment. "Maybe Ben should be the lawyer on this? Maybe you should have a co-producer, Sam." She was very reluctant to cast Ben aside.

"Maybe," Sam said evenly. He liked Ben enough. But partners and co-producers made him uneasy. He was used to working alone. Working with Alison was something else. For him it was an experiment, a kind of preamble to a marriage.

It took Lillie Mae Carter exactly thirty seconds to adjust to a long-distance call from Guadeloupe. She heard the funny languages, but she was used to that in her neighborhood, and then Alison's voice came on the phone, telling her that she wanted to do the script.

"Who wrote what?" Alison asked.

"Well, Roberto wrote the script. He's in the High School of Music and Art. He sits next to me in English. José and John-John wrote the music and lyrics together. They're one grade ahead. They're going to be seniors this year."

"You mean they're all minors?"

Lillie Mae wasn't sure whether that was good or bad. She remembered John-John had been arrested once, but his name hadn't appeared in the paper because he *was* a minor. She wasn't about to mention that though.

Instead, she asked, "What do you mean?"

"What I mean is, was this was all written by high school kids?"

"Well, what's wrong with that? We know where it's at!"

"I didn't mean anything bad, Lillie Mae. I told you I love everything about this. I'm just amazed that it came out of the heads of people so young. But if they're going to sign contracts for a movie, their parents will have to consent."

" A *movie*?" Lillie Mae screeched. "Oh, their parents, they'll consent all right."

Sam got on the phone and advised Lillie Mae to have her mother contact a lawyer. He even recommended one. Lillie Mae was certainly agreeable.

"Give me a lawyer and what do I sign?" she said.

"It's an option agreement. Not for you. For them. You didn't write any of this, did you?"

Lillie Mae considered for a moment. She had certainly been an inspiration to Roberto, who was now her boyfriend.

"Do I get more money if I did?" she asked Sam.

"You get a percentage of the option money and a percentage of royalties—"

"I wrote some," Lillie Mae assured him. "The boys will agree to that."

The phone call finished, Sam turned to Alison. "Whew, you could take lessons from that little street hustler. She's got a head for business."

Alison had decided overnight that it was dumb not to know about business. Now she listened, wrote down what she didn't understand, asked questions, annoyed Sam about details, but then he learned to love her interest. And then to respect her mind as well as her creativity.

Alison, in turn, was amazed at how quickly one could obtain money—if one had a certain amount to begin with. The bank in Houston couldn't have been happier to invest. It had only one question after negotiations had been completed. "Does the music have anything a body can hold *on* tó?" Alison understood the complaint. Sam reassured them.

The foreign tax-shelter money was even easier. They really didn't want to know much about the film, but were terribly interested in how much the risk would save them

in tax money. Here again, Sam knew all the men, had
dealt with them and their lawyers before, wined and dined
them in Amsterdam, Paris, Rome, Tokyo, Stockholm, London, and even Houston.

He called the Ellenfields. At first Anne-Marie wasn't
sure the project was cultural enough—fortunately it was
Sam who was on the phone; Alison would not have stood
for that—but when she heard there would be no stars,
that it would be shot on location in Central Park, and that
it had to do with Humanity and the Intermingling of
Cultures, she and Harry made a considerable contribu-
tion. Sam thanked them kindly.

"Eight million dollars and I never left this room," he
said with a grin. The others applauded. The only inhabitants of the house who were not happy with this activity
were Lucien and Marie-Claire. Their faces showed disapproval. This had been meant as a vacation spot. A place to
rest. Lucien's sumptuous meals were only half eaten. Marie-
Claire's great jubilant floral bouquets went unnoticed. There
was nothing but telephone calls and callbacks and conferences among the four of them. Lucien and Marie-Claire
did not approve of all this excitement. It was what these
guests were supposed to be running away from.

At breakfast the next morning, under a cloudless blue
sky, Alison suddenly asked Trevina, "Could you do the
costumes?"

Trevina, taken aback, said, "What costumes? These
are mostly street kids. What would they wear? For the
elegant joggers and cyclists, all you do is go to a sports
house, get their outfits wholesale or for a credit."

"No," Alison said, and began to describe the fantasy
look she wanted. "The Latin-American festival should look
like this." She spread her arms wide. "The handkerchiefs,
the colors, the madras, straw hats. Take it the next step.
Fantasy! The kids—look what they wear nowadays! They
are fantasy. The performers. Outrageous. Oh, Sam had
the right phrase for this film: Kick up your heels. That's
what I want."

Trevina, intrigued, brought out her sketch pad and
pencils. "Like this?" she asked an hour later.

"Yes!" Alison jumped up and down. "Like that. Oh, and let's have some high society, Astaire and Rogers, 'Dancing in the Dark,' you know. Oh," she said again, "we can have such fun with this one!"

"Nagy, come, you drive me," Trevina commanded. "We will go to the town. And then I will see what I want."

"You want Nagy to drive?" Sam inquired gingerly. Nagy was probably a perfect driver for the island. He drove like the French, with absolutely no regard for the rules of the road.

Alison found herself too revved up to sit still.

"Come on," she said to Sam, "let's take the Jeep, do something, explore the rain forest. See the Atlantic side of the island. Something!"

"I have got you hopping," he said, pleased.

"Absolutely. I cannot wait to get back. I figure we rehearse for six weeks and then shoot it."

"Six weeks? You'll be into the first week of July. You'll only have a month to shoot the film before the kids go back to school."

"I'll have to rehearse for three weeks then, and pick the cast fast. I know a lot of what I want. Oh, God, let them be available! What if they aren't?" She began to panic. Sam decided her first idea was a good one. They took the Jeep.

The Basse-Terre was like another world. The roads, narrow and tortuous, ran through tiny villages. On either side was a vibrant green jungle, huge trees, blazing flowers. The opposite of the neat peasant farmlands on their side of the island. Each little village had seven or eight houses, chickens that ran into the road, dogs that barked after them, cats that were sunning themselves, and two or three villagers who stared after them, sometimes answering a wave with a wave, more often just looking. The village would disappear and a small sign would point the way to the next one. Higher and higher they climbed, and still the forest seemed to envelop them until suddenly they were at the top.

They came upon a small restaurant with a hand-lettered sign that read BON REPOS, a building that was more than a shack but less than a house. Alison looked at it queasily. Sam was enthusiastic. And thirsty. He had Alison ask for a bottle of wine.

"*Tout de suite, Madame,*" the *patronne* said. Sam and Alison sat at a rickety table that tipped when one leaned on it. The *patronne* returned with the wine, fresh and cold, two glasses, shining clean, and a piece of paper to place under the table leg for balance. The paper did no good, but the wine was excellent. Alison and Sam sipped it and looked out at the wide expanse of the world from their little table. They were so high up, they could see the curve of the horizon.

The *patronne* offered them a menu and explained to Alison that she would be happy to prepare *une spécialité* for them. Three glasses of wine had released Alison's caution. She agreed and Sam ordered another bottle of wine. The lady returned in a half hour with a thick soup of mussels and crayfish and a salad of ripe papayas and avocados that was divided by large grapefruit slices and crisp lettuce; the salad was served with a dressing that was the perfect complement. Alison discreetly inquired about the ingredients. The *patronne* smiled sweetly and said, "Ah, Madame, we all must have our secrets. And now I prepare a dessert."

She slid away into her native world behind the screen and the bar.

Alison gingerly tasted the soup, put down her spoon, and began to laugh. Sam looked at her. "It's our lucky day," she said. "We struck it rich. Taste the soup."

It was Taillevent, it was Lutèce, it was the Café Chambord, Chantilly, Père Bise, Troisgros. It was nectar, it was fantastic. They had three bowls apiece and then the *patronne* stunned them with a mango pie topped with custard.

"*C'est pas bon repos. C'est Bon Repas!*" Alison exclaimed, and the *patronne* accepted the compliment with grace. They exchanged French franc notes and farewells and then Alison and Sam began the sharp descent. An hour later they reached the Atlantic side, where a majestic sea, surf rolling in, replaced the placid Caribbean. A strong breeze was blowing in from the ocean. Sam stopped the Jeep.

"Christ, will you look at that!" he said, Texas diminished for the moment.

"Oh, Sam, there's a beach over there," Alison said, pointing. In a small clearing, totally surrounded by giant palms, lay a stretch of sand.

"Can you believe this?" He looked around at the landscape. "Not a soul in sight. Not a single house." He was used to the relative sophistication of the other side of the island. "I feel like Columbus," he said, climbing out of the Jeep. "This is totally deserted. We're the first people ever to discover this place."

"Except the ones who built the road," she reminded him.

"Let's explore," he said, taking her hand and heading for the beach. Fringing it, before the jungle made its claim, lay a thousand different tropical blossoms, red, violet, a lush blue. A hundred feet away the breakers were rolling in, directly from Africa. There was the song of the Atlantic wind, the roar of the breakers, and no other sound in the entire world. The sun beat down on the beach. They sought the shade. The wine had made them sleepy. They relaxed into a somnolent, slightly tipsy embrace. Passion came upon them slowly, taking its own sweet time. They were lovers with all the time in the world. They tasted of wine and mango pie, a saltiness that was partly their bodies and partly the air around them. The fragrance of the flowers added to the sensuality. Slowly, slowly, Sam stripped off his cutoffs and unbuttoned the man's shirt Alison was wearing, unfastened her jeans.

They were naked in the shade of the palm leaves. He knelt over her, preparing to make love. Silently and slowly, like two lazy cats, they rubbed their bodies against each other, almost reaching a climax and delaying, not moving a muscle, feeling the waves of passion crest like the breakers beyond them, but not letting their own waves dissolve, but to crest even higher. It was delicious and tormenting, becoming an endurance contest to see who could hold back longer. Sam was very adept at this, Alison realized. A touch of jealousy struck her. He had learned before. Someone had taught him, some other woman. But it did not matter. Nothing mattered but the moment, and when it came upon them, Alison screamed out. She became a crazy person. Writhing with pleasure, her nails scratching the hard muscles of his shoulders, she desired to envelop his compact body completely.

He was the silent one; his body expressed everything. It knotted with desire, crashed into her, flowed, surrounded her, crushed her, ground and panted, lips kissed a thank-you of gratification, and finally they both were still, sated. Complete.

But that is never the case. Love only asks for more love. Enough is never enough. Alison rose from the pile of clothes and walked, nude, down to the ocean's edge. Sam followed her. Hand in hand they walked along, feeling the waves break at their ankles. The sensation of nudity was extraordinary. Alison felt like she'd been freed from a prison. She grew hot as the sun's rays touched her breasts and buttocks. She plunged into the ocean. Revitalized, she was aware of the water on every part of her body, cooling and caressing her. She dived underneath and came to the surface again and again. A mermaid, Sam thought, as he dived after her.

They swam until they were tired, then floated on the buoyant tide, letting the sun warm their bodies. Once again they swam, and entwined with each other, tasting the sea on each other's lips. And it came upon them again—this passion that was as overwhelming as the Atlantic. They began to couple in the water, but the swell of the tide made it impossible. He carried her out of the surf, bore her all the way to the edge of the beach and the shelter of trees. Still standing, he thrust into her. She climbed on him. Animals, leaning against a pliant tree, they both felt at the same time, the same power, the same sexual hunger. She felt the juices released, the whole giving up of herself to him.

She could not have said where her body left off and his began. They were one instrument, the male and the female, working perfectly in passion. Rhythms, tides. This time they both moaned and sighed and cried, and finally when she was dizzy from the increasing never-ending excitement of her orgasm, Sam let himself erupt in her. And he cried out. No one, no person on the earth had ever heard him cry so fully and so openly. Not a defense was left against this woman. It was a cry that was both exultant and as natural as a baby's. The cry of a man who has given all to his mate.

How wrong they had been to think that sexual pleasure had boundaries. They dropped to the mound of clothes and embraced, and each touch of her finger on his arm was the equal of another orgasm. It was an enchanted time for them both, when they fully understood the present that had been given to them in their bodies. They were beautiful humans. She was at the height of her glory. Her breasts were full and firm, her belly slightly rounded and feminine, her calves and legs smooth and long. And Sam was the male; the buttocks hard, the stomach flat, shoulders and upper arms muscled, the legs strong and graceful. They were loving creatures.

It did not stop when they donned their clothes. They were still in a state of excitement. Every movement caused a tremor. They were on the edge of passion as they walked back to the Jeep, as he put the vehicle into gear, when her hand grazed his thigh, his shoulder touched hers. They had no words to say to each other, they needed none. The late afternoon sun was blinding now and they drove along in a golden blaze. They were again in the flat countryside, where farmers were preparing for the night. The last of the day's chores at hand. The livestock to be fed, cows to be milked, supper to be prepared. And then, perhaps, man and woman would couple as they had, would feel the same sense of belonging to each other.

Even in Pointe-à-Pitre there are traffic jams. At five in the afternoon the tiny buses, the carts, the livestock, the French officials, the native pedestrians, the fascinated tourist, and the last-minute shoppers caused a melee.

As they crept along Alison suddenly saw Kenny Buck. He was in a station wagon with an assortment of musical instruments and faces masked by dark glasses. The station wagon bore the insignia SAMPSON STUDIOS, GOSIER, and had palm trees painted on one side. At first she thought she was mistaken, the face was so thin, the cheekbones so pronounced. But he was also staring at her. Auto horns, angry voices, moos, neighs, shouts, filled the marketplace.

Sam was swearing. Alison and Kenny simply stared at each other, pointing and laughing. How ridiculous for them to find each other again in a marketplace in Guadeloupe. Alison glanced in the Jeep's mirror and understood why Kenny had looked at her so oddly. Her blond hair, still wet from the ocean, was flattened to her head. She was wearing Sam's white shirt. Sam himself was bare-chested and almost as brown as some of the natives.

Kenny clambered out of the car. He was wearing a black vest and white pants. No shoes. She saw that he was painfully thin; he looked ill. She could see his ribs. There was something frantic—manic—in his movements. She couldn't put her finger on what disturbed her so about him.

"What a place to meet!" Kenny giggled in an unnaturally high voice. Alison introduced him to Sam. Mutual dislike on sight.

"We're here on vacation," Alison shouted over the din. "At Myra's."

"Oh."

"She died," Alison said.

"I know," Kenny said. Myra's death had no meaning for him.

"And you—what are you doing?"

"Making an album."

"What?"

"You know. Music. Tum-tum. Remember? I was a singer once."

"I remember."

"Diane brought me here for a couple of sessions with Stevie Wonder, and McCartney's coming in with Linda. Billy Joel. Linda Ronstadt. It's David's idea. Beautiful!"

Why was he dropping so many names? Why did he feel so insecure? she wondered. "Is Diane here?" she asked.

"Yeah. She and David are producing the album. He built a studio down here. Beautiful!"

He pulled out a card. "You must come round and see. This card'll get you by security. Security very tight here. But beautiful."

Sam was regarding Kenny. Kenny was ignoring Sam.

Suddenly the traffic dispersed. Kenny turned back to his car, then shouted to Alison.

"Hey, aren't you going to congratulate me? Best actor at the Cannes Festival."

"What?" Alison felt she had not heard correctly.

"Best actor!" Kenny repeated, exultant and laughing at the same time. "Me!" He pointed to his chest.

"Cannes? *The Ski Pro?*" Alison was confused. Ben had said New York, the New York Film Festival. He had never mentioned Cannes. Why was that? "Who else won?" she asked.

"Paul Masland best director. A Polish film won best film, but who gives a fuck about that? It's going to be a big one! Give a call! We'll come get you. It'll be beautiful!"

And he was back in the station wagon and gone, gone, leaving Alison stunned.

"What was he saying? Did you hear it? What does it mean, Paul Masland was voted best director? That was my film. I was called in. I made that film. There are people to prove it."

"We'll call when we get to Myra's. Just calm down."

"I won't calm down!" Alison snapped, as though it were all Sam's fault. "There has to be a mistake. I know. Maybe it's Kenny. He was high. Did you notice he was high?"

"I noticed."

"He's mean. Basically, he's just mean. He's mean enough to play that kind of joke on me. That's what it has to be. Some kind of joke."

It was no joke. Sam put through the call to Ben Sawyer. After the first two *I see*'s on Sam's part, though, Alison grabbed the phone away from him. There was an instinctive look of anger on Sam's part, but he relinquished the phone.

"Ben, tell me, it's me, Alison. What does this mean?"

Ben's voice on the other end of the wire was too cool and too distant, even for all the miles that separated them.

"Alison, it was all a contractual matter. Obligations."

Alison did not say "I see." "What the hell kind of double-talk is that, Ben?"

"We were contractually obligated to put Paul Masland's name on the screen as director. We gave you everything you asked for. We lived up to the letter of our contract." Alison realized this was a lawyer talking. She had forgotten that Ben knew all the angles. And had played them. Suddenly it all fit together, the picture came into focus.

"I understand. You had this planned from the very first. From the moment I signed the contract. No wonder Paul Masland was so easy to manipulate. No wonder Diane walked around pleased as a puss. She got what she wanted. She finally got her star to give a performance. She got her movie. She even got her director *credit*."

Ben was trying to protest. Alison steamrolled on.

"And that was why you kept saying, 'Credits to come' and why it was lucky I wasn't in Seattle, and why you lied to me about the Cannes Festival. You lied to me, Ben. You cheated me. You used me. And maybe you were like that all the time and I just never knew it. I liked you. I thought I liked your decency. I thought I liked your sense of honor. But don't blame David for this one. Or Diane. People don't allow themselves to be used unless they want to be." Then the tears of rage and frustration took over and she slammed down the receiver. Nothing settled. Nothing gained. Ben had won. As Diane had won. And Kenny too. Perhaps Kenny didn't know about this. But perhaps he did. She was in a fury to find out.

"Come on," she said to Sam.

"Hey, wait. You're in no condition to go anywhere."

"I'm going to find out from Kenny—"

"What? That you were mixed up with a bunch of bastards? I could have told you that from the first. I knew that. How come you didn't? You get thrown out on your ass—and you make a movie with the man who threw you out and the fuckin' bitch who helped to do it. You not only make a movie, you sit there and talk to him today—"

"It wasn't his fault."

"Bullshit, it wasn't his fault. *Her* fault. *Ben's* fault."

"Then why didn't you tell me?" she screamed at him.

"Because you never would have believed me!" he screamed back.

She stared at him for a minute. "Did you know about Cannes?" she asked, her voice quiet.

"No," he said, so simply that she had to believe him. She sat down. She got up. She paced. Nagy and Trevina returned, bubbling over with enthusiasm, sketches, a wonderful bistro, costumes, whole pads full of costumes—to be met with Alison's fury. By now she was so angry, she could not speak. Sam told the story. Nagy nodded. Nothing ever seemed to surprise him, but then, he had lived through a concentration camp. What was there left? Trevina tried to comfort Alison. Comfort was not acceptable.

"I'm going out there," she said. "I'll go alone if none of you will come with me."

"Where?" Nagy asked.

"Where Kenny is. This studio of David's."

She had the keys to the Jeep in her hand. She ran out, started the motor, and was off before anyone could stop her.

"The only thing to do is follow her," Sam said.

"Myra's Jeep is out back," Trevina said. The three of them took off in pursuit.

Alison knew vaguely where she was going. The night was pitch-black and the feeble headlights illuminated only patches of the tortuous twists in the mountain road. She was blinded by tears of fury. She raced the Jeep down the mountain path at breakneck speed. Villages, deserted by the night, whizzed by her. Dogs barked and chased her out of town.

Pointe-à-Pitre came in view with its signs and tourists. She leaned on the horn. People looked up at her angrily. She pushed the Jeep past them, her jaw set. She wanted to scream out at the night, at the darkness. The fury rose in her throat. She thought for a moment she might be sick. She pressed down the accelerator more firmly. Suddenly in front of her she saw a curve. She applied the brakes and swung the wheel. She could see only darkness, and then the edge of the road loomed up in front of her. Beyond that was nothingness. The edge came closer; the Jeep skidded. She was too terrified to scream. She just held her breath. The Jeep shuddered by the edge of the mountain pass, wavered, steadied. Stopped.

Alison closed her eyes. Gulped for breath. Sucked in the sweet night air. Her hands were shaking, but she was in control. Again she put the Jeep in gear and moved forward. She was no longer crying. Her fury was cold and white. She could taste it like bitter blood in her mouth. Always, always and always, she had trusted. And she had been hurt. She had trusted Kenny. He had hurt her. Had taken her love and destroyed it. Had almost destroyed her.

No, it was Diane. Diane was the destroyer and always had been. Whatever else happened, there was one constant and that was the bitch. The cruel bitch. Alison could picture the smile now, taunting her, just ahead in the night.

Then she saw lights. There was a barricade. A number of vehicles. Activity. She was stopped by the guards. They spoke to her in Creole. She didn't understand, so she addressed them in French. Their response sent her screaming past them, past the open gate into the compound.

By this time Sam, Nagy, and Trevina had caught up with her. Nagy asked the guard what had happened, and was silent after the guard had answered him.

"What is it?" Sam asked.

"It's Kenny Buck," Nagy whispered. "I believe they said he's dead."

Alison found Diane.

"Where is he? What have you done with him?" she screamed.

For once Diane had a look of fear in her eyes. She gestured. Kenny lay on a stretcher in the next room. They hadn't covered his face. He was, in fact, still wearing the black vest. He looked just the same, except now he was dead and his arm was flung carelessly over his belly, its strength gone somewhere else. Alison stared down at him and saw another crumpled corpse, another overdose, another headline for another day's paper.

"Beautiful!" She spat the word at Diane and the herd of groupies and roadies and druggies, some with blue hair and some with orange, some with beads and some with none. All of them with silly stupid trendy idiotic suicide-prone childish dumb faces. All of them except Diane.

She had to attack that face. Started to. Was restrained.

"Killer!" she shrieked in her fury. "Bitch! Killer!"

The words meant nothing.

Back at Myra's Trevina found a sedative and gave it to Alison. She swallowed the pill obediently, then laughed suddenly, hysterically.

"The one time I didn't have my camera ready. I could have made a fortune tonight. Last pictures of Kenny Buck!"

Sam took her to bed, comforted her, finally fell asleep. She rose and walked out on the terrace.

The moon was also alone in the sky. The Caribbean sparkled below. She sought Kenny somewhere in the vastness, the immensity of heaven. They had met so abruptly, from nowhere. She could recall the brilliance of that snowy day. She could recall their times of love, the passion he held for her, the tenderness he sometimes allowed to creep in. Then she pictured him as a little boy in the shack in Maine, surrounded by rusty junkheaps in the yard. She could see him crying, sitting cross-legged on a bed, letting the tears fall down his cheeks.

And then she thought of his baby. *Their* baby that had never been, that could have been. He would have been almost four now. And she would have seen to it that he never, never cried like Kenny had, was never abandoned, never cuffed around, never made to feel unwanted. She would have protected him, sheltered him in her arms. He would have had Kenny's eyes, the dark skin, the flashing grin. She could have kept a part of Kenny.

And now there was nothing but the moon sailing by, unconcerned in an unknowing night. *We live, sailing just like that,* she thought. *We do meet each other by chance and love for a while, leave each other or get left behind, sail away, float off, depart from this earth. And mostly it is as though nothing has occurred. The moon continues to cross the sky. The sea continues to sparkle.*

She stared the night down until dawn erased the moon and nothing was left but the sea, blue again in the light of morning.

Chapter Thirty-one

They returned to New York on the twenty-eighth of May. The news was out, of course. First the news of Kenny Buck's death. And the awards at the Cannes Festival.

Sam found himself in a bad way. He was being called a liar. He didn't take to that. But in the long run he had to swallow it and see most of his potential investment drop off.

Not the foreign tax-shelter money, however. Those people were just as happy. Risks gave them pleasure. The word was out, underground, that Paul Masland had not directed the film. Most insiders knew that Alison had been called in.

But the bank in Houston was conservative. It backed out of the deal. That was five million backing away. "She's a woman, Sam," they explained, "and, begging your pardon, but if you want to put that kind of money behind her, you go right ahead. We were going on your say so, but—again, Sam—nothing personal, maybe she did direct that ski film, and then again—"

"Forget it," Sam snapped, and hung up.

They were alone, just the two of them, Sam and Alison.

"That's probably good advice," Alison said slowly.

"What is?"

"To forget it."

"Do you want to?" he asked. She was looking at his hands. Fists, he had made fists.

"No," she said. "No, I don't. But you can't invest in this all by yourself."

"Let me tell you a story. A God-for-real Texas story. I got started in real estate. I couldn't get anyone to invest in oil. And I knew I had oil. 'You don't know diddly-squat about the oil business,' that's what the banks said, and they wouldn't loan me a cent. But I scraped together the money somehow—fifteen thousand. And that investment paid for itself in 40 days. After that it was easier to find investors. Then I got to drilling a well by myself. I didn't have all the money. It took twenty-five days for that well to come in. But it did. That was the longest holding of breath I ever did in my life. But I'm prepared to do it again. You know why? It's like living in high gear. It's more fun that way. Now—let's see how we can cut down on production costs."

Alison remembered Huttner one day mentioning there was a new electronic system for editing film that could cut twenty-five to thirty percent off the cost of making it.

"Holy shit, why didn't you say anything about it before?" Sam shouted.

"I didn't think about it till this moment," she shouted back. He got on the phone to Huttner immediately, and by the time he was through, Huttner had given him all the information and agreed to work on the film on deferral.

Yes, Alison thought, two days later when she had seen seventy five young actors for the various roles, this was living in high. She was so revved up with the need to work, to accomplish, she could survive on very little sleep. To her delight, she had her crew for the asking. Jimmy Smith drove east in a '52 Ford, giving up a trip to Tahiti to work on the film. Conti offered to orchestrate it. He was enchanted, as every one else had been, by the quality of the score.

"Who are these bastards?" he asked when he had heard the first three songs. "I'm going to kill them. Who needs the competition?"

Conti only wrote his own music. It was an honor to have him work on another composer's work.

Lillie Mae also had her own ideas. She could have cast the film in two days herself. She brought in friends, street kids she had hustled with and whom she had discovered when she began to work in the theater. She saw this as Star Time and was not about to be dissuaded by any little roadblocks such as money. Surprisingly, and then again maybe not so surprisingly, Alison agreed with most of Lillie Mae's choices. Lillie Mae, of course, played the girl from Harlem. A very handsome sweet-faced boy named Perez was chosen to play the young Puerto Rican emigrant who lived in New Jersey. Within a week Alison had her cast, her choreographer, had started rehearsals at Variety Arts. For three weeks her life was again a chain of cardboard coffee cups, rehearsal halls, routines that couldn't possibly work but magically did. Conti was incredibly patient, then got set back on his haunches. The kids came in with an improvisation. Two bars into it his finger went to the record button on the tape player. The kids improvised truer than he was able to approximate by writing. So he used their improvisations, left them free to work in their own way, then selected from the product.

Alison sped from breakfast meeting to rehearsal, to business lunch, to music session, to Trevina's atelier to look at the costumes. Once in a while she noticed the sun was shining, or the moon. Toward the end of the month she overheard someone say that it had been the most beautiful June in memory, one dazzling day after another. But this had no bearing on Alison's life.

Or so she thought at the time.

The shooting schedule had been planned like this:

Fourth of July weekend, film the concert in the park, plus the fireworks, which were, of course, the climax of the film. The concert itself would be presented as a benefit. Save Central Park. The Parks Commission, traditionally short of funds, had agreed enthusiastically. Particularly when Sam listed the performers: Loggins and Messina, Stevie Wonder, Mad Queen Bess. Sam had also stipulated that the production company would be responsible for cleaning up the debris that always followed one of these concerts.

Therefore with the encouragement of the Parks Commission, Sam had advertised widely. Articles appeared in *The Times, Post,* and *News,* plus a "Best Bets" in *New*

York magazine. Fliers were pasted to billboards by the thousands. A stage had been erected near the baseball field, beyond which spread the expanse of the Sheep Meadow.

Alison and Jimmy Smith had discussed the number of cameras to be used, the enormous amount of equipment that had to be moved, stored, hung, laid, or connected; wires, cables, lamps, scaffolding, microphones. The entire process was like planning a battle campaign. Surely Waterloo had been less arduous, Alison thought.

The very first day of shooting, the day before the concert, was splendid. The fifteen Winnebagos that served as makeup rooms, dressing rooms, canteens, and the like stretched like a gypsy caravan along the walkway bordering the 72nd Street pond. The scene between the girl and the boy involved the sailing of one of the tiny model battery-driven sailboats. A trek across a miniature ocean. The song—which had been prerecorded—expressed the boy's dream of taking her on a trip "across the sea so blue to Puerto Rico . . ." It could not have come off better. The weather was feathery early summer, fresh morning-cool. They started at seven and were finished by eleven, ahead of schedule. The two other locations involved the boy and girl meeting, and her showing him Belvedere Castle. Both scenes were shot during the afternoon. The cast was a dream to work with. Even New Yorkers who happened on the scene contributed to the infectious fun of the film. Alison and Jimmy looked at each other. They could not believe their luck.

The next morning rain set in. A dull gray sky and a dull steady monotonous rain.

Sam had rented a suite in the Sherry Netherland to use as office space. They drove there from SoHo and stared gloomily out the window. By nine o'clock the phones were ringing. The crew: Would there be a shoot that night or not? The press: Would the concert be postponed? The Parks Department: Had the production company provided for a possible rain date, in other words, another night for the concert? Sam fielded these questions as best he could.

Jimmy Smith entered the office and sat with Alison. Together they looked out at the park.

"It sure is green," Jimmy said.

"And wet," Alison said.

"Maybe it will clear. What's the weather report?"

"Unstable conditions."

"Well, that could work in our favor."

"It could."

It seemed to. At five o'clock, miraculously, the rain stopped and the sun appeared. Sam, Jimmy, and Alison whooped like children told they had been let out of school. They rushed across town to the Sheep Meadow. The crew had been on call. They were ready.

What shocked Alison was the crowd. They were kids and had been waiting there all day. Some of them were soaked to the skin but happy. They frolicked like puppies, throwing Frisbees, setting off firecrackers. Jimmy and Alison took one look and immediately set the cameramen to work. Yes, this was it! This was the feel. This was kick-up-your-heels time. A celebration. The rain had only added a kind of drama to it. A victory celebration, Alison thought. The team after a championship game. In the locker room. Everybody wet, and who could care? She was already visualizing the way she wanted to cut from Frisbee to face, from sky to eye, from laughter to love, kisses. Her mind returned to Woodstock. This scene had that same free quality, the quality that had been missing from America now for two or three years.

The outrageous Mad Queen Bess showed up in a long white limousine with an enormous jolly Falstaffian crony named Franklin, a manager, and two or three gofers. The crowd roared. Queen Bess waved back enthusiastically, blowing kisses.

Her manager stated his conditions.

"Any rain, no play. The musicians are afraid of being electrocuted."

"Why don't we just wait and see what develops?" Sam suggested with his West Texas drawl.

"I want it straight up front!" the manager snapped.

"Well, *we* don't want to see anyone *killed*." Sam started to dead-eye the man. Suddenly everything was getting heavy. Including the weather. Muggy. The sun disappeared. The atmosphere became oppressive.

"I got a band to protect."

"I got an entire production at stake."

Alison looked away. On the stage, Bess and her jovial Falstaff appeared, took one look at the threatening sky and broke into an impromptu Indian rain dance. Alison laughed.

But that was her last laugh for a long time. Almost immediately the first clap of thunder was heard. The clouds grew black. Lightning flashed and a torrential downpour began. The crowd ran for cover.

"That's it!" the manager ordered. "Bess does not perform."

"To hell with that!" Sam said, turning toward the police. "Get those kids away from those trees."

"Oh," the officer said. Born and raised in Brooklyn, he was street-smart but had no knowledge of nature whatsoever. However, a command was a command.

"Oh, my *goodness*," the bedraggled Mad Queen said as she joined them, "I didn't realize my *pow-er*." Then, seeing Alison's expression, she immediately became sympathetic. "Gee, I'm sorry."

"Well, it's not your fault," Alison said.

"Maybe it will clear up," Bess said hopefully.

"We are not staying around to find out," the manager interposed. The Mad Queen silenced him with a look and settled down in one of the wagons. "Any coffee?" she asked. Someone supplied her with a cup and two towels, one for her and one for Franklin, who was fiddling with straws and looking extremely uncomfortable. The camper was suddenly filled with a dripping, sopping, cursing crew. They were all carny folk, Alison realized, and they were losing the night's profits.

The storm turned violent as the wind rose. An enormous crash of thunder prompted an exclamation from the Mad Queen. A discussion followed about whether or not the Winnebagos were safe in a thunderstorm.

"They're metal. Metal attracts lightning."

"But they're on wheels. Rubber. It acts as an insulation. It's better to be in a moving vehicle during a thunderstorm."

"Yeah, but we're not moving."

Eventually they did. Limousines were lined up and stars, grips, producers, managers were all drenched by the rain. It lasted all night and Sam had provided no rain date.

"Now what?" Alison asked him the next morning. The rain had tapered off to a light drizzle.

"I don't know," he said. "There's some kind of tropical depression."

"You've been talking to the weather bureau."

"I've been talking to everyone. We might as well have gone on location in bloody London." He was not smiling. She noticed his hands were balling into fists, relaxing, then balling again.

"How much is this costing us, this delay?" she asked.

"It depends on how long the rain lasts," he said gloomily.

"I mean, how much per day?" she persisted.

"Don't ask me that. It'll upset me and just make you nervous. Pray for sun."

Prayers didn't work. Nothing did. The rain continued off and on for six days. The papers were already forecasting the wettest July on record.

Alison visited the troops. They were encamped, many of them, in the wagons, on call, on pay, advised that the rain might let up any minute. That was the worst part of the week. It constantly seemed to be clearing, and then another downpour would occur.

One group of men, very few of whom spoke English, were grouped together like a stranded soccer team.

"Who are they?" Alison asked Sam.

"The bicyclists. Stuntmen."

"You're paying them?"

"Every day."

"Oh." Alison was beginning to feel it was all her fault. They walked out into the soggy park.

Abruptly Sam began to yell to shake his fist at the heavens.

"Fucking weather! Drought ruined my daddy! And now you're trying to drown me with this rain! Well, fuck it all!" His outburst over and drenched once again, they returned in defeat to the Sherry Netherland, where a new doorman tried to deny them entrance. They were both sopping wet, Sam, unshaven, in his chinos, Alison in her blue jeans.

"I'm sorry, sir," the doorman said to Sam, blocking his entrance.

"Me too," Sam growled.

"What I mean is, you can't go in."

Sam looked at the man. "Why not?"

"Look at you!"

"We've been making a movie!" Sam shouted at the top of his voice. That evidently excused any kind of behavior, any kind of dress, because the doorman immediately became apologetic. A stream of *I'm sorry, sir*'s followed them through the lobby.

"Maybe we should take the freight elevator," Alison suggested as they waited, making great puddles on the marble floor.

"Not at these prices," Sam said. When it finally came, the passenger elevator took them directly to their floor.

Once in the suite, they stripped off their wet clothes. The air conditioning was running full blast and the room was freezing. They wrapped themselves in towels, then ordered more since there weren't enough. Then a bottle of bourbon and some steaks. They drank the bourbon and ate the steaks in front of the window, watching the rain ruin their production.

Around ten o'clock Nagy joined them. He took a glass from the bathroom and poured himself a drink.

"Here's to good times," he toasted them. They gave him a look that would have killed anyone but a Hungarian. "So, now, how far behind schedule are you?"

"One week and two days," Sam said.

"And our best effect was just rained out," Alison said, gesturing toward the window. Nagy figured rapidly that the delay in shooting was costing Sam half a million dollars a week.

Sam had confided to Nagy that when the majors had backed out and no investors had registered interest, he had called his bank in Houston and taken a loan at twenty-one percent interest, using his real estate holdings as collateral. But he could only afford such exorbitant interest rates for a short time. Eight weeks to be exact. He had figured that, with the new editing system, the film would have been completed by that date. Now the margin was down by a week.

Delay made Alison impatient. Sam was watching another hundred thousand dollars literally go down the drain. There was nothing Nagy could say. So he proceeded to get drunk with the two of them.

The following day the sun came out to mock them. The city was radiant. Clean. Glowing. The Fourth of July had come and gone, and Alison and Sam had missed their big chance. There was nothing to do but start shooting again and try to figure out some way of filming the concert.

For Alison the next four weeks were enormously creative. Everything cooperated—the weather, New York, the cast, and her own sense of vision. The episode involving the theft and the bicycle chase through a runner's marathon turned out to be hilarious. Lillie Mae had obviously fallen in love with her leading man. In classic fashion the tough little street singer had proved to be a soft touch. Right before the camera—and Alison's delighted eye—Lillie Mae turned into a woman. She bloomed like a flower, becoming a beauty. Alison made a note to reshoot the ending. It had been part of the first day's schedule. Lillie Mae was not the same person she had been a month ago. She could bring much more to the scene now, Alison speculated.

The only gloomy aspect during those weeks for Alison was Sam. He was unusually cranky. She could sense him looking over her shoulder every moment, silently urging her to shoot faster.

Half of New York was watching their progress. They stood behind police barricades, or, either uncaring or blissfully unaware, they jogged through scenes, walked their dogs past the cameras. Alison made it all part of the movie, part of the party. The kids were the intoxicant. The kids and the park.

One Sunday morning, growing nostalgic about her own first love, Alison took a mobile unit and began to shoot a scene that encompassed all different kinds of music. The brass quintet that played near the Plaza, the four different groups of folksingers who fringed the walkway to the 72nd Street Shell, the steel drum that banged away under the statue of Hans Christian Andersen while roller skaters whirled in front, weaving graceful patterns in and amid the grim-faced joggers. Watching them gave Alison an idea. She asked Lillie Mae and Perez if they could roller-skate. Both looked at her scornfully. Could a fish swim? She rented skates at 79th Street, then asked them to play a game using the joggers as obstacles. And so an impromptu dance sequence was formed—the graceful, flying lovers and their plodding, earnest elders. It was a lyrical sequence. Even Sam, who had taken to short, mysterious trips out of town, fell in love with the dailies. Moments like these made all the fatigue, the boredom of waiting, the anxiety of keeping schedules worthwhile.

But there was a merciless reality that Alison kept postponing until the last minute. There was no culmination to the film. There was the tender meeting, the amusing disagreement, the contrast between City Girl and Country Boy, the love story that was even more touching than Alison had realized, the celebration of the mixture of cultures that make up Central Park, the hilarious bicycle caper, all the wonderful songs, but no concert. And no hope of duplicating the event. Mad Queen Bess was off in Australia, and Stevie Wonder was rumored to be recording an album in a secret studio up the Amazon. There was no way to deal with the idiosyncrasies of the rock world. And yet the script demanded an Event.

They had shot the beginning of the concert, of course. Jimmy Smith had ordered a camera to be trained on Mad Queen Bess at all times. They had footage of her rain dance with the Falstaffian Franklin and the crowd's reaction.

What they didn't have was the vocal part.

Alison showed the footage to the cast, who laughed and applauded just like a regular audience. Then Lillie Mae jumped up.

"Did you see that?" she cried, doing a perfect imitation of the Mad Queen.

"Yeah!" Perez jumped up and joined her, portraying

the Portly Partner. It took exactly two seconds for Alison
to visualize the sequence. With that savior of most musicals, the Dream Sequence, they would dissolve from Bess
and Franklin to Lillie Mae and Perez becoming their
idols. From that thought it was only another second before
Alison conceived of having the kids perform the concert.
Street kids, street concert. And there should be some
song which summed up the joy of the picture. Her mind
was racing and for a second she thought of Paris. *Click!
Click!* Take everything. Do everything. Nothing was
impossible.

Was this?

She asked Lillie Mae and the kids if they could do a
real concert on the stage in Sheep Meadow. They could
hardly wait to get started.

How would they attract an audience again? They
didn't have time to circulate fliers.

"You want an audience?" asked Lillie Mae, grabbing
on to her chance for stardom. "Don't worry 'bout it. I'll
get you a crowd. I can do it, right, Perez?"

"I'll tell the world!" Perez said, and at that Alison
perked up.

"What?" she asked. "What did you say?"

"I'll tell the world!" Perez repeated, mystified. His
English was not perfect. He spoke slang, mostly, which he
learned from watching old Warner Bros. movies on
television.

Alison summoned José and John-John.

"I want to tell the world how wonderful the world is,"
she said, "how wonderful love is, and being young, and
being old and being alive and having friends—"

"We understand, we got it!" said José and John-John,
and off they went.

Sam called the Parks Department and refused to be
put on hold. In twenty minutes he got permission to use
the stage and the Sheep Meadow for the following evening.

About five o'clock the next night Alison's limo drove
up to the Sheep Meadow. She saw a sea of faces. Where
had they all come from? she wondered. There were maybe
ten thousand kids, and the number seemed to be growing.

She confronted Lillie Mae. "What did you do? How did you manage this?"

Lillie Mae shrugged. "You out on the streets long enough, you get to know people. Looks like I know enough!" She smugly surveyed the crowd. "Of course, only five thousand are *mine*. The rest is just what happens in New York when you got a crowd. When you got a crowd, you get a crowd!"

Sam arrived on the scene. His whoop was pure Texan excitement. "Get Frisbees!" he ordered a gofer.

"Where?" the gofer asked.

"How the fuck do I know?" Sam roared. "Get 'em. Steal 'em if you have to!"

Lillie Mae and the rock band rehearsed the song "I'll Tell the World."

"Catchy title," Alison said, grinning at José.

"We thought so," the lyricist agreed modestly.

It was not Alison's talent to be musical. She stood in awe of anyone who could even whistle. Therefore when she heard the kids—guitars, bass, keyboards, Lillie Mae, backup trio—begin to sing a song that had not existed twenty-four hours ago, she was totally speechless.

Still, at first she wasn't sure about the song. It sounded good, but how good could anything be on such short notice? She listened again. This time the performance was smoother. It was good. Maybe better than good. Catchy certainly.

When it was time, Alison appeared before the crowd to explain the proceedings. She described the debacle of the previous concert, then told the audience that this was a movie and introduced the cast.

When she was through, she nodded to Jimmy and signaled the sound engineer. A plane few overhead. They waited.

"If it ain't the fuckin' rain, it's the fuckin' planes," Sam shouted in exasperation. Alison studied him for a moment. Where had Mr. Cool gone to? She was allied with another crazy producer. It made her laugh.

Quiet. It was time for a take. Keep the cameras rolling, Alison had ordered. Jimmy, as before, had given

instructions that one camera was to remain on Lillie Mae
at all times.

The band started. Lillie Mae made her entrance.
Alison gasped. In some thrift shop or other Trevina had
found a spangly sequin gown Queen Bess would have
given her Australian bullion for. It was trashy, it was
flashy, and it suited Lillie Mae's dream perfectly. Little
Sequin Street Singer, Alison thought. Well, go to it, missy.
This picture lies in your hands right now.

Lillie Mae put down one track that was hot. Dissatisfied, she did another, forcing the band to focus all its
attention on following her. The amount of dynamic energy
that was being projected from that stage shook the audience. They may have come as strangers or friends, but
they stayed as fans.

Ten takes in all. Some of them were spoiled by noise
and mechanical difficulties. On the last take Lillie Mae
whipped the microphone around, swiveled her hips to the
beat. The gospel-rock rhythm gave her the chance to tear
loose. She moved. No choreographer could have come up
with such outrageous combinations. The backup trio mocked
her. They turned one another on. Lillie Mae had a brief
flirtation with the band and they stomped. Lillie Mae
whirled on the audience. She had never done that before.

"Come on, everybody. You oughta know it by now.
Tell me 'bout the *world*!" The audience roared out the
song, clapped in rhythm, started their own dance. Lillie
Mae glowed like a diamond in the dark. She left the stage
and threaded her way through the twisting bodies. Then
she was back onstage and built to one tremendous climax
whose decibel count had all the residents of the West Side
holding their ears. Finally it was over. Finished. A wrap!

"Print it!" Alison screamed, and rushed onstage to embrace Lillie Mae before the stage filled to overflowing
with grips, cameramen, props, scriptgirl, Sam, Jimmy,
Nagy, Trevina, street kids, gaffers, freaks, and bystanders.
It was August 12.

Chapter Thirty-two

Huttner came to town. Once again he began the process of piecing together bits of film to make a whole, a unit. Sam kept pressing them. When? When? He needed a deadline.

"When the film is finished," Alison screamed at him. Only Nagy knew the reason he was pressuring her. She worked. Jimmy Smith worked. Huttner labored over the Rem. At least the new electronic process cut the time in half. Huttner was gleeful. The rough cut was ready in twelve days. Impossible, everyone said. But it was the twenty-fourth, and they were watching it.

This sequence, too long, Alison scribbled on a pad. *Where is the build here!!! Edit the bike sequence.* She was hard on herself. At the end of the film, amid the general celebration, she dictated more notes to her assistant.

"What is this?" Sam demanded.

"Leave me alone. Editing. More work."

"No. No more work!" he said.

"It needs it."

"I'll give you two days."

"Two days! I need two weeks."

"You can't have it!"

"I have final cut," she yelled at him. One thing Alison had learned over the years was how to yell. But his next comment stopped her from speaking at all.

"In two weeks you won't have any film to cut! No more money for this project. The bank is closed!" Then, with a complete change of voice, he said, "I want you to meet a member of the committee for the New York Film Festival."

If she heard the name, she gave no indication. She had time only for her baby. She wanted it to be perfect, and it was being taken away from her while it was still ugly and misshapen. She needed time to fit, to reshoot, to—

". . . unfortunately, the Polish entry *Agony in the Mist* has not been completed. We have an opening in our schedule, and we would very much like to present your film. Particularly since it was filmed in New York, is about New York . . ."

Alison stared at the man. What had he been saying? She could only say aloud what she had been thinking. "It's not ready to be shown."

The man smiled tolerantly. He had heard this all before.

"Miss Carmichael," he said, "it is not unheard of for a film to be reedited following presentation at the Festival. And," he delivered his parting shot, "presentation at the New York Film Festival never hurt."

"We accept your offer," Sam said quickly before Alison could put a word in, then shook the man's hand. Pure Texas. The handshake, the word, was the bond. Alison reflected that Sam had a lot to learn about the entertainment industry. Sometimes, and she thought of David Samson, even a man's bond wasn't his bond.

But it was settled. It would be announced in the newspapers. *Kick Up Your Heels!*, an original musical directed by Alison Carmichael, would be included in the list of films to be presented by the New York Film Festival.

Also included was the Paul Masland film *The Ski Pro*, starring the late Kenny Buck. It promised to be quite an auspicious festival.

Chapter Thirty-three

Only when she saw the announcement in the paper did Alison ask, "Who titled this *Kick Up Your Heels!*?"

Sam, ready for an argument, said, "I did."

"Without asking me?"

"You're not the author."

"No, but—"

Sam had his ammunition ready. "You're not the producer."

"That's true."

"There is nothing in your contract that specifies you have approval of the title."

Alison took back what she had been thinking. Sam had already learned a lot about the business.

"Do you like it better than the other title?" he asked.

"What was the other title?"

"That's just the point. There wasn't any. *Untitled* was its title."

"Oh," said Alison, giggling. "Well, then, I guess I like this title better."

"Thanks," said Sam. "You see what it's like working with a creative producer." He kissed her. "I'll be back for the opening on the twelfth."

"Where are you going?" she asked, suddenly feeling abandoned.

"I got other empires that need fixing," he said, grinning. "Real estate and oil. Just like the movie business. If you don't look out, they'll steal you blind in a minute."

And he left her to spend two weeks in New York by herself.

By the third day she felt she was going crazy, and decided maybe Houston was better than going crazy. She called Sam, yelled at two private secretaries, got hold of him, and asked if she could come to Texas.

He tried not to let his pleasure show too much. He met her at the Houston airport, carefully whisked her into the air-conditioned limousine—not, however, before she had felt one blast of the Houston summer—and then surrounded her with a carefully selected group of funny, intelligent, international Houstonians who had been to New York and seen more plays and read more books than Alison had in the past four years. Their cosmopolitan concerns finally got on her nerves, but she found they all liked to drink. The men *and* the women. After two drinks everyone kind of fell apart and she learned all the dirt about who was sleeping with whom in Houston and had a perfectly lovely time waiting for Sam to finish with his empires.

Somebody at the New York Film Festival was either wildly funny or wildly bitchy. The opening program would this year be a double feature.

The first film (commencing at 6:30 sharp) was *The Ski Pro*, and would be followed at 9:00 by *Kick Up Your Heels!*, after which was a buffet dinner at Le Poulailler, across from Lincoln Center.

They were all there, Alison realized as she took her place beside Sam. No, she corrected herself, two were missing. Myra and Kenny. Otherwise the whole gang was there: David Sampson, who could have used two seats all by himself; Diane Landers, whose escort was program executive, Michael Eisner; Ben Sawyer, who was seated with Julie, the snow bunny. That made good sense, Alison thought, mentally wishing them well, then taking it back. Paul Masland, who looked extremely self-important with his gray hair, gray beard, and pearl-gray tuxedo. And then there was *her* group. Jimmy Smith, Huttner, Nagy, Trevina. . . .

Trevina, looking elegant and Oriental, was draped in

shawls. Diane wore a classic, very simple white gown, her jet-black hair pulled back like a flamenco dancer's. Ben, more the blond carefree playboy than ever, showed a grin as wide as the Sunset Strip. Nagy had all the allure of a Jean Gabin. Why had he never acted? Alison wondered. Next time she would use him in a film. There would be another film. This was not the end of the line. Or was it? She would not think about that. Films had been withdrawn from distribution following particularly disastrous receptions here. Well, wasn't that what it was all about? You kept on gambling, sometimes winning, sometimes not. She would think about Sam.

It was good to think about Sam. What was there about a westerner wearing formal dress that was so titillating? She supposed because it was so unexpected. Europeans, particularly the English—and all bogus nobility—constantly wore smoking jackets and tuxedos. But the look of a man who the day before had been up to his hips in oil or mud, or riding a horse, and who now appeared in black tie . . . The thought excited Alison.

She wore a backless black dress and had also drawn back her hair, though not nearly so severely as Diane. A very simple, very expensive diamond choker, Sam's gift to her, lay against her smooth white throat. Evidently the other empires were booming, even if this one collapsed.

No, she would not think negative thoughts, she instructed herself as the houselights dimmed and the credits began to roll for *The Ski Pro*. She could think *hostile* thoughts, though, she decided, when she saw Ben's name, Diane's, and finally the words *directed by Paul Masland* appear on the screen. Was it her imagination or had somebody hissed? No matter. The movie began.

It was as good as she had remembered, though having to watch it again was unbearable. But Sam held her hand and she endured.

Until the final scene. Kenny skiing that last run down the mountain. How she remembered the day, the chill of the alpine wind on her cheek, the sun and the shadows, the figure weaving down the slope, the rise of the mogul, his leap—and then, frozen forever in time, exultant, a man flying. She began to weep; she could not control her tears. The memories were too much to bear. The life they had shared, their triumphs and tragedies, overwhelmed her. Before the lights came up she got up from her seat on the aisle and made for the exit.

They were applauding as she ran up the aisle. The movie was a success. Of course, Kenny's death was a big plus, said cynical-sentimental Hollywood. It had been rumored there were Oscar nominations in store. The number of bookings Ben and Diane had already secured following the Cannes showing was staggering.

None of it mattered. She found her way to the powder room. Elegant and sleek, a model of modern design, as was all of Lincoln Center, but no place to cry one's heart out for a love that had once existed, a life that was gone. She sought refuge in one of the toilet stalls. After a few minutes she began to see the humor of wearing a black evening gown and a diamond choker and hiding from the world in a toilet stall. Her tears stopped, and she was able to face the world again. She emerged from the powder room and went to find Sam.

"Well," she said, taking a deep breath, "that's over."

"Is it?" he asked, not referring to the film.

"Yes, Sam, it is," she answered. And then she kissed him on the cheek, close to his ear, and thought she could smell the outdoors still on him, but perhaps it was only after-shave.

The publicist for *Kick Up Your Heels!* rushed down the aisle and knelt by Alison's seat. She was a nice working girl, still carrying great clumps of leaflets and brochures, which were out of keeping with her demure evening dress.

"They'll expect you to take a bow," she whispered to Alison.

"Who will? When?"

"At the end. You will rise and take a bow after the houselights come on. I always count to five before I get up."

Alison was confused. "Do you take a bow?"

"Of course not," the girl said, as though she were talking to an idiot. "I mean, my client. I tell them count to five and then get up."

"Got it," Alison whispered, and the publicist scuttled away.

"I pay her good money," Sam said. "Now you do what she says. Besides the others all had their turn. Even the Old Gray Masland. I'm sorry you missed it."

"I'm not."

"There were some boos."

She was horrified. "For the film?"

"For Masland."

"Oh." Her voice changed. "Those things happen."

The houselights flickered a warning. The audience returned to their seats. The critics were on the aisle so that they could run for their deadlines.

Alison nudged Sam. "Isn't that the man I poured spaghetti on? What's he doing reviewing movies?"

"Moonlighting," Sam whispered, and then the movie started.

The first hint of success was an audible gasp as the opening shot moved from the dew on the leaves to the dewy eyes of Lillie Mae. The combination of her street-smart shrewdness and vulnerability charmed the audience. From there it was simple because the film was simple: a eulogy to all our first loves and fantasy adventures. Their delight continued. A spontaneous burst of applause accompanied the roller skating–jogging ballet. Lillie Mae followed Mad Queen Bess with "I can do that!" and the audience laughed at her youthful confidence, then grew silent as Lillie Mae proceeded to blaze away on the screen. When she reached a third chorus and began a roulade of improvisational notes that carried an incredible burst of energy, the audience could no longer contain itself. In midsong applause broke out. It was like a gospel meeting, Alison thought—cry and response. At the end of the number half the house stood up and bravoed. When the film was over, the other half joined them.

There was tumult. The houselights came on. Alison sat frozen. She counted to five, but did not dare move. Everyone else was standing. Who would notice her?

And then she saw that the head of the Festival had appeared before the screen and was gesturing. Gesturing to her. She rose from her chair, held out her hand to Sam. He declined. This was her moment. She left him and ran down the aisle. Someone helped her onto the stage. On the other side of the stage, dressed like a princess, the wonderful sassy Street Singer no more, was Lillie Mae. They met in the middle of the stage, both of them in tears. They embraced. The flashbulbs popped, blinding them; the roar of the crowd drowned out all thoughts of speech. Instinctively they turned to face the audience and together, bowed.

Chapter Thirty-four

Everyone had kind words. Everyone edged with the elbow, attempting to be the first to set up future dates for projects. For stage productions. Films. Whatever she wanted. Finally, Alison thought. Finally someone might entrust the direction of a play to a woman. It was about time. She smiled and nodded and thought, *When the time comes, I will consider all offers, but that time is not now. The time now is to enjoy what I've got.* The phrase Ben had used about Kenny came back to her. *The high life.*

Well, this was it, wasn't it? She had managed to climb to the top. She had directed her film. She had directed plays. She was going to direct more. Stage works. Operas. What else? Produce? She looked at Sam. He was back to doing what he liked best—or second best, she amended. Dickering with the Majors. Distribution deals. Percentages. Only she could see the relief in his eyes. Another gusher had come in, she thought. Sam, you hit another winner. Their eyes met. He didn't even have to wink. His look said, *Ain't this fun, ain't this worth everything? What did I tell you?*

Ben Sawyer wove his way through the crowd to congratulate her. Flashbulbs caught their handshake, their cordial smiles. That much was recorded. Paul Masland, never one to be overlooked, joined Ben and offered Alison his hand. Alison, still smiling, refused it.

Sam approached with Michael Eisner, Diane on Eisner's arm. Sam introduced Eisner to Alison.

"Congratulations, a beautiful film," Eisner said, clasping her hand respectfully.

Sam said, "We have just completed a deal, Mr. Eisner and I. His company will handle the distribution rights. What do you have to say to that?"

Alison was speechless. Gulf & Western. That was not bad.

"Say thank you," Diane purred.

Alison couldn't believe her ears. "What?"

"Learn to say thank you," Diane repeated. She had taken total possession of Eisner's arm. Alison looked at her, her gypsy makeup, her masked smile, and it all came rushing at her—Kenny, the humiliation, the hurt, the death, the evil, the rottenness of the woman standing in front of her smiling at her.

Alison simply hauled off and socked Diane right in the face.

Flashbulbs caught that, too, and so did Michael Eisner. Diane fell flat on her ass.

Doris Lilly sighed and wrote her headline DESPERADESS STRIKES AGAIN. Perfect for page one, *first* section.

They were in his limousine streaking across the Triboro Bridge.

"Oh, God!" Alison moaned. "Did I spoil your deal?"

"No. I'm sure Eisner's used to wildcats."

"What got into me?" she wailed.

"I don't know, but I got you out before you could do any more damage."

"I never had a chance to say good-bye, or thank you."

"Write notes," Sam advised.

"You're not angry?"

"Naw. Publicity only helps the picture. We got a shot at the Oscars too. Same deal as Ben's. So may the best man win. Or in this case, woman." He kissed her. It was a kiss that said *You're mine and I want you, for as long as you want me.*

"Sam, where are we going?" she asked.

"Houston. As long as you're specializing in personal attacks, I thought I'd teach you to shoot a gun."

"I don't believe in violence," she said primly. That made him laugh a lot. Her next question didn't.

"Sam," she said, going for broke, "will you marry me?"

"Will you come and live with me in Houston?"

"No. Will you live with me in New York?"

"No. But I'll visit you a hell of a lot."

"It'll be hard. Hell." She paused. "But it'll be fun," she decided, and looked to him. "So what's your answer?"

He let her wait a bit.

"Yes," he said.

Finally.

Generations of love, war, betrayal—
And a dream that would not die.

THIS PROMISED EARTH

Lee Raintree

The South—lush, fertile, built on a foundation of pride and wealth, torn by rebellion and war, rooted in tradition and heritage. From the sprawling plantations to today's dazzling cities, here is a magnificent, richly human novel that intertwines past and present in the moving story of a man and a family you will never forget.

Don't miss *THIS PROMISED EARTH*—available September 1, 1985, wherever Bantam Books are sold.